# Mistaken Identity

## BIG MISTAKES SERIES - BOOK ONE

by

### SUZIE PETERS

GWL
PUBLISHING

# Dedication

For S.

# Chapter One

———

*Livia*

"What about Saturday night?"

I know I should pretend I need to check my schedule, but who am I kidding? For Cole Shepherd, I'll make myself available. Not that I've got anything planned. But if I did, I'd cancel. Who wouldn't for the most handsome man in the building… possibly in the entire city?

He's just over six feet tall, with dark blond hair, cute dimples and the bluest eyes I've ever seen. I should know. At this precise moment, they're gazing right at me, and a smile is twitching at his lips as he tilts his head, waiting for my reply.

"Saturday is great for me."

I don't mention the fact that it's only Monday morning, and it seems a little early in the week to be making plans for the weekend. Maybe he likes to be organized. Who knows? Who cares?

It can't be that he's keen. We've both been working here for over six months, and this is the first time he's made a move. It's actually the first time he's spoken more than ten words to me.

Cole's one of the product designers who works on the third floor, while I'm the personal assistant to the CFO, two floors above. We met on my first day here, which also happened to be his, and which was probably the last time he spoke to me at any great length, when he did his best to put me at ease, sensing how nervous I was as we rode up together in the elevator. Little did he realize it wasn't the prospect of starting my new job that was making me anxious. It wasn't even that I'd moved to Boston from a small town in Maine, and was terrified of being on my own in a big city. Both of those things made me uneasy, but what was really getting to me was being in the presence of perfection.

It's been the same ever since. Whenever he wanders past my desk, I find myself staring, wishing he'd do more than nod in my direction, or drop me a smile.

That's why it was such a surprise today, when he walked by, then stopped, and doubled back, coming around to my side of the desk to ask if I'd like to have dinner with him… as though I'd be the one doing him a favor.

"You'll need to give me your address," he says, pulling his phone from the back pocket of his pants.

"My address?"

"Yes. How else will I know where to collect you from?"

He's going to call for me? I'd assumed he'd expect me to meet him somewhere, and I wonder how I'm going to get out of this…

"The thing is, I don't live locally."

He frowns. "Where do you live then?"

"Allston?"

His frown changes to a grin. "So… a ten-minute drive. It's hardly the moon."

I guess he has a point, and I smile back, feeling a little foolish.

He tilts his head, waiting again, and I remember I need to give him my address, hoping the next five evenings will give me enough time to tidy my tiny apartment. Saturday itself will be spent entirely on preparing myself for an evening with Mr.

Perfect, so I've only got until then to get the apartment ready. Of course, that's assuming he'll want to come up, rather than wait outside for me, but it's better to be safe than sorry.

He finishes typing my address into his phone and looks up at me again. "And your number?"

"My number?"

"In case I get held up. A gentleman should never keep a lady waiting."

I smile, nodding my head and recite my cell number, while thinking about the fact that he's a gentleman. Of course he is. How could he be anything else?

With any luck, that means he'll be tolerant of my inexperience... my innocence... my total lack of knowledge, when it comes to men.

Hopefully, his expectations for our first date won't be too high, either. I'm envisaging drinks, dinner, lots of talking and gazing into each other's eyes, holding hands, and maybe a kiss at the end of the evening. Anything more than that would be beyond me. I might daydream about Cole all the time. I might even dream about him occasionally, but I want to get to know him properly before we...

"I'll pick you up at seven." His voice breaks into my thoughts and I blush as I realize how presumptuous I've been in assuming that he'll even want to kiss me on our first date, let alone do anything else.

"O—Okay."

He smiles down at me and steps away from my desk, winking as he moves back around it and disappears down the hall, and I almost slide off of my chair to the floor. I grip the arms, holding myself steady, and let my head rock back, unable to control the grin that forms on my lips.

I've got a date with Cole Shepherd... well, who'd have thought?

I swivel around in my seat, staring out across the Boston skyline, and let out a deep sigh. Could it get any better than this?

"Livia?" I startle at the sound of my boss's voice. "Can you come in here for a moment, please?"

I jump to my feet, push my chair in under my desk, and walk over to his door, looking to the right.

"Yes, Mr. Wicks?"

He smiles up from behind his large oak desk, shaking his head. "How many times do I have to tell you to call me Lucian?"

"Sorry… Lucian."

I step inside, and he lowers his dark head to the document in front of him while I wander over, and stand on the other side of his desk, facing him.

According to his profile on the company's website, Lucian Wicks is thirty-four. He's married, with twin girls, who are eighteen months old, and who look down at him from a large framed photograph on the wall beside his desk, cheeky grins adorning their angelic faces. They're beautiful children, but that's not surprising… they have beautiful parents. I've met Lucian's wife on a few occasions, and she's a stunning red-head, and a former model. As for Lucian himself, beneath that short dark hair, he's got gray eyes and a clean-shaven, handsome face, which is now looking up at me again, his eyebrows raised.

"What did Cole Shepherd want?"

I hadn't expected him to ask that. When Lucian's door is open – which is most of the time – he can see the comings and goings outside, but he can't see what actually happens at my desk… and I'm starting to think that's a good thing.

"Oh, nothing in particular." I decide against mentioning Cole's invitation to dinner on Saturday. As far as I'm aware, the company doesn't have any policies against employees dating each other, but I don't want anyone to gossip. I've always been quite shy, and although I'm sure Lucian is the soul of discretion,

I think it's best if I keep quiet about my relationship with Cole… at least until I know I've got one.

He nods his head and returns his attention to the document in his hands. "Do you remember this?"

"What is it?"

He doesn't hold it out to me, but puts it back down on the desk, so I have to walk around, standing beside him now, to see what he's talking about.

"Oh… it's the report." The one we've been working on since the beginning of the month. "I thought that was all finished with."

He nods his head. "Yes. So did I. But unfortunately, I was sent some new information on Friday, and I spent the weekend amending all the figures, which means it now needs modifying… for about the twelfth time." He looks up at me. "I'm really sorry. I'm sure you thought you'd seen the back of this."

I don't know why he's apologizing. This is my job, after all.

"It's fine," I say, picking up the report and flicking through it. There are a lot of changes, including some new graphs that he's drawn in by hand, and I can't help the slight sigh that escapes my lips.

"It's not fine." He sighs too. "To make up for it, I'll order us something for lunch from that new deli."

"You don't have to do that."

"Yes, I do."

I smile down at him. "When do you need the report completed?"

He frowns. "Ideally, last Friday."

"I see."

"That's why I need to buy you lunch. You won't have time to leave your desk."

I roll my eyes. "No, I won't."

"I really am sorry, Livia."

I smile. "Stop apologizing. It's not your fault… and I didn't have anything planned for this evening." *Other than tidying my apartment, which I guess can wait until tomorrow.*

He shakes his head. "I don't know what I'd do without you. I honestly don't."

It's nearly five-thirty, and although my back's aching and my eyes are stinging, I feel like I'm on the home stretch now.

Lucian was as good as his word and ordered a delicious lunch from the deli down the street. He came out to my desk at around twelve-fifteen and showed me the menu on his phone. I chose a garden salad with grilled chicken. He had a turkey sandwich, and it was all delivered about thirty minutes later.

"How's it going?" I look up to see Lucian leaning against his open door frame. At some point today, he must have taken off his jacket, although this is the first time I've noticed, and for once, he's undone his tie and top button, which is unusual for him. He's normally fastidious about his appearance… not that he looks anything but tidy, even now.

"Nearly there," I say as I turn my attention back to my computer screen. "I think I should be finished in about an hour."

He nods his head. "I'll just call Shelby and let her know I won't be home in time to see the girls before they go to bed."

"You don't have to stay." I glance up at him again. "I can manage by myself. The worst of the changes are done, and the rest are self-explanatory. I'll email the file to you when it's finished."

He comes over to my desk, perching on the edge. "I wouldn't dream of leaving you here all alone. Do you want me to get you something to eat?"

"No, thanks. I'd rather just finish up and go home."

"And how do you usually get home?"

"On the bus."

"Not tonight. I'll take you."

I drag my eyes away from the computer screen again and look up to find he's staring down at me, his brow furrowed. "I'll be fine, really, Lucian. You don't need to wait… or take me home."

"Yes, I do. It's my fault you're having to work late, and I'll feel happier knowing I've seen you to your door."

He gets up and goes back into his room, making it clear the decision has already been made. I could argue, but I'm too tired, and besides, I like the idea of being driven home rather than waiting for the bus.

I get back to the report, vaguely aware of people leaving the office for the day, and Lucian's voice in the background as he talks to Shelby. She must be very understanding, because I can hear him laugh. Within fifteen or twenty minutes, though, everything goes much quieter. Lucian has clearly finished his call, and everyone else has gone. Although I'm still busy, still concentrating on the job at hand, I'm glad Lucian said he'd stay. I'm not sure how I'd feel about being completely alone in a deserted office.

I flick through to the end of the report. There are six pages left, and I stretch my arms above my head. I've got a niggling pain in my back and I long to get up and walk around a little, even though I know that will only delay me further… and Lucian too, for that matter.

The next page only has two amendments and I complete those quickly, turning it over, just as my phone beeps, letting me know I've got a message. It's in my purse, and I know I could ignore it. Except it's probably my mom. She often contacts me at this time, knowing I'll have just finished work. I don't want her to worry, so I save the document and reach down to my bag, opening it and pulling out my phone.

I frown as I gaze at the screen. The number is 'unknown', and it looks like there's an attachment to the message. I click on it and let out a gasp.

What's going on?

What is this? I mean… I know what it is. It's a picture of me, standing outside the office doors. But why is someone sending it to me? There are no words, just the photograph, and I study it a little more closely. It wasn't taken today, that's for sure. I didn't wear this jacket today. I wore it on Friday, though, because it was raining… and I put my hair up then, too, just like it is in the picture, which I didn't today, because I overslept and didn't have time for anything so fancy. It could have been taken any time, I suppose, but either way, it's creeping me out and I delete it, blocking the number, and shuddering slightly before I put my phone back in my purse.

I know it sounds odd, but I feel like someone's watching me now, even though I know there's no-one in the office, except Lucian and myself, and although I try to focus on the document, and getting it finished, I can't help wondering who could have taken that picture, and why they'd want to send it to me.

Lucian parks his BMW outside my apartment building, having followed my instructions to get here.

"Thanks for bringing me home," I say as I turn and look up at him, smiling.

"You don't have to thank me, Livia. I'm the one who made you work late. Bringing you home was the least I could do."

I open the door to get out. "Well, I'm grateful."

He nods his head. "See you tomorrow."

He doesn't offer me the opportunity to come in late, but I didn't expect him to. He's got an eight-thirty meeting with several department heads, and I'll need to be there to take notes.

I give him a wave, closing the door, and he pauses for a second or two before he pulls out into the traffic as I turn, crossing the sidewalk and entering my apartment building.

It's quite old, red-brick, and doesn't have an elevator. I don't mind that. I like the exercise of climbing up to my studio apartment on the fourth floor, although today I take the stairs more quickly than usual, opening my front door and slamming it closed behind me, before I finally let out a long sigh of relief. Why did I do that? It's not as though there was anyone following me. But that photograph has left me feeling nervous.

I open the small closet to my left, hanging up my coat and purse, and then wander past the kitchen area, into the living space. I do my best to keep it tidy in here, but I have to eat, live and sleep in this one room, so it's not easy. My attention is caught by the piles of books, and the magazine lying open on the floor, beside the cup and plate I left there from my breakfast this morning, and I wonder if I could try harder. The room is dominated by my bed, which, by rights, should currently resemble a corner couch. Except I rarely bother to change it back in the mornings. I just leave it like this... an unmade bed, with the pillows and covers scattered. Unlike most things in this place, though, they actually have a home. The shorter end of the couch can be raised to reveal a handy storage space, perfect for bedding... when you're not the kind of person who just leaves it lying around, that is.

Still, there's no point in converting the bed back into a couch at this time of night, and I go over to the walk-in closet in the corner, changing out of my work suit and blouse, and putting on some gray pajama bottoms and a pink t-shirt before I make myself a quick stir-fry. I sit cross-legged on the bed and eat, with the TV on in the background, while I survey the mess that is my apartment.

What I really need are some bookshelves. I'm an avid reader, and have never thrown away a book in my life, as a result of which, I'm inundated. The problem is, space. I don't have much of it. But I suppose I might be able to squeeze something in underneath the window… if I can find some shelving to fit.

Once I've finished eating, I waste thirty minutes looking for a tape measure, and then write down the length of the space beneath the window, before going onto my laptop and taking over two hours to find something that will fit… just. The only problem is, it won't be delivered for two weeks, and while it's still a fantastic solution to my book storage problem, it's not much help for this weekend.

I suppose the best answer will be to stack the books there in the meantime. Apart from anything else, it'll stop me from using them as glorified end tables, like I'm doing now with my glass of wine. And it'll mean that, if Cole decides to come up here, at least he won't be falling over piles of books.

I'm not in the mood for starting that now, though. I'm tired, and once I've washed the dishes, leaving them to drain, I check the door's locked and turn out the lights, getting into bed and pulling up the covers. It would be easy to be haunted by that photograph, but I refuse to think about it. Instead, I snuggle down and I let my mind drift off to thoughts of next weekend and an evening spent gazing into Cole's eyes.

I'm feeling rather pleased with myself today.

It's only Wednesday and, because Lucian said I could go home earlier than usual last night to make up for staying late on Monday, I got a lot of the books moved, and my apartment already looks tidier. There's still a little more to do, but I'm feeling confident I'll achieve it now.

I'm just finishing a letter for Lucian when my phone beeps and although it's the middle of the day and I should probably leave it, I check it anyway, taking it from my bag, just as it beeps twice more.

My fingers shake as I study the screen. There are three attachments this time… photographs of me again. I can tell from what I'm wearing that they were taken yesterday morning. One is as I'm getting off of the bus, the next is me walking to the office and the third, and perhaps most spooky of all, is of me, inside the elevator, taken from the foyer, just as the doors are closing. Whoever took them, it seems they were following me. But how could I not have noticed?

"Livia?" I jump, dropping my phone as I realize Lucian is standing in his doorway, and I turn to look at him. He frowns. "Is everything okay? You've gone very pale."

"I'm fine."

He steps forward. "Are you sure?" he says. "You don't seem fine."

I hesitate, my hand over my phone, and then I decide I might as well show him. At least one of the photographs was taken inside the office building, so maybe there's something he can do.

"It's just… I've been sent these pictures."

He perches on the edge of my desk as I hand him my phone and he swipes to the left, studying them before he looks down at me.

"It seems you have an admirer," he says, smiling.

"This doesn't feel like something an admirer would do." Not the kind of admirer I want, anyway. This feels intrusive, like the person who's sent them has invaded my personal space. "What's really odd is that I had one of these pictures sent to me on Monday, and I blocked the person's number… so how are they able to send more?"

"Maybe they're using a different phone."

"But why? If someone was doing this as a joke, or because they liked me, and for some reason thought it was a good idea, then surely they'd stop once they realized I'd blocked their number. They wouldn't go out and get a new phone and start all over again... would they?"

He stands, putting my phone on the desk, and folds his arms across his chest. "I don't know," he says. "And in any case, I'm not sure there's very much I can do about it. This is your personal phone, isn't it?"

"Yes." He knows I'm not entitled to a company one.

"And the photographs were all taken in public places?"

"Except that last one. That was taken in the elevator, downstairs."

"Yes, but the company doesn't own the elevators, Livia. There are several offices within this building. The foyer and elevators aren't owned by us and what happens there isn't our responsibility."

He sounds quite reasonable, and a lot less sympathetic than I'd hoped. He's probably worried I'm going to sue the company, or something, but that doesn't help me. It also doesn't feel very good to know he's more concerned with the business and its reputation than with my welfare.

"Maybe I should report it to the police..."

"The police?" He raises his voice slightly and then coughs, putting his hands on my desk and leaning over so he can whisper, "Why on earth would you want to go to the police?"

"Because this feels like – I don't know – like stalking, or something."

He smiles, shaking his head. "You've been watching too much television, Livia."

That's not fair. I hardly watch television at all. "You don't think the police would be able to help?"

"I'm not even sure this is a crime. It's not as though the person doing this is threatening you in any way," he says, standing again. "Just delete the pictures and put it behind you... okay?"

I nod my head and watch him walk away into his office. It's the first time since I started working for Lucian that I've felt disappointed in him. It's also the first time I've wondered whether this is really the place for me. If profits mean so much more than people, I'm not sure I belong here.

*Hunter*

"Hunter?"

I look up from my computer screen as Doreen comes into my office and I try not to smile. Everything here is very informal. So informal that I'm sitting here on a Wednesday morning in jeans and a white button-down shirt, with not a suit or tie in sight. Which makes it even more strange that I still can't get used to my secretary calling me by my first name. That says a lot more about her than it does about me, though.

Doreen has been here almost since the beginning. She was my father's first full-time employee. Even when he was still using freelance artists and copywriters, Doreen was a permanent fixture. She still is, and although I've got my doubts, I keep hoping she always will be. I'd be lost without her. She knows the advertising industry inside out, and just about everyone who works in it, too. She also knows what they're doing, and usually who they're doing it with, and while I'm no gossip, a little inside information can sometimes go a long way.

I save the file I'm working on and focus on her. "Yes?"

She comes and stands opposite me. "I need to speak with you."

I nod toward the chair that's just behind her, and she turns, sitting down and straightening her skirt, before she looks up at me again. She's a very attractive woman. I know from her personnel file that she's fifty-six, although she looks a lot younger. She always dresses smartly and wears her blonde hair in a neat bun behind her head.

"How can I help?" I ask.

"I ought to have put this in writing, I know… and I will do later today, just to make it official, but I wanted to tell you in person first that I'm leaving."

I feel as though I've entered an entirely different realm, where nothing feels quite right, and I know it never will again.

"Y—You're what?"

I sit forward, hoping I heard her wrong.

"I'm leaving." My shoulders sag as she dashes my hopes. "I'm sorry," she says. "But after your father died, I knew I wouldn't be able to stay on forever."

"It's been a year, Doreen." If she wanted to leave, why has she waited until now to do so?

"I know. And I feel that's long enough for you to have settled in."

"And for you to have done your duty to my father?"

She doesn't answer, but she doesn't need to. I've always known her loyalties lay with him, and not with me.

It's still his name above the door… Theodore Bennett Associates. In the sixteen months that I've sat behind this desk, first as acting CEO while Dad was in the hospital, and then permanently after his death, I've made a few changes. I've had the company logo and website re-designed, altered the ethos of the business quite drastically, re-modeled the office interiors and hopefully made this a more pleasant place to work. But even I know some things never change. Doreen is one of them. And, while I might have been lulled into a false sense of security by her having stayed for so long, I know there's no point in trying to dissuade her. As much as I value her, I don't need someone working for me who doesn't want to be here.

"I'm supposed to give you three months' notice," she says, biting on her bottom lip, and I wonder what's coming next.

"I know."

"The thing is, my daughter is due to have my first grandchild in just over two months, and I'd really like to be there."

"Right…"

"Only she and her husband live in Plymouth."

I'm not sure what her problem is. "So… about an hour away?"

She smiles. "I don't mean Plymouth, Massachusetts," she says. "I mean Plymouth on the south coast of England."

That puts things into a different perspective. "Oh… I see."

She sighs. "I—I was wondering if I could leave in six weeks. I know it's a lot to ask, but I want to fly out to the UK before the baby's born, so I can help my daughter, and then stay there for a few weeks afterwards."

I suck in a breath. "I don't wish to be difficult, but you must have known your daughter was going to give birth, and roughly when. Why have you waited until now to tell me?"

"Because they waited until yesterday to invite me over there," she says, with a hint of steel in her voice.

"You could just take some time off work. You know that, don't you?"

She looks at me and tilts her head slightly to one side. "Yes, but…"

She stops talking and I nod my head, both of us understanding the other, I think. I might bear my father's surname, but there the similarity ends. Personally, I think that's an advantage. I can't remember ever liking my father very much, let alone loving him, but I think Doreen might have done. God knows how. He was the most unpleasant man I've ever known. But maybe she saw something the rest of us didn't.

"I'll arrange it," I say, smiling at her, so she knows there are no hard feelings, even though her departure is likely to cause me some serious headaches.

"I'll happily help with handing over to whoever you get as my replacement."

*Assuming we can find someone before you leave.* "That's very kind, and I'm grateful for everything you've done to make the last year a lot easier for me than it might have been."

She blinks rapidly as she gets to her feet. She's clearly finding this an emotional moment and I don't know what to do. I feel as though any more words will only cause her further upset, but I don't know her well enough to hug her... even though I've known her all my life.

She saves me the embarrassment of trying to work it out, and leaves the room, while I stare at my computer screen for a moment, feeling a little lost, before I realize I need to act... and act quickly. I bring up my email app and start typing...

*'Miles,*

*Doreen is leaving in six weeks, so I need you to find me a replacement ASAP.*

*Keep me posted on developments.*

*Hunter'*

I press send and get up, wandering over to the coffee machine in the corner of the room and making myself a cup of very strong espresso, which I bring back to my desk, just as my phone rings. It's lying face-down, and I pick it up, rolling my eyes when I see the name 'Miles' on the screen. Why am I not surprised?

"Yes?" I say, snapping out my greeting, although that's not unusual with Miles. He has a habit of annoying me, like many of the people who were here in my father's time and whose contracts I gained, along with the title of CEO.

"Six weeks?" he says, not bothering to greet me, either. "You know that anyone who's any good is going to need to give three months' notice at their current job?"

"Of course I do."

"But you're only giving me six weeks?"

"No. Doreen is giving me six weeks."

"And you're letting her?"

"Yes, Miles. It's called loyalty. And when I want your opinion, I'll ask for it."

He sighs, but clearly knows when to stop arguing. "I take it you want someone with experience?"

"Ideally. It's not vital that they've worked in advertising before, but some experience of being a PA would be useful."

I hear him suck in a breath. "Okay. I'll see what I can do."

Anyone would have thought I'd asked him to solve the climate crisis, or bring about world peace, but before I can say anything, he hangs up, and I stare at the phone, wondering why I so rarely feel like I'm in charge around here.

I try to get back to the proposal I was working on, but I can't settle, and after twenty minutes, I pick up my phone again and connect a call to the only other person on this planet who understands what it feels like to be Theodore Bennett's son... my younger brother, Drew.

"Can I call you back?" he says, sounding rushed.

"Sure."

"Sorry. I'm right in the middle of a shoot and the model's being a pain in my ass."

"I heard that, Drew." The sound of a disgruntled female voice in the background makes me chuckle.

"Look... you're busy, and I ought to be working too, so why don't you come over to my place tonight? We'll order in pizzas, and..."

"And you can tell me what's wrong," he says, finishing my sentence.

"Who says anything's wrong?"

"I do... I'll be over around six-thirty. Okay?"

He hangs up on me, just like Miles did... but in Drew's case, I don't mind in the slightest. I'm looking forward to seeing him. It eases the prospect of another night spent staring at the walls of my apartment, or taking work home, so I can pretend I'm too busy for the social life I don't have anymore.

It's closer to seven by the time my intercom buzzes. I let Drew in, although it takes another few minutes before the elevator doors open and he steps out directly into my apartment, or rather into the small lobby that leads to my apartment.

I have to smile... not because he's late, but because looking at him is a little like looking in a mirror. Or it would be, if he didn't have the beginnings of a beard, which is a significant difference to his usual clean-shaven appearance, and my carefully maintained stubble. Okay, so he's also two inches shorter than I am, and his eyes are more milk chocolate than dark, but we both have a very similar build.

"Have you given up shaving?" I say as he pulls off his leather jacket, throwing it over the back of one of my couches. As usual, he's wearing jeans and a t-shirt, and while there's nothing wrong with that, he looks like he's seen better days.

"Don't." He shakes his head, turning to me. "Just don't. The agency I'm working for allocated me a day and a half to do a shoot that should have taken three. I'm so tired, I don't even know which way is up."

I wander past him and through to the kitchen, grateful that Mrs. Edmonds has been in to clean today, so the place looks immaculate. Drew follows, waiting while I fetch some beers from the refrigerator, handing him one. "Don't expect any sympathy from me. I know you love your job, and I know you'll have spent the entire day looking through a lens at some of the most beautiful women in the world... so quit moaning."

"I will, if you'll tell me what's wrong."

There's no point pretending, but before I tell him, I lead us both back to the living area and sit on one of the four enormous leather couches. He takes a seat opposite and stares at me, waiting. "Doreen's leaving, and she's only giving me six weeks' notice."

His eyes widen, and he sips from his beer bottle before he nods his head. "Is there a reason for that?"

"For her leaving, or for the lack of notice?"

"The lack of notice." I explain about Doreen's daughter and my secretary's wish to travel to England to be with her. "Sounds like the perfect excuse," he says.

"She didn't need one. I might have wanted her to stay, just because it makes my life easier, but I think I always knew she'd go, eventually. Dad was her link to the company, and when he died, she had no real reason to carry on. She admitted that herself."

He tilts his head, his brow furrowing. "Do you think there was something going on between them?"

"Who? Doreen and Dad?"

"Yeah." He shrugs his shoulders. "She's a very attractive woman, and her husband died years ago."

I might think Doreen worshipped my dad. I might even believe she loved him in her own way. But a physical relationship? That I'm not so sure about. "You mean, you think she and Dad...?"

"I don't know, but I've always wondered. He left her a lot of money in his will."

"Yes. Because she'd been his loyal assistant for decades."

"Or because he was sleeping with her."

"You don't know that."

"Maybe not… but when Mom left, Dad spent a lot of time at work, didn't he?"

"He spent a lot of time at work, even before Mom left. That doesn't mean he was having an affair with Doreen. It just means he was an asshole who didn't know when to come home to his family."

Drew shakes his head, although he doesn't disagree with me. "I wish I could remember that time."

"Why? Our childhood wasn't anything to write home about."

"I know, but I was only six when Mom left, and I can't remember anything about it."

"Can you remember Mom?" I ask.

"Bits of her."

"Well, I guess that makes us both luckier than Ella. She doesn't remember Mom at all."

"She was only three," he reasons, and I nod my head. "Did Mom and Dad argue on the day she left?" he asks, like a thought has suddenly occurred to him.

"Not that I'm aware of. Mom had an accident."

"What kind of accident?"

"I don't know. I was reading in the library, you were playing in your room, and I think Ella was asleep. The next thing I knew, Mom was bundling us into a cab, and taking us to the hospital. She said she'd had an accident, and when we got there, a nurse took us all to a separate room. A while later, Dad arrived. He talked with the doctors for ages, and after that, he took us home."

"Dad did?"

"Yeah. He said Mom needed to stay in the hospital overnight. The next day, she didn't come back… or the day after that.

When I asked him where she was, he said she'd left us, and she wasn't coming back, and he told me not to talk about her again."

Drew nods his head, like he's remembering something, too. "I don't have any memory of that whole hospital thing, but I do recall Dad would always refuse to talk about what happened that day." That's not strictly true. Dad mentioned Mom's departure again. But that was much later, and there's no way I'll ever tell Drew about it. "What about the guy who stole all the money?" he asks.

"Ken Bevan?" I might have only been eleven years old when our mother left us, but that man's name is permanently etched in my memory.

"Yes."

"What about him? You're not suggesting he and Mom were having an affair, too, are you?"

"How would I know? But don't you think it's odd that Mom left, and the CFO of Dad's company was caught embezzling millions of dollars from right under his nose, all within the space of a couple of months?"

"In a six-year-old's head, I can see how you could have joined the dots between those two events, but you've got them the wrong way around. Dad discovered what Ken Bevan had done and had him arrested at his family's home late that summer. Mom didn't leave until the day before Thanksgiving."

"Oh, yeah… you're right. I'd forgotten that."

"I hadn't. I'm not saying I don't think there was a connection between what Ken Bevan did and Mom leaving, but it wasn't the one you're thinking."

"What was it, then?"

"I've always thought that was the final straw for Mom."

"What? Dad nearly losing everything? Was she really that fixated on money?"

"No. Not at all... not that I can remember. And that's not what I mean. She'd put up with his moods, his crazy hours, his selfishness, his absence from the family home, and for all we know, his affairs, too. But his attitude over what Ken Bevan did, and the way it changed him... I think that was just too much for her. I think she faked the accident to get away."

"Really?"

"Yes."

He stares at me for a moment, like he's struggling to take that in. "You're not just saying that because it makes Mom look less guilty of abandoning her children?"

"No."

He frowns. I might never have suggested this theory out loud before, but that's only because he and Ella have never quite seen eye to eye with me about Mom leaving us. For that reason alone, we rarely discuss it. After all, it's bad enough that we were 'abandoned', as they like to put it, without the three of us arguing over who did what.

"How did it change him?" he asks. "What was it about the episode with Ken Bevan that made Dad so different?"

"Don't you remember?"

"No."

"Lucky you." I shake my head and unlock my phone, tossing it to over him. "Choose a pizza, will you? And forget about Mom and Dad... and Doreen. Even if the two of them were having an affair, it's not something we're ever gonna be able to confirm."

"Isn't it?"

"No. I'm sure as hell not gonna ask her about it, and neither are you."

He studies my phone. "How did he survive it?" he asks, after a moment or two's scrolling.

"Survive what?"

"Ken Bevan stealing all that money." *We're back on that, are we?*

"I don't know. I guess the cops must have got it back. Either way, he worked it out."

"And now you're running the show." He looks up at me again, handing me back my phone so I can choose my own pizza.

"In a way."

He frowns. "You might try to seem a little more cheerful about it. You chose to go into advertising long before Dad got sick, just like I chose to become a photographer, and Ella chose to flit around Europe learning to cook."

"You're assuming she's still doing that? She only lasted two years at college before she decided it wasn't for her. Knowing Ella, she's given up the cookery school, left Paris, and has moved to the Alps to study mountaineering, or something."

He chuckles. "I'm not sure you can study mountaineering, but nothing she does would ever surprise me." I order the pizzas, choosing the same as Drew, but with extra chili, and put down my phone, taking a sip of beer. "Are you unhappy about running the business?" Drew asks, watching me closely.

"No. Like you say, I chose this career."

"Whatever else Dad got wrong, at least he never tried to force us into doing something we didn't want."

"Because he was never at home enough to notice what we were doing, and he never cared enough to ask."

He waits a second or two and nods his head. "Okay. But the point is, he's not responsible for you being the CEO, is he? When he died, despite being a lousy father, he left us the house in Rhode Island and a serious amount of cash each. He didn't leave you the business, or put you in charge."

"He couldn't, Drew. TBA wasn't his to leave anymore. He took it public not long after his cancer was diagnosed."

"Yes, because running it by himself was too much for him. The guy was sick."

"Don't be so naïve. Dad wasn't running the business then. I was. He'd already brought me back in by that stage." I shake my head, smiling at him. "The only reason Dad went public with TBA was to ensure none of us could inherit the company outright from him."

"I know you think he didn't care about us, and I don't disagree, but if that's the case, why did he leave us all his money?"

"I don't know. He never believed in any of us, so he probably thought we'd give up our jobs and blow it all on fast living."

"Even if that is the case, he still left us his shares," he says, like he's trying to justify what Dad did.

"You mean shares in the business we have no control over, even if we have the controlling interest? Everything is run by the board, not by me. I might be the one who carries the can, but Dad didn't want me to do things my own way, and if he wasn't going to be around to control me, he made sure the board would be there instead."

"Are they holding you back, then?"

"I don't know if that's the best way of putting it, but I'm wondering if they knew something I didn't when they confirmed my appointment."

"Like maybe you're the best man for the job?" I shake my head and he sits forward. "You are, Hunter."

"I was already in the job when Dad died. It was easier for them to keep me on than to find someone else."

He frowns. "Has something happened… other than Doreen announcing her resignation?"

"Nothing specific, but since Dad's death, we've lost several of the older clients; the ones who were loyal to him, but not necessarily to me."

"Have you been able to replace them?"

"Some of them, but not as many as I'd like."

"Do you know what the problem is?" he asks.

"I think so. There are a few of the account execs who aren't pulling their weight. Some of them are fifteen or twenty years older than me…"

"Wow… that's really old. Do they still have their own teeth?"

I narrow my eyes at him. "Hilarious. You'll be twenty-eight next year… just you wait."

"Hmm… you see, the problem with that argument is that you'll be thirty-three. No matter what happens, that five-year gap will always be there."

"Don't I know it."

He tilts his head, frowning at me. "Are you sure your problems are all about work?"

"Why?"

"I don't know… I just get the feeling you're fobbing me off with all this crap about Doreen and Dad, and account execs."

I hate that he can see through me so easily.

"Okay… if you must know, I'm bored… and lonely." That sounds like too strong a word when I say it out loud, but before I can retract it, Drew perches forward on the edge of the couch, putting his beer bottle on the table between us.

"When was the last time you went out with anyone… other than me?"

"Sadie."

His shoulders drop, and he shakes his head. "Sadie? But that was three years ago."

"I know."

"I get that it's not every day you find your girlfriend having sex with the man you thought was your best friend, but three years? I didn't think you were even that serious about her."

"You're starting to sound like Dad."

"Like Dad…?"

"Yeah. He told me I was crazy to go out with her, insane to move her into my place, mad to trust her."

"What made him say all that? He barely knew her."

Neither did Drew. He was away a lot at the time, and I've never really talked about Sadie since. "Dad didn't know her at all. He'd never even met her. The problem was, she worked in a bar and came from the wrong side of town, as far as Dad was concerned... which was why he sent me to Europe for four months."

"In the hope you'd get over her?"

"There was nothing to get over. He sent me in the hope she'd prove herself unfaithful in my absence... which, of course, she did." There was more to it than that, but I'm not going into it now. It's ancient history.

"So, he did you a favor."

"He wasn't being altruistic, Drew. He just wanted to be right, that was all."

He frowns. "Wait a second... is that why you left TBA and went to work for the opposition?"

"Of course. I wanted to hurt Dad, like he'd hurt me."

"Wasn't it Sadie who'd hurt you? And Austin?"

"Yeah. Austin more than Sadie, if I'm being honest. But I was lashing out. When I got back and found her and Austin together, Dad told me I was stupid not to have seen it coming. Maybe he was right about Sadie, but I never thought Austin would do something like that to me. And in any case, there was no need for Dad to be so vindictive about it. I decided, there and then, to hurt him back the only way I could."

"By going to work for Moss and Dixon?"

"Yes. They were our biggest competitors back then. And the truth is, I'd probably still be there if you hadn't called to tell me Dad was sick."

"You know he asked me to do that, don't you?"

"Yes. I guessed as much when he told me he wanted me to come back to TBA. He didn't ask you to call me out of sentiment, because he wanted to reconcile with his son. He needed me to come back and run the company for him. I think even he realized there was no-one inside the organization who was capable, and he didn't want to bring in fresh blood at that level. I was his only option."

Drew shakes his head. "I didn't realize. I thought it was a genuine olive branch."

"From Dad? You're kidding, right? If he hadn't needed me to take charge of things at TBA, he'd never have bothered to contact me again."

"If you knew all that, and you hated him so much, why did you agree? You could've said 'no'."

"I know. And don't think it didn't cross my mind to walk right out of his hospital room and leave him to it."

"Then why didn't you?"

"Two reasons…"

"Which are?"

"At the time, he hadn't taken the company public. He didn't tell me he intended to, either. As far as I was aware, that was our inheritance. I wanted to protect it. For all of us. You, me, and Ella."

He raises his eyebrows, smiling at me. "What's the other reason?"

"To prove him wrong."

"How?"

"He made it very clear he'd be watching, just to make sure I didn't screw up. He didn't trust me in the slightest. I understood that, even if I knew nothing of his plans for the business, and his intention of hog-tying me with a board of directors and shareholders. Back then, I thought I could make an enormous success of things in his absence, and show him he'd misjudged me… again."

"I guess you never got the chance, did you? No-one could have known he'd be dead within four months."

"You think? You think he didn't know how aggressive his cancer was?"

He frowns. "Of course not."

"I think he did. If he'd believed he was going to survive, he'd never have signed the business away. He'd have kept it in private hands, so he could take it over again when he got better."

"So, you think he knew he was dying?"

"Yes. It's the only thing that makes sense. He knew he'd never get back behind his desk again. He put me in charge, and then almost immediately took steps to ensure I had to work with at least one hand tied behind my back at all times. I often used to imagine him lying in hospital, laughing at me."

"But you've made a success of it," he reasons.

"No, I haven't. I've tinkered around the edges, but I've achieved nothing... other than to lose a few clients."

"Will you stop putting yourself down?" he says, raising his voice, and I sit back, staring at him. "You need to get out more... to get a life outside of work. Hell... you need to get laid once in a while."

"Get laid?"

"Yes. Surely you can remember what you used to be like before you met Sadie?"

"Of course I can remember. I'm just not sure I wanna be that guy anymore."

Drew laughs, shaking his head. "Are you kidding me? You don't wanna be the guy who had a different woman on his arm every night?"

"Not every night. I wasn't quite that bad." At least, not most of the time.

"Maybe not, but the principle stands. You know what they say about all work and no play..."

Drew left about thirty minutes ago, and I've cleared away and grabbed a quick shower.

Coming out, with a towel wrapped low around my hips, I gaze at my empty bed and wonder about what he said. Could it be as simple as that? Is it just that I need to have sex?

I sit on the edge of the mattress and rub my hands down my face, allowing the thought to filter through my mind. I picture myself with a beautiful woman… the two of us writhing around on the bed, our limbs entwined, our bodies joined. My cock hardens and I lie back, closing my eyes and immersing myself in the scene as the woman gazes down into my eyes, her body rising and falling, a breathless need written in every sigh and moan. I roll her onto her back, raising myself above her and she reaches up, touching my cheek with her fingertips, matching my every move, giving herself to me. I give myself back, even as I'm holding her, thrusting into her… taking her.

"Oh, fuck…" I open my eyes, staring up at the ceiling. That wasn't sex. That was making love… and that's the last thing I need. Making love implies a relationship. It implies feelings, and worst of all, it implies trust. That's something I'm incapable of. I'd like to say that's because of what Sadie did. It would be the simplest explanation. But the truth is, Drew was right. I didn't love Sadie and whatever problems I've got, they go a lot further back than that. It's been years since I've trusted anyone.

Maybe that's something else I have to thank my dad for… or maybe it's connected with Mom, as well. Who knows?

I sit up and then stand, ignoring my hard-on, and wander back to the bathroom to brush my teeth. Staring at myself in the mirror, I overlook the tiredness around my eyes and the sadness behind them and I wonder if thirty-two is too old to have casual sex.

Is that the problem?

I'm just getting too old for this shit.

"I guess there's only one way to find out…"

# Chapter Two

———~~~———

## *Livia*

"How's work going?"

My couch is still a bed, even though I've just finished eating dinner, and I lie back on it, holding my phone to my ear. Mom sounds concerned, but that's normal for her, and while I'd love to tell her it's great, I settle for, "It's fine."

I still feel disappointed Lucian wasn't more supportive when I spoke to him yesterday, but there's no way I can tell her about that… or the photographs, or my thoughts about whether I really want to keep working for Lucian at all. I haven't decided how I feel about that yet, and until I do, I think it's best to keep it to myself. Mom wasn't sure about the idea of me moving to Boston in the first place. Leaving home was one thing. Finding my own feet was fabulous. Settling in such a big city was something else altogether. If she got so much as a hint that I was uncertain about my future, she'd be booking me a ticket on the next bus out of here.

"How's Dad?" I ask, changing the subject. She sighs and I prepare myself for bad news, wondering if that might be the real reason for her call. "Mom? He is okay, isn't he? He hasn't had another stroke or anything?"

"No, sweetheart. He's fine. He's just a bit low at the moment."

"Why? What's happened?"

"Nothing in particular. But you remember what he was like when he first had the stroke?"

"Yeah. He was absolutely convinced he was gonna get back to normal in no time at all, even though he couldn't move one side of his body, and struggled to speak."

"Exactly. I'm not saying I didn't admire his optimism, but now and then, the reality proves a little hard for him to accept."

"He's improved so much, though."

"I know that," she says. "And you know that, but sometimes it's hard convincing him. He hates that he's so slow, that he's still having to use a walking stick, and he gets really frustrated when he can't think of the right words."

"How's the therapy going with his hand?"

"He keeps trying with it, and we practice every day, but this far down the line, I'm not sure it's gonna get much better now."

"So he still can't write?"

"No. I think that's the hardest part for him."

That makes sense. My dad was an academic. Writing was a huge part of his life. I can't imagine how difficult it's been for him to give that up.

"Do you want me to come home at the weekend?" I ask.

I know I'm supposed to be seeing Cole, but I'm sure he'd understand if I had to cancel… as long as I explained.

"That's why I called," Mom says. "I wanted to check you *weren't* thinking of coming, because we're going away."

"You are? Where to?" I think I already know the answer to my question, but I ask it anyway.

"Oh… I just thought I'd take your dad to visit Uncle David for a few days."

That's exactly what I expected Mom to say. My dad's brother lives in Jackson, New Hampshire, along with his wife, Elizabeth and their two golden retrievers, in a lovely home that has views across the mountains. "That sounds perfect. And just what you both need."

Every so often, Mom needs to get away. She says it's so Dad can spend time with Uncle David, and it is. But it's also so she can get a break, have some down-time, and let off steam at Aunt Elizabeth.

"That's what I thought. But I realized I ought to check you didn't have any plans to come for a visit."

"No, I haven't." For a second, I wonder about telling her I've got a date, but I decide against it. I can tell her after the event… assuming there's anything to tell. For now, I think I'll just keep quiet.

"You'll come up soon, though, won't you?"

"Of course I will."

I might even take Cole to meet them. Who knows?

Once we've finished the call, I go onto my banking app and transfer some money to my parents. I do this every so often, when I can afford it, and on this occasion, my mom sends a text message within minutes.

— *What's the hundred dollars for? xx*

— *It'll help pay for the gas to get to Uncle David's. xx*

— *We can afford it. xx*

— *I know you can, but let me do this. I want to, and I can afford it, too. xx*

There's a pause before her next message.

— *Thank you, Livia. Love you xxx*

— *Love you, too, Mom xxx*

Just like yesterday, I've hardly seen Lucian all day. He's had back-to-back meetings, and my presence hasn't been required in any of them. I can't say I'm sorry about that. My disappointment in him hasn't diminished, and now I'm just relieved it's Friday, which means I won't have to even think about him for two whole days.

I haven't had any more photographs, either, although what I'd do about them if I did, I really don't know.

As it is, the phone and email are keeping me busy, and I've forwarded dozens of messages to him already. I've just pressed 'send' on the latest one when I get a tingly feeling down my spine, like someone's watching me, and I look up to see Cole, leaning against the wall opposite my desk, his arms folded across his chest and his eyes fixed on me.

"Hello." I smile at him, and he smiles back, unfolding his arms before he pushes himself off of the wall. He wanders slowly around my desk and gazes down at me.

"Hi."

"Have you come to see me?"

"Of course. I wanted to make sure you're still okay for tomorrow night."

My smile widens. "I'm flattered you've taken the time, but you could've called, or texted me. You've got my number, remember?"

"I haven't forgotten, but phoning or texting wouldn't have worked for me."

"Why not?"

He leans back on the edge of my desk, lowering his voice. "Because I wanted to see you."

Oh… what a lovely thing to say. "That's nice."

He stares into my eyes. "Yes, it is… and while we're on the subject of phoning and texting, I realized earlier that you don't have my number."

"Do I need it?"

"You might. Who knows when you might want to talk to me?"

"In that case, you'd better give it to me."

His eyebrows flicker upwards and a smile touches the corners of his lips as he recites his phone number. I don't have my phone to hand, so I write it down, and he stands and walks away, although he looks back, giving me a wink, just before he disappears from sight, and I sigh deeply, leaning back in my chair.

Maybe working here has its benefits after all…

Lucian's door opens and I sit up straight as he says goodbye to his latest visitor, shaking the man's hand before he leaves.

"That's it for today," he says, checking his watch. I know already that it's nearly five and, like him, I can't wait to go home for the weekend… and my date with Cole tomorrow night.

"I've forwarded all your messages."

He looks down at me. "I haven't been checking my mail. Are any of them urgent? Or can they wait?"

"Zach Fowler called twice, and your wife phoned three times."

He rolls his eyes. "Okay. Can you do me a favor and email Zach? Tell him I'm still in a meeting and I'll call him first thing Monday morning. I'll phone Shelby now and see what she wants."

He walks back into his office, closing the door again, and I let out a sigh, quickly typing the email as requested and wondering why he can't be as solicitous with me as he seems to be with his wife.

Because I can't make his life a misery, I suppose.

It's almost time to go home, but before I do, I need the ladies' room, so I grab my purse and make my way down the hall before Lucian comes out and gives me something else to do.

There are six stalls in the restroom, two of which are occupied, so I take the one at the end, smiling as I close the door and realize the women in the other two stalls are carrying on a conversation.

"He's going away for the entire weekend?" one says. "Are you sure about that?"

"Yes. He said he's leaving early tomorrow morning, and won't be back until late Sunday." I can hear the disappointment in her voice.

"How can he do that to us? I've been looking forward to seeing him all week."

Us? I lock the door as quietly as I can, wondering what she can mean.

"I know. It's so unfair."

I hear a toilet flush and wait until the room falls silent.

"Do you think we could find someone else?" The second woman's voice is coming from over by the wash basins now.

"Of course we could. Show me a guy who'd turn down the chance to watch us bring each other off and then join in." I put my hand over my mouth to stifle my gasp. "The problem is, it wouldn't be the same, would it?"

The other toilet flushes, and I strain to hear as they continue their conversation. There's something muffled that I can't make out, but as the noise quietens, I hear, "… had a dick that felt so good."

"Hmm… I wasn't thinking about his dick, I was thinking about his tongue. No-one's ever made me come so hard… or so fast."

"Do you know, if it wasn't Cole we were talking about, I could feel insulted by that."

Cole? She definitely said Cole. My skin freezes and my heart pounds in my chest. It's not the most common name in the world, but I suppose it doesn't have to be my Cole, does it?

"Why don't you call him? Ask if he'll meet up with us tonight… or maybe Monday?" I'm not sure which of them is talking now, and I don't care. I just want to know who they're talking about.

"You don't think that makes us look a little desperate?"

"Who cares? We are desperate. There's no way I can wait until next weekend."

I hear a rustling sound and then silence, followed by the noise of a phone being dialed. She's calling him on speaker? Oh, God…

"Hi, Cole? It's Casey."

"Hey, babe."

It's him. It's Cole. I recognize his voice. He called her 'babe', and I clench my fists, anger building inside me.

"I've got Gina with me."

"Hey, sexy."

Sexy? Is that worse than 'babe'? I don't know.

Either way, it's Gina who replies to him. "We know you said you're going away over the weekend, but we were wondering if you wanna meet up tonight?"

"Sure. I didn't realize you guys would be available, but if you're free, I can come to your place."

He sounds so carefree, so blasé, and I have to unclench my fists because they're hurting.

"Can you stay over?" Casey asks.

"No. Not this time. But my dick's already aching for those perfect pussies."

She laughs. "We're aching for your cock, too."

"I guessed as much." God, he's so arrogant. "When shall I come over?"

"Around seven?" Gina says.

"Okay."

They end their call, and Casey says, "How could he not think we'd be available? For him, I'd cancel everything on my schedule… including Christmas."

Gina laughs, and I hear the door open and close, their giggles fading into the distance.

I shake my head, recalling very similar thoughts about my own schedule flitting through my head on Monday, when Cole asked me out to dinner… a dinner I won't be attending now.

I open the door again, almost falling out of it, and make my way over to the basins. There are mirrors above them and the reflection looking back at me is pale, my blue eyes wide and glistening.

I will not cry… not over Cole. He's not worth it. Although this shock coming on top of the photographs, and Lucian's attitude is enough to make any woman weep. I could kick myself for being blinded by good looks and charm, but I can't help thinking what a lucky escape I've had. Or I will have done, when I break off our arrangements for tomorrow.

I wash my hands, dry them quickly, and walk back to my desk. Lucian's door is still closed and I sit down, finding the piece of paper with Cole's number on it before I pull my phone from my purse. I go to my message app, my fingers hovering over the keypad, before I realize I need to do more than send a message, and I abandon that idea and dial his number.

"Livia?" he says, answering on the second ring, and making it clear he's saved my details, which is a compliment I won't be returning. "Is something wrong?"

"That depends on your definition of wrong." My voice is quiet and impersonal and he picks up on that straight away.

"Are you okay?"

"Why wouldn't I be?"

"You sound… kinda weird."

"Do I? I wonder if that's because of the conversation I just overheard."

"What conversation was that?"

"One that took place in the ladies' room just now. There were two women in there at the same time as me. One of them was called Casey, and the other was Gina. They're friends of yours, I believe?"

"Oh… shit."

"Hmm… it was an interesting conversation. Impossible not to overhear, too. They were saying how they'd had a really great time last weekend, with someone called Cole. That's your name, isn't it?"

"Yes, but… but it's not what it seems."

"Oh? You know, I wondered about that. It struck me as a little odd, because they said that the Cole they knew was going away this weekend, and I thought it couldn't be you, because you're not going anywhere as far as I know… other than out to dinner with me on Saturday night."

"Exactly. It must be a different guy." He's trying to sound lighthearted, but he just comes across as fake… which is exactly what he is.

"A different guy who sounds exactly like you?"

"Sounds exactly…?"

"I heard them call you, Cole. I heard everything you said, including how much you ache for them – or certain parts of them – and your arrangement to go to their place tonight at seven." My words are greeted with silence, although I can still hear him breathing, so he hasn't hung up. "The thing is, I'm intrigued," I say eventually. "I can't help wondering what your plans were for our evening together."

"To have dinner, of course."

"And you expected that to take all weekend, did you? You told your friends you were going away, for the sake of a dinner? Or were you assuming that dinner would lead to sex, and that sex would turn into spending the night together… presumably either in your bed, or mine?"

"A guy can dream, can't he?"

"Yes… and in your case, you'll have to keep right on dreaming. At least as far as I'm concerned."

"Hey… come on. It's not like we're actually seeing each other yet."

"I know. You're a free agent, Cole. You can do whatever you like, with whoever you like. Only you won't be doing anything with me… including having dinner."

"I don't get it. You just admitted I'm a free agent, so what does it matter who I fuck between now and tomorrow night?"

"It doesn't. I couldn't care less what you do. I'm just so damn grateful I found out what you're really like before I had to sit through dinner with you. Goodbye, Cole."

I end the call, putting down my phone, my hand shaking even as I take deep breaths and try to calm myself. It's a struggle and I notice the time on my computer, realizing I can leave, thank God. Lucian still hasn't come out, but that doesn't matter. I put my phone back in my purse and power down my computer, shrugging on my jacket as I get to my feet, my eyes wandering over my desk.

No matter how I look at it, I definitely don't belong here… not any more.

I'm sitting cross-legged on my bed, the covers scattered and the pillows behind my back propping me up. I've got a coffee in one hand and I'm staring at my laptop screen.

"I know nothing about advertising," I mutter to myself, reading through the job description for a third time. Should that stop me from applying, though? I knew nothing about robotics when I applied to work for Lucian, and to be honest, I still don't. I don't need to. "Oh, to hell with it."

I click on the button that says 'apply', and between sips of coffee, fill in the online form, attaching my resume when prompted. At the end, after just a second's hesitation, I press 'submit', and let out a long sigh. It's late on Sunday night and I've spent almost the entire weekend scouring the Internet, looking for a job, and while there are plenty of secretarial vacancies, this is the only one that's offering the same rate of pay that I'm getting now. It's a little depressing that, having decided to leave my job, I'm struggling to find something new, but I console myself that it's only the first weekend. If nothing comes of this application, there will be others, and in the meantime, I'll keep my head down, do my job, and hope I never have to see Cole Shepherd ever again.

I turn off my laptop, put my coffee cup on the floor beside my phone and settle into bed, pulling the covers over me. I've tried not to think about Cole all weekend, and I refuse to start now, even if he is the reason I'm looking for a new job. Obviously, Lucian's attitude to my plea for his assistance over the photographs didn't help, but the thought of having to face Cole was the final nail in the coffin. Hopefully, whoever these advertising people are, they'll treat their employees with more respect...

I wake to the sound of my phone ringing and sit up with a start. *Have I overslept? What's happening?* I grab my phone from the floor, knocking over the empty coffee cup I left there last night, and try to focus on the time, which says seven-thirty-two. It's not my mom, but who else would call me at this time of the morning?

I press the green button and turn the phone to speaker.

"Hello?"

"Good morning. Is that Miss Hopkins?"

"Yes."

"Hi there. This is Miles Hampton, from TBA."

TBA? Who the hell are they? And who on earth does Miles Hampton think he is, calling at seven-thirty in the morning?

"Oh?"

"You applied for the position of personal assistant to our CEO."

Oh, my God... that's who he is. I swing my legs around, shimmying to the edge of the bed, and I put my feet on the floor, in the hope it'll ground me.

"Yes... yes, I did." *Really late last night.*

"I'm so sorry to call this early, but I was just checking my mail over breakfast and I saw your application. I wanted to catch you before your day got started, because I wondered if we could set up a meeting. It's not an interview, you understand... just a preliminary chat. Your interview – if you have one – would be with Mr. Bennett himself. He's the CEO. Initially, though, I'd like to arrange a video call between the two of us, maybe sometime today, if that's possible?"

It might be, if he'd stop talking long enough for me to get a word in.

"Would twelve-thirty be okay? I can come home during my lunch break."

"Certainly. I'll set it up and send you an email."

"Okay. Thank you."

We end the call, and I stare at my phone for a few seconds. That was a strange way to wake up, but I can't help smiling, wondering if my luck might be about to change.

Still, there's no time to dwell, and I pick up the coffee cup, taking it over to the sink, before I head for the bathroom.

I've spent most of the morning watching the clock, and as it ticks around to noon, I start to get nervous. Miles Hampton might have said this wasn't an interview, but it feels like one to me. In fact, it feels worse, if anything, because if I don't make a good impression, I know I won't get to the next stage of meeting the man I'm going to be working for... Mr. Bennett.

I told Lucian when I got here this morning that I had a dental appointment at twelve-thirty, so he's not surprised when I pop into his office and announce I'm leaving.

"I'm not sure how long I'll be," I say, and he looks up from his desk. "My dentist is renowned for running late." That's not true at all, but I'd rather concentrate on my conversation with Miles Hampton than spend my time clock watching.

"Don't worry. I've got a fairly easy afternoon."

"Okay. Thanks."

A small part of me feels guilty about lying to him... and about looking for another job in the first place. But I still can't escape that feeling of disappointment in him. Lucian has changed in my eyes, and I don't think he'll ever change back. I don't think I'll ever feel comfortable working here again, either. A lot of that is down to Cole, though, not Lucian...

Still, I refuse to think about Cole. Mostly because I feel so foolish when I do.

Fortunately, the bus is on time, and I use the journey back to my apartment to revisit some of the research I did earlier. In between checking the clock and doing my job, I've also found a few minutes to look up TBA. I probably should have done that before applying for the job, but I thought I'd have more time than this, and although I've only scratched the surface, I've discovered they're a public company, established thirty-six years ago, that their last declared turnover was eye-watering, and that TBA stands for Theodore Bennett Associates. Theodore... that's quite an old-fashioned name. As I'm riding home on the bus, I wonder if he prefers to be known as Theo, or maybe even Teddy. I can't help smiling at that thought, picturing an image of the 26th President of the United States, and wondering if Mr. Bennett of TBA might be middle-aged and cuddly...

I shake my head. I need to stop daydreaming and focus.

The company's website is really stylish, but I suppose it would be. They're an advertising agency. They probably do this kind of thing day in, day out. Even so, it's also very comprehensive, and I've only had time to check out a few of their better known clients before the bus stops opposite my apartment block.

I should have spent more time studying the company's profile, the services they offer, and the people who work there, but it's too late now, and I let myself into my apartment, just slightly out of breath.

I've got five minutes before my scheduled call with Miles Hampton and I set myself up on the bed. I know that sounds weird, but I don't have a table or a desk, so the bed is my only option, other than the floor, and at least here I've got a blank wall behind me.

Once I'm comfortable, allowing for the nervous churning of my stomach, I open the email Miles Hampton sent me early this morning and click on the link within it, following the instructions to join the meeting he's scheduled. I've done this dozens of times for Lucian, so I'm not fazed by any of it, although the moment I'm able to see my own image on the screen, I quickly adjust my hair. I hadn't realized it was so untidy and I could kick myself for not checking in a mirror before starting this call.

"Hello." Miles Hampton looks to be around thirty years old, and when he smiles at me, his blue eyes sparkle and dimples appear on his cheeks... and I almost groan. He reminds me far too much of Cole, but with blonder hair, and I suck in a breath, telling myself not to judge.

"Hello, Mr. Hampton."

"Call me Miles, please." I nod my head and he glances down at something in front of him, although I can't see what it is. When he looks up again, he's still smiling. "I know you're on a tight schedule, so we'll get right down to it, shall we?"

"Okay."

"You're currently working as a PA to the CFO at..." He glances down again. "At SKJ Robotics. Is that right?"

"Yes."

"I notice you haven't been there for very long. Why do you want to change jobs already?"

I've been dreading this question, but I've thought it through and I give him my rehearsed answer.

"I only moved to Boston six months ago. To be honest, I took the first job that came my way, but finance doesn't really interest me and neither do robotics. As I said in my application form, I'm looking for fresh challenges."

"I see... okay. Your resume says you're originally from Maine?"

"Yes."

"Whereabouts?"

"Falmouth. Do you know it?"

"No. But I think I'd like to." That feels like an odd thing to say, but before I can ask why, he puts his next question. "I notice you got great grades in high school... and yet you didn't go to college."

"No."

"Was there a reason for that?" he asks, tilting his head.

"Yes. It was personal." *And none of your damn business.*

He pauses for a moment or two and when it becomes clear I'm not going to add anything, he continues, "It says here you only have to give one month's notice to your current employer. Is that correct?"

"Yes. After a year, that would be extended to three months, but as I haven't been there for that long..." I let my voice fade and he frowns slightly.

"So you're on trial for the first year? Because I'm guessing they only have to give you a month's notice, too, during that period?"

"Yes." Although I've never thought of it like that.

"And what about your benefits? When do they kick in?"

"What benefits?"

His frown deepens. "Don't they offer you a benefits package?" he asks.

I remember the ad for the position with TBA mentioning a benefits package, but it didn't say what that entailed.

"There's health insurance, but that doesn't start until after twelve months."

He nods his head. "Well... just so you know, if you were to be employed here, we do things a little differently."

"Oh?"

"Yes. Mr. Bennett recently instigated a new system... so we only operate a ninety-day trial period, after which your full contract would come into force. That's when your benefits would start, including medical and life insurance, extended vacation allowance, flexible working hours, a retirement plan and gym membership. In your case, there would be two exceptions to that rule."

"There would?" I'm still reeling from the idea of gym membership... and wondering what I'd do with it.

"Yes. Your phone and company car would be given to you on your first day."

"I'm sorry? Did you say car and phone?"

"Mr. Bennett likes all the senior staff to have reliable transportation," he says. "And the phone is so we're all using the same system. It makes life easier."

"Okay." I can't believe I'm hearing this, or that I'd be considered 'senior staff' in Mr. Bennett's organization.

"I have to say, you've impressed me, Miss Hopkins. Although I hope you don't mind if I call you Livia," Miles says, and I try to focus on him, even if I'm still in shock. "How are you fixed for getting together sometime soon?"

Did he say what I thought he just said? He can't have done, can he? "I'm sorry... did you just ask me out?"

"Um... no. I asked you when you'd be available to get together for a meeting with Mr. Bennett. I think I explained to you this morning, that's the next stage of this process."

I can feel myself blush and I want to bury my head... or better still, my entire body.

"I'm so sorry. That was really stupid of me."

"Hey... don't apologize," he says, as he leans in a little closer to the screen. "And don't dismiss the idea, either."

I'm not sure how to reply to that. I'm not even remotely interested in him... not in that way. But I can't say anything to put him off, having been responsible for the misunderstanding in the first place.

"I'm happy to fit in with whatever Mr. Bennett needs." That sounds like a reasonable response, keeping it professional, and about his boss, not him.

"Okay. I'll check his schedule and get back to you."

We end the call and I wait until the application has closed before I let myself fall sideways onto the bed, my head hitting the mattress as I groan out loud.

Could that have gone any worse? Probably. Although I can't think how. And the job sounds so perfect for me, too. Not only is the package incredible, but Mr. Bennett seems like someone who really cares about his employees.

It's just a shame I won't be one of them, because even though Miles said he'd get back to me, after that little performance, I seriously doubt I'll ever hear from him again.

# Hunter

I know it's only been a couple of days since I tasked Miles with finding me a new PA, and I'm probably jumping the gun in expecting him to have achieved anything yet, but I've heard nothing from him and I'm getting anxious. In reality, I know my anxiety doesn't stem entirely from Miles's silence. It stems mostly from the fact that I've just finished a meeting with my team of account execs, and it could have gone a lot better than it did… in all kinds of ways.

First and foremost, Doreen proved how invaluable she is, and how much I'm going to miss her, by correcting Preston Tucker, when he claimed he'd heard one of our competitors is going out of business. That would have been great news for us, if it had been true, because their clients would have been looking for a new agency, and we'd have had the chance to step in. However, it seemed Preston had his wires crossed. That's unusual for him. He's usually on the ball, but I guess we all have bad days.

"They're not going out of business. They're looking to merge with Banks, French and Stanley," Doreen said, before Preston had even finished his explanation.

"Really?" I turned to her. "I hadn't heard that."

"I only found out about it myself an hour ago. I was going to tell you after the meeting."

"But if the merger goes ahead, it'll make them the biggest agency in the city."

"Yes, it will. Although I have to stress, nothing's been agreed yet. The word is, the board at Banks, French and Stanley are still looking through the financials. It could all come to nothing."

She must have been able to see the worry written on my face, and was doing her best to appease me. Not that it helped, especially considering the men and women sitting around the table had just given me their poor appraisal of the next three months' projections. I called the meeting to a close then, feeling the need to think things through.

Revenues are down, and while the business isn't exactly in trouble, we need to get creative. That shouldn't be a problem. Getting creative is what we do. But like I said to Drew the other day, a lot of the people around me date back to our father's time. They've worked for the company for years, and I think they resent me coming in and taking over. Naturally, it doesn't help that I worked for the opposition for a while, and poached a few of Dad's clients from under his nose when I left TBA. I did that just to spite him, and although I know I could probably poach them back again, given the right incentives, I'm not going to. I'm trying to do things differently now… trying to be a better man, if I can.

On the bright side, it's Friday. It's the weekend, and I'm spending it at our property in Rhode Island. That's not unusual for me, and I packed a bag this morning and left it in the trunk of my car, ready to start the drive.

It doesn't take me long. I'm familiar with the roads and I pull through the gates at just after seven, feeling myself relax already. There's something about this place that has always made me feel at home. Maybe it's the fact that our father rarely came here. As a very young child, I don't remember being bothered by his absence. Our mother was still here then, and she was all we needed, so I didn't mind when he missed birthdays and Christmases.

I remember the arguments between him and Mom, though, when he occasionally remembered he was supposed to be a husband and father, and not just a businessman.

It was after she left, I suppose, that his absences became more noticeable. That was when he employed Patricia and Michael Ferguson to look after us and the house, and although they never tried to take the place of our parents, they became like a beloved uncle and aunt… known to all three of us as Pat and Mick.

I park in front of the double garage and get out of the car, retrieving my bag from the trunk and wandering over to the front door, although it opens before I get there.

"Good evening, Hunter." Pat smiles at me, tilting her head to one side. I've got no idea how old she is, and I've never dared ask, but if I had to guess, I'd say she's in her early-sixties now. She's slim and diminutive, wearing a plain skirt and blouse, with silver streaks in her auburn hair, and green eyes that can see right through me.

"Hello, Pat. How are you?"

"I'm very well, thank you."

She holds the door open while I step inside, and then closes it, reaching for my bag, although I pull it away, keeping hold of it. We don't have this confrontation every time I come here… just every other time.

"Are you trying to make me feel old?" she says, narrowing her eyes at me. This is a different response from her usual one, which is to tell me it's her job to take my bag.

"No. But I'm quite capable of carrying my own luggage, thanks."

"Oh? So you don't need me anymore, then?"

"I'll always need you, Pat. You know that."

If I didn't, I wouldn't have kept her on after Dad's death… especially as we'd all essentially left home by then. I only come back here on the weekends. Drew comes back every so often, but when he does, he lives in the guest cottage, not the main house, and Ella's been in Europe for the last four years, barring vacations. The place wouldn't be the same without Pat and Mick, though, and there's no way I'd even consider letting them go.

She nods her head, smiling. "I've got some sea bass for your dinner."

"Sounds perfect."

Clearly giving up with the battle of the bag, she turns, going through the archway and into the living area, and then onward to the kitchen at the back of the house. "Ready at seven-thirty?" she calls over her shoulder.

"Thank you."

I head up the stairs and turn right at the top, going around the landing to my room, which is the second door on the left. Inside, I let out a sigh. I love this room. It's so tranquil, and Pat's left the window open, so the drapes are billowing in the breeze. I wander over, looking out across the lawn to the woodland beyond, and dump my bag on the couch, sighing even more deeply. I might love it here, but I wish…

"Oh, stop it," I mutter to myself. There's no point in wishing. I learned that a long time ago.


"Is there a reason you seem a little quieter than usual?" Pat says as I swallow the first mouthful of my sea bass.

I'm sitting at the island unit in the kitchen, in one of the wicker chairs, and she's clearing up the mess she's just made while preparing my dinner.

"Am I quieter?"

"Yes."

"It's just work," I say, putting down my fork and taking a sip of white wine from the long-stemmed glass before me. "Sales aren't great, it looks like two of our competitors might be merging, and to make things worse, my PA has just handed in her resignation."

"I see. And that's it, is it?"

I look up at her. She's standing now, with her back to the stove, her arms folded across her chest and her eyes boring into mine. It's quite unnerving.

"Isn't that enough?"

"I don't know," she says. "I just got the feeling you were pining for something."

I don't know why it still surprises me that Pat can read me like a book, but I'm not giving in that easily. "Like what?"

"Like someone to share all this with, maybe?" Dammit. How does she know that's exactly what I was just wishing for, right before I convinced myself there's no point in wishing? Not that I'm about to admit that. I'll stick to going on the offensive instead.

"If you think I'm pining for Sadie, you're wrong."

She shakes her head. "I wasn't thinking about Sadie. She was never right for you."

"My father used to say that, and I'd rather not hear it from you."

She smiles. "Just because you don't wanna hear something, doesn't make it any less true."

"How would you know, Pat? You never met her."

"Exactly," she says, like she's stating the obvious. "You dated her for six months. You even moved her into your apartment. But you never once brought her here."

"You're forgetting, I was away for a lot of that time."

"No, I'm not. I remember you going to Europe. But what stopped you from bringing your girlfriend here before you went?"

"She preferred to stay in the city." That sounds better than admitting I never felt comfortable about inviting Sadie here. I hated not coming to the house while we were together, but it seemed better to deal with an enforced absence than bring her here when I knew it would feel wrong.

Pat steps forward, so she's on the other side of the island unit. "You're sure it was Sadie who felt like that?"

"You know I prefer being here to anywhere else, Pat."

"I know you're willfully misunderstanding me," she says. "This is your home. We both know that. I'm not questioning the fact that you love it here. I'm questioning the fact that you never seem to want to share it with anyone else."

"I haven't met anyone I want to share it with."

"In three years?" She frowns, shaking her head. "Are you even trying?"

"Not really."

She lets out a sigh. "And you still maintain you're not moping over Sadie?"

"I'm not."

"So, you're honestly telling me you weren't hurt by finding your girlfriend with another man?"

"I was shocked. I'll even admit to feeling humiliated. But I wasn't hurt."

"Then why are you pining?"

"I didn't say I was. You did."

"Oh, Hunter... any fool can see you're lonely, but don't you think it's time you tried dipping your toe in the water again, with someone new?"

She turns, stepping away, and picks up her cloth again. She knows me well enough not to push me on any subject... but especially this one, and she gets on with what she's doing, leaving me to think...

She's only saying the same thing as Drew did the other night. Their language might be slightly different, but they mean essentially the same thing, and although I've avoided thinking about it for quite a while now, maybe I need to face up to it.

"You're right."

Pat turns around, raising her eyebrows. "I am?"

"Yes. There's no point in denying it. I'm lonely. I told Drew when I last saw him. Only after I'd said it, I thought I was exaggerating. Except I'm not. It's how I feel. The problem is, the only person who can do anything about it is me."

She puts down her cloth, coming back and standing right in front of me.

"I don't see why that's so much of a problem."

I wish I could believe that.

Admitting to being lonely is one thing. Working out what to do about it is something else altogether.

I wound up spending the entire weekend by myself. Pat and Mick were at the house, obviously, but they were as unobtrusive as ever, and I only saw Mick once, when he was mowing the lawn on Sunday morning.

Knowing me as well as she does, I think Pat sensed I needed some thinking time. Not that it did me any good. I don't feel as though I'm any further forward than I was on Friday.

Part of me wishes Drew had been at the house this weekend. Even when he is, we normally don't live in each other's pockets. He has sole use of the guest cottage, so we can both have some privacy when we need it. But if he'd been there, we'd have been able to talk... or more likely just sit in the den watching movies, or hang out by the pool with a beer. Of course, if Ella had been there, I wouldn't have had any peace at all. She might have her own apartment now, in the west wing of the house, but she prefers company, and isn't necessarily that sensitive to anyone else's need for solitude... or silence. Fortunately, as far as I know, she's still in Paris, and will be until later in the summer.

So far, my Monday has been about as uneventful as my weekend. I'm busy enough, but I can't seem to settle, and I've made it to early afternoon without feeling as though I've achieved anything.

I'm contemplating yet another cup of coffee, when my computer pings letting me know I've received an email, and I open the app, sitting forward when I see the message is from Miles, and that the subject is 'Doreen's replacement'.

"About time," I mutter under my breath, clicking on the message and reading...

*'Hunter,*

*I think I've found the perfect replacement for Doreen.*

*Miles'*

That's it? That's all he's going to give me? I know he's expecting a tit-for-tat... that I'll reply, asking for more information and he'll drip feed it back to me, like this is some kind of game. Except it isn't.

I grab my phone as I stand and put it into my back pocket, heading for the door.

Doreen is sitting at her desk, and she looks up as I come out, raising her eyebrows.

"I'll be back in a minute."

She nods and returns to typing, while I walk out of her office and down the hall, turning the corner at the end, by-passing the stairs and the elevators, and moving a little further along, knocking on the third door on the left. I barely wait for Miles to say, "Come in," before I push open the door and try not to smile as he sits back in surprise, his eyes darting up from his computer screen and his mouth popping open.

"Expecting an email, were you?"

"Well... um..."

I move further into the room, closing the door behind me and stand opposite him, using my height to full advantage. "You think you've found a replacement for Doreen?"

"Yes... I..." He's flustered, and while I don't normally like making people feel uncomfortable, I can't help making an exception in his case.

"Tell me about her... assuming it's a woman."

He taps on his keyboard a couple of times. "Oh, it's a woman," he says, his confidence returning, along with his smile. "Her name is Livia Hopkins. She's twenty-one, and..."

"And, let me guess, she's beautiful?"

Miles is a couple of years younger than me, and for some reason, my father appointed him head of HR not long before his cancer diagnosis. In my opinion, that was a big mistake, but I wasn't here then to give an opinion on the matter, and even if I had been, Dad wouldn't have listened to me. The problem is that Miles has a reputation with women, and while my own track record makes it impossible for me to criticize, I've heard rumors about the way he talks to some of the female employees, and the way he behaves around them, too. All the while they're only rumors, there's nothing I can do, though... and I think he knows it.

He doesn't need to answer my question, and I can tell he doesn't intend to, in case he incriminates himself. Instead, he just smiles. To me, that seems like the perfect reason not to employ Livia Hopkins, just to keep her out of his clutches.

"Have you only got the one candidate?" I ask.

"Yes. I've interviewed five others..."

"This is news to me."

"I know, but I didn't tell you about them, because they all needed to give at least three months' notice to their current employers."

"And Livia Hopkins doesn't?"

"No."

"Is she even employed?"

"Yes. She's working as the PA to the CFO of a robotics company, and has been for around six months. She's qualified to do the job, Hunter."

I'm not sure he's qualified to judge, but I can see the problem. It's the one we always knew we'd have… namely, finding someone who can fill the position within such a short time-frame.

"Okay. I need to see her sooner rather than later." If she doesn't fit the bill, I'll have to give Miles more time to find someone else, and if she does, the earlier she can start, the better. It'll give Doreen at least a few days to hand over the reins.

"She said she can fit in with your schedule." He looks up at me, tilting his head expectantly, and I pull out my phone, going to my calendar.

"I'm slammed with meetings later in the week, but I'm free for most of tomorrow. Do you think she'll be able to manage that?"

He shrugs his shoulders. "There's only one way to find out."

"Okay… well, the morning would be better for me, but if it has to be in the afternoon, I can work around it."

He nods his head. "I'll call her and get back to you."

"Fine."

I turn, leaving his office without another word. I know I should probably thank him, but I can't bring myself to. As I'm about to close the door, I hear him connecting a call to Livia Hopkins, and I get a strange feeling, like a gust of ice cold wind brushing over my skin. I shiver against it, wondering if it was the tone of Miles's voice as he said her name, or the name itself. There's something about it… something familiar.

I close the door as quietly as I can and stroll back down the hall, playing her name over in my mind. *Livia Hopkins… Livia… Livia…*

Why do I know that name?

I get back to my office and sit behind my desk, racking my brain, trying to think about where I might have met someone called Livia before. I come across all kinds of people in my professional life, but I don't think it's got anything to do with work. We don't have any clients who deal in robotics, and to my knowledge, we never have, so it can't be that...

My computer pings, and I click on my email app, sitting forward to read a message from Miles. He's letting me know he's confirmed an appointment with Livia Hopkins for tomorrow at ten-thirty. I reply with a quick, 'Thanks', just as an awful thought crosses my mind.

What if I've slept with her?

I've always known the names of the women I've slept with at the time, but I can't honestly say I can remember them all. Not now. I can't imagine how embarrassing it will be if she walks in here tomorrow morning, and we both have recollections of a night of intimate passion... or worse still, if I recall it and she doesn't. At least, I think that would be worse. I'm not altogether sure.

"Don't be an idiot," I mutter to myself.

I can't have slept with her. Miles told me she's only twenty-one years old. I haven't slept with anyone since Sadie. Livia Hopkins would have only been eighteen then, and I haven't slept with an eighteen-year-old since I was eighteen myself.

I smile, thinking back through those fourteen years to my first time...

Her name was Raven, and it suited her. She had jet black hair and bright blue eyes, and my eighteen-year-old body craved her, like oxygen. The feeling was mutual, it seemed, and one evening, after we'd made a pretense at dating for the third or fourth time, we found our way back to her place. Her parents were out, and we barely made it through the door before we started tearing at each other's clothes. It wasn't her first time, and I don't think she realized it was mine. I certainly wasn't going to tell her. I can't claim it was spectacular, but it was good enough that we both felt like repeating the experience… multiple times. It was a purely physical attraction, born of lust, not love, and when her parents decided to move out of state, we parted like old friends, knowing we'd had a great time… but that there was greater still to come. We both knew we hadn't found 'the one', if such a thing exists…

I sit forward, just as my phone beeps. The appointment with Livia Hopkins has automatically migrated to my calendar. It will have synched with Doreen's too, and a reminder window has popped up on my screen, letting me know. I glance down and shake my head. *Livia… Livia.*

It must just be a coincidence… or else my jaded mind is playing tricks on me.

# Chapter Three

*Livia*

I need to stop shaking… although I'm not sure how.

I hadn't expected Miles Hampton to call me back at all, let alone to do it so promptly, but he phoned not long after I got back to the office yesterday afternoon, asking if I'd be free to have an interview with Mr. Bennett this morning. I could hardly say 'no', having said I'd fit in with whatever Mr. Bennett needed, and to be honest, I was just so relieved to have been given the opportunity, having messed up so badly with Miles, I said 'yes', on the spot.

Of course, that left me with the problem of what to tell Lucian.

He was between phone calls, so I went straight into his office, standing on the opposite side of his desk, and I looked down at him, remembering why I was doing this. The lies fell off of my lips more easily that way…

"I'm sorry, Lucian, but I won't be able to come in tomorrow morning."

He looked up, putting the lid back onto his fountain pen and frowning. "Tomorrow?" I knew he wanted to say something about the short notice, but instead, he just asked, "Why?"

"I have to see my doctor." I tilted my head slightly, raising my eyebrows, and he nodded his head, as though he'd understood the secret code for 'you don't want to ask what about'.

"Okay. It's nothing serious, is it?" He might not have been asking for details, but he seemed concerned, and I felt a little guilty for deceiving him.

"No. It's just routine."

He nodded. "In that case, can you contact Zach Fowler and bring our meeting forward to this afternoon? He wants to talk through the provisional marketing budgets for the next two quarters and I'll need you to sit in, to take notes."

"Sure." My guilt ratcheted up a notch, but didn't go so far that I was prepared to cancel my interview… which is how I've come to be standing outside this four-story, red-brick building, a knot gathering in my stomach. I'll admit that's partly because I still haven't had time to do any research on Theodore Bennett, or his company, and I'm scared it's going to show. That's not entirely my fault, though. The meeting with Zach Fowler ran on longer than anyone expected, and Lucian didn't offer me a ride home, so by the time I got back last night, I barely had time to eat before I fell asleep.

I swallow down my nerves, pulling at the hem of my dark gray jacket, before I push on the door in front of me and walk in.

I've left behind a bright and sunny spring morning, but in here it seems even brighter still. The foyer is huge, with white painted walls and a really high ceiling. There are scarlet couches and chairs dotted around, and to the left, a large meeting area, hemmed in by glass, inside which is an enormous table, surrounded by over a dozen chairs.

In front of me is a white, semi-circular desk with the TBA logo emblazoned on the front, and behind it there's a woman wearing a pale gray blouse and a smile, her dark hair cut short around her pretty face.

"Hello. How can I help?"

"I'm here to see Mr. Bennett."

"Miss Hopkins? Is that you?" I turn at the sound of my name and see Miles Hampton approaching from the elevators on my right. He's around six feet tall, or maybe a little less, and while he might be wearing a button-down shirt, he's also got on a pair of dark blue jeans. I'm surprised by how informally he's dressed, but I plaster on a smile, taking the hand he's holding toward me.

"Miles…?" I turn around again, as the lady behind the desk calls his name. "Would you like me to let Doreen know Mr. Bennett's appointment is here?" She nods her head in my direction, with a smile, which I return.

"No, thanks, Miranda. We'll just go on up."

She frowns now, but shrugs her shoulders, and Miles puts his hand in the small of my back, spinning me around again, to face the elevators. Even as we start to walk, he keeps his hand where it is, and although I feel uncomfortable, I'm not sure what to do. I certainly don't want to make a fuss, or be accused of misunderstanding his actions… not after what happened during our video call.

Fortunately, the elevator doors open almost immediately, and I take the opportunity of stepping away from him, and once inside, I move over to the side wall and keep my back against it. He follows me, standing opposite, and once he's pressed the button for the top floor, he gazes at me, tilting his head slightly to the right.

"It's good to see you again," he says, and I smile, unsure how to reply as his eyes rake up and down my body, making me feel even more uneasy. "Do you always dress like this?"

"For work… yes."

He raises his eyebrows, smiling. "And for a date?"

I feel myself blush. "That depends on the date, I suppose. But generally, no, I wouldn't wear a suit."

I wish he'd leave me alone, but it's quite difficult in such a confined space, and I almost sag with relief when the doors open.

I step out to be faced with the head of a staircase immediately opposite, and the option to turn either left or right. Rather than just saying which way I should go, Miles once again places his arm around me and steers me to the right.

"All the executive offices are up here," he says. "Including mine."

"Oh?" I'm not sure why I should be interested in where his office is, unless he's trying to brag that he's one of the 'executives'.

We turn a corner, making our way down a shorter corridor, until we come to the end. The door in front of us is open and Miles waits, letting me pass through ahead of him, although he follows close behind.

Inside, there's a desk in front of the window which overlooks the city, and behind the desk is a lady who glances up, frowns, and gets to her feet. She's probably in her early-fifties, with neat blonde hair, tied up in a bun behind her head and as she steps out from her desk, I can see she's wearing a skirt and blouse, which are smart, but not as formal as my outfit. Her shoes are more sensible, too.

"This is Miss Hopkins," Miles says, and the woman glances at him. I could swear she narrows her eyes, but it's only for a moment before she looks back at me with a smile.

"I'm Doreen," she says, with a gentle voice. "I'm so sorry. If I'd known you were here, I would have come down to greet you myself." She turns her attention back to Miles again, and this time there's an unmistakable hardening of her features. "I'm sure you've got things you need to be doing, Miles?"

He hesitates for a moment, but then backs up toward the door. "I'll see you later," he says, not taking his eyes from me.

I'm not sure he will, but it seems wise to be polite. "Thank you for bringing me up here." He smiles and ducks out of the room, and I turn back to Doreen. "The lady downstairs offered to call you," I say, and she rolls her eyes.

"I'm sure she did. Miranda's very efficient. It's Miles who's nothing but trouble." I stifle a half-laugh. She joins in and I feel a tingle over my skin. It's an odd sensation, and by no means unpleasant. In fact, it's the exact opposite. I feel like I belong here, even though I've never been here before. "I'll show you in," she says, moving toward a doorway in the corner of the room. The door itself isn't closed and I follow, waiting while she announces me as 'Miss Hopkins', and then I enter.

The room is large, taking up a significant corner of the building, with windows on two walls. The furniture is modern, comprising an enormous desk, roughly in the center of the room, and over on the far side, two long, black leather couches, with a low, glass coffee table between them.

There's a man sitting behind the desk, and the moment he gets to his feet, everything stops.

What was I thinking?

Who was I kidding?

This is no teddy bear.

He's no grizzly, either. At least, I don't think he is. But there's no getting away from it, the man before me exudes power.

That could be because of his build, I suppose. He's around six foot four, with broad shoulders, his white shirt fitting closely to his muscular arms and chest, just like his jeans hug his thighs.

Or maybe it's his dark, brooding good looks, the way his eyes are boring into mine, heating me like a furnace.

I have no idea what makes him seem so commanding. I just know I'm drawn to him... like a magnet.

I also know the silence between us is stretching, and one of us needs to say something. I open my mouth, but he beats me to it. "Please come in. Take a seat."

His voice suits him perfectly; it's so masculine, so controlled, and I somehow put one foot in front of the other, making it across the room to the chair in front of his desk. He waits until I've sat down and then resumes his seat, gazing across his desk at me.

It's my turn to talk now – or it feels that way – but what to say? Would 'I think I love you' be okay?

*Don't be ridiculous…*

"Everyone dresses very casually in your office."

Does that sound like a criticism? I hope not. It wasn't meant as one. It was meant as an observation, and a distraction from the way he makes me feel… which is seriously overdressed in this suit.

*What's happening to me?*

His eyes wander lazily up and down my body, but unlike when Miles did this earlier, I don't feel uncomfortable. I don't feel self-conscious, either. I welcome Theodore Bennett's gaze as it slowly meanders back up to my face, a slight smile settling on his lips.

"There's no proper dress code here," he says, his voice sounding just a little deeper, and he coughs before he continues, "I insist on people being decent, but basically comfort is more important than anything else. People work better if they're comfortable."

"So, you'd be okay if I wore a suit to work… assuming I got the job, of course?" I blush. I wouldn't normally be so presumptuous, but I'm very distracted.

"Are you comfortable wearing a suit?" he asks.

I think about his question for a moment. "I'm most comfortable in leggings, or jeans… or better still, pajamas. But they're for relaxing in… for lying in bed, reading a book. And we're talking about work, aren't we? In a work environment, I'd have to say, yes, I'm most comfortable in a suit."

He pauses, takes a deep breath, and shifts slightly in his seat. "Why?"

"Because dressing like this puts me in the right frame of mind for doing my job."

He nods his head. "I can see that."

"But it doesn't apply to you?"

He smiles and although I feel I should apologize for being more forward than I've ever been in my life, he doesn't give me the chance. "I've been known to wear a suit, and even a tie, when I have to. I have a whole drawer of them at home. And if you feel better wearing a suit, please don't let me stop you."

His smile widens, and he sits forward, averting his gaze from me for a moment, while he taps on his keyboard a few times and then looks back at me.

God, he's gorgeous. I've never seen anyone who looks like he does. Not even in a magazine. His eyes are a dark, chocolate brown, and his jawline bears a hint of stubble, like it's meant to be there, not like he couldn't be bothered to shave. I suck in a breath, wondering what it would be like to be kissed by him... how it would feel to have those bristles abrade my skin.

But then I'm reminded of the fact that I used to think Cole was perfection on legs... and look where that got me.

*Focus, Livia. Focus.*

---

## Hunter

I feel like I need to keep telling myself to breathe, as though without the constant reminder, my heart is going to stop, and I'll die... right here, right now.

I'll die happy, though, because I'll be looking at the most beautiful woman in the world. And who could ask for anything more?

*Breathe… breathe…*

Yeah. Breathing would be good. It would be a lot better than dying, anyway. Especially as I'd like to get to know her… to find out how she can do this to me so easily. I was only going to dip my toe in, not my heart. I hadn't been looking for love. And yet, here I am, falling for the woman who's right in front of me, captivating me… capturing me.

There's something ethereal about her. I know that's partly because she's sitting in the sun's rays, and they're giving a magical glow to her long, blonde hair. But the sun doesn't account for the sparkle in her sky-blue eyes, or the perfection of her porcelain pure skin. It doesn't make sense of the fact that, although she doesn't seem to be wearing very much makeup, there's a pink hue to her cheeks, and a glossy sheen on her lips… or that I want to kiss her.

Man, do I want to kiss her.

*Breathe, Hunter. Breathe…*

She's staring at me, looking right into my eyes, and I could happily stay here forever… held captive in her gaze.

Except I need to pull myself together. I need to stop thinking about her lying on my bed in those sexy pajamas she was just talking about, a smile touching her lips as she smiles up at me…

*Get a grip, man.*

She's here for an interview. It's a process I've been through many times before. The problem is, I can't think of what to say next. I've already screwed up by focusing too much on what she's wearing, my only excuse being that her tight gray suit is too distracting for words.

But now I need to concentrate.

And breathe…

With great reluctance, I tear my eyes away from her and glance at my computer screen, pulling up her resume, before I look back at her again, smiling.

"I'm sorry. We haven't been formally introduced, have we?" I offer my hand across the desk and she takes it. Her skin is soft against mine and I take a moment to get used to the sensation before I add, "I'm Hunter Bennett."

She withdraws her hand, like I just scalded her. "I—I thought I was seeing Theodore Bennett. I mean, I thought I was applying for the position of PA to the CEO," she says, looking confused, and sounding it too.

"You are. I'm the CEO. Theodore Bennett was my father."

"Was?" she pales slightly.

"Yes. He died a year ago, and for some reason best known only to themselves, the board put me in charge."

"Oh, God. I am so sorry. I didn't…"

"Hey…" I hold up my hand. "Please don't worry about it. It's a simple mistake to make." *It's also something Miles should have put you straight on… damn him.* "Although I like to think my father and I are very different men. At least, I hope we are."

Her brow furrows, but I'm not about to go into my family history. Not now.

"I'm still really sorry," she says.

"Don't be." I hate seeing her like this. I need to change the subject… quickly. "Your name…"

She sits forward, the movement interrupting me. "Oh, yes. Sorry. I forgot to introduce myself."

I smile. "You don't need to. I know your name is Livia Hopkins."

"Oh… of course you do." She blushes again, and while I hate the fact that she's so flustered, I can't help smiling. She's so damn beautiful.

"I was just wondering, is Livia short for Olivia?"

She shakes her head. "No. My name is Livia. It's not short for anything."

"It's odd, but when Miles told me your name, I felt sure I'd heard it before. Not the Hopkins part, you understand, just Livia."

"You mean you've met someone called Livia before? Because I never have."

"Neither have I. Not necessarily. That's what I'm trying to say. Your name is familiar, but I can't think where from."

"I see. Well... if you remember, let me know."

"I will."

We stare at each other for a long moment and then my phone beeps, reminding me I've got another meeting in an hour.

"What was that?" she asks.

"Just a reminder. I've got a meeting scheduled..."

She sits forward. "Sorry. I'm taking up too much of your time."

I shake my head. "No, you're not. The meeting isn't for another hour." *And even if it was sooner, I'd make time for you. I don't want you to go... ever.*

She relaxes slightly and I glance at her resume, wishing I'd studied it more closely before she arrived... wishing I'd taken her application for the job more seriously, instead of dismissing it as one of Miles's flirtations. I clench my fists, just for a second or two, the thought of Miles flirting with Livia making my skin crawl... the thought of him doing anything more making my blood boil.

"I see you didn't go to college?" I say, trying to focus.

"No."

"But your high school grades were excellent."

"Yes. There were... personal reasons I couldn't go to college."

She hesitates as she's speaking, and I sense there's a lot more to her answer than she's willing to say. It's not relevant to her working here, though, and it's none of my business… although I'd like it to be. I'd like everything about her to be my business.

"So, you started work when you were eighteen?"

"Yes. My first job was as the secretary to the manager of a small electronics company close to my home."

I check her resume again. "That's in Maine?"

"Yes. In Falmouth."

"I don't think I've ever been there."

"It's right on the coast, just a few miles from Portland." The sparkle in her eyes intensifies and her smile widens as she speaks. "I wouldn't call it a bustling town. I don't think there are more than two thousand people living there… but it was a great place to grow up."

"You miss it." I'm not really asking a question. I'm stating a fact based on instinct.

"Yes, I do."

"Why did you leave?"

She tilts her head, and although that's probably one of the cutest things I've ever seen, I'm slightly distracted, wondering if her departure from her home town might have had something to do with a man. Could she be running away from someone?

"I was looking for something more," she says.

"Something more?" What does that mean?

"Yes." She sits forward slightly. "Leaving home was a huge wrench for me, and I know I could have probably found other opportunities in Portland, and not left Falmouth at all, but I wanted to spread my wings."

"Personally, or professionally?" I have to ask.

"Oh, professionally. I might not have gone to college, but I felt I had a lot more to offer, and Boston seemed like the place to find out if I was right."

My lips twist upwards into a smile, which has nothing to do with the fact that she's made no mention of a man. It's got everything to do with her conviction. She doesn't come across as over-confident, but she knows herself; she knows what she wants, and in my experience, those are rare qualities, not to be ignored.

"So, you moved here and got a job at…" I glance at her resume again. "SKJ Robotics?"

"Yes. I've been there for six months, working as the PA to the CFO." She takes a deep breath. "I know that's not very long, and I know my employment history isn't great, but I'm very methodical and thorough."

Does she think she has to sell herself to me? If she does, she's wrong. I'm already sold.

"I'm sure you are. Unfortunately, I'm not… either methodical or thorough."

She chuckles, and the sound reverberates through my body, all the way to my rock hard cock, making it twitch against my zipper.

"Are you saying you're disorganized?" There's just the slightest hint of a tease in her voice and my cock responds to a painful extent, although I still manage a smile.

"I wouldn't go that far, but I'm in need of constant assistance."

Her eyes sparkle, and she sucks in a breath, letting it out slowly.

*God… could she be any more sexy?*

I'm aware that time isn't on our side, though, and there are things we need to discuss… like when she can start working here. Because I'm going to hire her. I decided that the moment she walked in the door.

"I believe you only have to give a month's notice to your current employers. Is that right?"

She nods her head. "Yes."

"Good." Her eyes widen slightly. "And did Mr. Hampton explain to you about the package we offer here?"

"He said something about a car, and a phone, and a ninety-day trial period."

"I think we can waive that."

"Which one? The car, the phone, or the trial period?"

"The trial period. Although I suppose I ought to ask... can you drive?" There isn't much point in me arranging a car for her if she can't.

"Yes. I don't at the moment. But I used to, when I lived in Falmouth."

"Okay."

She blinks a couple of times, her eyes truly shining now. "Are... are you offering me the job, Mr. Bennett?"

"Yes, but only if you agree to call me Hunter."

"Okay... Hunter."

My name on her lips is about the sexiest thing I've ever heard, but I need to regain some control. I'll have to show her out of my office fairly soon, and at the moment, that would be embarrassing... for both of us.

"It'll all have to be handled through HR," I explain, grabbing a file from my desk.

"I see. Does that mean I'll be hearing from Mr. Hampton?"

She sounds doubtful, bordering on worried, and I drop the file, sitting forward. "Would you rather not?"

"I—I don't want to cause any trouble."

"You're not. Doreen can liaise with you, if that's easier?"

I'd love to say I'd do it myself, but I'm not sure that's a wise idea, given how I feel about her. To be honest, I'm not even sure it's a wise idea to be hiring her. But I can't let her go. I don't think I'll ever be able to let her go.

"W—Would that be okay?"

"Of course."

She smiles and gets to her feet. I copy her, picking up the file again and holding it in front of me as I follow her to the door. I don't even remember what's inside this file, and I've got no intention of doing anything with it, other than using it as a shield, but Livia doesn't seem to notice and when we get outside, she turns and looks up at me.

"I'll be hearing from you, then?"

"Yes, you will."

She holds out her hand and we shake, before she turns to Doreen and says, "Goodbye," with a smile, and I watch her walk down the hall, my eyes fixed on her perfectly formed ass, until she turns the corner and disappears from sight... for now.

"Ahem?" Doreen's exaggerated cough brings me back to reality and I look down at her as she raises her eyebrows. "She seemed nice."

"She is nice," I say. In fact, she's way more than nice. She's perfect. "Can you contact Miles and get him to send me a copy of our draft employment contract?"

Doreen frowns. "You don't want him to handle it?"

"No. Something about Miles seemed to make Miss Hopkins uneasy. I told her you'd liaise with her. That's okay, isn't it?"

"Of course."

I move a little closer to her desk, letting the file drop to my side, its shielding purposes no longer required. "She didn't mention anything to you, did she? About Miles?"

"No, but he was the one who showed her up here."

"He was? Why didn't Miranda call to let you know Miss Hopkins had arrived?"

"She offered, evidently... at least that's what Miss Hopkins said."

"So Miles just happened to be in the reception, did he?"

Doreen shrugs her shoulders and picks up her phone. "I've got to speak with him about the contract... do you want me to ask?" she says.

"No. Leave it for now."

I don't want to make a big deal out of it, and I wander back into my office, sitting down behind my desk and looking at the chair Livia just vacated.

Have I just made the dumbest decision of my life?

I'm not talking about falling for her. That wasn't a decision; that was an instinct... like breathing in and out, which I'm getting to grips with again, now she's gone. What I'm talking about is hiring her to work here... with me. Was it wise to do that, knowing she already owns my heart, and that I'd like nothing more than to give her my body?

Possibly not. There are rules about things like that, when I'm the boss, and she's my employee... and I have a feeling I'm about to break every single one of them. The thing is, though, this is different. She's different.

And it's too late to turn back.

# Chapter Four

*Livia*

Today is my first day at TBA, and although I was thrilled to be offered this opportunity, the month that's gone by since my interview with Hunter Bennett has been a maelstrom of confused emotions.

I suppose it didn't help that I fell for him the moment I walked through his door. After all, getting involved with people at work doesn't seem to end well for me. Not that I'm suggesting Hunter would be interested in me in that way, although he was kindness itself when I mistook him for his dead father... a result of my lack of research.

I heard from Doreen the very next day, relieved that Hunter had picked up on my discomfort about having to deal with Miles Hampton. She emailed me a copy of my employment contract and I read it through, noticing that there was no reference to a trial period, and that all the generous benefits would be starting on the very first day of my employment. Happy with its content, and more than happy about the prospect of working with Hunter Bennett, I signed the contract and returned it to Doreen... and then I typed out my resignation letter to Lucian.

I wondered about leaving it on his desk, but that felt cowardly, so I took it in to him personally, handing it over and waiting while he opened it, with a puzzled expression on his face.

I'd kept the letter brief, offering no explanation for my imminent departure, and once he'd read it, he looked up at me, frowning.

"Why?" he said, his voice unusually cold and detached.

I'd already rehearsed my answer, and I gave it. "It's got nothing to do with the job itself. My reasons are entirely personal."

He might not have supported me when I needed him, but I didn't want to bring that up, or even mention the photographs. They seemed to have stopped, so what was the point?

"Personal?" he asked, frowning.

"Yes."

He stared at me, waiting, and then got up, coming around to my side of his desk. I was standing, but he still used his height, getting too close, and intimidating me.

"You're leaving me in the lurch like this, and all you're gonna say is 'it's personal'?"

"Yes."

I took a step back, putting some space between us, and the movement seemed to startle him back to reality. He shook his head and leaned on the edge of his desk, his shoulders dropping.

"Fine." He sounded resigned, and I left the room, feeling relieved.

I'd made the right decision.

Since then, working for Lucian has been a nightmare. He's taken to sulking, and has only spoken to me when absolutely necessary, which seems incredibly childish. His wife even called me a few days ago, asking if I'd reconsider.

"He's been so difficult to live with since you told him you're leaving. I don't suppose there's any way you could…?" She left her sentence hanging, but I knew what she wanted, and the answer was, 'no'.

As for Cole, I've avoided seeing him at all, and I'm not sorry about that. I'm not sure what I'd have said to him, but I doubt it would have been polite.

I didn't expect a party when I left on Friday, but it would have been nice if my leaving could have been marked somehow. A card, perhaps? Or even just a fond farewell?

Instead, I packed up my desk and walked out the door without so much as a 'goodbye'.

It reminded me of why I didn't belong there... especially as I'd received more photographs in the last few days and had no-one to turn to. I deleted them all, knowing I'd be getting a new phone as soon as I started at TBA, and that would be the end of it.

It was the end of the first chapter of my time in Boston... and hopefully the beginning of a much happier one.

At least, that was what I'd hoped, until I spent the weekend doing some proper research into my new employers... or more specifically, into my new boss.

Almost as soon as I'd started, I wished I hadn't. Not because I couldn't find out very much about him, but because the Internet was awash with articles. They weren't the kind of articles I was looking for, though. They were gossip columns, almost all of which described him as 'Hunter Bennett, millionaire playboy'. That phrase left me cold... and wondering.

He didn't come across as a playboy, although I wasn't sure I could trust my own judgement when it came to men. Even so, the Hunter Bennett I'd met had seemed like a gentleman. He came across as fun and exciting, but also – dare I say – tender and considerate.

I'm not sure now which version of him is the right one, but as I climb down from the bus outside TBA's offices, I realize I'm about to find out.

Maybe...

*

"Miss Hopkins… it's good to see you again."

Doreen greets me in the reception, before I've even made it to the desk, and I shake her hand. "It's good to see you, too. And please, call me Livia."

She guides me toward the elevators, pressing the 'up' button. "I've been meaning to ask, do you prefer Livia to Olivia, or Liv… or Livvi?"

I can't be bothered to explain that Livia is my name, and it's not a derivation of anything, so I just say, "Livia is fine."

The doors open and I let her get in first, noting that she looks almost exactly the same as she did the last time I was here, except her skirt is navy blue today, instead of the black one she wore when I came for my interview.

"I don't know whether Hunter explained," she says as the doors close, "but I'm only going to be here for this week, and then I'm leaving."

"Oh… I see."

"I'm going to guess from your reaction that he didn't mention it."

"It must have slipped his mind."

She smiles. "I admire your loyalty. Hunter will appreciate that."

I want to ask her if loyalty to Hunter is a problem around here, but I can't see why it would be, and I imagine she's just making conversation.

"Where are you going? When you leave, I mean?"

"England."

"Oh?" I hadn't expected that. I'd assumed she'd say she was going to work somewhere else, or maybe that she was retiring.

"My daughter and her husband live there, and they're about to have my first grandchild, so I'm going to stay with them for a few months."

77

I nod my head, just as the doors open and we both step out. "Is it going to be a boy, or a girl... or don't they know yet?"

"It's a girl," she says, beaming. "They're going to call her Phoebe."

"That's pretty."

She tilts her head. "I wasn't sure about it to start with, but it's growing on me."

We get to her office, which I guess will be mine soon, and she waits, letting me enter ahead of her. The door to Hunter's room is open, but there's no sign of him, and I walk over to Doreen's desk, unsure what to do. I don't feel as though I can sit down, not when she's still here, but she solves the problem for me.

"If you want to leave your purse in the bottom drawer, along with mine, I'll take you on a quick tour of the offices."

I'm not sure why she didn't give me the tour on the way up here, but I'm not about to question anything she does, and I just smile and say, "Okay," before I go around to the other side of the desk, depositing my purse as instructed. Then I straighten my jacket and follow her back out into the hall.

"When Theodore Bennett first started the company," she says as we walk along, "he just rented the room that's now Hunter's office."

"Did you work here, even then?"

"Not straight away. I joined after about a year, but I was Theodore's first full-time employee, and to start with, I had a desk in the corner of his office. It was my first job, too. I was straight out of college and I've been here ever since, except the few months after my daughter was born." It's obvious that leaving is going to be a wrench for her, but before I can say anything, she continues, "I was grateful for the work when I first came. I knew nothing about advertising." That sounds reassuring. "I was engaged, too, and my fiancé and I were saving for our first home. Theodore needed an assistant, and luckily, I seemed to fit the bill."

"The company's obviously grown since."

She smiles. "Yes. For the first few years, he outsourced everything. Then, slowly but surely, he brought it all in-house and took over the entire building."

"And does TBA own it now, or is it still rented?"

"Oh, no... the company owns it." We stop at the top of the stairs, by the elevators. "This is the executive floor," she says.

"Miles Hampton explained that when I came for my interview."

She nods her head. "I'm sure he did." She sounds very dismissive of him, which makes me smile. "The executive officers can be a little self-important, but don't let them get to you. Hunter's in charge, and you work for him, not them."

I nod my head, and she puts her foot down on the first step before she turns back to me.

"I forgot to say, there's a board room further along the hall. They have quarterly meetings of all the board members, and you're expected to take notes... but don't worry about it; they've only just had one, so you've got a couple of months to get used to who's who and what's what."

I feel like I'm being thrown to the lions, but try not to show my trepidation as we head down the stairs, stopping at the floor below.

"The account executives and administration staff hang out here," Doreen says, looking at me with a smile.

"Account executives? Shouldn't they be on the fourth floor?"

She smiles, shaking her head. "Account executives are responsible for looking after the clients. Essentially, they're the sales force of the business. That's over-simplifying their role, and they'd probably all walk out in protest if they heard me describing them like that… but that doesn't make it any less true."

"So, they're kinda self-important, too?"

"You could say that. Don't get me wrong, the company couldn't function without them, but they never let you forget it." She says those last few words under her breath, and I have to chuckle.

Making our way down another floor, she explains that this is home to the design teams, that there are several of them, and that they each have different functions.

"Don't look so worried."

I hadn't been aware that I was. "There's a lot to take on board."

"And no-one expects you to learn it all in a day. That's why I'm not introducing you to anyone yet." We continue down to the first floor, coming out into the foyer. "To be honest, most of the people you need to meet will come to you, because they'll need to see Hunter. Or they'll think they need to see him."

"Is it my job to stop them?"

"No. It's your job to assist him. The clue is in your job title. Although, to be fair, Hunter doesn't require much assistance."

"Really? That's not what he told me."

She smiles. "Then he was being modest."

We wander past the reception desk, and I give Miranda a smile. Apart from Hunter and Miles Hampton, she's the only other person I know here, so I feel I shouldn't neglect the acquaintance. She smiles back, but Doreen moves on toward the glass-framed meeting room on the far side.

"Why is this here, if there's a board room upstairs?" I ask and she turns, her lips twitching upwards.

"This is one of Hunter's additions," she says. "I can see the value of it, I guess. Clients don't have to wander around the building, and it certainly looks good."

There's a slight hint of disapproval to her tone, but I get the feeling her loyalty to her boss won't let her voice it.

She stops and turns around, glancing over my shoulder, a slight smile forming on her lips.

"Would you excuse me, just for a minute?"

I nod my head and she darts away, hurrying over to a woman who's just come in through the main entrance. Doreen kisses her on both cheeks, and then pulls her aside, the two of them talking and the other woman shrugging her shoulders a couple of times before the stranger departs.

Doreen rushes back, her smile even wider, and a definite spring in her step.

"Well... that's gonna make Hunter's day."

"What is?"

"The news I've just received." She turns. "Shall we go back up to the office?"

"Sure."

I've got no idea what she's talking about, but I follow her to the elevators, getting in with her the moment the doors open. She's positively fizzing with excitement, although she doesn't say anything more, and as soon as we get to the top floor, we make our way back to her office again.

Once inside, she heads straight for Hunter's open door while I hang back. She clearly senses I'm not with her though, and turns.

"You need to come with me," she says, frowning slightly. "Everywhere I go this week, you go with me... except the ladies' room, obviously. It's the only way you're gonna learn."

I nod my head and straighten my jacket again, then follow her into Hunter's room, noting that she doesn't knock... not even on the doorframe.

He's sitting behind his desk, staring at his computer screen, but he looks up the moment we come into the room, and then stands when he sees me. He's wearing jeans and a white button-down shirt again, and although my heart still skips a beat, just at the sight of him, the words 'millionaire playboy' ring around my head.

"Livia… I'm sorry. I should have come out to greet you."

"It's okay. Doreen's been showing me around the building."

He nods his head, smiling down at her. "Thank you," he says.

"Why are you thanking me?" She sounds confused. "It's my job."

He pushes his fingers back through his thick, dark hair before he looks back at me again. "What did you make of it all?"

Doreen rolls her eyes. "She'll get used to it," she says, answering before I get the chance. "But that's not why we came to see you."

"Oh?" Hunter sits down again, looking up at us, his brow furrowing. "Has something happened?"

"In a manner of speaking." Doreen moves a little closer to his desk, and I follow her, doing as she instructed, and acting like her shadow. "Do you remember last month at that sales meeting, when Preston Tucker said he thought Palmerston's were going out of business, and I told you they weren't…"

"But you said they were merging with Banks, French and Stanley," Hunter says, finishing her sentence.

"I said they might be, if the financials stacked up. Well… my friend who works at Banks, French and Stanley has just told me the deal's off."

Hunter leaps to his feet, his face lighting up. "You mean the merger isn't going ahead?"

"Exactly."

Hunter stares at her for a moment and then walks to the window, staring out at the skyline. I can see his shoulders relax, like there's been a built-in tension that he's finally releasing, and he sucks in a breath, his muscles flexing, as he turns back around again.

"What are Palmerston's chances?" he asks, his eyes alight as he comes back over to the desk again.

"Not great," Doreen says. "Without the merger, I'd say they've got weeks, rather than months."

Hunter nods his head. "I agree. We need to act fast."

"Shall I get all the account execs together for a meeting this afternoon?"

"Yes. And I don't want any excuses. I don't care what they're doing. I want them all there."

He's like a different man. Not that I know him very well, but compared to how he was at my interview, he seems much more driven... determined... forceful.

Doreen heads for the door, and I follow in her wake.

"Sorry, Livia." I stop, turning, as Hunter says my name and I see he's smiling at me. "You probably didn't understand a word of that."

"You don't have to apologize." I look from him to Doreen, and back again. "I get how important this is. From what I could gather, one of your competitors was in trouble and was going to merge with another one?" He nods his head. "Only that's all changed now, and the company that was in trouble is likely to go out of business in the next few weeks. You want to make the most of the situation by getting your sales team together, presumably so you can... I don't know... swoop in and pick up their clients?"

There's a very brief silence, of no more than a couple of seconds, and then Hunter laughs, throwing his head back. The sound is glorious and echoes through my body.

I turn to Doreen, and she smiles. "You're gonna fit in just fine," she says, and we both leave the room.

\*

I doubt Doreen would still think so highly of me if she knew how little I'd understood of the meeting between Hunter and his account executives. It finished over thirty minutes ago, and my head is still spinning.

There were nine of us around the desk in the glass meeting room downstairs, including Hunter, Doreen and myself, and I can't remember any of the other people's names… except for Preston Tucker. I think that's only because Doreen had already mentioned him, though. No-one was formally introduced to me. There wasn't time, and Hunter was clearly keen to get on with the meeting. He took control, exerting his authority and making sure everyone knew what was required of them. It seemed to go well, even if I didn't understand everything that was said, and everyone left seeming much more invigorated than when they'd arrived.

I can't believe I've almost reached the end of my first day already. It's been complicated and busy, but great fun, and I've enjoyed it enormously. Everyone I've met has been friendly and relaxed, and although I'm exhausted, I'm looking forward to tomorrow… and the next day.

"Livia?" I look up to see Hunter standing on the other side of Doreen's desk, smiling down at me. We moved another chair in here this morning and I've been sitting beside her, getting to grips with the computer system… when we've had time.

"I meant to give these to you earlier, but it's been a slightly crazy day, even by our standards."

He hands over a box, which contains the latest iPhone, and on top of it, a set of car keys. I can't contain my gasp when I notice the Mercedes logo on the key fob.

Seriously? A Mercedes?

"Um… thank you."

He smiles, and my heart lurches in my chest. I need to get a grip. He's my boss and even if I have fallen for him, it's not practical – or sensible – to think about him in any other way. I have to keep telling myself he's a playboy, and ignore the heat in the pit of my stomach, and the fact that he's staring at me, and that I like it. Doreen coughs and he turns to her, clearing his throat. "Do you know where Livia's car is parked? No-one told me."

"It's in bay twelve," she says, looking at me. "That's bay twelve of the parking garage in the basement of the building."

"I see. Thank you so much. This is so, so kind."

Hunter seems confused by my reaction, his brow furrowing, and he hesitates for a moment or two before returning to his office.

Doreen leans over. "If you want to head off, you can."

I check my watch. "But there's still fifteen minutes to go."

She smiles. "I know, but as Hunter said, it's been a crazy day, and it was your first… so go find your car and head home. We can do this all over again tomorrow."

"Exactly the same?"

"No. That's the best part about this job. No two days are ever the same. Tomorrow will probably be even crazier than today."

"Really?"

She shrugs her shoulders. "Who knows?"

I get up, retrieving my purse from the drawer. "Are you sure about this?"

"Absolutely. Have a nice evening."

"You too." I nod toward Hunter's office. "Should I say 'goodbye'?"

"Don't worry. He seems kinda preoccupied for some reason."

"Probably everything that's going on with Palmerston's."

She frowns, shaking her head. "Things like that don't normally affect him… not like this. But don't worry about it. I'll let him know you've gone."

"Okay."

"See you tomorrow."

I give her a wave and head for the elevators, feeling a mixture of relief, tiredness, and satisfaction. As far as I know, I did okay today. I certainly didn't screw up. I didn't tell my boss I'm in love with him, or actually drool while in his presence… and that's the main thing.

The elevator takes me to the parking garage, where I easily find bay twelve, and the gray convertible Mercedes that's parked in it. I giggle, pressing the button on the key fob, and climb inside, throwing my bag onto the passenger seat as I look at the controls. I'm not sure I'll ever work out what they're all for, but I lean back in the seat, taking a deep breath and absorbing that 'new car' smell, before I giggle again.

*— This is my new number, Mom. I'd call, but I'm exhausted. Love you. xx*

I'm already in my pajamas, and am sitting on the bed, having transferred all the details from my old phone to my new one. My dinner is cooking, and with any luck, I'll stay awake long enough to eat it.

Mom replies promptly, which isn't unusual for her at this time of night.

*— We can talk at the weekend, but I'm dying to know, how was your first day? And how's the car? xx*

I smile, recalling the journey home. It went better than I'd expected, considering I haven't driven for months.

*— My first day was busy, but really good. I enjoyed it. The car is great. xx*

I don't tell her the car is a Mercedes, or that it took me nearly ten minutes to work out how to put the roof down. Instead, I sit back, checking out some of the features on my new phone, which beeps with Mom's response.

— *You'll have to drive up and show us. I meant to say, Uncle David said he'd sent you a 'good luck' email. xx*

— *Okay. I'll check it out. Thanks xx*

I go onto a browser and log in to my mail account, where I find a few unread messages. There's one from my uncle, wishing me luck in my new job... and much to my surprise, there's one from SKJ Robotics. The subject reads 'Payroll Discrepancy', and I click on it, reading...

*'Dear Miss Hopkins,*

*There has been a minor discrepancy in your final paycheck. Can you please call me on the number at the bottom of this message, at your earliest convenience?*

*I look forward to hearing from you.*

*Howard Dawkins'*

I don't remember anyone at the company called Howard Dawkins, but I had very little to do with the payroll or HR departments, and the message seems legitimate. The logo is definitely familiar. It used to appear automatically on every email I ever typed for Lucian. I wonder what the discrepancy is, but I hope I won't need to repay them anything. Money is tight enough as it is.

I know I shouldn't be so worried about a supposedly 'minor discrepancy', but what's minor to a corporation like SKJ Robotics could be major to me, and I've hardly slept at all. It might only be eight in the morning, but I know a lot of people used to get into the office early, and I can't wait any longer. I dial the number on the email, half expecting it to go to voicemail, and almost jump out of my skin when a man answers.

"Is that Howard Dawkins?"

"No. He's not due in for another thirty minutes. Can I take a message?"

*Damn...*

"Sure. Can you tell him Livia Hopkins called?"

"Ahh... you're the one with the problem paycheck."

He makes it sound like it's my fault, even though I had nothing to do with it. "Yes, although I don't know what the problem is. I don't suppose you can help?"

"I'm afraid not. Howard's dealing with it. I can get him to call you, though."

"Okay." I give him my number. "I started my new job yesterday, so if I don't answer, he'll have to leave a message and I'll get back to him."

"I'll let him know."

I feel even more frustrated now, but I end the call and swallow down a quick cup of coffee before setting off for work.

It takes me less time to get to the office than I'd expected, and I'm parked in bay twelve well before eight-thirty. I'm not due in yet, so I sit in the car, hoping Howard Dawkins might call back, and while I'm waiting, I watch some of my new colleagues arriving to start their day. Most of them are dressed down, like Hunter was yesterday, and I smile. I like the relaxed atmosphere of this place, even if I am still wearing a suit myself... and I intend to keep on doing so. Like I said to Hunter, I find it easier to focus.

When I'm not thinking about him, that is...

My phone rings and I jump, even though I'd been expecting the call, or at least half hoping for it. I answer straight away, recognizing the number as the same one I dialed this morning.

"Is that Livia Hopkins?" The man's voice has a higher pitch than most... or maybe I'm just getting used to how deep and masculine Hunter sounds.

*Stop it!*

"Yes, it is. Is this Howard Dawkins?"

"Yes. Thanks for phoning earlier. Sorry I wasn't here to take your call."

"That's okay. I understand there's a problem with my paycheck?"

"There is. I just need to find the document..." I can hear papers rustling, but the sound is drowned out by another. It's the throaty noise of a car engine, and I look out through the windshield to see a bright red sports car drive past, the driver reversing with ease into a bay at the end of the garage. I admire the car, noting the prancing horse logo on the hood, and I smile... who wouldn't? It's a beautiful Ferrari, and I'm still gazing at it when the door opens and Hunter steps out. I don't know why I'm surprised. It's the perfect car for a playboy, and I imagine him with beautiful models on his arms, arriving at restaurants and opening nights.

God... what a depressing thought.

"Ahh... here we are. Found it." Howard's voice permeates my frozen brain. "It seems we made an error. You had some unpaid vacation allowance, which we failed to add to your last payment."

I drag my eyes from Hunter, who's leaning into his car, retrieving something, and I focus on Howard. "Are you saying the error is in my favor?"

"Yes." I can't help smiling. "The problem is, although we still have your employment file, I'm afraid your banking details were removed from our systems when you left."

"So you can't transfer the money?"

"No, but we can send you a check, if that's okay... unless you'd rather give me your bank details again?"

"No, a check will be fine."

To be honest, I'm so relieved I don't owe them anything, I don't care how they're going to send the money.

I wait, while he verifies my address hasn't changed, then we end the call and I let out a sigh, glancing out the windshield again, and gasping when I see Hunter is still by his car. The door's closed now, though, and he's just standing there, looking in my direction. Is he looking at my car, or at me? I can't be sure, and I wonder if I should wave, or get out and go over to him. I hesitate, giving it a moment's thought… but it's a moment too long, and before I can do anything, he shakes his head and turns, walking away.

*Well… that was weird.*

I've made it to Friday, and while I don't normally celebrate getting to the end of the week, I feel as though congratulations are in order.

It's been hard.

Okay, so it's been fun, too, but I don't think I've ever felt so tired.

There's been so much to learn, but Doreen has made it easy, giving me the benefit of her years of expertise and experience. She's stepped back a little further every day, gradually letting me take over, and although Hunter seems a lot more efficient than he implied, I've seen how much he relies on Doreen, and I've wondered on more than one occasion, how I'm ever going to fill her shoes.

This afternoon, there's a party being given in her honor, although I knew nothing about it until this morning, when Miranda called to say the caterers had arrived, and wanted to know where they should set up. I had to ask Hunter, who took over and dealt with everything, and it was then that I realized he'd organized the entire event without me even knowing.

It feels like everyone who works here is rammed into the boardroom. Hunter makes a speech and presents Doreen with gifts, one of which is from the staff, and the other from him. Doreen's close to tears, but I grab a few minutes alone with her not long afterwards.

"I can't thank you enough... for everything."

She smiles up at me. "You don't have to thank me, Livia. You're gonna be just fine." She tilts her head. "I think you're just what Hunter needs."

I'm not sure what she means by that, but before I can ask, one of the account executives, whose name I can't remember, comes and whisks her away.

A tingle shudders down my spine. I feel as though I'm being watched, and after what happened with the photographs, it's not a comfortable sensation. I turn, my eyes darting around the room, until they quickly settle on Miles Hampton, who's staring straight at me. Fortunately, there are too many people here for him to get any closer, but he smiles and winks. I smile back, just to be polite, and then turn away again. God, he gives me the creeps.

My eyes are instantly drawn to Hunter, who's standing over by the windows, talking to two women. I feel a claw of jealousy clutching at my heart, but I ignore it. What right have I got to be jealous of my playboy boss? None at all.

Their group is joined by a man and another woman, and while they all talk, I notice Hunter take a slight step back, and then raise his head, gazing across the room, directly at me. It's as though he knew exactly where I was, and although I think about looking away, I don't want to. There's a hum of conversation continuing all around us, interrupted by peels of laughter and the clinking of glasses, but regardless of all that, we just stare...

For ages...

And ages.

I might be inexperienced with men, but do playboys really do things like this?

Do they capture your heart and hold it so gently?

I don't know.

What I do know is that I'm really struggling not to tell him I don't want him to be a playboy, but that I want to be his... always.

—~~—

## *Hunter*

Doreen's been gone for a week now, and it's the strangest thing... even though she'd been here almost since the beginning of time, and I often wondered how I'd ever cope without her, it already feels like she was never here at all.

In just a few short days, I've grown used to waking up with a feeling of excitement in the pit of my stomach because I'm looking forward to coming in to work. I've become more accustomed to the way my heart flips over in my chest every time I see Livia sitting behind her desk... because it's her desk now, not Doreen's. I'm slightly better at controlling my reactions to hearing her voice on the phone when she transfers calls, although I still struggle when she wanders into my room, and I look up to see her standing there, so beautiful, before me.

I think we work together really well, and she's fitting in perfectly, although it took her a couple of days to get used to not knocking on my doorframe before coming in.

"You don't have to do that, you know?" I said from behind my desk, when she'd done it for the third time on her first morning after Doreen had left.

"Do what?" She looked a little startled, evidently unsure what I was talking about.

"Knock on the door… or even the doorframe."

"Oh. Are you sure?"

"Positive."

"But what if you were…" She blushed, which I found both arousing and intriguing.

"What if I was what?"

"In the middle of something private." Her blush deepened, and I wondered what she could be thinking about. I was tempted to ask, but she was embarrassed enough already.

"Then I'd close the door."

"I see."

"But you don't need to worry. I've never done anything that private in here."

Her eyes widened, and she sucked in a deep breath, and even though she was wearing her suit, with the jacket still done up, I noticed the way her breasts heaved. It made my cock ache, and I regretted my decision to tease her.

She smiled then, depositing the file she was carrying on my desk before she left. I wondered if I'd gone too far, and part of me wanted to follow her out, to ask. Except we weren't on those kind of terms.

We're still not. Not yet.

I hope we will be, though. Very soon. And even where we are now is better than where we've come from…

The month I spent waiting for her to start working here was torture. It was also the longest month of my life. I counted every hour of every day, doubting my sanity for employing someone

I'd fallen for, but wanting her so much, it hurt. The time dragged, and I only got through it by keeping busy. As well as all my normal activities, I made a point of dealing with everything related to Livia's employment, including selecting her phone and car. The phone was easy; I just got her exactly the same one as mine.

As for the car, I checked what employees on her pay-grade are normally allocated and discovered the make and model varies.

"It's dictated by price," Miles said when I asked the question. "We go wherever we can get the best deal."

"I see. Can you send me the details of what we can get for Miss Hopkins?"

"Why don't I just order the car?"

"Because I'm asking you to send me the details."

I could tell he was confused, but I wasn't in the mood to offer an explanation, and about an hour later, an email landed in my inbox containing a list of cars, all of which were perfectly adequate and perfectly dull.

I wanted something more than that for Livia, and after a couple of minutes' thought, I picked up the phone...

It took three weeks for the car to be delivered, and when it was, news traveled fast.

"A Mercedes? You've got her a fucking Mercedes?" Miles said, walking right into my office and up to my desk, staring down at me. It's one thing for Livia – or Doreen in her time – not to knock, but I object to anyone else doing it. Especially Miles.

"Good morning, Miles. Do come in." I couldn't contain my sarcasm and didn't bother trying.

"You realize her car cost more than mine, don't you?"

"And?" I said, putting down my pen as I sat back in my chair.

"There's a hierarchy. I'm a department head. Livia Hopkins is going to be your PA."

"I'm aware of that."

"Then why did you get her a car that's more than thirty thousand dollars over the allocated budget?"

I stood, towering above him, although he didn't flinch, which was annoying. "Go speak to the Finance Department. They'll tell you the car is on budget."

He narrowed his eyes. "You can't be serious," he said. "Are you telling me you got a Mercedes for twenty-five thousand dollars? Because if you are——"

"I'm sorry, Miles, but you'll have to leave." Doreen's voice cut him off mid-sentence and we both turned to see her standing in the doorway. "I'm afraid Hunter has an appointment in ten minutes, and he can't be late."

Like everyone else in the building, Miles knew better than to argue with Doreen and, although I could tell he had more to say, he backed out of my office. Doreen stepped aside to let him leave and then came further into the room.

"I don't have an appointment, do I?" I looked over at Doreen once he'd gone.

"No. But I can tell when you're about to lose it, and it sounded like you were getting there."

"Yeah, I was," I said as I sat back down, shaking my head. "Miles is such an asshole."

Her lips twitched upward, but she didn't say anything, and turned away, although as she got to the threshold, she looked back.

"Did you really get a Mercedes for twenty-five thousand dollars?"

I gave her a smile, but didn't reply, and after a second or two, she went back to her desk.

The only person who knows my secret is Marcus Fisher. He's the Chief Financial Officer, and I got him to handle the transaction for Livia's car, knowing I could trust him. I appointed him not long after I took up my position here, and I know he's loyal. He won't tell anyone that, while the company usually leases its vehicles, on this occasion, we bought it, and that although TBA paid twenty-five thousand dollars to the Mercedes dealership, I made up the deficit from my personal account.

I don't know what Miles made of that episode. I haven't bothered to ask. But I'm fairly sure Doreen guessed what was going on. That was why I had to be careful around her, once Livia actually started working here. I realized she'd see right through me if I spent too much time around my new PA, and I didn't want anyone – not even Doreen – to think I'd employed Livia because of how I feel about her, or because of how she looks. So, I kept my distance last week, while Doreen was showing her the ropes, just in case I gave myself away.

Even then, it was a struggle. Every moment I was in Livia's presence, it took all my concentration not to focus on my need for her, which hadn't diminished in the slightest. That first morning, when she and Doreen came into my office, I wanted her so much, it was like a physical ache, deep inside me, and it was a real effort to listen to Doreen, rather than walk around my desk and take Livia in my arms.

What Doreen had to tell me was important, though. It wasn't as important as Livia, but it was important nonetheless. She came with the news that the dreaded merger between Palmerston's and Banks, French and Stanley, was off. There was the potential, within that news, for a massive uplift in business for TBA, and although Livia had only been here for roughly an hour, she picked up on what was happening straight away. I was impressed by that. I was also impressed by how she helped Doreen arrange the impromptu meeting we held that afternoon. What pleased me a lot less was the way in which all the male account execs around the table responded to her. None of them had met her before, and they couldn't take their eyes off of her.

I wanted to reprimand them for leering at her like a piece of meat. I couldn't say a word, though, because I knew I'd give myself away... maybe not to them, but to Doreen.

And possibly to Livia, too.

Oddly, that didn't worry me. I didn't care if she knew how I felt. In fact, I welcomed the idea that she'd realize how much she means to me, or even that I might be able to tell her one day. I can't wait for her to know that I fall asleep thinking of her, wake up longing for her, and spend every second in between dreaming of her.

I guess that's why I didn't shy away from what happened at Doreen's party. I knew I wouldn't be able to spend any time with Livia – especially not at a social gathering, where tongues were more likely to wag – but there was a moment...

It sounds like a cliché, but our eyes met across the crowded room, and it was just perfect. Neither of us could look away. We were drawn to each other, like magnets, and we stared and stared, for what seemed like forever. I felt a connection between us then, and there was something in Livia's eyes that told me she felt it, too. At least, I hope she did... because it was magical.

This week, since Doreen's been gone, it's been slightly easier. That's to say, I haven't had to hide my feelings. Being around Livia doesn't get any easier in itself, but to be honest, we've been so busy, neither of us has had time to think straight, let alone anything else. We certainly haven't found the time to mention that 'moment' at Doreen's leaving party, but I keep hoping that means we don't need to.

Like I say, she's fitting in here perfectly as far as her work is concerned, and the situation with Palmerston's means she's been thrown in at the deep end. I've had back-to-back meetings, which she's had to attend, and as well as reports and evaluations which I've had to prepare, I've also taken over doing all the proposals, so the account execs can work on more important things… like getting in front of potential clients, and persuading them that TBA is where they want to put their business. Livia's taken it all in her stride. She's sensible enough to know when to ask if she's unsure what to do, but generally, she just gets on with things, which is a godsend.

I wish we hadn't been so busy… that it hadn't all been about work, and that I'd been able to find the time to talk to her. I'm dying to know more about her. Specifically, I want to know if she's seeing anyone.

Naturally, that's because I want to start seeing her myself.

But I feel an even greater need to find out after I saw her in the car park one morning last week. I think it was her second day here, and I was surprised to find her Mercedes already parked up in bay twelve. My first thought was that she'd probably come in a little early to make a good impression – not that she needed to – but then I realized she was on the phone, and there was something about her face, about the smile on her lips and the way her eyes lit up, that made me wonder if she might be talking to her boyfriend. The thought made my chest ache, and I considered waiting for her and riding up in the elevator together, so I could try to find out. I changed my mind in the end, discretion proving to be the better part of curiosity, and since then, she's made no mention of anyone special. She hasn't taken any private calls that I'm aware of, and has worked late on two evenings, without feeling the need to mention it to anyone… so I'm starting to wonder.

And hope.

The clock ticks around to lunchtime, and although I've still got three emails to send, one of which is going to be relatively long and detailed, I can't stop thinking about Livia.

Would it hurt to go out and talk to her? I've got the perfect excuse, after all. I can ask how she's been getting on since

Doreen's departure. It's the end of her first week and now seems like an excellent opportunity to see if she needs help with anything. I know that's still making the conversation about work, but hopefully I'll be able to turn it around.

All I've got to do is take the chance…

I get up, swallowing down the unexpected nerves that rise from my stomach, and I take a deep breath before walking over to my door. It's open, as always, and I go straight out, my blood boiling in an instant, when I see Miles Hampton, perched on the edge of Livia's desk.

He's leaning over her, and although she's pulled her chair back, edging it away from him, he's not getting the hint.

"Are you here to see me, Miles?"

He jumps up and turns to face me. "Um… I was, but I can't remember what about now."

He expects me to believe him? "In that case, maybe you should leave and come back when you've remembered," I say, glaring at him. "I'm sure you've got work to do. And so has Livia."

His eyes darken, and I can tell he'd love to bite at my comment. He's wise enough not to, and just says, "Okay… I'm going," instead.

I wait, watching him until he disappears around the corner, heading back to his office, and then I turn to Livia, who's blushing to the roots of her light blonde hair.

"Sorry," she says, speaking before I get the chance, although her voice is a low whisper.

"What for?" I make my way over to her desk, standing at the end of it.

"You were right. I should have been working."

I feel terrible now. "I didn't… I mean, that remark wasn't aimed at you."

"That doesn't make it any less true."

I move closer, and although I don't sit on her desk, like Miles was, I lean against it, looking down at her. "Please don't feel uncomfortable. That's the last thing I want." Her eyes widen slightly and she gazes up at me. "I only came out to ask how you've been getting along this week." She frowns, looking doubtful. "What's wrong?"

"Miles just asked the same question," she says.

"Oh, I see. And this feels like a conspiracy?"

She smiles. "I'd say coincidence more than conspiracy."

"Ahh… but the difference is, I care about your answer." Her gasp is almost inaudible, but the flush on her cheeks is unmistakable. "I mean it, Livia. I want to know how it's been, if there's anything you need, or anything I can do to make things better for you… easier for you?"

She blinks, her eyes fixed on mine, and her smile widens. "You've been so kind already."

Have I? I'm not aware of having been especially kind. I'm just aware of loving her so much it hurts. I can't mention that, though, so I stick to work… for now.

"You call it kind that I've made you work late?" I ask.

"You didn't make me work late. You asked me to. Although I'll admit, I'm looking forward to the weekend."

"Oh? Are you seeing your boyfriend?"

What the hell is wrong with me? I might have been dying to know if she's free, but why did I have to blurt out the question like a desperate teenager? She must think I'm such a loser now. But what can I say? I can't tell her that love does crazy things to your brain. That would mean explaining how I feel about her, and while I don't mind her knowing, I don't think now is the best time… not given the shocked expression on her face.

"I—I meant I was looking forward to sleeping for as long as possible."

Her voice comes out as a staccato whisper, like she's struggling to believe I just asked her that, almost as much as she's wrestling with giving me a sensible answer.

"So, you don't have a boyfriend?"

It doesn't seem so bad asking the second time. And, allowing for certain ambiguities in her response, I really need to know. Besides, I've already made a fool of myself once...

"No. I don't. Unlike you."

Even before she finishes speaking, she claps her hand across her mouth, her cheeks flaming red. She definitely didn't mean to say that, but now she has, I'm more than intrigued and I lean in just a little closer to her, lowering my voice.

"I don't know what you've heard about me, but I don't have a boyfriend, either."

She lowers her hand. "Sorry," she says. "That wasn't what I meant. I just thought... I mean, I read..." She stops talking again, incapable of finishing a sentence.

"What did you read?"

She lowers her eyes, staring at the desk. "That... that you're a playboy."

"Oh, I see." She looks up again, and it's impossible not to see the glistening in her eyes. Does that mean she's going to cry? I edge closer, but she doesn't move away. Thank God. "I know what they say about me, Livia, but I promise, that's all in the past. I'm not that man anymore."

She sucks in a slightly stuttered breath, biting on her bottom lip and smiling as she does so, and my heart feels like it's bursting in my chest. Can it be? Can it be that my answer meant something to her? Is it possible that I mean something to her? Please don't let me be imagining that...

She opens her mouth to speak, and I hope against hope she's not going to shoot me down in flames.

"I—I…" Whatever she was going to say is cut off by the ringing of the telephone on her desk, which makes her jump. She takes a breath, then reaches over and answers it, "Hunter Bennett's office. How can I help?"

I'm not sure I'm capable of coherent thought, let alone speech, but she sounds so professional. Did I read her wrong? Was she going to tell me she didn't believe me… or that she didn't care? I watch her as she listens to whoever's on the line, my mind in turmoil, my heart in stasis.

"Just one moment, please," she says, and then she glances up at me, her brow furrowed, and a look of hurt filling her eyes. *What's happened now?* She reaches forward, putting the call on hold. "It's someone called Ella… for you."

That slight hesitation tells me everything I need to know. She thinks I've lied to her.

I let out a sigh, getting to my feet. "You've gotta love little sisters. Their sense of timing is immaculate."

Livia's face clears in an instant, and I smile when I hear her sigh of relief. I was right. For a second, I think about taking the receiver from Livia and telling Ella to call back, but I don't want to over-react. I could be reading too much into a few very simple gestures.

Except I don't think I am.

I walk to my office door, pausing on the threshold and looking back at Livia. She's staring at me, her eyes alight, her lips parted, and I stare back, unable to move, unwilling to breathe, to break another of those moments.

"Y—Your call," she says eventually and I remember Ella and nod my head, going into my office and sitting at my desk, before I pick up the phone.

"Sis?"

"Take your time, Hunter. I've got nothing better to do with my evening."

I can hear glasses clinking, a hum of voices and music, and a woman laughing. "It sounds like it. Where are you?"

"In a little bar we've discovered."

"Who's 'we'?"

"Just me and some friends."

She's being evasive, but I'm not sure I want to know exactly what she's doing, or who she's doing it with. "As long as you're being careful."

"Oh… lighten up, will you?"

"You're still my little sister."

"And I suppose you're gonna fly over to Paris to protect me, are you?"

I sit forward slightly. "Do you need protecting?"

"No. I need you to stop fussing, and tell me who just answered the phone. It sure as hell wasn't Doreen. She didn't even know who I was."

"Why should she? You're not a world-famous chef yet, you know?"

"I'm never likely to be. But who was she?"

"My new PA."

"What happened to Doreen? Did you finally drive her away?"

"No. She left of her own free will to spend some time with her family in England."

"When did this happen?"

"She resigned a while ago, but only left last week."

"And nobody told me?" She's not hurt. I can hear the smile in her voice.

"If you called a little more often, you wouldn't be so far outside the loop."

"Okay, okay. So, Doreen left, and you employed a child in her place, did you?"

"Livia isn't a child."

She isn't, but I'm suddenly reminded of how young she is… that three years ago, when I was where Ella is now, in Paris, keeping busy, and blissfully unaware that Sadie was cheating on me, Livia would have probably just graduated high school.

*Dear God…*

"She sounds very young." Ella's voice brings me back to reality with a bump.

"She is. Was there a reason you called?"

"Is there a reason you just tried to change the subject so abruptly?"

"Of course not."

There's a second's silence and then she says, "I believe you… not."

"Oh, grow up, will you?"

She chuckles, unable to take anything seriously. "Even if I do, I'll never be as old as you."

I wish she'd stop talking about age. It just reminds me of the gap between myself and Livia, and while I guess I've always been aware of it, having it put into context is a little sobering.

"I have work to do, Ella…"

"I know."

"Why didn't you call my cell?"

*It would have saved you from finding out about Livia.*

"I did," she says. "You didn't pick up."

I reach out, flipping it over, and see I've got a missed call. The volume's turned down, but even if it wasn't, I've been so engrossed with Livia, I doubt I'd have heard it.

"Sorry."

"That's okay. I just wanted to let you know I'm coming home."

"Really?" Drew and I have always known she'd be back sometime soon, but she's never put a definite date on it, which I guess she still hasn't…

"I haven't booked my ticket yet, or anything."

"Does this mean you want me to collect you from the airport?"

"Probably not. I think I'm gonna be staying in the city for a while."

"You are?" That doesn't sound like Ella at all. She hates the city and always prefers to be at home in Newport.

"Yeah. Believe it or not, I've got a job."

"A job?"

"I know. It's shocking, isn't it?" It is, but I don't say so. "I'm not due to start for a while, but I'm flying back early so I can find somewhere to live." She sighs. "It's all happened so fast."

"So, what's the job?"

"It involves cooking, before you suggest I've wasted the last four years… but it's not in a restaurant."

"You're being very cagey."

"Hmm… because I'm not supposed to say anything about it yet."

"Oh, I see." I don't, but knowing Ella, this is probably just a tease. I only hope her four years of training won't result in her flipping burgers at a fast-food joint. "Do you want to stay at my place while you're looking for somewhere of your own?"

"Thanks, but I'll probably crash at Drew's. I tried calling him earlier to let him know… or rather to ask him, but he's not picking up either, so can you tell him? And can you say I'll text him when I know my flight details, or when I get back… or something?" She sounds just as disorganized as ever.

"Sure, but you're welcome to stay with me, you know."

"I know, but Drew's place is easier. It might be smaller than yours, but he's less likely to be there."

"Have I done something to offend you?"

She chuckles. "No. But I'd hate to cramp your style."

I'm not sure I have a style. My head's in too much of a turmoil over Livia. But then it occurs to me Ella might be more worried about me cramping her style. Maybe she has a reason for wanting to be by herself... a male reason. I don't want to think about that, though. She's still my little sister.

As I end the call with Ella, I sit back in my seat, thinking about our conversation. I'm not worried about her coming home, or her mysterious job, or even the fact that she's choosing to stay at Drew's place instead of mine. They're a lot closer in age, so even when Drew's there – which he isn't very often – the two of them have more in common than Ella does with me. What I'm most concerned about is that I've just realized that my 'little sister' is three years older than Livia.

Does that mean I should back off? Can I? Is it even possible to ignore my feelings for Livia?

"Hunter?" I sit up as she comes into the room.

"Yeah?" She's carrying a sheet of paper and is studying it as she crosses the floor toward me.

"Can I check these figures with you?"

"Sure."

She comes around my side of the desk, placing the page before me, and leans in, close enough that I can smell her scent. There's something fresh and floral about it, and I struggle not to groan out loud.

It doesn't matter how young she is, I've already gone too far down the path of falling in love to turn back. Given the way she reacted earlier, I just hope she's on the same path with me.

# Chapter Five

---

*Livia*

I'm so close, I can smell the slight spice of his body wash and see the prickly stubble on his chin. I want to reach out and touch, to feel the spiky hairs against my skin.

If only I were braver, I could tell him how I feel, or at least drop a hint of some kind about what he means to me. I'd never be able to tell him I love him, but I wish there was some way I could let him know he's so much more to me than just my boss…

"You're quite right. It doesn't make sense." He looks up at me with a soft smile, breaking my train of thought. "I probably shouldn't be let loose on things like this when I'm so tired."

I lean in slightly, using my pen to point at the figure I think is incorrect. "It's this one, isn't it?"

"Yes. It looks like I've used the wrong hourly rate. But how did you know?"

"Because it's so different to the proposal I typed last week, when Doreen was still here. I can't remember the client's name, but the job seemed quite similar, and added up to a lot more than this."

He nods his head, smiling more broadly. "I'm impressed."

I can't help smiling myself, and I wait while he corrects the figures, relieved that my earlier indiscretions don't seem to have affected his good opinion of me as his assistant.

I can feel myself blush, even thinking about what happened, and I suppose I should be grateful that I got the chance to explain, even if that meant revealing I'd been checking him out. His response was beyond my wildest expectations, and the look on his face when he told me he wasn't like that anymore... well, it was as though I'd died and gone to heaven. I was reading too much into it. I think I knew that even then, but I was saved from making an even greater fool of myself by that phone call. The woman's voice was playful, and very young, and it brought me back to earth with a bump. I assumed he'd been lying to me... just saying what I wanted to hear. But he explained that Ella was his sister, not the girlfriend I'd suspected her of being. He came into his office to take her call, and although I knew I ought to be getting on with this proposal, and that his personal life has nothing to do with me, I couldn't help watching him as he walked away. The odd thing was, he stopped on the threshold of his room and stared back at me. It was a moment that mirrored the one at Doreen's party. I felt his gaze melt through me, heating me from the inside out, and I wondered if he knew what he was doing... if he had any idea of the effect he was having on me. He didn't, of course, and eventually I came to my senses and reminded him of his call.

He came into his office then, the moment broken, and although I could hear the murmur of his voice, I focused on my work and not his private conversation... or I tried to.

"Hunter?" I startle, looking toward the door, and my body tenses when I see Miles Hampton standing there. He notices me and grins, stepping into the room, uninvited.

"Ever heard of knocking?" Hunter says, surprising me, considering he made such a big deal about me not having to knock before coming in here.

Miles ignores Hunter's comment. In fact, he ignores Hunter completely and walks over, staring straight at me. "I forgot to tell you earlier... that color really suits you."

"What color?" I ask. I'm wearing a gray suit and a white blouse with black stockings and shoes. The reality is, I'm a vision in monochrome.

"Your lipstick."

It's called 'Nude Touch'. It barely qualifies as 'color'. I know he's flirting, and doing a pretty poor job of it, and even though there's a desk between us, unlike earlier, when he insisted on getting way too close and sitting right beside me, I still feel uncomfortable.

"We're in the middle of something here, Miles. What do you want?" Hunter's voice is harsh, and I step back in surprise. I've never heard him speak to anyone like that before... not even when he came out of his office and found Miles sitting on my desk.

Miles looks down at him. "I remembered what I came to see you about."

"Oh?"

"I got the point that we'll need to take on new personnel if we pick up any extra work from Palmerston's, but did I hear it right that we won't be employing people on a permanent basis?"

"Not to start with, no. Everything's very fluid at the moment, and I don't want to commit the company to anything long term."

Miles nods his head and rests his hands on Hunter's desk, leaning over it slightly. "Okay, but in that case, we're gonna need to look at our freelance contracts."

"Why?"

Miles stands again and looks at me, rolling his eyes, like we're in some kind of co-conspiracy against Hunter, and then he puffs up his chest, a slightly smug smile on his face. "Because we haven't employed any freelancers for years. We need to make sure the contracts are up-to-date."

"I know we do." Hunter leans back in his seat, looking as relaxed as you please and gazing up at Miles, like he hasn't a care in the world. "Or rather, you do, Miles. Because that's your job. You shouldn't need my help with a minor issue like that, and it's up to you to ensure *all* our employment contracts are up-to-date. Of course, if you can't handle it..."

"I can handle it," Miles says. "I just thought I should make you aware..."

"I already was." Hunter tips his head slightly, raising his eyebrows. "Was there anything else?"

"No."

"Fine. In that case, if you don't mind, we're busy. And next time you come into my office, damn well knock."

Miles looks like he wants to say something, but thinks better of it, and without another word, he turns and leaves.

Hunter sits forward, letting out a long sigh, and then he looks up at me, a frown quickly forming on his face before he gets to his feet.

"Hey... are you okay?"

His voice is concern itself and I gaze up into his molten brown eyes, trying to remember how to swallow.

"Y—Yes."

"You're not, are you?" He grabs his chair, pulling it closer and then gently places his hands on my shoulders, sitting me down.

I shift forward to get up again. It feels wrong to be sitting here. But he crouches in front of me, his hands on the arms of the chair, so I can't move.

"Tell me what's wrong, Livia?"

I stare into his face, worry written in his eyes. "Nothing's wrong."

"Then why do you look so… so scared?"

"B—Because you were angry."

He leans back, his shoulders tensing, his muscles clenching, and then he takes a deep breath. "Are you saying you were scared of me? Because you know I wasn't angry with you, don't you? I wasn't raising my voice to you, Livia. I don't think I could."

He sounds almost fearful and I want to reach out, to touch him and reassure him that, even if his tone startled me, I'm not scared of him. I know he'd never hurt me. I don't know how I know it, but I do.

"I—I…"

"It's Miles," he says, getting to his feet and pushing his fingers back through his hair. "He has that effect on me."

I sit back, relieved I didn't say anything… didn't touch him. I misunderstood. This is about work, not me. Not us. There is no us.

"He's very full of himself."

Hunter looks down at me. "He is. But it's more than that. I don't like the way he talks to you. The problem is, it's difficult for me to do anything about it, when…"

"When he's not really doing anything wrong." I finish his sentence for him.

"That wasn't what I was going to say."

"Wasn't it? Well… it's true. Commenting on someone's lipstick is hardly a federal offense."

"Maybe not, but if it makes you uncomfortable…"

"I'll have to grow a thicker skin." I get to my feet and he steps back a little further, giving me some space. "A—Are the figures ready yet?"

"Yes… sorry." I'm not sure why he's apologizing, but he reaches over, handing me the piece of paper from his desk.

I don't want to look up at him. I feel embarrassed now for having misunderstood his concern and almost acted on it.

Instead, I stare down at the page before me and walk from the room, taking care not to rush... not to make it look like I'm keen to get away.

I'm not really, but that's the first time there's been any palpable awkwardness between us... and I don't like it.

*

I was glad that episode happened on Friday, and that I could spend the weekend at home in my apartment, trying to come to terms with my feelings for Hunter.

I couldn't, of course.

Every time I thought about him, my mind and my heart did battle, muddled thoughts and confusing emotions racing through me. In my heart, I know how much I love him. It's like a physical ache, touching every part of my body and putting all previously held thoughts and convictions into perspective. I might have believed Cole was perfect, but I was so wrong, and that realization hits home whenever I think about Hunter... which is pretty much every moment of the day. I long to be held by him... to be wanted by him. My need for him is no different from my need for the other basic elements in life; food, water, warmth... love. In my head, though, there's a voice that keeps saying none of this is real; that it's fantasy. Wanting Hunter, needing Hunter, loving Hunter... they can't happen in the real world. I've known that all along. I've been misreading his reactions, and it's my inexperience with men that's causing the problem here. Just like it did with Cole.

No matter which part of me was winning the battle over the weekend – whether it was head or heart – I was grateful I hadn't said anything to really embarrass myself. I hadn't told him how I feel, or what he does to me. My secrets are safely locked away, and they're going to have to stay that way.

It's for the best.

By the time Sunday night came around, I'd convinced myself of that. I'd told myself, over and over, that the real world was the best place to be. It was simpler and much less complicated than any fantasy involving Hunter Bennett.

That worked absolutely fine… until I came into work on Monday and saw him again, and all my grand ideas flew straight out the window.

Even now, at the end of another week, no matter how hard I've tried to separate myself from my feelings, I'm still struggling. I gaze at him every time I'm in his presence, trying not to fantasize about what it would be like to be held, and touched, and kissed. But when I look at his arms, his fingers, his lips… I want him more than ever.

Fortunately, I'm going to Mom and Dad's for the weekend. Hopefully, while I'm away, I can get some proper perspective and come back on Monday with a renewed determination to leave Hunter in the 'dream' zone.

I'm packing away my things, looking forward to driving my lovely car up to Falmouth, and seeing Mom and Dad for the first time in ages, when I look up and see Hunter standing in his doorway. I've got no idea how long he's been there, but I haven't been aware of him, and I sit back, tilting my head.

"Is something wrong?"

"No." He comes over, walking around to my side of the desk and leaning against it, like he did last week. I take a long breath, trying hard not to react to having him this close. "It's been a crazy week, hasn't it?"

"It has. I thought last week was busy…" I don't need to finish my sentence. We both know how insane it's been.

"Can I assume you're looking forward to catching up with your sleep again this weekend?"

I wonder why he's asking, but knowing my capacity for misunderstanding almost everything he says, I decide to play it safe and keep it about work.

"Did you need me to come in, then?"

"No. We might be busy, but we're not that busy, and besides, you've done so much already…" His voice fades and he sucks in a breath, his chest expanding, and then deflating as he lets the breath go again. "I was just wondering what you were doing, that's all."

He sounds a little quiet, maybe even slightly dejected, and although I don't understand why, I decide to tell him my plans. It seems the easiest solution.

"I'm going home for the weekend."

"To Falmouth?"

*He remembered?* "Yes. I haven't been for a while, but I'm driving up there tonight. I can't wait."

He smiles. "It must be nice to have that kind of relationship with your parents."

"What kind of relationship?"

"One where you look forward to seeing them."

The smile is still touching his lips, but his eyes are so sad, I can't leave it there. "You don't have that kind of relationship with yours?"

He shakes his head. "I can't. My dad's dead…"

I could kick myself. "Of course. I'm sorry."

"Don't be."

I'm almost scared to ask… "What about your mom?"

"She left us. Years ago."

"And you don't talk to her anymore?"

"I haven't spoken to her since the she day she walked out. None of us have."

"None of you?" I lean a little closer to him, my confusion making it hard for me to remember that this is the real world, not a dream.

"Yeah, my brother and sister."

"I didn't know you had a brother *and* a sister."

He nods his head. "My brother's name is Drew."

"And none of you have spoken to your mom?"

"No. She left when I was eleven." My mouth drops open, although I snap it shut again. "Drew was six and Ella was only three. Neither of them really remembers her... but I do."

The sorrow in his voice makes my heart ache for him and looking into his eyes, I don't see a man, but a lost and lonely little boy.

"What do you remember?" The question leaves my lips before I can stop it, but I don't want to take it back. I want to know. I want to listen... to help him find his way back, if I can.

Part of me expects him to tell me it's none of my business. But he doesn't. He gazes down at me. "I remember her smile, her laugh... the sadness in her eyes."

"Sadness?"

"Yeah. My dad used to make her sad. He made her cry... a lot. I used to hold her and tell her it would be okay. Deep down, I knew it wouldn't be, but you know how it is when you're a child and you think you can make everything better, just with words and gestures?" I nod my head, knowing exactly what he means. I feel like that myself, right now. Only I'm not a child.

"It wasn't your job to make it better, Hunter." He frowns, like he doesn't agree. "You were eleven years old."

His frown deepens. "I hated him for hurting her."

"Was that why she left? Because he hurt her?"

"It wasn't as simple as that." I sense there's something he's holding back; something he doesn't want to talk about... or maybe doesn't know himself.

"She never contacted you?"

He shakes his head. "I imagine she made a new life for herself... and I'm happy for her, if she did."

"Really? You don't blame her for leaving you?"

He smiles, although it still doesn't touch his sad eyes. "How can I? I'm confused by why she left, and it hurt that she didn't take us with her, but until I can understand what happened and why she did it, I can hardly blame her for going."

I reach out, needing to feel a connection, even if he doesn't. "I'm sorry, Hunter."

He startles as my hand comes into contact with his arm, and I pull it away again. "It's okay," he says.

I know it's far from okay, but I can't presume to doubt him. "What about your dad?" I ask instead. "How did you get along with him?"

His brow furrows. "My relationship with my dad was always hard, even before Mom left. I never understood him, or his absences, or why he treated her the way he did, and we rarely spoke to each other, even after I finished college and joined the company."

"You came to work for him, even though you didn't get along?"

"Yes. I'd decided to go into advertising, so there was no way he was gonna tolerate me working for someone else. Then, years later, I fell out with him, and as I was walking out the door, vowing never to set foot in his office again, he yelled at me that Mom had left us all behind because she didn't love us enough to take us with her."

I suck in a breath, tears welling in my eyes. "That's such a cruel thing to say."

"He was a cruel man." He looks troubled, and then moves a little closer, lowering his voice. "I've never told Drew or Ella about that… about what Dad said to me. Would you mind keeping it to yourself?"

"Of course not." I blink back my tears. "Surely you didn't believe him, though, did you?"

"I don't know. Like I say, I've never understood it."

My heart aches for him. "If you don't mind me asking, if you fought with your dad and walked out, what are you doing back here, running things?"

His lips twitch upwards. "Good question. It's one I often ask myself. Our argument was over something… personal." I notice his hesitation, but I don't feel I have the right to ask about it. "I wanted to hurt him, so I left TBA and went to work for one of our major competitors, just to spite him."

"Did you only come back here after he died?"

"No. Drew called me when Dad's cancer was diagnosed… at Dad's request."

"He wanted to make things up with you?"

"He wanted someone to run the business while he couldn't. Although I use the word 'run' very loosely."

"Why?"

"Because his very next step was to take the company public."

"Meaning…?"

"Meaning I have to answer to the board and the other shareholders. I have no autonomy. He made damn sure of that."

"What if he'd recovered from the cancer and wanted to come back? He'd have regretted giving up control then, surely?"

"Maybe. But I think he knew he wouldn't recover. That's why he put me in charge."

"You underestimate yourself." Once again, my mouth has run away with me, but the words are out there now, and they seem to have confused Hunter almost as much as they have me.

"I do?"

I've started now, so I may as well finish…

"Yeah. It's not the first time you've said something like that."

"Oh?"

"At my interview, I remember you saying that the board made you the CEO for reasons known only to themselves. Didn't it occur to you they might have thought you were the best man for the job?"

He laughs, his eyes sparkling for the first time in ages, and I have to smile, although I don't know why, except that he looks glorious… like he's finally let loose the child inside the man he had to become when he was eleven years old.

"Have you been talking to my brother?"

"No. I didn't even know you had a brother until a few minutes ago. Why?"

"Because Drew said something like that to me not very long ago."

He's staring right into my eyes, and even though my head is telling me to stick to the real world, my heart isn't listening. It wants the dream.

I'm drawn to him. I'm joined to him, and he needs to know…

"There was something else you said to me at my interview…"

"What was that?"

"You said you thought you and your father were very different men."

"I think I said I hoped we were."

"Based on what you've told me, I don't think there's any doubt, and I think you should…"

"You think I should what?"

"I think you should step out from his shadow. Stop waiting for his criticism. It can't come now, other than in your own head, and you know you're better than that. Live your own life, Hunter, and be the man you want to be." I blush, wanting to bite back my words. They might be true, but I shouldn't have said them. "I'm sorry."

"What for?" He frowns.

"I shouldn't have said that."

"Why? Don't you believe it?"

"Yes, I do. Completely. But it's not my place…"

"Not your place? Are you gonna curtsey to me next?"

I manage a smile. Just. "No."

"Thank God for that. I—"

My phone rings and I look down at the screen, seeing the word 'Mom'. "I'm sorry. I need to take this."

"Go ahead."

I connect the call, holding the phone to my ear.

"Hey, Mom."

"Thank God you're okay. I've been getting worried." She sounds it, and I feel guilty.

"I'm sorry. It's my fault. I got held up at work, but I'm just leaving. I'll be on my way in five minutes."

"Won't you have to go home first, to get your things?"

"No. I packed my bag this morning. I've got it in the trunk of my car."

"Oh… okay. So, we'll see you soon?"

"You will."

"Drive safely, won't you?"

"Of course."

"Love you, Livia."

"Love you, too, Mom."

I disconnect the call, noticing that Hunter's standing now. He looks down at me, his eyes clouded again… although it's not with sadness. This looks more like disappointment.

"I should let you go," he says.

"Yeah." I grab my purse, putting my phone into it. "Sorry about that. I always call when I'm setting off, even when I'm taking the bus. Mom was fussing because she hadn't heard from me yet."

"She was caring, not fussing. Mom's do. Even I remember that."

I want to hold him. I want to put my arms around him and tell him I care, too. And that no matter what my head says, I'm never going to stop.

*\*\**

## *Hunter*

I take the drive down to Newport fairly slowly, giving myself time to think and to recover. I won't deny, I'm a little disappointed. That might sound unreasonable after everything that happened between Livia and me before I left the office, but the thing is, I wanted more. Call me greedy, but that's how it is. I went out there with the express intention of asking her to have a drink with me after work, hoping drinks might turn into dinner, and that dinner could become… well, more.

And while what I got was so much better than anything I'd expected, I still can't help wondering what might have happened if I'd been able to ask her… if I'd gotten a chance at more.

I don't know why, but the moment she noticed me, I lost my nerve and asked her about work, and then fumbled out a question about her plans for the weekend. I was desperate to keep her there, hoping the words 'come for a drink with me' might somehow find their way out of my mouth. But then the conversation turned, and I don't even know how.

She told me she was going home to visit her parents, and the next thing I knew, I was telling her about my relationship with my dad… or the lack of it. I talked about Mom, too. I told her things I've never told anyone… not even Pat or Drew. Some of it shocked her, like hearing that Mom walked out when I was only eleven, and that she left the three of us behind. But the way Livia handled that was so compassionate, it took my breath away. She talked, or rather, she listened and let me talk, and she said the right things, at exactly the right moments, encouraging me, helping me to open up… and I did, like never before. The memories came flooding back. And I let them, pouring them out. I'd buried a lot of it for far too long, but it helped to acknowledge my impotence… my inability as the eleven-year-old man of the house, to help my mom through all the pain my dad inflicted on her. I might have stayed silent, but deep down, I've always felt inadequate, like I could have done more, should have tried harder. Although Livia was right. I was a child. It wasn't my job.

Hearing someone else absolve me was like having a twenty-year weight lifted off of my shoulders. I wanted to thank her, but it seemed she had yet more to give.

She told me to forget my pointless feud with my father, to step out from his shadow, and be the man I want to be. I don't know how she understood me so well, but hearing her words was like seeing the dawn break for the very first time.

I wanted to keep talking; to tell her more, to ask her more, to hold her and kiss her and never let her go, but her mom called, and she had to leave.

I've realized since, though, that our conversation changes everything. I think I worked it out even before I left the office, but I know for sure now. Not only do I love her, but I trust her. I must do, otherwise I couldn't have opened up like that, not so readily.

Love and trust go together. Everyone knows that. Even me. But trust has always been a huge barrier for me. After that conversation with Livia, I'm pretty sure that's because of my parents and what they did. It's not just my dad, but my mom, too. Like I said, I don't blame Mom for leaving, but the fact is, she left… and it hurt. It still hurts. Your parents are the people you're supposed to be able to trust above and beyond anyone else. And mine let me down.

Now, though, it feels as though I've taken an enormous leap of faith. I've broken that barrier and nothing can stand in my way anymore.

Not even me.

"What are you doing here?" I hadn't expected to see Drew in the kitchen, but he smiles up at me, taking a sip from the beer bottle in front of him.

"Um... I live here? At least, I live in the cottage, but I felt like a decent meal tonight, and I thought, as Pat was gonna be cooking for you..." He lets his voice fade and turns, fluttering his eyes at Pat, who's standing on the other side of the island unit, her arms folded across her chest. She's staring at him, but with such affection, it's hard not to smile.

"You thought you'd take advantage of my generosity?" she says, shaking her head, and he gets up, going around to her and enveloping her in a bear hug.

"You know I'm your favorite, out of all of us."

"You're no such thing. I don't have favorites."

"And if she did, it would be me." I dump my keys on the island unit and sit down, giving Pat a wink, which she returns, shooing Drew away.

Once he's released her, she straightens her blouse and gets down a glass, pouring me a beer and passing it over.

"Thanks."

She tilts her head and narrows her eyes at me. "You're looking relaxed."

"I'm feeling relaxed."

I clink my glass against Drew's bottle and take a sip. "Who is she?" he says.

"Who's who?"

"Whoever's taken the edge off."

I'm not in the mood for talking about Livia... not yet. "Who says there has to be a 'she'?"

"I do."

"Leave your brother alone, or I'll send you back to the cottage with no dinner." We both turn to Pat, who's folded her arms again and is staring at the two of us, although her gaze is more sternly fixed on Drew. He holds up his hands in surrender.

"There's no way I'm going anywhere until I've had my chili."

I look over at Pat. "You've made chili?"

She nods her head, and my stomach growls, making us all laugh. "Guess someone's hungry," she says.

"Well... at least we know he can't be in love, not if he's still got an appetite." Drew chuckles at his own joke, but it hits a little too close to home for me, and I shift uncomfortably in my seat.

"And what would you know about love?" Pat turns to him.

"Absolutely nothing, other than my love for you, dear Pat... and your chili, of course."

She rolls her eyes, turning away to fetch the dishes, muttering, "Dear Lord," under her breath.

Pat's chili is second to none and has always been a firm favorite in this house, and while Drew and I eat, she cleans up the kitchen. When we were younger, she and Mick used to live in rooms in the main house, but now they have an apartment over the garage and I know she'll have cooked enough food for them to eat later. Even so, she's always made a point of hanging around while we have our meal. She did it when we were kids, taking the time to make sure we were okay, letting us know we could talk to her if we needed to. I'm not sure why she does it now. Probably for the same reason, knowing Pat.

"I've been meaning to call you," I say, taking a sip of beer between mouthfuls of chili.

"Who? Me?" Drew twists in his seat, so he's looking at me.

"Yeah."

"You'd have been lucky to get hold of me. I've been up to my eyes in work." He lets out a long sigh. "Was it anything important?"

"Only that I spoke to Ella last week."

Pat turns around and Drew raises his eyebrows, like he's slightly fearful about what's coming next.

"How is she?" he asks. "It's been ages since I've spoken to her."

"She's fine."

"Did she call for a reason?"

"Yeah. To let us know she'll be coming home soon."

"That's fabulous news." Pat's clearly keen to see her.

"Believe it or not, she's got a job lined up."

Drew drops his fork and Pat's mouth falls open. I laugh and, after a couple of seconds, they both do too.

"Ella?" Drew says. "A job?" He's as disbelieving as I was.

"I know. I felt the same when she told me." Although thinking about it, why should she be any different to Drew and me?

"What's she gonna be doing?" Pat asks.

"She wouldn't tell me. She said it involves cooking, but it's not in a restaurant."

"And we're supposed to guess, or something?" Drew shakes his head, heaping chili onto his fork and into his mouth.

"No. She said it was a secret, and she's not allowed to tell us... or anyone else."

"Why do I get the feeling she's gonna end up working in a diner, or a burger bar?" Drew says, smiling.

"Oddly enough, I thought the same thing. But I guess that's Ella for you."

"I think you're both being very unfair. I'm sure she'll tell us when she can." Pat turns to me. "Should I get her apartment ready?"

"Not yet. Her job is in the city, so she's gonna stay there while she finds herself somewhere to live." I can see the disappointment on Pat's face. Ella was still really young when Pat and Mick moved here and started looking after us. She's close to all three of us, but I think she took on the roll of Mom far more with Ella than with Drew and me, and she's missed her since she's been away. "She'll come home as soon as she can," I say, because even though Ella didn't mention coming to Newport, I want to make Pat feel better, if I can.

And I guess that just goes to show, a part of me still feels like that eleven-year-old kid.

"Is she gonna stay with you while she's looking for somewhere of her own?" Pat asks, smiling at me.

"No. She's gonna crash at Drew's place."

He flips his head around. "Is she? It's nice of her to ask. And it's good of you to wait so long before telling me."

"Sorry. I've been busy." And distracted. "But anyway, she said you're never there, so…"

"Actually, she's not wrong," he says. "Sometimes I wonder why I bother to keep an apartment in the city."

"I'm sure Ella will appreciate it, even if you don't."

"No doubt she will. Do you know when she's coming back?"

"She hadn't booked her flight when we spoke, but she said she'd call you."

He nods his head. "Okay. At least she has her own key."

"Why? Are you going somewhere?"

"Yeah."

"Oh?" Pat says. "Where are you going?"

"The Caribbean."

"How long for?" I ask.

"That depends on whether the shoot goes to plan, but probably around three weeks."

"Oh… poor you."

"It's work, not a vacation."

"Yeah. We really sympathize, don't we Pat?"

She chuckles and turns, getting back to clearing up, while we continue to eat our delicious chili.

Drew doesn't seem to be in any hurry to go back to the cottage, and I'm not that keen for him to leave, either. When he does, I know I'll end up thinking too hard about Livia, about the fact that she's in Maine, and I'm here, unable to do anything about my feelings for her.

We could sit out by the pool, but it's a little breezy this evening, and in any case, I prefer being in the library. It's at the back of the house, its longest wall comprising floor-to-ceiling windows that overlook a vast expanse of lawn. The rest of the room is filled with books, lining the walls, on oak shelves. There are three enormous leather couches around the fireplace, as well as four or five wing-backed chairs, which are dotted about the room, each with a lamp beside them, perfect for reading in solitude.

"Now we're alone, I can tell you about my visit to the office the other day."

I've barely settled on one of the couches, but I shift forward in my seat, staring across at Drew, who's sitting opposite. He's clutching a cup of coffee, but I put mine down, just in case I drop it.

"What the hell were you doing at the office? And why didn't you come see me?"

"Because I know you're even busier than I am right now."

"And? I can still make time for you. Unless you didn't want to see me, of course." I narrow my eyes at him. "I notice you haven't answered my question about what you were doing there. Please tell me you're not screwing around with someone who works for me."

He rolls his eyes, shaking his head at the same time. "No, I'm not," he says. "I came to do some detective work."

"Detective work?"

"Yeah. Now Doreen's gone, it felt safe to ask around the office about her and Dad."

I let out a groan. "I think I'd feel happier if you were fucking around."

He chuckles. "Sorry, but I'm not. Not at the moment. I'm too damn tired."

I ignore his remark. I'm not interested in his sex life… at least, not as interested as he appears to be in our father's. "Who did you ask?"

"Just some of the old-timers… the ones who've been working there long enough to know the answers."

"To know the gossip, you mean. I don't see how any of them can claim to know the answers. Who does, when it's someone else's relationship?"

"I suppose… but the point is, they all told me the same thing."

"All of them?"

"Yeah."

"Which was?"

"That Dad and Doreen were having an affair, and had been for years. It started not long after her husband died, evidently."

I think back, trying to remember when that happened and how old I was. "Wasn't… wasn't that before Ella was born?"

"I don't know, but what I did find out was that it continued right up until Dad's death."

For some reason, I'm surprised by that. "All that time?"

"Yeah."

"How do they know this?"

"Evidently, quite a few people were aware of what was going on, even though Dad and Doreen tried to keep it a secret." He pauses, taking a sip of coffee, and then looks at me over the rim of his cup. "Do you think Mom knew about it? Do you think that's why she left?"

"I don't know. If they started seeing each other before Ella was born, it doesn't make much sense that Mom would wait until Ella was three years old, and then leave…"

"Unless she only just found out."

"Mom wasn't stupid. If Dad was having an affair, and half the people working for him knew about it, I imagine she'd have known too."

"In which case, I don't understand why she…"

"What's the point of this, Drew?" He startles slightly at my raised voice.

"What do you mean?"

"I mean, why are you doing this? What are you trying to prove? Whatever it is, it won't change anything. Mom left over twenty years ago. We haven't heard from her since, and speculating about what happened between her and Dad, or Dad and Doreen, isn't gonna alter a damn thing."

"Other than the fact that neither of our parents knew how to be faithful."

"You don't know that."

"Why else would Mom have left us all behind? It's the only thing that makes sense."

"Is it?"

He nods his head. "I know you think she faked that accident to get away, but who's to say there wasn't a guy waiting for her somewhere, and that he didn't want her bringing her kids along for the ride?" I can hear the bitterness in his voice and it makes me soften mine.

"Maybe that's true, and maybe it isn't." I stand and walk around the table between us, sitting beside him. "I get how much of a hole she left in our lives, Drew… but we've been okay, haven't we?"

He leans in to me. "Sure, we have." He looks up, giving me a half smile. "Why do you always defend her?"

"I don't. I just don't judge her. If she was sitting here now, I'd have just as many questions as you and Ella."

"Would you?"

"Yes. Only I can't see the point in asking them when there's no-one to give us any answers. I know you think I'm looking back with rose-tinted glasses, but I'm not. When she left, it hurt. I was angry, and confused, and lost… just like you. But the thing is, I don't recall her having a cruel bone in her body. I don't think she'd have gone if she didn't have to."

He frowns. "You think Dad made her go?"

"Maybe not in the literal sense. He may not have thrown her out, but he made her life so damn miserable, she had no choice but to leave." He opens his mouth, but I hold up my hand, stopping him before he can say anything else. "Speculating won't get us anywhere. We'll never know what happened between them, and frankly, I don't particularly want to waste my time theorizing about two people who aren't here anymore."

He lets out a long sigh and nods his head, and although I'm not convinced I've gotten through to him, I think he's gonna let it lie… for now.

It's hot tonight, despite the breeze, and I lie naked on top of the bed, not bothering with the covers. I'm tired. In fact, I'm desperate for sleep, but my mind won't stop churning.

I hadn't realized the relationship between my dad and Doreen was so serious… or even that there had been a relationship at all, come to that.

What bothers me more, though, is the similarity between Dad's situation and my own. Okay, so I'm not married. I don't have children. But other than that, the parellels are obvious. And, for someone who's always prided himself on being different, that thought makes me very uncomfortable.

The problem is, there's nothing I can do, other than remind myself that I'm not him. I'm still me, and I'm still in love with Livia... even if I am her boss.

# Chapter Six

*Livia*

"You didn't say your new car was a Mercedes."

Mom comes out to greet me, staring at my car, although she takes the time to give me a hug.

"I thought I'd surprise you."

I open the trunk, using the key fob, and she chuckles. "That's impressive."

"I know."

I rescue my bag, carrying it into the house, and she follows, closing the door behind us. Dad's in the living room and I dump my bag in the hall and go straight in to him. He gets to his feet, but I'm across the room before he's even halfway out of his chair.

"Don't get up, Dad."

He lowers himself down again, and I lean over and give him a hug. He returns it with his left arm only, and I let my cheek rest against his before I stand up straight and look down at him.

He seems well, although I hate the fact that the stroke has left him looking older than his fifty-four years. I remember how jealous Mom used to be that he didn't have a speck of gray in his hair, and now it's more gray than brown, as is the beard he's grown since I was last home.

"What's this?" I say, rubbing my fingers over his bristled chin.

"Your mom found shaving me too t—t…" He stops and looks at her. She's moved toward the fireplace, which divides this part of the living area from the dining room beyond.

"Time consuming?" she says, guessing at his meaning. He shakes his head. "Terrifying?" She has another stab.

He smiles. "Terrifying."

"You could always use an electric razor." It makes sense to me, but he frowns.

"They don't shave as close." He rubs his fingers over his whiskers. "Besides, this makes me look…" His brow furrows, and I wait. He hasn't looked for help, so we don't offer it. "Distinguished," he says eventually, with a satisfied smile.

"Distinguished is a good word, Dad."

He grins up at me, and I perch on the arm of his chair, so he can put his left arm around me, the right one lying limp on his lap.

"Your mom's made chowder for dinner. The smell has been driving me crazy."

"We can eat, if you want," Mom says, looking at me. "Everything's ready."

"Okay."

"Why don't you come help me with the table?"

"Sure."

I get up again and follow her through the formal dining room and into the kitchen, where there's a smaller table. We eat in here when it's just us at home, but I'm surprised to find Mom's already set out the silverware and glasses, and that there's crusty bread on the board in the middle of the table, and I stand by the doorway as she goes over to the stove.

"You didn't need my help at all, did you?"

"No, but your father sometimes has trouble getting up."

"In that case, shouldn't I go help him?"

"He won't thank you." She rolls her eyes. "He'd rather manage by himself."

"Even if he falls?"

"Worst-case scenario, he only usually falls back onto the chair."

"Usually?"

She turns, holding up her hands. "I know, Livia. It might not be the safest thing in the world, but what can I do? Have him yell at me every time I try to help?"

"Oh… I'm sorry, Mom." I walk over to her and gather her up in a hug. She lets me, just for a few moments, but then she steps back, tears welling in her eyes.

"It's okay," she says, even though it clearly isn't.

I'd hoped the visit to Uncle David and Aunt Elizabeth might have helped ease the strain a little, but it seems not.

She's about to take the lid off the stock pot when I stop her. "Why don't you go out tomorrow? Maybe get your hair cut, or have a manicure, or something?"

"Are you saying I'm a mess?"

God… she's sensitive. "Not at all, but wouldn't you like to get out, without having to worry about Dad?"

She sighs, like she's thinking. "It would make a change."

"Then go. Enjoy yourself."

"You wouldn't mind?"

"Not at all."

I notice the sound of Dad's shuffling footsteps behind us, and as I turn around to face him, I move away from Mom, so she can get on with the dinner, and I can distract Dad from seeing the tears in her eyes.

"Come and sit down, and I'll tell you about my car."

He's focusing on putting one foot in front of the other, but once he's reached his seat, he looks over at me. "What car?"

"The car that's parked outside… the one that goes with my new job."

"Oh yes? What is it?" He sits, using his stick for support, and then leans it up against the table.

"It's a Mercedes."

"Wow… the neighbors are gonna think we've gone up in the world."

My parents actually live in a very nice neighborhood, but I know they both resented having to sell the cars they had before Dad's stroke. Mom's Lexus was her pride and joy, but it was impractical for their new needs, and Dad loved his Porsche. Once it became clear he'd never drive again, though, there was no point in keeping it, just to let it gather dust. There's nothing wrong with the SUV that's parked in the garage, but it's not what they wanted… like a lot of things these days.

"Tell us about your job," Mom says, bringing the bowls of steaming chowder to the table. I sit next to Dad, the incredible aromas making me realize how hungry I am.

"This looks delicious, Mom." She smiles, her eyes still glistening.

"It does," Dad says, and then he turns to me. "Go on, Livia… tell us about your job."

I wait for Mom to join us, bringing her own bowl, and then I look at the two of them. "I don't have much to tell…" *Other than the fact that I've fallen for my boss.* "I've been so busy, I don't really know what I'm doing most of the time."

"I find that hard to believe," Mom says, passing around the bread. I help Dad to a slice, leaving it on the plate beside his bowl, and noting how he holds his spoon with some difficulty. He doesn't ask for help, though, so I leave him be.

"All I can say is, there's a lot going on, and I've had to work late… although my boss apologized for that." Right before he asked if I had a boyfriend, if I remember correctly. "I don't know all the details, but it's got something to do with one of the company's competitors going out of business, and our sales team trying to pick up the slack."

"And you say you don't know what you're doing?" Dad says, looking at me with a smile.

"Sometimes I'm not sure I do. I'm learning a lot though, and it's interesting... even if the deadlines can be crazy."

Dad finds eating exhausting and once we've finished, he's too tired to sit up any longer. Mom needs to help him get ready for bed, so I offer to load the dishwasher. The look she gives me is one of relief, mixed with gratitude, and I wonder now if leaving home and moving to Boston might have been the most selfish thing I ever did.

Everything is cleared away, and Mom still hasn't come back, so I wander through to the library. This is my favorite room in the house, even if it's not really a library. It used to be my dad's study, when he was teaching. This was where he did all his writing, and the main wall is filled with books, a few of which bear his name.

Now, it's where my mom works, as a para-legal, although how she finds the time, I honestly don't know. The desk is a lot tidier than when Dad used to work in here, and I can't help smiling at that as I sit on the couch and gaze at the bookshelves, letting my eyes wander over the leather-bound volumes.

Within moments, though, my mind drifts to Hunter. It's an instinct that hasn't diminished with the physical distance the weekend has put between us, and I sigh as I recall our conversation this evening, before I left to drive up here. I saw a different side to him then... a sad and vulnerable side that I'd never even realized existed. It made me love him even more, if that were possible. Sure, I can still hear that small, quiet voice in my head, telling me to stick with reality, but it's being drowned out by memories of the way he spoke to me, of the honesty in his voice, the trust in his confessions… and the hope he instilled that maybe dreams can come true.

I twist around, putting my feet up, and lie back, staring at the ceiling. It's at times like this that I wish I understood men a little better… or at all, actually. But the truth is, I know nothing. As a teenager, I was always studying, and I spent most of my time in this very room, with my head in a book. Then, of course, Dad had his stroke, and all thoughts of boys, boyfriends, and dating took second place… and somehow, I never got around to making them a priority again.

Until now.

Hopefully…

"Livia?"

"Yes, Mom?" I sit up as she comes into the room, and she smiles, which is a relief.

"I knew you'd be in here."

"I guess some things never change."

She shakes her head and comes to sit beside me. "Dad's settled. He's reading a book, but no doubt he'll fall asleep soon."

I sit forward slightly, looking down at her. "Can I ask you something?"

"Sure."

"Would it be easier for you if I moved back here again?"

She frowns, and then sighs, and then moves closer, taking my hand in hers. "It's not as bad as all that. Honestly."

"Really? You said earlier that Dad yells at you, just for trying to help him."

"No, he yells because he's frustrated. I wanna yell too, sometimes, but it's like howling at the moon. It wouldn't do any damn good. We both want things to be how they were, Livia. Only that's not gonna happen."

"I get that, Mom, but my question stands. If it would make life easier for you, I can move back."

"I wouldn't hear of it. We didn't raise you to look after us. We raised you to have a life of your own. You've already sacrificed enough by not going to college, and there's no way I'm gonna let you give up what you're doing now. Not when you've worked so hard for it. I might worry about you, and I know I fuss, but that's my job."

"I worry too, Mom… about both of you."

Her eyes glisten and she blinks hard a few times. "We're fine, Livia. It's just that some days are harder than others. Most of the time, I'm too busy to think, and when I do, I'm just grateful that your father is still here, and that he survived. Although I'll admit that, every so often, I sit in here and wish we'd gotten on and done something with our lives, instead of planning and talking."

"Like what? What do you wish you'd done?"

She smiles. "All kinds of things. Your dad always said he'd take me to Europe… to some of the places he visited when he lived over there. We used to sit in here in the evenings, and he'd tell me about Paris, and London… and especially Florence. He used to come alive, describing the paintings in the Uffizi Gallery, and how he'd stood for hours, just staring at a particular Botticelli." She laughs. "He used to say he'd take me there and show it to me, and I used to tell him there was no way I was standing in front of a painting for hours on end, no matter how good it was."

"And what did he say?"

"He told me to wait until I'd seen the painting first." Her smile fades as she's speaking and she falls silent.

"Couldn't you still go? I know the practicalities are daunting, but…"

She shakes her head. "It's not just that. I—I worry that he'd get there and the frustration would be overwhelming. Not just for him, but for both of us. He always talked about it as something romantic for us to do together. But I know we'd end up worrying about transport, and medications, and food, and all kinds of other mundane things that run our lives these days. The very last thing it would be is romantic."

I get the sense that romance isn't anywhere on their list of priorities anymore, and I lean over and put my arm around her.

I'm not sure whether that helps… but I don't see how it can hurt, either.


"Where's Mom gone again?" Dad asks, even though she explained where she was going before she went out, just fifteen minutes ago.

"She's gone to the beauty salon."

"That's nice."

"Do you want to do a puzzle?"

It should keep him occupied for a while, and besides, it's part of his therapy. Puzzles help with his hand-eye coordination and dexterity. They're also marginally more entertaining than picking up paperclips and putting them into a pot, which is what he used to do.

"Sure."

"I'll go set one up in the dining room."

I leave him to stand by himself, knowing better than to watch him, or offer to help, and I wander through to the dining room, where I open the cabinet and find several puzzles stacked up. They're designed for people with dementia, and although that doesn't include Dad, they're perfect for him, too. The pieces are large enough that he can pick them up, but the pictures are more satisfying than the cartoon versions, usually aimed at children. I rifle through, finding one with a flower bed on it, and pull it out.

"Oh, that's a nice one," Dad says, as he comes into the room. It's hard to tell from the tone of his voice whether he's saying he remembers doing it before, and enjoyed it, or whether he has no recollection at all, and just likes the picture. I decide against asking and pull out the chair at the end of the table, waiting for him to sit. Then I open the box, letting him remove all the pieces while I take a seat beside him. He's supposed to do this by himself – or as much of it as he can – and I don't interfere, while he gathers all the edges together, putting them methodically to one side.

"How long will Mom be, do you think?" he asks, not taking his eyes from the puzzle pieces.

"I don't know. Why? Is something wrong?"

"No. I just miss her, that's all."

I reach out, putting my hand on his arm, and he glances up at me. "Can you do something for me, Dad?"

He puts down the puzzle piece he's holding and focuses on me. "Sure, sweetheart. What do you need?"

"Can you tell Mom that you miss her?" He frowns, like he doesn't understand. "She needs to feel loved."

"She is loved."

"I know that, Dad... and so does she. But knowing it and hearing it are two different things."

"And she needs to hear it," he says slowly, like the thought is sinking in, as he shakes his head. "We're so preoccupied just..." He stops talking and looks to me for help.

"Getting through the day? Dealing with all the crap life's thrown at you since you had your stroke?"

He smiles. "All of that, and more." He reaches across, placing his hand over mine and giving me a squeeze. "You're right. I need to get her to stop dashing around and sit down with me for five minutes so I can apologize for being so grumpy."

"You're not grumpy."

"Yeah, I am," he says. "I don't mean to be, but I am. And while I'm about it, I also need to tell her she's the only woman I've ever loved, and how utterly perfect she is."

I smile. "She'd like that, Dad."

He squeezes my hand again. "Now, if you go make some coffee, I'll get on with these daffodils."

I glance at the picture on the box. "They're not daffodils. They're tulips."

"Your mom calls them daffodils, so they're daffodils."

I chuckle, getting to my feet, and kiss the top of his head. "Whatever you say, Dad."


Hunter's waiting for me when I get into my office, and just the sight of him has me feeling a little flustered.

My drive back from Falmouth last night was pretty straightforward and I must confess, although I was really worried about my parents, I'm less so now. They seemed like different people yesterday, and I guess that must mean Dad found the time to sit Mom down and remind her how perfect she is. Even now, the thought makes me smile, and Hunter tilts his head, my expression clearly confusing him.

"How was your weekend?" he asks.

I'm not about to share my family secrets with him, so I just settle on, "It was fine, thanks," and then add, "How was yours?" as I step into the room, moving closer to my desk.

"It was…" He pauses, like he's thinking. "Enlightening."

I don't know what that means, but before I get the chance to reply, two things happen; the first is that he steps forward, moving closer to me, and the second is that the phone on my desk rings, making us both jump. Hunter sighs, pushing his fingers back through his hair, and I pick up the phone.

"Hunter Bennett's office. How can I help?"

"Is Hunter there? It's Preston Tucker."

"I'll find out if he's available. Can you hold?" I don't wait for his reply and put the line on hold, turning to Hunter. "It's

Preston Tucker for you." I remember him from the meeting of account executives, and smile as Hunter rolls his eyes.

"I guess I'll have to take it," he says, and turns, going into his office. I give him a minute and put the call through. Then I sit at my desk, stash my purse in the bottom drawer and finally turn on my computer.

I wonder how long Hunter had been waiting for me. I'm not late, but surely he can't have been standing out here for too long... can he? And what did he want? Asking about my weekend was nice of him, but if the number of emails in my inbox is anything to go by, we're too busy for pleasantries. Dear God, there are hundreds of them.

I let out a groan, just as my cell phone beeps. I can hear it, even though it's tucked away in my purse, and although I know I ought to ignore it, I can't. It could be Mom.

I open the drawer and reach in, retrieving my phone and turning it over. The number isn't one I know, and it's certainly not my mom, and I feel my stomach lurch when I realize the message contains attachments.

This is like déjà vu.

Except it can't be happening again... can it?

I click on the message and let out a gasp as I see the images come up on my screen. They're all of me... and all were taken either last night or this morning. I can tell by the clothes I'm wearing. There's one of me getting out of my car yesterday evening, outside my apartment. One of me taking my bag out of the trunk, and another of me entering my apartment block. A fourth one shows me at the grocery store last night, when I went to buy milk. The final one shows me getting into my car this morning, wearing exactly the same clothes I've got on now...

I thought this was all over, but evidently it's not.

Is there no escape?

I can't help it. I drop my phone on my desk and sob.

## Hunter

Preston's timing sucks.

I came into the office early this morning, desperate to see Livia, to talk to her, and find out whether there's a hope for us.

I never got the chance, though, because even though I started the conversation, and got as far as telling her I'd had an enlightening weekend, Preston's call has brought everything to an abrupt halt.

That means I wasn't able to explain what I meant. I couldn't tell her I've spent a lot of time over the last two days examining my feelings for her.

And that now I'd like to examine them with her.

Or I would, if there weren't so many goddamn interruptions.

With great reluctance, I go into my office, and sit at my desk, having time to get comfortable before Livia buzzes the call through.

"Preston?"

"Good morning, Hunter." He sounds pleased with himself, and I'm hoping that's a good sign. We could use one.

"What can I do for you?"

"Nothing at the moment, but I wanted to let you know, I've got a meeting this morning with Jim Nichols at Ecstatic Sports."

I'm impressed. I know that Ecstatic are one of Pemberton's biggest clients, so I guess this means they're looking to move. At least, I hope it does.

"You know who I'm talking about, don't you?" Preston says, after a few seconds' silence.

"Of course. They used to make running shoes."

"That's ancient history. They've been the leading suppliers of home fitness equipment for the last five years."

I'm aware of that, but I don't say so. I'm just relieved he's got an appointment.

"Do you know Jim Nichols?" I ask.

"Not personally, but I met him at the golf club yesterday and we got talking."

I knew there was a good reason for employing account execs. It means I don't have to play golf.

"And he arranged the appointment there and then?"

"No, but I gave him my card, and he emailed me this morning. He seems keen to meet up."

"Okay. Let me know what happens."

I end the call, wondering if this might be the break we've been hoping for. It's often the way that, if one company jumps ship, others follow, and maybe Jim Nichols might be the metaphorical Pied Piper in this scenario. I sit back, letting out a sigh, and try not to feel too optimistic. It's way too soon for optimism, but it's not too soon for coffee, and I'm just getting up when I hear what sounds like crying coming from outside... from Livia's office.

I make it around my desk and to the door in seconds, going outside, where I find her, huddled over her computer keyboard, her head bent, her shoulders shaking... a picture of agony. My heart contracts painfully in my chest, but I ignore it and rush to her.

"Livia? What's wrong?"

She startles, looking up at me, and the pain in my chest intensifies as I see tears trickling down her cheeks, and more waiting to fall. She opens her mouth, but then closes it again, and reaches for a Kleenex from the box on her desk, wiping her eyes, before fresh tears fall. Whatever this is, it's bad, and I long to hold her. I can't, but I need to do something...

"Livia… tell me what's wrong. Let me help." *Please. This hurts.*

"M—My phone." Her words come out on a stuttered breath, and I look at the device, lying face-down on her desk.

"Your phone?" She nods her head, but says nothing more, and I pick it up. "You need to unlock it."

She sits up slightly and I hold the phone in front of her face, waiting a moment while it recognizes her, and then I turn it around again. It's unlocked now, and I swipe upwards, frowning as I stare down at a photograph of Livia getting into her car. From the looks of things, she's wearing the same dark suit that she's got on now, but I don't understand.

"There are more," she says, gulping down her tears.

I swipe to the right and see another photograph, this time of her coming out of a grocery store, clutching a carton of milk. She's wearing jeans and a blouse, and is smiling contentedly. I swipe again. The next picture is of her, wearing the same clothes, but entering what appears to be an apartment block, and the next is of her taking a bag out of the trunk of her car. I stop there, suddenly realizing I'm in her message app, not her photos… and the meaning of this becomes clear.

"You're being stalked?"

She looks up, her face paling. "I—It feels that way, yes."

I clench my fingers around her phone, trying to control my anger and my fear.

"Come with me." I don't care whether what I'm about to do is right or wrong. We need to be alone. We need to talk in private. I put my arm around her and help her to her feet, ignoring how soft and sensual she feels as I guide her into my office. She doesn't seem to mind the close contact. In fact, she leans in to me as we're walking, and when I close the door, I'm almost certain I hear her sigh. Perhaps she feels safer in here with me.

*I hope so.*

As much as I'd like to keep hold of her, it's not practical, and she needs to sit, so I guide her past my desk to the couches on the far side of the room, sitting her down on one of them. For a moment, I contemplate taking a seat beside her, but then I remember the circumstances and realize she might want some distance, so I perch on the edge of the couch opposite, putting her phone on the table between us.

Her brow furrows as she looks down at it, but then she sucks in a deep breath, stuttering it out again, and I can tell how much she's struggling.

"How long has this been going on?"

It's more than just today, that much is obvious from her reactions.

"It started a couple of months ago, I guess. Then it stopped for a while, and then just before I left SKJ, it started up again. Obviously, it all went quiet when you gave me my new phone… except it didn't, did it, because it's happening again. Although I don't know how. I mean…"

I can hear the panic in her voice, and it's too much for me. I get up and move around the table, crouching right in front of her.

"It's okay. You're safe."

"I don't feel safe. It was bad enough before, when they were sending me pictures of myself at work, or getting off the bus outside the office, but these…" She waves her hand toward the phone. "These are more personal. Whoever it is, they're following me. They know where I live."

"I know. And I don't like it any more than you do."

I try to stay calm, despite the waves of fear rising inside me, made worse when I see the terror in her eyes.

"I—It's not your problem, Hunter."

She's got to be kidding. "Yeah, it is. I'm making it my goddamn problem."

She frowns, like she doesn't understand. "Y—You mean you want to help?"

"Of course I want to help." I don't know how, but from somewhere, she finds a smile. It's only slight, but it's there, and it takes my breath away. "What's wrong?" I ask, finding my voice.

"Nothing's wrong... not really. It's just that, when I went to my old boss and asked him to help, he told me that because the messages were on my personal phone, it was nothing to do with him, or the company."

"In that case, I'm not surprised you left."

"It was one of the reasons... obviously not one I wanted to talk about," she says, and I nod my head. I can understand that, and I don't blame her for not mentioning it. "I guess because this is a company phone..." She nods toward it again, although she doesn't finish her sentence.

"That's got nothing to do with it. I'd help you regardless of whose phone it was."

"You would?"

"Yes."

I get the feeling she wants to ask why. I wonder, if she did, whether I'd tell her it's because it's the right thing to do, or whether I'd be completely honest and say it's because it's the right thing to do, and because I love her... because protecting her is wired into my DNA, so I know no other way of being.

It doesn't matter in the end, because she doesn't ask the question. Instead, she says, "I'm not sure what you can do."

*Anything. I can do anything it takes, if it keeps you safe.*

"To start with, we need to find out who's behind this."

"I know. But how?"

"I have a friend... well, a kind of friend. It's someone I used to know, anyway. They're a detective."

"The police?" She sounds doubtful.

"No. A private detective, but they might be able to find out who's doing this. Do you want me to call and see if they can help?"

She hesitates for just a few seconds and then lets out a breath. "Would you?"

I smile. "Of course." I stand up, regretting the distance I have to put between us, as I wander to my desk, picking up my phone. Keira's number should still be on here. I hope. Because I can't remember her surname... not after all this time. Scrolling seems to take forever, but I find it eventually, connecting a call and switching it to speaker, so Livia can hear us. It feels important that she knows everything that's being said about her.

After four rings, Keira finally answers.

"Hunter Bennett... after all this time."

"Are you talking to me these days?"

"Why wouldn't I be? It wasn't your fault things ended up the way they did."

"No, it wasn't." I take a breath. "I have a favor to ask, although I'll pay you the going rate for your time."

"You want to use my services?"

"Yes. But it's a personal matter. Do you think you could come see me?"

"Where? At your apartment?"

"No. At my offices?"

"Sure. I'll happily take your money. I've got an opening at noon today, if that works for you?"

"That works perfectly. I'll see you then."

I end the call and glance over at Livia. She's frowning now, although I don't know why.

"Is everything okay?"

"Y—Yes." She stands before I can get back to her, picking up her phone from the table at the same time. "I—I should get back to work."

"You don't have to, Livia. You can stay in here, if you'd prefer."

"No. It's okay. I've got a lot to do today, and I'd rather keep busy."

I guess that makes sense, but I get the feeling she's holding something back. I'm not sure what, though, and I can hardly make her tell me, can I?

I step to one side, so she can pass me, and she does, without looking up.

"Keira will be coming by at noon."

"I know. I heard."

I'd swear there's a crack in her voice. "Livia? Are you sure you're okay?"

"I'm fine… thank you."

She's not fine at all, but I guess I can't blame her for that, and as she leaves, I stare after her, muttering, "Fuck it," under my breath.


It's just after noon, when I look up at the sound of knocking on my doorframe. I'm surprised to see Livia standing there. She hasn't knocked for ages, and I frown at her.

"Is something wrong?"

"No, but your… um… friend is here."

I notice her hesitation before she says the word 'friend', and for a moment, I wonder who she's talking about, before I remember Keira.

"Oh, yes. Of course. Show her in."

Livia turns, stepping aside and looks out into her own office. "This way please," she says and I stand as Keira walks into the room.

She's just as stunning as I remember her. Keira might be a PI, but she dresses like a catwalk model and has the looks to match.

Today, she's wearing a pale blue dress that's practically glued to her slim figure, and heels that can't possibly be practical in her line of work. She's changed her hair, though. It's shorter than I remember, and a shade blonder, perhaps, and I can't help smiling as she walks over, holding out her hand for me to shake.

"That's very formal."

"This is business, Hunter."

My smile becomes a grin, and I offer her a seat, just as Livia turns to leave.

"You should stay, Livia."

She looks back, and I can't fail to notice her despondent expression.

"You want me to?"

"Yes. I think it would help Keira if she heard the story from you, rather than me."

Livia shrugs, like she couldn't care less, but comes into the room, closing the door behind her, and sits on the other chair, next to Keira. She holds her hands in her lap, and stares at the back of my laptop, like she'd rather be anywhere than here. I guess that's understandable, considering she doesn't know Keira, but I wish she'd relax and accept we're only trying to help.

"So, what can I do for you?" Keira asks, looking at me, but then turning to Livia. "Or should that be you?"

Livia looks up at me with a pleading expression in her eyes, and I smile at her. "Do you have your phone?" She goes to hand it to me, but I nod toward Keira and Livia gives it to her instead. "Livia's being stalked," I say, starting the explanation, because one of us needs to. "Someone sent her some photographs which were taken outside her apartment building and at the grocery store."

Keira raises her eyebrows and looks down at the phone, before turning her gaze on Livia. "You'll need to unlock this for me." She hands the device to Livia, who unlocks it and gives it back. Keira swipes her finger across the screen a few times, and then takes a deep breath, looking up at Livia again. "There's nothing intimate here, but I can see why it would have freaked you out. Whoever's sending these pictures has been following you."

Livia nods her head. "It happened before… before I came to work here. I had a different phone then, and…"

"Were the pictures the same?" Keira asks, interrupting her.

"Similar. Although none of them were taken at my apartment. They were all taken around my old office."

"So whoever it is, they're escalating things. They're making it more personal."

"It feels that way, yes."

Keira looks back at the phone again. "I'm going to ask you a few questions now. Some of them will seem really dumb, but bear with me, okay?"

"Okay."

Keira takes another breath. "Have you noticed anyone taking pictures of you?"

"No."

I glare at Keira, but she ignores me. Even by dumb standards, that was a really stupid question. Doesn't she think Livia would have said something if she'd noticed a guy taking photographs of her?

"No-one's asked you any unusual questions, or taken an interest in what you're doing?"

Livia glances at me, and I wonder if she's thinking about that time when I asked if she had a boyfriend. That was pretty unusual, in the circumstances.

"No," she says eventually.

"Have you broken up with anyone recently? Someone who'd know your movements?"

"No, but…"

"But what?" Keira sits forward, and I copy her.

Livia frowns, like she's thinking. "It's never occurred to me before, but there was a guy where I used to work."

"Right?" Keira prompts her. "What about him?"

"His name was Cole Shepherd, and he… he could be responsible for this."

"Why?" I get the question out before Keira does, and she turns and scowls at me. I scowl back, but we both focus on Livia.

"Because he asked me to go out with him, and I said yes, but then I changed my mind when I found out he'd slept with two other women." A blush creeps up her cheeks as she's talking, but before I can say anything, Keira shakes her head.

"Can I get this straight? You refused to go out with this guy because he'd slept with someone else?" She doesn't give Livia a chance to answer before she says, "I'm sorry, but how old are you?"

Livia turns to her, frowning. "I'm twenty-one. Why?"

"How old was this guy?"

"I don't know. Twenty-six, I guess."

Keira huffs out a sigh of frustration. "And you're surprised he'd only slept with two other women? Seriously? You expected the guy to be a virgin, at the age of twenty-six? Are you…?"

"That's not what I meant." Livia raises her voice for the first time since I've known her, and I can't help smiling. Keira can be a little overbearing at times.

"Okay. What did you mean?"

"Just that I prefer men who sleep with one woman at a time."

"Don't we all." Keira rolls her eyes. "But there are a lot of men out there who think monogamy is over-rated."

"No. You still don't understand. I'm not talking about monogamy. Not really. What I mean is, I didn't want to be with someone who thought it was okay to have two women in bed with him… at the same time."

Livia's blush has now reached the roots of her blonde hair, and she lowers her head to hide her embarrassment.

"Oh… I see what you're saying." Keira smiles, and Livia looks up again.

"That's a relief. But the point is, he had my address and my phone number. He'd have been able to follow me."

Keira nods her head. "He seems like a good place to start. I'll look into him. You said his name was Cole?"

"Yes. Cole Shepherd."

"Okay. And you can't think of anyone else?"

"No. No-one at all."

Keira gets to her feet, handing Livia her phone as she stands too.

I get up, and Keira looks across at me. "Invoice your hours directly to me, will you? Don't put anything through the company."

She frowns slightly. "If that's what you want."

"It is. I wouldn't like anyone here to gossip about this."

She shrugs her shoulders and turns, looking at Livia. "I'll find my own way out, and hopefully I'll be in touch soon."

Livia nods her head, and Keira leaves without bothering to say goodbye.

Once she's gone, Livia steps away from my desk, but I don't want her to go yet.

"I—I'm sorry that guy treated you so badly," I say and she stops, looking back at me.

"It's not your fault." She glances out the window and I move around the desk, so I'm standing in front of her.

"How did you find out? About his past, I mean?"

She turns to face me. "It wasn't really his past. It was his present."

"I don't under—"

"He asked me to have dinner with him," she says, interrupting me with a sigh. "I accepted, but then I overheard a conversation between two other women while I was in the ladies' room. They were… they were talking about him, and what they'd all done together the weekend before, and how they were going to miss doing it all again that weekend, because he'd told them he was going out of town. I couldn't believe they were talking about the same guy, but then one of them called him. They'd put the phone on speaker, so I heard his voice. I knew it was him, and I heard them arrange to meet that evening… all three of them."

"Even though he was supposed to be seeing you?"

"Yes. The very next night."

"The guy was an asshole."

"I know he was, but our conversation was still humiliating."

"Conversation?"

"Yes. I called him right away and told him what I'd overheard."

"Really?" I love her style. "How did he react?"

"He tried to deny it… until I named the two women and told him I'd overheard his phone call with them. Then he told me it didn't matter what he did, because we weren't seeing each other yet."

"Was he serious?"

"He seemed to be." She shakes her head. "To be honest, in the end I was just relieved I'd found out what he was like before I had to sit through a meal with him… and his ego."

I laugh, unable to help myself, and although she smiles, she still turns to leave. Without thinking, I grab her hand, pulling her back, and she looks up into my face, her eyes widening.

"I'm sorry."

"What for?"

I can't think what to say… I'm not sorry for holding her hand, or for being this close to her. I'm not even sorry the guy turned out to be an asshole, because it means she's here, now… with me.

"I'm sorry you had to go through that with Keira. She can be quite bossy at times. She always was."

Livia seems to shrink away from me, pulling her hand from mine.

"It's fine. I'm grateful for your help."

I don't want her to be grateful. I want her to stay here with me, and let me hold her and comfort her and make it better. But she seems determined to leave, edging toward the door as she's speaking, and I can't stop her. I wish I could, but I have to let her go.

For now.

# Chapter Seven

*Livia*

I've got so much work to do, but I can't seem to settle to anything, and the more I try to concentrate, the worse it gets, the more I struggle not to burst into tears… again.

Obviously, I'm upset about the photographs, but it's more than that.

It's Hunter.

I'm grateful to him for offering to help. His response couldn't have been more different from the one Lucian gave me, and I don't think I'll ever forget how wonderful it felt when Hunter put his arm around me and took me into his office. I'd been so scared, felt so vulnerable, and suddenly, with that one move, he made me feel safe again. Leaning in to him, craving more, felt like the most natural thing in the world, and I was so disappointed when he sat me on the couch, and then took a seat opposite. I wanted to have him close again… needed to feel the warmth of his touch, the strength of his arms. I could feel the panic rising inside me. Even when he came back and crouched in front of me, he wasn't close enough. I needed more. But then he said he'd help. He said he *wanted* to help, and the relief was overwhelming… until I realized what that meant.

I didn't mind that he was asking for assistance from a friend. It was the nature of their friendship that bothered me. When he'd said he knew a private detective, I had images of a slightly overweight man in a crumpled suit. I never envisioned that he'd call a woman, or that she'd be an ex-girlfriend of his. One of many, no doubt.

I could hear their conversation, and just like that one I overheard in the ladies' room between Casey, Gina and Cole, I wished I could be anywhere but in his office, listening to things I didn't want to know… like how they broke up, or that Keira didn't consider it to be Hunter's fault. I presume that meant it was hers. In that case, though, would he have been asking a favor of her? I wasn't sure. I'm still not. Is that the kind of thing people do when they've broken up? Or does that mean it wasn't anyone's fault, and they just went their separate ways? And if that's what happened, does he still love her?

God… I'm so confused.

I'm confused about everything, except the fact that, no matter how much I love Hunter, I know nothing can ever happen between us. Not now I've met Keira.

When she arrived, there wasn't a crumpled suit in sight, and I couldn't help staring at her. She oozed sex appeal and sophistication, her blue dress hugging her svelte figure, and her makeup flawless. Her perfume was spicy, with a hint of musk, and while it wasn't overpowering, it stifled my more delicate scent and knocked it into submission.

I followed quickly behind.

As I walked into Hunter's office, deciding to knock, for some reason, I realized that if Keira is the kind of woman he's used to going out with, there's no way he'd give me a second glance, outside of the confines of my job.

If that's true, though, can I stay here? Can I work for Hunter, knowing how much I love him and want him, and that he'll never feel the same way about me?

"Is Hunter available?" I look up at the man standing in front of me, his head tipped slightly to one side and a smile on his lips. He's somewhere between thirty-five and forty, and is just under six feet tall, with mid-brown hair and attractive hazel eyes. He's vaguely familiar and I wrack my brain. I remember him from the meeting of account executives, and suddenly I recall his voice from this morning's telephone call.

"You're Preston Tucker."

His smile widens.

"Well done. I'm impressed you remembered."

I smile back and get to my feet. "I'll just check to see how Hunter's fixed."

He nods and I feel him watching me as I walk to Hunter's door, knocking on the frame again. He looks up from behind his desk, frowning.

"Preston Tucker's here to see you."

He nods his head. "Okay. Just come in for a second, will you?"

I hesitate, but only for a moment, and then walk into his office, right up to his desk. "Is something wrong?" I ask, feeling more nervous than I have since my first day here.

"I don't know. You tell me." I frown, unsure of his meaning. "Why have you started knocking on my doorframe again?"

I look down at the surface of his desk, unwilling – unable – to gaze on his perfect face for a moment longer, knowing that what I want can never happen.

"I guess I'm just not thinking straight."

"Because of this morning?" He gets up, coming around to me.

"Yes." *But not in the way you think.*

"Okay. As long as it's nothing I've done wrong."

"No. Of course not."

It's not 'wrong' of him to be attracted to women who are the polar opposite of me.

It's just unfair.

He nods his head. "I don't know what Preston wants, but he went to an important meeting this morning, so can you come back in with him and take notes?"

"Sure." He smiles and I return the gesture, because I know that's all it is now, and then I go out to my office again, picking up a notepad and pencil. "Hunter can see you now," I say to Preston, and he follows me back into the room.

Hunter's sitting behind his desk again, and Preston takes a seat opposite him. I pull the second chair closer to the window, so I'm a few feet away. I'm hoping to be unobtrusive, but I can't help noticing how both men stare at me as I sit down, even though it means Hunter has to twist in his seat to do so.

Once I'm settled, I fully expect Hunter to turn around again, but he doesn't. Instead, he smiles over at me. "Preston went to see Jim Nichols this morning."

I frown. "Who's Jim Nichols?" Is this someone I should have known about? Have I messed up?

"He's the CEO at Ecstatic Sports."

"The people who make fitness equipment?"

Preston laughs. "It's good to see your PA is up to speed, boss... even if you're behind the times."

Hunter shakes his head, and I wonder if I've said the wrong thing. "It wasn't that I didn't know they make fitness equipment," he says, turning to Preston. "It's just that I remembered where they started out."

"Making running shoes, you mean?" I blush, wishing I could remember when to speak, and when to stay silent.

"How did you know that?" Hunter looks back at me again, a smile tweaking at his lips.

I shrug my shoulders. "I thought everyone knew how their story started. It's all over their social media pages."

Preston laughs again. "I like her."

Hunter turns to him, frowning slightly. "I'm sure you do. Now, tell me about your meeting with Jim Nichols."

"It went well. He's heard the rumors that Pemberton's are on rocky ground and he's definitely looking to move, out of choice, rather than necessity."

"Here?" Hunter asks.

"He hasn't decided yet. He wants to talk things through with his board, and I'm seeing him again on Friday."

Hunter nods his head. "Okay. Is there anything we need to do in the meantime?"

"Not really. If we get the account, we'll get everything. I know that much. But until we get it…"

"We just sit tight and wait." Hunter finishes his sentence for him, and Preston nods his head, getting to his feet.

That seems to be all he came to say, and I wonder why Hunter asked me to sit in. There were no notes to take, although I suppose he didn't know that.

Preston leaves, giving me a smile, and I turn to Hunter.

"This is important, isn't it?"

"Yes." He sits back in his seat, turning it and gazing in my direction. "It might sound really cutthroat, but we need to make the most of Pemberton's bad fortune."

"Before it turns into ours?"

He shakes his head. "Things aren't that bad. We'll be okay, whatever happens." He gets up, moving around his table and leans on the edge, facing me. "I just…"

"You want to prove yourself?" There I go again, speaking without thinking. "I'm sorry."

"Why? And for Christ's sake, don't tell me it wasn't your place to say that. You hit the nail right on the head… as usual." He crosses his legs at the ankle and folds his arms across his expansive chest. "We lost a few clients when Dad died, and I took it personally."

"That's understandable. It must have felt as though they didn't trust you."

His eyes light up. "That's exactly how it felt... as though they thought the business would crumble without him, and probably this building with it. They weren't willing to take a chance with me."

"More fool them," I murmur under my breath, but I wonder if he's heard me... especially when he tilts his head slightly, his brow furrowing. He doesn't comment, though.

"The thing is, we don't need lots of new clients. We couldn't handle that much work. If we can just pick up one or two of Pemberton's bigger accounts, like Ecstatic Sports, it would make a world of difference to how we're perceived."

"And it's all about perception, is it?"

"In this business, yes. Perception is everything."

I get up and he pushes himself off of the desk, uncrossing his arms and stepping closer.

"I'll get back to work," I say, looking up at him.

"Are you okay?" He stares down into my eyes, and while I wish I could tell him I'm very far from okay, it's all about perception, isn't it?

"I'm fine."

He frowns, and I sense he doesn't believe me, but he steps back, letting me leave the room.

I might be tired – both physically and emotionally – but I'm dragging out that moment when I have to leave. I don't know whether my stalker will be watching me, whether he'll be outside the office, at my apartment, or somewhere in between. It could be Cole, or it could be anyone, and the uncertainty of all that is playing on my mind and giving me a headache.

I can't stay here all night, though, and I power down my computer, opening the bottom drawer of my desk to pull out my purse.

"I thought I heard you turning off your computer." Hunter's voice makes me jump, and I look up to find him standing by the door to his room. "Are you ready to go?"

"Yes. Why?"

"Because I'll take you."

"But you can't."

"Why not?"

"It would mean leaving my car here. How would I get to work in the morning?"

"I'll come get you."

I shake my head, standing up. "I'm sure you've got better things to do. Really. I'll be okay."

I know he thinks he's helping, but I can't let him do this. His kindness will be my undoing, when I know what I want, and that he doesn't. Tears well in my eyes and before he sees me cry again, I grab my purse and run.

"Livia! Come back!" I hear his voice, but ignore him and bolt straight for the stairs, ignoring the elevators, and heading down to the parking garage, where I hurry to my car, opening it as I approach and jumping in. With shaking hands, I start the engine and slam the car into reverse, backing out of the parking space, and then driving up onto the street.

It's busier than usual, the traffic much heavier than I'd like, and my journey is full of stops and starts, which gives me time to look around, and get more and more nervous with every passing yard. I can't see anyone looking at me, or pointing a phone in my direction, but I feel like I'm being watched... being followed.

As I get closer to home, the traffic eases a little, and I'm able to speed up, driving faster than I usually would and eventually parking outside my apartment block. I turn off the engine, taking a few deep breaths before I get out, grab my purse, and run as fast as I can into the building. I don't look back, I just run, and once I'm inside, I go straight up to my apartment, opening the door, slamming it shut behind me, and locking it before I slide to the floor and burst into tears.

I'm so damn scared, and the thought of making that journey in reverse tomorrow morning is terrifying. It makes me wish I'd accepted Hunter's offer… but as I crawl like an infant over to my bed and climb up onto it, curling into a ball, I realize there wouldn't have been any point. He was only being kind, and while kindness is lovely, I want so much more.


It's Thursday already, and while I'm not sure where the last few days have gone, I'm no less scared, no less tired, and no less emotional. I've done my best to hide it all from Hunter, but I don't think I'm doing a very good job. He keeps asking if I'm okay. I always say I am, but he doesn't seem convinced.

I don't think I've screwed up at all at work, despite my exhaustion. Hunter certainly hasn't mentioned anything being wrong. I've continued to knock on his doorframe, but he hasn't picked me up on it – not since that first time – and I'm wondering if I've started to see it as a necessary barrier between us; one that I have to knock on to gain entry into his personal space because I have no right to be there.

Or maybe I'm just overtired and reading too much into every nuanced action.

I'm aware of Keira's perfume before she says a word and I look up to see her smiling down at me.

"Sorry to come in without an appointment," she says, parting her lips into a perfect smile. "But I've found your stalker."

I stand, wishing I could hug her. Except she's far too immaculate for hugging.

"You have?"

She nods her head and then tilts it toward Hunter's office. "Is he free?"

"Yes." I might feel elated by her news, but my heart is still heavy at the thought that she'd rather see Hunter than me. Not surprisingly.

I get up and wander to Hunter's door, knocking on the frame, and he looks up as I enter.

"Keira's here."

His face lights up and he stands. "Oh, yes? Show her in."

I step back, but don't announce her, or even guide her in. She knows the way well enough, and as she passes me, I realize – yet again – why I don't stand a chance. We might both be wearing business suits, but they couldn't be more different. Mine is navy blue, with a fitted jacket and a skirt that ends just above my knees, and beneath it, I'm wearing a white blouse, open at the neck. Keira's suit is cream-colored. The jacket is tailored, and while I'm sure she's wearing underwear, that's the only thing between her and the suit itself, the skirt being short enough to show off her tanned thighs. She looks incredible, and I can't blame Hunter for his taste in women. It's just that I'm not made that way.

"I was just telling Livia," Keira says before she's even sat down, "I've found her stalker."

Hunter looks over at me. I'm still standing by the door, but he ushers me into the room and I go over to his desk, sitting in the other chair. Hunter resumes his seat, turning his attention back to Keira.

"Was it the guy Livia thought it was?" he asks.

"No." She turns to me. "It was your old boss… Lucian Wicks."

I shake my head, disbelief welling inside me. "But that can't be right. Lucian is a family man. His wife is a former model. Shelby Wicks is beautiful. Why would Lucian be interested in me?"

Keira tilts her head, smiling. "Have you looked in a mirror lately?"

I can feel myself blush and I glance at Hunter, who's staring straight at me. "But Lucian's married," I whisper.

"Married or not, he's admitted to being besotted with you," Keira says, and I look back at her. "Those were his words, not mine, by the way. I don't think I've ever used the word 'besotted' in my life."

"Are you sure about that?" Hunter says, clearly struggling not to smile, and she turns to him and frowns.

I don't want them to get into reminiscing about old times, so I ask, "How did you find out about Lucian?"

She looks back at me. "I accessed your old phone records and discovered that he'd sent the first images from his personal phone."

"Really?" Hunter's as shocked as I am, and it shows in his voice.

"I'm surprised you didn't recognize his number," Keira says, still staring at me and ignoring Hunter.

"I didn't have his number."

"Seriously?"

"Yes. I never needed it. We worked right next door to each other. Why would I need his number?"

"Because he was your boss?"

"So? I don't have Hunter's number."

Keira rolls her eyes. "No, but he has yours, I'll bet." She looks over at Hunter.

"Of course I do."

"Typical," she says, and then turns back to me again. "Lucian told me that after you blocked his number, he realized his mistake. He was also worried his wife might find out what he was doing, so all the subsequent messages came from burners."

"I can't believe I went to him for help."

"No, neither could he, evidently. He told me he panicked then, especially when you said you were gonna report it to the cops."

"Is that why he played it down... tried to pretend it was all in my imagination?"

"Yeah. He got scared. That's why he stopped sending the photographs... at least for a while. Just before you left SKJ Robotics, he sent a few more."

"Why did he do that?" I ask.

"He claimed he wasn't sure, but I got the feeling he was hoping you might turn to him for help again."

"Why would I when he'd been so dismissive before?"

She shrugs her shoulders. "Don't look for logical explanations here. There aren't any. And like I say, that's just my gut feeling. He never really explained why he did that... not with any degree of satisfaction, anyway."

"Okay... but having stopped after I left, why did he start up again?"

"Because he didn't really stop," she says and I shake my head, feeling confused. It's easily done. It comes from being so tired.

"What does that mean?" Hunter puts my question for me and we both stare at Keira, waiting.

"It means he carried on following you, taking photographs of you, and after a few days, he tried sending them. Except they bounced back."

"Yeah, because I'd changed phones."

"Exactly. He didn't know that though, so he kept trying for a while, until he worked it out for himself. He said he was desolate after that, believing he'd never be able to communicate with you again. Until the discrepancy was found in your final paycheck."

"What discrepancy?" Hunter looks from Keira to me, raising his eyebrows.

"It was nothing, really. They'd forgotten to pay me some vacation allowance, that's all. I had to call them, and they sent me a check."

"They couldn't just pay you electronically?"

"No. My bank details were wiped from their system when I left."

He nods his head and looks back at Keira. "Wicks wasn't responsible for the problem with the paycheck," she says. "But he found out about it, and overheard someone in the HR department saying they needed to contact you. He realized then that he might be able to get hold of your new number through them. He knew he was going too far with the whole thing... that he'd already gone too far, really, and that what he was doing was wrong. Only by that stage, he didn't know how to stop. He said he knew he'd upset you, and asked if you could forgive him."

"I—I don't know if I can do that. I've spent the last three days living in fear, running to and from my apartment, barely sleeping, cowering every time I hear a door slam or a raised voice. He's made me feel unsafe in my own home and in my own car, and pretty much everywhere else, too."

Keira leans over, putting her hand on my arm. "Hey... don't beat yourself up over it. He might want your forgiveness, but that doesn't mean you have to grant it. He's to blame for what's happened, no-one else... certainly not you."

"Why did he do it, though? I mean, if he was besotted, that's one thing. I don't understand why he would be, but if he says he was, then he was. But why send the photographs to me? Surely he had to realize they'd scare me? I'd already told him as much myself, when I went to him for help, so why would he want to do that? And keep doing it?"

"It wasn't about scaring you, it was about getting your attention. It's a stalker thing. They become obsessed. In his case, he followed you around, doted on you in his own way, and took photographs whenever he could."

"I understand that, but why send them to me?"

"So you'd know he cared…"

"Cared?" Hunter scoffs, but Keira ignores him.

"He did it so you'd realize he was there," she says. "Watching you wasn't enough. Having your photographs wasn't enough. He needed you to be a part of it, too, even after you'd explained how frightening it was for you. That wasn't what he wanted to hear, you see… so he ignored it." She lets out a sigh. "It's like when you fall in love, and you want the other person to know, and understand… and feel it, too, even if they don't."

"This isn't love," I murmur, unwilling to think about that sigh and what might have happened between her and Hunter.

"No. It's weird and creepy," she says, shaking her head. "But to him, it was love."

"Tell me you're gonna inform the cops," Hunter says.

Keira gives him a pitying look. "I gave all the details to one of my contacts this morning. They picked him up before I came here."

"What about his wife and his daughters?" I'm mumbling, barely able to speak, the relief is so intense.

"They're not your problem," Keira says.

"She's right." Hunter gets up, coming around the desk and crouching beside me. "He made vows to his wife. He broke them. It's not your responsibility, Livia. It was his."

I look into his eyes. They're shining into mine, and although I know it can't happen, I long for him to hold me, to take all the scattered, muddled pieces of me and put them back together again.

"I'll be going," Keira says, getting to her feet and breaking the spell. Hunter stands and goes to her, shaking her hand, which seems very formal for two people who were once lovers. But then he said that to her the other day, didn't he? Or words to that effect.

"Don't forget to invoice me, not the company," he says.

"You can count on it."

She leaves and I struggle to my feet. I might be relieved, but it's like a wave of fatigue sweeping over me, as though the lifting of my worries has left me sapped of energy, and I realize I've been living on adrenalin and very little else for the last few days.

"You should go home," Hunter says, and I turn to face him.

"I'm fine."

"No, you're not. You're dead on your feet. You said earlier you've barely slept since this started, so go home."

"A—Are you sure?" I feel guilty, but I'm too tired to be useful here.

"Positive."

"Thank you." He turns away. "Hunter?" He spins back, looking at me. "I mean it. Thank you. For everything."

He shakes his head. "You don't have to thank me."

"If you let me know how much Keira's invoice is, I'll…"

He holds up his hand, stopping me mid-sentence. "Don't even go there."

"But…"

"This is on me, Livia."

I don't have the energy to argue. "Th—Thank you."

"You're welcome. Now, go home and get some rest." I turn around, getting to the door before he calls me back. "There's just one thing."

"Yes?"

"It doesn't matter right now because he's not here…"

"Who's not here?"

"My brother."

"Your brother?"

Hunter nods his head. "Yeah. The thing is, you haven't met Drew yet, and like I say, he's away right now, in the Caribbean. He's not due back for a while, but I'm sure he'll call, or just walk in the door sooner or later… and when he does, it would be better if you didn't mention Keira."

I feel a stabbing pain in my heart, but swallow it down. "Oh?"

"Yeah. It's kinda awkward. He probably wouldn't like me borrowing favors from his ex-girlfriend, but she's the only private investigator I know, and she's really good at her job."

"She's your brother's ex-girlfriend?" I can't believe I'm hearing this. It can't be true, can't it?

He nods his head, confirming what he's just said. "They dated for a while, but Drew ended it and Keira didn't take it too well."

"So, when she was talking about falling in love, she was thinking of him?"

"I imagine so."

"I see. I—I'll keep quiet then."

"Great. Thanks."

My relief is overflowing now, and I turn around and float out of his office and back to my desk.

---

## *Hunter*

What a week…

I feel like I'm on a rollercoaster, and I don't know how to get off.

From the moment Livia showed me those photographs, it's been a never-ending stream of worry. Obviously, the pictures themselves were a cause for concern, as was the mystery of who'd sent them, and what else they had planned. But then, there were so many other strange things happening, too. For example, I couldn't understand Livia's reactions to Keira. She was grateful for Keira's involvement – any fool could see that – but she was also being really weird. She withdrew into herself whenever Keira was around, or even when I spoke about her. To start with, I put that down to Keira being a stranger, and Livia not wanting to share her story, but even after Keira came here yesterday and revealed that she'd discovered who Livia's stalker was, there was still something odd about Livia's behavior. I tried to make allowances for her tiredness, for the stress I knew she was under, but it seemed there was more to it than that. Except she's not been in a fit state for me to ask her.

She's been quiet all week – understandably – and I sent her home yesterday. I think the relief of knowing it was all over had finally gotten to her, and she looked like she was going to collapse. I wanted to go with her, but there was too much to do here, and I wasn't sure she wanted my company. She'd run out of here when I offered to drive her home, so I didn't think she'd welcome the prospect of me actually going back to her place with her for an entire afternoon.

I can't deny I was disappointed, and surprised, when Livia wouldn't let me see her home on Monday. I'd kept her close all day, inviting her into my office, even when she didn't need to be there… like when Preston came down to tell me about his meeting with Jim Nichols. Her presence wasn't required, but having her there proved to be yet another revelation. She really knew her stuff, and it couldn't have been that she'd done her research, either. She didn't know Preston had gone to see Jim Nichols that morning. Come to that, she didn't even know who

Jim Nichols was until I told her. But she knew about Ecstatic. She knew what they did, and their background, and that impressed me.

It didn't impress me as much as what happened after Preston left, though. She took so much interest in the business, then, showing an amazing understanding of what was going on. But it was more than that... it was better than that. She understood me, and why this matters so much. I desperately wanted to thank her for caring, but I could see how vulnerable she still was and I knew I'd have to bide my time.

Even so, I wasn't taking no for an answer about seeing her home, and although she bolted, clearly in tears, and didn't come back when I called her, I wasn't about to let it lie. I ran back to my office, grabbed my keys, and followed her. I kept my distance, so I wouldn't spook her if she noticed me, and I stayed behind her, all the way back to her place... which is in Allston, in a worryingly insecure apartment block. The street itself is nice enough, with houses opposite, and family cars outside. I parked further along the street, far enough away that she wouldn't see me, but close enough that I could watch her in my mirrors, and I waited until she'd gone inside. She ran all the way, clearly still scared, and a part of me wished I'd insisted on bringing her home, or better still, taking her back to my place. She could have stayed in the guest room... no strings. I might ache for her, but even I know this last week hasn't been the time for thoughts like that.

It's been a time for worrying, and for following her everywhere she's been. So, after I'd seen her safely home on Monday evening, I drove back to the office and picked up my jacket and laptop, before driving back to my place. I didn't sleep very well, but the next morning, I got up early and drove over to Livia's apartment again, waiting outside until she appeared, and then I followed her into the office. That evening, I repeated the process, having decided I wouldn't suggest I'd see her home again. I wasn't sure I could handle being rejected a second time. Besides, she'd driven really erratically on Monday night, and I didn't want a repeat performance. It was bad enough that I felt she was under threat from an unknown stalker, without worrying about her dangerous driving.

We carried on like that, morning and evening, and I'd have gone on for as long as it took, but after Keira came to say she'd found out who Livia's stalker was, I felt like I could stand down… which was weirdly disappointing. Livia didn't need me anymore. Not that she'd needed me in the first place, of course. She'd dismissed my offer of help… and that hurt more than I'll ever be able to tell her.

I keep thinking that, when I came in here last Monday morning, I had such plans…

I was desperate to talk to Livia, to find out if she might feel the same way about me as I do about her… if there was any hope for us.

Having been so readily dismissed, I'm not sure I can face those questions now. Except I still want to know. I still need to know. The problem is, asking her now would look as though I was capitalizing on her situation, and my role in resolving it.

It seems I can't win.

Not only that, but we've been so busy this morning, I've barely had time to think.

Livia clearly got some rest after she went home yesterday afternoon, and she's come in this morning looking much more refreshed. She's also been in and out of my office, driving me crazy. It's not her fault. She doesn't even have to try to look sexy. She just does.

I stare at my computer screen, trying to focus on the email I'm supposed to be reading, my mind filled with thoughts of Livia and the depressing prospect of another weekend which looks like it'll be spent alone… again.

I wish Drew was home. If he was, I could talk it through with him. Although I'm not sure that would help. I know exactly what he'd say. First of all, he'd call me a cliché for falling for my PA, especially as she's so young. And then he'd tell me to stop being so serious about life and fuck her out of my system. Except I don't want to fuck her. Well, I do. Obviously. Even if I don't. I want to make love with her… and I want so much more than that, too.

How on earth I'm going to achieve that, I don't know. What I do know is that I'm going insane… and achieving nothing.

I take a breath and sit forward in my seat, paying more attention to the screen, just as my desk phone buzzes and I pick it up, bracing myself for hearing Livia's voice.

"I've got Preston Tucker on the line for you," she says, and I nod my head, only just remembering to speak.

"Okay, thanks."

The line clicks and although my head is still filled with images of Livia, and the sound of her voice, I hear Preston saying, "Hunter?"

"Yes?"

"I've just got back from my meeting with Jim Nichols." He sounds a little out of breath.

"Do you want to come up to my office? It'll be easier to talk."

"Sure. I'll be there in five minutes."

"Okay."

I hang up and then stand, going to the doorway and leaning against the frame, staring out at Livia, who's concentrating on her computer screen, her fingers flying across the keyboard.

I'd like to stand here and gaze at her all day, but I can't, and I cough to get her attention. She turns and looks up at me.

"Preston's coming up here in a minute. He's been to see Jim Nichols about this contract."

"Do you need me to sit in again?"

"If you don't mind."

"Of course I don't mind."

Her smile is mesmerizing, and I struggle to focus. She's still gazing at me, and although I know I should go back into my office, I can't seem to move.

"Hey… Hunter." Preston's voice startles me and I turn to face him, realizing that either those five minutes passed really quickly, or that Livia and I just got lost in another of those moments. I wish I had time to think about that – about why it keeps happening – but I don't.

"Preston… come on in."

Livia stands, Preston and I both wait, letting her go through to my office first, then I follow, with Preston bringing up the rear. Livia sits off to one side again, and I take my seat behind my desk, waiting until Preston is comfortable opposite me.

"So… what happened?" I ask. He's not smiling, and I'll admit I'm a little worried.

He sits back, crossing one leg over the other, and tilts his head. "Jim wants us to pitch for all their work," he says and I feel a slight shiver of excitement run up my spine. This is what the job's all about as far as I'm concerned.

"Why am I sensing a but?" I can tell there is one. It's obvious from his demeanor.

"We're not the only agency in the running."

"I didn't think we would be."

He nods his head. "And they need the proposal back by Monday morning."

There it is. That's the glitch.

"So, this is our first test. This is a massive proposal, but if we fail to deliver on time, they'll rule us out straight away. They're giving us no time to get this right, but if we get it wrong, we won't stand a chance."

"That seems unfair," Livia says and Preston and I both turn to look at her.

"All the other agencies will no doubt have been given the same brief," I say, and she shrugs her shoulders.

"It still seems unreasonable."

"It's their way of seeing what we're made of… whether we're willing to put ourselves out." She nods this time, like she's understood, even if she doesn't agree with the tactic. I turn back to Preston again. "It looks like we'll be working the weekend, then."

His brow furrows, and he stares down at my desk rather than at me. "Um… I've got a slight problem with that, boss."

"Oh, yeah?"

"Yeah. I obviously had no idea Jim was gonna do this, but it's my tenth wedding anniversary this weekend, and my wife has booked us into a fancy hotel. I already got balled out for not organizing anything myself, but she's arranged for the kids to go to her mom's and everything, and although I could cancel…"

"She'd probably divorce you?"

He shakes his head. "There wouldn't be any need. She'd kill me first."

I can't stop myself from smiling, even though his revelation hardly helps the situation.

"Can I do anything?" Livia's voice makes me jump, and I turn to face her, my smile becoming a grin when I see the expectant look on her face.

"I couldn't possibly ask that of you. It would mean working the entire weekend."

"I know, but I don't have anything else planned."

Preston stands up, clearly in a hurry to get out of here, presumably relieved that he can go away for the weekend with impunity now… thanks to Livia. "I'll email you the full brief," he says, backing away from my desk.

"Okay. Make sure I've got everything, though, won't you?"

"I will."

He leaves with haste, and I turn to Livia again. "Are you absolutely sure about this? It's a big contract, worth a lot of money to us."

"I realize that, and I'm not sure how much help I'll be..."

"That's not what I meant. I'm sure you'll be invaluable. What I meant was, even without knowing the full brief yet, I know it's gonna be a lot of work. We'll have to start early in the morning, and probably won't finish until late at night."

"I'm okay with that. I get how important this is."

A thought suddenly occurs, and I get up, walking to the end of my desk and leaning against it, looking down at her. "I don't suppose..." How do I ask her this, without it coming out wrong?

"You don't suppose what?"

"I don't suppose you'd come to my house in Newport with me, would you?"

She frowns. "When?"

"This weekend."

Her frown deepens. "But I thought we were gonna be working."

"We are. But I've just realized, I'd have been going there anyway, and I've got a full office set up down there with everything we'd need. And, at the risk of being presumptuous, we'll probably be able to work even longer hours. It's my home, so we can cook and eat without leaving the building, and all we'll have to do at the end of the day is fall into bed." I realize what I've just said and notice the blush creeping up her cheeks. "Separately... of course."

*Shit. Why did I say that? Because she's blushing? Because she's embarrassed? Yeah... but she looks so disappointed now. At least, I think she does.*

If only I could ask her; if only I could be sure. But I need to keep this about work, because if I'm wrong, the consequences don't bear thinking about.

"I'm not coming on to you," I say, although I'm not sure that helps… not judging by the sadness in her eyes. "We don't have to go, if you'd rather not."

"N—No. It sounds sensible."

I nod my head. "We'll certainly be more comfortable there than we would here. We can leave early, so we can get some work done this evening, and I'll bring you back on Sunday night."

"You want to leave this afternoon?"

"We'll need to, if we're gonna stand a chance of getting this proposal finished by Monday morning."

She nods her head. "Should I go home and pack a bag?"

"Yes. I'll come by and pick you up in…" I check my watch. "In an hour from now."

"Okay." She stands. "I'd better give you my address. It's apartment twelve…"

"It's okay. I already know where you live." I regret the words the moment they've left my lips.

"You do?"

"Yeah. It's… it's in your personnel file."

"Oh… of course."

That was close. I almost gave away that I've been following her to and from work all week… but at least now I know her apartment number without having to look it up.

She turns to leave, but I reach out and touch her arm. She spins back around, looking up at me.

"I wasn't coming on to you." *I was, but I don't want you to feel uncomfortable with me… especially not now.* "You've had a horrible time this week and I just… I just want you to know, you'll have as much space to yourself as you want this weekend. The house has six guest rooms for you to choose from, plus there's a separate apartment, which my sister lives in when she's home… and a guest cottage, which is a couple of hundred yards away from the main building. My brother lives there when he's not jetting around the world."

"It's quite a small place, then?" she says, smiling.

"Yeah… it's just your average family home." She shakes her head and I step closer. "What I'm trying to say is, apart from when we're working, you won't even have to see me… not unless you want to."

She opens her mouth, like she's going to say something, but then snaps it shut again. Was she about to say she wanted to?

God… I hope so.

# Chapter Eight

*Livia*

Hunter told me the journey would take about an hour and a half, and although the scenery is pleasant enough, I've spent most of my time absorbed by what's inside his car. His Ferrari is beautiful, but so is he, and watching him drive is mesmerizing.

I'd only just finished packing when he knocked on my door, and I opened it to find him standing there, still wearing his jeans and shirt, and I felt relieved that I hadn't changed. I hadn't been able to decide if I should, but in the end, I ran out of time. Since getting home, all I'd done was try to work out what to take with me, while doing my best not to read too much into the things Hunter had said in his office.

I have to admit, I was disappointed when he said he wasn't coming on to me. Especially as he said it twice. Although there was something about the look in his eyes, and about the way he fumbled over his words. I'm not sure what it was, but at least I stopped myself from saying I wanted to spend as much time with him as possible. It was a close call. I think I even opened my mouth, remembering just in time how good I am at misunderstanding, and I snapped it closed before I completely humiliated myself.

Again.

His car eats the miles, and during the journey, he spends some of the time talking with Preston, never losing concentration on the road, but going through the brief that Preston emailed over, to make sure he's understood everything. They've been talking for quite a while already and I'm doing my best to keep up.

"Thinking about their social media," Hunter says, "do they want us to place the ads as well as designing them, or will they be doing that in-house?"

"They want us to place them as well." Preston's voice fills the car and I wonder if I should have been making notes.

"Okay. So will we be adding them to our online account and acting as their agent, or will we be getting access to theirs?"

"They'll be giving us access to theirs."

"In which case, I won't need to allow for an ad budget, just for the setup, copywriting, and design costs."

"Exactly," Preston says. "Was there anything else I didn't make clear?"

"I don't think so," Hunter says with a smile. "I just don't want to disturb your weekend and be responsible for your wife facing a homicide charge."

Preston laughs. "I'm sure she won't mind if you have to call or text me."

"I'll try not to."

"I'm just sorry I can't help more, but…"

"It's okay. I understand. I'll see you early on Monday to run through everything before we put the proposal in, okay?"

"Fine. I'll come by your office at eight."

"That's perfect." Hunter ends the call, pressing a button on the steering wheel as he glances at me. "Are you okay?"

"Yes. Was I supposed to write any of that down?"

He smiles. "No. We're nearly at the house now. I'm sure I can remember it all for the next few minutes."

I smile back at him, knowing he's a lot more efficient than he's suggesting. He recalled the content of Preston's email, which he can't have had more than a few minutes to glance at before leaving the office.

He grabs a small device from the space between us and presses a button, then signals to turn left, spinning the wheel and replacing the device at the same time. I glance out the window, my breath catching when I see wrought-iron gates opening, and Hunter drives the car through them onto a long driveway.

Suddenly, I'm more focused on what's outside the car, and I take in the wide lawns, the mature trees and… eventually, the extensive house that comes into view. I'd expected it to be big, just from Hunter's description, but this is enormous. It's painted white, and is formed in a 'U' shape around a courtyard. There's a double garage off to one side, but he parks out front, opening the door and getting out, before coming around to help me. I'm in a daze as I climb out, holding onto his hand and staring at the stately building before me.

"You can't see the guest cottage from here… or the pool."

"You have a pool?"

He smiles. "Yes, but it's around the other side of the house." I turn, glancing at the double garage behind me. "Pat and Mick live over there," he says, and I look back at him.

"Who are Pat and Mick, and why do they live in your garage?"

He laughs. "Pat's the housekeeper and Mick is her husband… and they don't live in the garage. They live in the apartment above it."

"Oh, I see." I can feel myself blushing.

"They look after this place, and have done since Mom left, when Dad employed them to take care of everything… including his children."

I can hear the bitterness in his voice and I release his hand and move around, standing in front of him and looking up into his eyes. "Are you still resentful about that?"

"Not anymore, no. But I used to be." He stares at me for a long moment and then blinks, biting his bottom lip. "I—I probably should have mentioned… they're not here this weekend."

"Who? Pat and Mick?"

He nods his head. "They've gone to visit Pat's sister, but I'd forgotten… until now. Obviously, Drew's in the Caribbean and I'm not entirely sure where Ella is. If she's back from Paris, she'll be at Drew's place in the city, but…"

"What you're trying to tell me is, we're alone."

"Yeah. Sorry. That wasn't intentional."

He looks so contrite, I have to smile. "It's okay, Hunter. I trust you."

His eyes widen, and after just a second's hesitation, he smiles. "Shall I show you around?"

"Sure." He pops the trunk and grabs my bag, along with another – presumably his own – which is made of dark-tan leather, and looks very expensive next to mine. Then he closes the trunk and pauses, just for a moment, offering me his hand again. I take it and let him lead me to the front door. He drops the bags, putting his key in the lock, and then lets me enter ahead of him, although he keeps a hold of my hand the entire time. I gaze around me, vaguely aware that he's closing the door, and I stare at the enormous space before me. The floor is oak, the walls are white and the stairs are right ahead of us, stretching up to a galleried landing above. There are five doors, and to our left, an archway.

Hunter dumps the bags and takes me straight through the archway into a huge living area with a vast fireplace and several brown leather couches. There's no television in here, and not a book in sight, although there are some very nice paintings hanging on the walls.

"I don't often use this room," he says, leading me through it, into the biggest kitchen I've ever seen in my life. In common with the rest of the house, it seems, there's a lot of white in here, from the floor, to the cabinets. The countertop is a very pale gray, and at the island unit are some slightly darker wicker chairs.

"But you spend a lot of time in here?" I ask.

He turns and looks down at me, smiling.

"Yeah, I do. There's a more formal dining room, as well. But I eat in here."

"I can see why. It's lovely."

The back wall comprises glass doors, and Hunter wanders over to them, taking me with him. He opens them, letting us out to the pool area, the magnificence of which is breathtaking. Surrounded by a wide terrace, the pool itself is rectangular and enormous, with loungers on both sides.

"There are changing rooms in the pool house," he says, pointing to a building over to my left, on the far side of the azure-colored water, closest to the steps that lead down into its depths. "And if you come with me…" He turns, leading me around the terrace to the other side of the house, where we stop and he nods toward another building in the distance, a footpath leading between the two properties. "That's the guest cottage."

"Right." I've never been anywhere like this before and it feels like so much to take in.

We wander back into the house, through the kitchen and living room, and then into the lobby, where he opens one of the five doors… the one nearest the front of the house. "This is my office," he says, although we don't go in. "You'll be seeing more than enough of it over the next couple of days, so we'll leave that for now."

We move further down the hall and he opens the next door, which leads into a less formal living room, where there are more couches, covered in softer material this time, two in dark blue, and two in a slightly paler shade. There's also an enormous television mounted above the fireplace. This has more of a homely feeling about it, and I turn and look up at him.

"You spend time in here?"

"I do... although it's not my favorite room."

"What's your favorite room?"

"I'll show you in a second... but first, the dining room."

We go back out and across the hall, where he opens the door and I peer inside to the formal dining room. The furniture is dark wood and a little oppressive and I can see why he prefers to eat elsewhere.

"The door at the end leads into the kitchen," he says. "So it's not entirely impractical. Just inhospitable."

"You don't like it in here?" I'm slightly relieved about that, although I do my best not to let him see.

"No. I haven't changed this room since Dad died... and it shows."

I can't help chuckling and he closes the door again, and leads me right to the back of the house. There are two doors here and he nods to one, which has a lock on it. "That's the entrance to Ella's apartment," he says, and then pauses for a second before he opens the last door.

"Your favorite room?" I say, looking up at him as I enter.

"Yes."

He seems nervous for some reason, and I wonder at that as I turn and catch my breath, gazing at the most perfect library in the world.

"Oh, Hunter. It's lovely."

He sighs. I actually hear him sigh, and I turn and look at him, to see he's smiling.

"I hoped you'd like it."

He did? I'm not sure what to make of that, but I'm too taken with his library to ask, and I release my hand from his and wander further into the room, gazing at the shelves and shelves of books.

"We have a library back home in Falmouth," I murmur. "But it's nothing like this. We don't need one of these to get to any of our books." I run my hand over the wooden rungs of the ladder that hangs down on a rail, and slide it along, unable to help myself from giggling. Hunter chuckles and I look over at him. He's standing with his hands in his pockets, just gazing at me. "I can see why this is your favorite room. It's the most perfect place to lose yourself."

"Yes, it is. Anytime you wanna come in here, just… well, just feel free."

"Thanks. I might take you up on that. If I have time."

He frowns. "Yeah. I guess we'd better get started, hadn't we?"

I go over to him and he waits while I leave the room ahead of him, although he doesn't close the door, and follows me back toward the front of the house.

"Can I assume you like reading?" he says and I turn to face him, walking backwards.

"I love reading. I have piles of books at home."

"Piles? Not shelves?"

I shake my head. "They ought to be on shelves, but that's one of those things I haven't gotten around to. I bought the shelves, and they were delivered a while ago, but finding the time to actually construct them seems to have evaded me."

He tilts his head to one side as we come to a stop outside his office door. "That's my fault," he says.

"No, it's not." I've had the bookshelves since before I left SKJ, but Lucian was making life difficult in those last few weeks, and since I've been with TBA, I've had other things to think about… like the man standing before me.

He pushes the door open a little wider and we go inside, although he hesitates on the threshold. "Sorry… did you wanna freshen up? I can show you to your room…"

"No, it's fine. I think we should get some work done, don't you?"

It's warm in here, and unusually for me, I slip off my jacket, placing it over the back of the chair in front of Hunter's desk. He stops, staring at me for a moment or two, and then walks around his desk, sitting down, and turning on the computer.

"Where do you want me?" I ask, with my hands on my hips.

He looks up, taking a deep breath. "That's an excellent question."

We've got a surprising amount done in the last few hours, but it's getting late now.

"We'll stop," Hunter says. "You must be exhausted."

I get the feeling he could carry on, and while I'm tempted to say it's okay, I know I'm past performing at my best. He doesn't even wait for my answer, but gets up from behind his desk and stands, looking down at me.

"I'll take you upstairs and show you to your room. You can freshen up while I make us something to eat."

I stand and follow him from the room, waiting while he grabs the bags, and then I let him lead me up the stairs.

"My room is around there," he says, nodding to the right as we reach the top. He pauses, leaving his bag, and then turns to the left, and we walk along the hall, stopping at the second door, which he opens. I pass in ahead of him and pause, letting out a sigh. "Is it okay? It's probably the most feminine of the guest rooms, and the view is pretty good."

I turn and look at him. "Pretty good? It's beautiful."

How could he think otherwise, when I'm faced with a view over the harbor, and the evening sun pouring in across an enormous bed, made up with pristine white sheets, and a lilac-colored throw that matches the drapes?

"I'll open the window for you." He puts down my bag at the end of the bed and walks to the window, opening it wide to let in the gentle breeze. "The bathroom is through there." He nods toward a door in the corner.

"Okay."

"Take your time and make yourself at home." He moves back to the door, hesitating on the threshold. "Can you find your way back to the kitchen?"

"I think so."

"Okay… that's where you'll find me whenever you're ready."

I nod my head, smiling, and he smiles back, closing the door as he leaves.

I turn around again, taking in the splendor before me, and while I'd like to lie down and rest, and absorb all this magnificence, I know I can't take too long, whatever Hunter said. If he's making dinner, I need to shower and change, and get back down there… not keep him waiting.

I pick up my bag and carry it over to the couch beneath the window, setting it down there, and slipping out of my clothes before I wander into the bathroom.

I can't help giggling as I'm faced with yet more opulence. This isn't a bathroom at all, but a wet room, the walls and floor of which are covered with white marble, and I walk in, standing beneath the shower head and turning it on, luxuriating in the splendor of it all.

It doesn't take me long to shower, or to find one of several white fluffy towels to wrap myself in. I braid my hair, rather than letting it drip over my shoulders, and then open my bag, pulling out stonewashed jeans, my pink blouse, and some underwear, wasting no time in putting it all on.

Once I'm ready, I rush back downstairs, going through the living room and into the kitchen, where I find Hunter, on the other side of the island unit, chopping bell peppers. He looks up, without me saying a word, and drops the knife he's holding, his eyes drifting down my body, and slowly back up again. That ought to make me self-conscious, but it doesn't. There's a hunger in his eyes I haven't noticed before, and I like the way his gaze makes me feel… little shocks, like pin-pricks, bubbling over my skin.

"I—I hope it's okay that I brought casual clothes for the weekend."

He frowns, his eyes settling on mine at last. "Why wouldn't it be?"

"Because we're here to work, and as I told you at my interview, I normally function better in suits. It's just…"

He holds up his hand, and I stop talking. "It's fine. As I told you at your interview, I want you to feel comfortable."

He picks up the knife again, resuming his chopping, and I wander over. "What are you cooking?"

"This is the salad that's gonna go with our chicken."

I nod my head. "Where did all the food come from?" We certainly didn't bring it with us.

"If Pat isn't here – which doesn't happen very often – she always leaves the refrigerator stocked."

"So, you come here every weekend, do you?"

"Yes."

"And is that why the bed in my room was made up, and there were towels in the bathroom?"

He puts the knife down again and leans closer to me. "The beds are always made up."

"In case you should bring a guest?"

He shakes his head. "I'm not in the habit of bringing people here."

"Why? It's lovely."

"I know. But this is my home. It's where I come to unwind… to get away from it all."

"Then why am I here? Why did you invite me? We could have worked at the office just as easily."

He leans in across the island unit, at the same moment as his phone rings and he closes his eyes, muttering, "Shit," under his breath. "Sorry," he says, and I shake my head as he pulls out his phone and frowns at the screen. "It's Keira… I'd better take it."

He steps away, pressing the screen and holding the phone to his ear.

"Hi," he says and then waits, glancing over at me. "I'm with her now. Shall I put the phone on speaker?" She obviously says 'no', because he doesn't, and he tips his head to one side, his brow furrowing. "What does that mean?" he asks and then listens for a minute or two. "Okay. I'll let her know. Thanks for calling."

He hangs up and comes back over, putting his phone on the countertop.

"What did she want?" I ask.

"To tell us that your former boss has been officially charged with stalking."

I feel a claw of fear creep up my spine. "Does that mean I'll have to go to court?"

"I don't think so. Keira said that because he's confessed, she thinks he's likely to plead guilty, which means you won't have to testify. But if you do, I'll be there with you… I promise."

I let out a sigh. "Thank you."

He moves closer again, although there are still three feet of island unit between us. "Do you really wanna do something to thank me?"

That claw of fear is replaced by a tingle of anticipation. "What did you have in mind?"

"An explanation."

I can't describe my disappointment, but I swallow it down, along with my anticipation. "An explanation of what?"

"Why you were behaving so strangely around Keira?"

I hadn't expected him to say that, and I feel myself blush. "I wasn't."

"Yeah, you were. You're doing it now, and all I did was mention her name." He shrugs his shoulders. "I mean, I get that the whole stalking thing was really stressful. I get that you were scared. You had every right to be. That's why I offered to take you home that night."

"I know, and I'm sorry I was so ungracious about that. To be honest, I regretted saying 'no' the moment I walked back through my apartment door. I felt like I was being watched all the way home…"

"You were."

"I'm sorry?" *What's he saying?*

"You were being watched. By me. I followed you."

I gaze up at him. "You did what?"

"I followed you. Did you actually think I was gonna let you drive home by yourself? I wasn't being creepy or anything. I just followed you in my car, waited until you'd gone inside, and drove away again… and then I came back in the morning, and followed you to work."

"I can't believe this."

He frowns. "You're not mad at me, are you?"

"No, of course not. I'm just shocked."

"I—I followed you every day until Keira came and told us she'd found out who your stalker was."

"You really did that? Every day?" I move around to his side of the island unit, staring up at him.

"I just wanted to know you were safe. And I'm only telling you now because I want you to know I understand how scared you were."

"It was very kind of you." I want to hug him, but I can't.

"That's not the first time you've said I'm kind, and I don't understand."

"Why I say it?"

"Yes."

"Because you are."

He shakes his head. "Kind or not, you still haven't explained why you were behaving so strangely around Keira. And don't tell me you weren't, because you were. You were quiet and withdrawn... not with her, but with me. I thought I must've done something wrong, but I couldn't work out what."

"You didn't do anything wrong."

"In that case, why won't you tell me?"

"Okay... if you must know, I thought Keira was an ex-girlfriend of yours, and it made me feel uncomfortable." Not as uncomfortable as I'm feeling now, having to explain it, but uncomfortable, all the same.

He frowns and takes a moment. "I don't understand," he says. "Why would you think that? I explained, she dated Drew, not me."

"Yes, you did... afterwards. But before, when you were telling me about her, you said she was a 'sort of' friend, and I thought..."

His frown deepens. "You thought she and I were an item?"

"I thought you must have been at some stage. You had her number on your phone," I say, trying to justify myself.

He nods his head and leans back against the countertop, folding his arms across his chest. "Yes, I did. When Drew broke up with her, she struggled for a while. She loved him a lot more than he realized."

"She didn't want them to break up?"

"No. His job means he has to fly off all around the world, often without very much notice, and Keira got fed up with his lifestyle. I don't think it helped that he spends a lot of his time surrounded

191

by semi-naked models. Keira couldn't get her head around it, and when he told her he was leaving for Australia, she freaked out."

"Australia?"

"Yeah. He'd been offered an assignment there. It was a big one, and he was excited about it. Keira wasn't. She asked him not to go. The way Drew told it, she begged him not to go. I think she thought he loved her as much as she loved him and that he'd sacrifice the job for her. Except he didn't."

"Love her? Or want to sacrifice the assignment?"

"Both. Either. He was fond of her, but that's not the same thing, is it?"

"No, it's not." I lean against the refrigerator door and sigh deeply.

Hunter stares at me for a second or two, and then coughs. "After a lot of arguing, Drew ended it with Keira, and took the job in Australia. He was gone for three months."

"Three months?"

"Yeah. That was why she didn't want him to go."

"I—I can't say I blame her. Three months is a long time."

"I know. She really struggled with it. She used to call me sometimes, just to talk."

"Did she hope to get back together with him?"

"No. She knew it was over. He'd made that very clear. I think she just needed to talk to someone who understood him."

"Like you?"

"Yeah. After a while, her calls stopped, which was why I wasn't sure if she was still talking to me. She never really explained why she went silent on me."

"Maybe she met someone else, and didn't want to admit it, having made such a fuss about your brother."

"Probably. I wasn't about to call and ask. It was none of my business. I wasn't even sure I still had her number, but the fact that I did means nothing. Honestly."

"I know. Although I wasn't so sure when I saw the way your face lit up the moment she walked into the room."

He frowns. "If it did, that's only because she was the person who was gonna put an end to your problems. I wasn't attracted to her, Livia. I never have been."

"Okay."

He stares at me, and I wonder which one of us would most like to change the subject. I know I would, and it seems Hunter feels the same as he pushes himself off of the countertop, looking down at the chopped bell pepper. "Sorry," he says. "I need to get some cucumber."

I'm in his way and I step aside, watching as he opens the refrigerator door. He pauses, although he doesn't take anything out, or even reach inside. Instead, he slams the door and grabs me, one arm around my waist and the other hand cupping my face as he leans down and crushes his lips to mine.

I'm shocked. I can barely breathe, and although I want to respond, to return his kiss, I'm frozen and I can't do a thing.

He pulls away in an instant, guilt written all over his face, and I feel the loss of him intensely.

---

## Hunter

I step back.

Oh, shit… what I have done?

She stares up at me, wide eyed, shaking her head.

"Please forgive me, Livia. I'm sorry. I—"

"Don't." She shakes her head even more vehemently.

"Don't, what?"

"Apologize."

"How can I do anything else? You didn't want me to kiss you."

That much was obvious. She might have just thrown me by confessing that her strange behavior around Keira was based upon her misconception that I'd been in a relationship with Drew's ex. I misinterpreted that admission as a sign that Livia was interested in me, that maybe she was jealous, and I stupidly acted on that misinterpretation and kissed her. What I hadn't expected was for her to freeze me out, and my only solace now is that I didn't pursue the kiss. I stopped the moment I realized it wasn't what she wanted. Now, I just have to work out how to get back from here without doing any more damage.

"I—I…"

"It's okay. This is my fault, Livia."

"No, it isn't," she says. "You don't understand."

"Yeah, I do. I'm really sorry. I thought…"

"Will you stop apologizing?" She puts her thumbnail in her mouth, chewing on it for a second before she removes it again, gazing up at me. "Why do you think I was having such a hard time over you and Keira?"

"I don't know." I thought I did, but it seems I don't… not based on that kiss, anyway.

She sighs and looks around, desperation clouding her eyes. She seems lost, like she's searching for inspiration, and I wonder if maybe I didn't misunderstand at all. It's beyond the bounds of all hope, but nothing else makes sense.

"Would it help if I withdrew my apology?" I say and she returns her gaze to me, her eyes sparkling and a smile tugging at her lips. *Oh, God… can it be?* I let out the breath I didn't realize I'd been holding and move closer to her again, looking down into her upturned face. "Would it help if I told you I'm not sorry I kissed you at all… as long as you're not?"

Her smile fills out, and she nods her head. "Yes. It would help enormously."

"Okay." I feel like I'm on the edge of a precipice and, despite the nerves swirling in my stomach, I can't wait to take that first leap.

"I'm sorry if I got that wrong," she says. "I—I just wasn't expecting you to kiss me... or that you'd want to."

"You didn't think I'd want to kiss you?" She shakes her head, and without hesitating, I take that leap... all the way in. I grab her around the waist and pull her right up against me. She yelps in surprise, but her smile turns into a grin as she gazes up into my eyes. "Livia... I've thought of nothing else since the day you first walked into my office."

Her eyes widen. "You mean you've wanted to kiss me all this time?"

"Yes."

"I—I didn't realize."

"Why would you?" *It's now or never...* "You had no way of knowing I'd fallen in love with you."

She gasps. "Y—You did?"

"Yeah. And I've been battling my conscience ever since."

"Why?"

"Because you're so young, and because you work for me. There are rules... not about age gaps, but about bosses hitting on their employees."

"And is that what you're doing? Hitting on me?"

"No. It's more than that."

She nods her head slowly. "In that case, I don't see that the rules matter."

"Neither do I," I say, smiling.

"And is your conscience still giving you trouble?" she asks.

"Not in the slightest."

I hear her exhale a long sigh and she brings her hands up between us, resting them on my chest. The feeling is breathtaking, and I gaze down into her eyes. "Thank God for that."

Okay… now I'm confused again. "Why do you say that?" I ask.

"Because I'd hate for your conscience to get in the way of me telling you that I'm in love with you, too."

I close the gap between us, crushing my lips to hers, hearing a low growl which I guess must be coming from me. Livia makes just the slightest of moans as I brush my tongue against her lips and she gasps, but opens up to me, and as I let my tongue dance with hers, I bring up my right hand, cupping her jaw and letting my thumb stroke against her soft cheek.

I keep telling myself this can't be happening… and yet it is. I can feel her hands coming up to my shoulders and resting there. Her breasts are pressed hard against my chest, and it takes all my strength not to move my hips… not to let her feel what she does to me… what she's been doing to me since the moment I first saw her.

I tilt my head though, changing the angle and kissing her deeper… harder, pulling her closer to me, even though it's torture. It's wondrous torture. Her moans become sighs as she breathes hard against me. She's too much and I have to slow this down…

I ease up a little, sucking gently on her bottom lip, and then I lean back, staring down at her.

A smile forms on her slightly swollen lips, her eyes shimmering as she blinks and lets out a slow breath. "I—I've never done anything like this before," she whispers.

I bring up my other hand from behind her, cupping her face. "Like what? Falling in love? Because I have to say, it's a first for me, too."

She lowers her eyes to my lips. "That's nice to know, but it wasn't exactly what I meant."

"Oh…" How could I be so slow? I've been telling myself how young she is, ever since I realized I'd fallen for her. "I see what you mean." She looks up into my eyes again. "It's okay. We don't have to do anything now, if you don't want to. We can wait."

She bites on her bottom lip, making me want to bite it back again, although I restrain myself. "I—I don't think I like the sound of that."

"The sound of what?"

"Waiting."

My cock twitches against my zipper, and I make a conscious effort to pull back just slightly. The last thing I need right now is for her to notice my arousal and feel pressured to do anything about it.

"Then what do you want?"

She shrugs her shoulders. "To be honest, I don't know."

"You don't have to decide anything right now, Livia. We can take this however slow you want."

"I don't think you understand."

"Then explain it to me." She takes a breath, stuttering it out. "Are you nervous?"

"Yes."

"Don't be, baby. Not with me."

She smiles. "I—I have no experience of this. None at all. You say I don't have to decide, but I don't even know what I'd be deciding on. That's what I meant when I said I don't know what I want."

"But you want me?" I think I've got that right.

Her smile widens. "Oh… God, yes."

I sigh out my relief. "Okay. Come with me."

I release her, leaning over to switch off the oven, and then take her hand, leading her from the kitchen, back into the hall and up the stairs. At the top, I turn to the right and she follows, pausing with me on the threshold of my bedroom.

I look down at her perfect face, all innocence and sensuality. "We're gonna take this slow… one step at a time. If you wanna stop, at any stage, just say, and we'll stop. Okay?"

She nods her head and I open the door, letting her enter ahead of me.

She stands still, looking around, and although I can tell she's admiring the room, she doesn't say a word. I wonder if nerves have stolen her voice, but I don't ask. This isn't the time for questions like that.

I close the door again and, keeping hold of her hand, I lead her to the far side of the room. Beside the window – which is open, letting in a gentle evening breeze – there's a wide, full-length mirror. It's free-standing and leans back, just slightly, against the wall. I stand Livia in front of it, facing me, and keeping my eyes fixed on hers, I slowly undo the buttons on her blouse. Her breathing is unsteady, like she keeps forgetting and then suddenly remembers. I know how that feels. It was what happened to me when I first saw her. Her lips are parted and the bottom one is trembling, but I can tell it's with excitement, not fear, just from the sparkle in her eyes.

When the last button is undone, I push the blouse from her shoulders, letting it fall to the floor, and then kneel before her, unfastening her jeans. They're tight and I have to tug to pull them down, raising my hand for her to hold while she steps out of them. She's not wearing anything on her feet, and I push her clothes aside and then stand, turning her to face the mirror.

I'm behind her, looking at her over her shoulder, and I kiss her neck.

"You're beautiful," I whisper, raising my head and looking at her in the mirror.

She blushes and I smile, kissing her neck again. Her breath hitches in her throat and I feel her pulse quicken beneath my lips.

Standing upright again, I take a half step back and pull my t-shirt off over my head before reaching out and unclipping the fastenings of her bra. Then I pull the straps from her shoulders and drop it to the floor, reaching around in front of her and cupping her firm breasts.

I look at her in the mirror again. She's studying my movements, but then raises her face, her eyes locking on mine. "You fit my hands perfectly." She nods her head, her eyes alight. "You like that? You like my hands on you?"

"Y—Yes. How can you tell?"

"Because your nipples are so hard."

I pull my hands away, revealing her pebble-hard nipples, and I capture them between my thumbs and forefingers, tweaking them gently. Livia gasps, her head rocking back.

"W—What just happened?" she says.

"I don't know." I kiss her neck again. "Describe it to me."

"It… it was like a shock of electricity rushing through my body."

I tweak her nipples again, eliciting the same reaction. "Like that, you mean?"

"Yes. How did you do that?"

"I didn't. That was all you."

She lets her head fall back, resting it against me, although she keeps her eyes fixed on mine the entire time, while I pinch and squeeze her dark pink nipples, until she's breathless and squirming against me.

I let my right hand wander slowly downwards, over her flat stomach to the top of her white lace panties, my fingers delving inside. Livia sucks in a sharp breath, breaking eye contact with me and watching the progress of my movements in the mirror.

"You're so wet," I murmur in her ear, kissing her neck still, as I slide my fingers between her soaking folds, brushing them over her swollen clit. She bucks against me, and then slowly grinds her hips as I circle around that precious pearl.

I alternate the pressure; hard and soft. I change the tempo; quick, then slow. Her breathing becomes ragged, and she parts her feet, shuddering against me as she reaches up and back, clasping her hands behind my neck.

I move my left hand over, clamping it around her right breast so I can hold her up. "It's okay, babe. I've got you."

She raises her eyes to mine, and that seems to be enough to tip her over the edge, her body surrendering to a crescendo of pleasure.

"Hun… Hun… ter. Oh, yes! Please… yes…"

She writhes against me, and I take her weight, holding her body tight to mine as she convulses through a shattering orgasm.

Calm returns in slow stages, her limbs still twitching, and I wait until I know she can support herself before I pull my hand from her panties and let her go. Our eyes are locked, and keeping them that way, I raise my hand, sucking on my fingers, one at a time, licking them clean. She gazes at me, hypnotized by my movements, before she releases her hands from behind my neck. I don't know what she's got in mind, but before she can turn, I move around in front of her, momentarily blocking her view in the mirror. She looks up into my eyes, still a little breathless, and while a part of me wants to ask if she's okay – if she's ready for the next step – this doesn't feel like the time for conversation. She knows she can ask me to stop, if she wants to, so I gaze into her eyes for maybe ten or twenty seconds, and then without a word, I kneel.

I'm still looking up into her perfect face, even as I place my thumbs in the top of her panties and slowly pull them down. She steps out and I push them aside, finally lowering my gaze to the most beautiful sight before me.

She has a triangle of neatly trimmed blonde hair, through which I can see her swollen, glistening lips. I shimmy forward and raise my hands, using my fingers to expose her, and then I lean in and gently lick her clit.

"Oh, God…"

She parts her legs, clearly wanting more, and I oblige, flicking my tongue over her again as I raise her left leg, putting it up on my shoulder to give me better access, so I can lick, suck, and gently bite on her.

She clamps her hand on the back of my head, her fingers twisting into my hair as she grinds her hips into me.

"That's so… that's so… Oh, Hunter…"

Her voice raises to a wailing crescendo and although I hadn't expected her to come again so soon, I raise my hands, grabbing her waist and holding her up, just as she succumbs, screaming my name as her juices pour into my mouth and I drink them down.

She seems to take less time to calm this time, and although she's still breathless, I lower her leg, making sure she's stable before I stand, gazing down into her eyes.

"You taste so sweet," I whisper.

"Do I?"

I nod my head and then lean in and kiss her briefly before pulling back. She runs her tongue across her lips, tasting herself, the fascination in her eyes capturing my heart.

I dip my head and kiss her again. Harder. My arms around her waist, I pull her closer, her breasts crushed against my chest, as my tongue finds hers. She moans, her hands drifting up my arms and resting on my biceps, staying there, her fingers tracing the contours of my muscles.

When I pull back, I gaze down into her eyes.

"Do you like how you taste?" I ask.

She nods her head, smiling. "Yes, I do."

"Good." I bring a hand up, caressing her cheek with the backs of my fingers. I may have felt this wasn't a time for conversation, but the next step is different. "Do you want to stop?" I ask, and her smile fades, her brow furrowing.

"Why? Do you?"

"Hell, no. I want to be inside you so damn much."

Her eyes widen, and she swallows hard. "Then… then why are you asking?"

"Because this next step is the biggest one of all. I need to be sure it's what you want."

She mirrors my action, moving her hand up and stroking my cheek. "Of course it's what I want, Hunter. I love you."

I smile, kissing her again, just briefly. "I love you too, baby."

I'd love to take her, here, now, standing in front of the mirror, so we can watch each other, but I think for her first time, it would probably be better for both of us if we were lying down. I'm gonna need more control than I'll have if I'm standing up, and after two orgasms, Livia's legs could probably do with a break.

I pull back and take her hand in mine, leading her to the bed. She gazes up at me and I kiss her, hard and deep, lowering her to the mattress without breaking the connection.

When I lean up, her body beneath mine, I have to take a moment… take a breath.

Can this really be happening?

Yeah… it seems it can.

I kneel and then stand, undoing my jeans and pushing them down, along with my trunks. Livia shimmies back on the bed a little, leaning up on her elbows and gazing at me, although she keeps her eyes fixed on mine, and I wonder if she's nervous about seeing me naked.

I place my knee back on the mattress, and am about to crawl up over her, when an awful thought occurs.

"Shit…" I kneel up again and Livia sits, looking into my eyes.

"What's the matter?"

"Condoms… I don't have any." What's wrong with me? How the hell did I let things get this far without remembering that I don't have condoms here? "I'm so sorry, baby. I feel like such an idiot."

"Why?"

"Because I should've thought."

A smile tugs at her lips. "I'm kinda glad you didn't. I'm not sure how I'd have felt if you'd had condoms lying around in your nightstand, especially as you told me earlier that you don't usually bring people here. And it would have been even worse if you'd brought condoms with you. I mean… that would have been incredibly arrogant… and presumptuous."

I can't help chuckling. "Maybe. But that doesn't help us much now, does it? I'll have to get dressed again. I'm pretty sure there's a drugstore in the center of Newport that opens late."

I go to get up, but she reaches out and in a strange, but I think entirely instinctive moment, she grabs my cock. The contact is breathtaking and I freeze, then gaze down to see her tiny hand wrapped around me, her fingers barely meeting with her thumb. I don't know whether she's followed the line of my gaze, or whether she's suddenly realized what she's done, but she snatches her hand away.

"I'm sorry," she murmurs and I look up again to see her blushing, bright red.

"Don't be. I liked it. I like you touching me."

She smiles, although she's still blushing. "I—I just wanted to get your attention."

"Well, you certainly did that."

Her smile widens. "It's just… I wanted to say, you don't need to go out."

"Yeah, I do. We can't…"

"Yes, we can. At least, as far as I'm concerned, we can."

What's she saying? Is she such an innocent that she doesn't understand? She can't be… and that only leaves one alternative.

I kneel back on my ankles. "I love you, Livia, with all my heart, but it's too soon to think about… I mean, I'd love for us to have kids one day, but…"

She giggles. "So would I, but that's not what I mean. What I was trying to say was, I take birth control pills."

Okay… what just happened there? It was like someone stopped the world for a split second, and now it's spinning way too fast.

"Y—You do?"

"Yes. And don't look so shocked. I've taken them for years, because I've always had issues… with my periods."

The world slows again, returning to its normal speed, and I feel like even more of an idiot. "Oh… I see." I lean in, my lips no more than an inch from hers. "As you might have gathered from my half-witted response, I've never had sex without a condom before."

She smiles, like she's pleased to hear that. "So this is going to be a first for you, too?"

"Yes, it is. But that wasn't why I told you that. I have a medical every year. I'm clean, Livia… I promise."

"I understand that. You love me, Hunter. I know you'd never do anything to hurt me."

"No, I wouldn't." I close the gap and kiss her. "Except…"

"Except what?" She frowns up at me.

"Except I'm gonna have to hurt you."

"You are?"

"Yeah. What we're about to do is gonna hurt you, babe." I hate that thought, but there's nothing I can do about it.

"It's not gonna hurt for very long, though."

"No, but I don't like the idea of hurting you at all."

She smiles, but doesn't say a word and, with her eyes fixed on mine, she lays back down again. I place my hands on either side of her head, parting her legs wide with my own, the tip of my cock nudging against her. She gasps, and I balance on one arm, taking her hand in mine and lowering it between us.

"Hold my cock," I whisper. Her eyes widen, but she does as I say, wrapping her fingers around me again, and I release her hand, putting mine back up by her head again. "Now… you're in control."

She sucks in a breath and slowly strokes me, along the length of my shaft.

"Oh… Oh, no." Her words come out on a stuttered breath.

"What's wrong?"

"I didn't realize before, but…" She strokes me again, from base to tip.

"But what?"

"It's too big."

I smile down at her. "It's not, babe. It'll be fine. I promise."

She blinks a couple of times and parts her legs a little wider, raising them up as she gently pulls me in to her, pausing as the head of my cock penetrates her.

"Oh, God… that's huge." She stares up at me. "It's never gonna fit, Hunter."

"It'll fit. Just relax."

She lets out a long breath, and after a moment or two, she relaxes and pulls me in a little deeper, raising her hips slightly.

"That's… that's better," she says, with a smile. It is. She's so damn tight, I've never felt anything like it.

"Good… but we're not at the painful part yet."

Her brow furrows. "We're not?"

"No. Take your hand away." She does, although she lets her fingertips dwell for a moment, stroking me, and I smile. "That felt nice."

"Hmm…"

"Grip my arms, or the bedding… or anything else you wanna grab hold of." I'm not sure giving her choices is a good idea, and she takes a moment before placing her hands on my arms, grasping them. I keep my eyes locked with hers and take a breath. "I love you," I whisper, plunging into her.

She cries out in pain, her nails digging into my skin, and I hold still, deep inside her, lowering myself to my elbows. I keep my weight off of her, but lean in and dust my lips over hers in the gentlest of kisses. Within moments, she brings her hands up from my arms, wrapping them around my neck, our tongues clashing in what quickly becomes a heated dance. We're there. We're finally there… and I have to move. I can't wait another second.

I pull almost all the way out of her, and slide back in, slowly to start with, but I repeat the movement, over and over, getting a little faster with every stroke.

Livia breaks the kiss. "I love you," she murmurs, staring into my eyes, and I raise myself up again, her hands on my shoulders now.

"I—I love you." My voice falters. She feels so good, it's hard to take in, and I struggle to focus, although I make the effort. I don't want to forget this… not as long as I live.

She's gripping me so tight, I know I can't take much more, and I change the angle slightly, swiveling my hips as she gasps, then moans. "Please… yes…"

That's it. That's too much. "Come with me, baby."

Two more strokes… then another, and another, deeper and harder, and she tips over into a screaming, wild orgasm. I follow, the howl of her name starting in the pit of my stomach and filling the room as I pour myself into her, our bodies pulsing together in perfect harmony.

I fall to my elbows, spent, then turn us onto our sides, facing each other, but still connected… always connected. Livia gazes up at me, then touches my cheek with her fingertips, like she needs grounding… needs confirmation this is real. I know how she feels. It seems like a dream… and yet it isn't. She's here, in my arms. I can feel her, and she's mine, at last.

"Are you okay?" I whisper. She nods her head.

"Are you?"

"Oh, God… yeah."

She smiles and nestles in to me and I hold her close, feeling her soft skin against mine. All the worries of the last few days and weeks seem to drift away like a cloud on the breeze. I know it's early days for us. We only said 'I love you' for the first time an hour or so ago, but I've never felt this happy… or this hopeful.

I wake up, my arms wrapped around Livia. She's asleep, and I can't help smiling, holding her closer, as I recall that, after we'd been lying together for a while last night, I realized we still hadn't eaten.

"Are you hungry?" I said to her, and she pulled back, tilting her head, like she was thinking about it.

"I guess."

"Shall I fix us something and bring it back up?" She smiled then, and I kissed her. "It's okay. You don't have to get out of bed."

"Thank heavens for that. I don't think my legs are working yet."

I chuckled and, after another couple of kisses, I resisted the temptation to take her again, and got up, going downstairs, where I finished the salad I'd started making earlier, and added the chicken, which had cooled off in the oven. I poured us both a glass of white wine and put everything onto a tray, carrying it upstairs again. Livia had unfastened the braid in her hair, and sat up in bed, greeting me with a tired smile.

"We'll eat this and go to sleep," I said, handing her a bowl, while leaving her glass of wine on the nightstand.

"Oh?" I couldn't miss the disappointed note to her voice, or fail to notice the way her eyes dropped to my hard-on, and I chuckled as I got back into bed beside her.

"You want more, do you?"

She turned to face me. "More…?"

"Of me."

She blushed, biting on her bottom lip, although she was smiling. "Yes, I do."

"I'm relieved to hear it. But I think it's gonna be better if we wait until the morning."

"Why?" Again, there was that hint of dismay.

I shifted a little closer, leaning in to her. "You're probably sore."

She paused and then said, "I am… but only a little."

"A little sore is sore enough for me. Hurting you once was bad enough. I'm not doing it again."

She took a bite of chicken and gazed up at me. "H—Have you done that before?"

I frowned down at her. "Which part?"

She lowered her eyes, staring at her bowl. "Have you… have you slept with someone like me before?"

I reached over, placing my finger beneath her chin and raised her face, until our eyes met. "There is no-one like you, Livia. There never could be."

"That's not what I meant." I suddenly realized what she was trying to say.

"You mean, have I slept with a virgin before?" She nodded her head. "No, I haven't."

"Then how do you know?"

"Know what?"

"Everything."

I smiled at her. "I don't know everything."

"Yes, you do. You knew when it would hurt. You knew I'd be sore."

I shrugged my shoulders. "Those are just instincts."

"Instincts?"

"Yes. A lot of this is instinct… knowing where to touch, where to kiss, where to lick."

She closed her eyes for a second, shuddering slightly, and I knew she was remembering what we'd done. "And how am I supposed to know where to touch, where to kiss, where to lick?"

"I'll show you, if you like."

"You won't mind?"

I grinned. "No, baby. I won't mind at all."

Now, lying awake and watching her sleep in my arms, I can't think of anything I want to do more than teach her everything I know.

As though she's sensed my impatience, her eyes crack open, and she looks up at me, smiling.

"Hello." She sounds sleepy, and so, so sexy.

"Hi, beautiful."

She smiles. "It's morning."

"Yes, it is. Do you want breakfast?"

"No, thank you."

"Do you want me?"

Her smile tips into a grin. "Yes, please."

I lean back, taking her hand and get out of bed, pulling her with me. She stands and looks up, surprise written all over her face. "Lesson number one… bed isn't the only place you can make love," I say, and her eyes sparkle with anticipation.

"Where are we going, then?"

"The shower."

She giggles and I lead her through to my bathroom. "Oh… how beautiful." She stops in the doorway, gazing at the picture window ahead of us. It has a view over the harbor and in front of it is the bathtub, set into a raised platform. It's huge, and oval-shaped, with a seat at one end, and Livia turns, looking up at me, her eyebrows raised.

"We can make love in there, too… but not right now."

"Why not?"

"Because it'll take time to run the water, and I need to be inside you."

She sucks in a breath and I lead her to the shower, turning on the water, and pulling her into my arms, kissing her deeply. She responds, pressing her body against mine, and within seconds, we're both breathless.

"W—What do I do?" she says, breaking the kiss and staring up at me.

"That depends. Do you want to be able to see my face?"

"Of course."

I smile. "In that case…" I lift her into my arms. "Wrap your legs around me and hold my shoulders."

She does as I say. "I feel so…"

"So what?"

"Exposed."

"Good. You're meant to be."

Holding her up with one arm, I reach around with the other, palming my cock, and finding her entrance. Then I rest my hands on her ass and lower her downwards. She gasps as I give her my entire length. "That's… that's so good."

"It is, and it's gonna get so much better."

I raise her up, lowering her a little harder this time, and she moans, low and deep, the sound reverberating through my body.

"More…" she whispers. "Please?"

"You want it harder? Deeper?"

She nods her head and I turn, shifting slightly, so her back is against the tiled wall. Then, without disconnecting us, I change position slightly, hooking her legs over my bent arms, one at a time.

"Oh… now I'm really exposed."

"I know. And that's exactly how I want you. Now… keep hold of my shoulders. Don't let go."

"Okay."

I plant my feet firmly on the floor and pull out of her before slamming all the way back in again.

"Yes!" Her scream echoes around us and that's all I need to hear.

Using the wall for support and holding her up in my arms, I take her. Hard. The room fills with the sounds of our lovemaking. Her sighs, my groans… skin against skin. I kiss her, biting on her bottom lip. She yells for more, and I give her everything I've got. It's frenzied, and intense, desperate… and everything I've ever wanted.

I feel the moment her orgasm begins, deep inside her… the tightening at her core that echoes and ripples all the way down my cock and into my balls. She seems to pull me in even deeper, and as I thrust into her, her whole body clenches and for a second, everything stops. She stills, gazing at me, right on the precipice… and then she tumbles. My body is hers, and hers mine, and as I let go inside her, I lose sight of everything, except Livia, and my love for her… my consuming, aching love for her.

"This paragraph doesn't read very well," Livia says, looking up at me from her place on the other side of my desk. She's using my laptop, typing the proposal from the notes I keep handing her.

We got dressed eventually, in between kisses, and even made it downstairs to have breakfast. I kept it simple, fixing us some scrambled eggs and toast, and we've been working for the last three hours.

"What's wrong with it?"

"I don't know, but I think you got muddled."

"Let me see?"

She turns the laptop around. "It's the third paragraph down. The one above is about app development, but here, it seems to me you're talking about the website."

I scroll back up, reading what came before, and then continue on, immediately seeing what she means. "Yeah. You're quite right. Where are my notes?"

She hands me the pages she's been working from and I find the relevant paragraph, crossing out a few lines and re-writing them before I hand it back. "There... how's that?"

She bends her head, studying the passage, and I watch her, smiling. She looks up. "That's much... what's wrong?"

"Nothing."

"Then why are you smiling at me?"

"For all kinds of reasons. Mostly because you make me so damn happy I can't help smiling, but also because I've realized you don't need me to teach you anything."

"About work?"

"About work, sex, life, or anything else. You're perfect, Livia."

"No one's perfect."

"You are." I tilt my head. "Come here."

"But I need to…" She reaches for the laptop, but I pull it away from her.

"Come. Here."

She stands, walking slowly around my desk and standing beside me. I turn my seat, so I'm facing her and, looking up into her eyes, I reach out and undo her jeans. She steps closer, resting her hands on my shoulders as I pull them down, followed by her panties.

"Step out," I whisper, and she does, breathing hard already.

"W—What do we do now?"

I rub my thumb against her swollen clit and she shudders, grinding her hips. "Do you wanna sit on my cock?"

"Sit on it?"

"Yeah."

She looks down at the pronounced bulge in the front of my jeans. "Yes, please."

I unfasten my belt and tilt my head again. "Why don't you do the rest?"

She leans forward, fumbling over the button and zipper of my jeans, but gets there eventually, and I raise my ass, so she can lower them, and my trunks, my cock popping free. I unbutton my shirt, but keep it on, and look up at her, asking her the same question as I did in the shower.

"Do you want to be able to see my face?"

"Um… yes." She looks confused, and I smile, putting my legs together.

"Put your knees on either side of mine."

She does as I say, kneeling up on the seat, and I place my hands on her ass, pulling her closer and raising her up above me.

"What now?"

"I'm all yours, babe." She chuckles, but as she lowers herself, she closes her eyes, her face an image of ecstasy. "Take it slow. There's no rush."

She inches down over my cock, settling onto me, and then she waits. While she's getting comfortable, I undo her blouse, pushing it from her shoulders, and dropping it to the floor. Her bra follows, and I cup her breasts, then capture her hardened nipples, squeezing them between my thumbs and forefingers. She squeals and raises herself up before she slams back down again, screaming my name as she comes.

Fuck... I didn't expect that. She rides me hard, thrashing against me, but I hold on, waiting until she's calmed.

"Don't stop, Livia... don't stop."

She takes a breath and, grabbing the arms of my chair, she leans back slightly and gets into a rhythm, a rise and fall, taking me hard. I move one hand down, my thumb grazing over her clit, rubbing against it, and she bucks her hips.

"H—Hunter... give me more, please? I need you."

I can hear a desperation in her voice and I wonder if she's tiring. I move my hands around behind her, clearing a space on my desk, and then I stand, supporting her ass, as I sit her right on the edge. She raises her legs, wrapping them around my hips, and clings to my shoulders, leaning back just slightly. There's no holding back now, and once I've positioned my feet where I need them, I pound into her, harder and harder with every stroke.

"Touch yourself," I murmur, a film of sweat forming on my chest. She looks up at me. "Rub your clit, babe. I wanna watch you."

She moves her right hand from my shoulder and reaches between us, her fingers tentatively sliding between her folds, and she shudders as she gently massages them around and over herself.

"Is that what you want?" she says, and I look into her eyes again.

"Yes. That's so damn hot. Make yourself come, Livia... please..."

She breathes hard, her breasts heaving, and I look down at the narrow space between us, her fingers playing ferociously against her clit now.

It takes no more than a few seconds before her body convulses into a powerful climax, and I feel her contract internally as she screams my name. I can't handle that. It's too much, and I slam into her, coming hard, whispering my love as I struggle to breathe.

Our foreheads are touching, our breath mingling, but eventually we pull back and stare into each other's eyes.

"Thank you," I murmur.

She shakes her head. "Don't thank me."

"Why not? You've made everything so much better than it's ever been before."

"Except for the mess that's now on your desk."

I look down at the mass of papers I just pushed aside. "Yeah, but it was worth it."

"It was."

"And it was my own fault. I'm afraid the need to take you got the better of me."

She grins. "I'm not complaining."

"No. I noticed." I lean in and kiss her. "Unfortunately, though, if we're gonna get this proposal finished…"

"I should probably get off of your desk."

"I wish it wasn't true, but…"

I step back, separating us, and she hops down from my desk, although she doesn't move away and stands in front of me, naked and looking up into my eyes. "I love you, Hunter."

"I love you too." I pull her into my arms, holding her close. "We'll take a break for lunch in a little while, and then do some more work this afternoon… and then this evening, after dinner, I'm gonna take you to bed again."

Her eyes sparkle as she smiles. "Really?"

"Yeah." I kiss her forehead. "And if you're really lucky, I might even let you get some sleep."

# Chapter Nine

*Livia*

It wasn't 'after dinner' that Hunter took me to bed. We couldn't wait that long, so we took dinner to bed with us, although food was the last thing on my mind. I was keen to learn more, and Hunter was only too willing to teach me.

We fell asleep eventually, in each other's arms, both of us exhausted but so, so satisfied, and I'd have happily stayed that way... except Hunter set an alarm, even though it's Sunday, because we've still got work to do.

He leans over, switching it off, and then turns back, kissing me, as I stretch my arms above my head.

"Are you sore?" he asks.

"Where?" I look up into his molten brown eyes, and melt a little more myself.

"Anywhere?"

"No... I don't think so."

He smiles. "In that case, would you like to take a bath with me?"

"Do we have time for a bath? I thought you said yesterday it would take too long..."

He kisses me into silence. "That was because I was desperate to be inside you yesterday."

"And you're not today?"

"Of course I am, but I'm getting in some practice."

"What for?"

"Showing a little more self-control around you."

"Why do you need to do that?"

"Because we'll be back at work tomorrow. I don't think it's a very good idea if I take you over your desk in the middle of the afternoon, do you?"

I shudder at the thought, and he smiles. "No. I suppose not."

He tips me onto my side, facing him, his hand on my ass as he pulls me close. "*My* desk, on the other hand, with the door firmly locked…" He wiggles his eyebrows and I giggle, which makes him laugh. "I'll go run us a bath."

He gets up, walking away toward the bathroom, and I admire his muscular back, my eyes drifting down to his toned ass as I lie back with a sigh.

I can't believe what's happened to me since Friday evening… how much has changed, and how much I've learned. From Hunter's first 'I love you', to that moment in front of his mirror, when he touched me… to making love in the shower, and in his office… it's all been so magical, and I know I'll never forget a single moment of it, even after the ache in my muscles has long worn off.

I feel as though I know Hunter so much better than I did before, and I know more about myself, too. I never realized physical love could feel like this, or that I'd crave it as much as I do, but even a few minutes away from him is making me impatient, and I sit up, wondering whether I should follow him into the bathroom, or wait for him to call me… just as a dreadful thought occurs. We're going back to Boston tonight, which means he'll take me home to my apartment, and then he'll return to his. We'll be apart. And although I know it's pathetic, that thought fills me with dread. He's said he loves me, over and over, and I know he's not going to stop, just because we're not sleeping together. But how am I supposed to survive an entire night without him? I've already grown accustomed to being held in his arms, to feeling his warm, powerful body beside mine, to hearing his soft, gentle breathing and matching it with my own…

"Bath's ready." His voice startles me out of my thoughts and I leap from the bed, running through to the bathroom. He's standing straight ahead of me, and I throw myself into his arms, wrapping my arms and legs around him. "Whoa… what's this?" He holds me close, looking down into my eyes.

"Nothing." I can't tell him how insecure I feel. What would he think of me? "I'm just pleased to see you, that's all."

He grins. "In case you haven't noticed, I'm pleased to see you, too."

His arousal was more than obvious when I rushed in here, even though I was more concerned with being held… being comforted.

"I'm glad to hear it."

He chuckles and carefully climbs the steps that lead up to the bath, holding me in his arms still, as he drops down into it, and then slowly sits on the seat at the far end, away from the faucet, careful not to let the water overflow.

I'm still wrapped around him, his erection between us, and as I get comfortable on his lap, I glance out the window, across the harbor.

"This is a lovely way to take a bath… and it's such an amazing view."

I turn to him to see he's gazing into my eyes.

"Yeah, it is." He coughs, clearing his throat. "I—I was gonna give you a couple of choices this morning, but I'm wondering…"

"Choices?" I forget about the view, that now familiar tingle of anticipation coursing through my body. It's been like this every time since Friday evening, when he stood me in front of his mirror, and let me watch his every move.

He smiles. "Yeah. Obviously, at least one choice still stands…"

"It does?"

"Yeah. Do you wanna make love?"

I grind my hips into him, his arousal pressing hard against my core, and his smile widens. "What do you think?"

"I'll take that as a 'yes'. In which case…" He reaches around, unwrapping my legs, and I release my arms from behind his neck, wondering what he's going to do. Before I can ask, he flips me around, so my back is to his front, and places his hands between my knees, parting my legs. I love being exposed to him like this… like I was in the shower yesterday morning. I also love not knowing exactly what's going to happen next, and I hold my breath, waiting, until he lifts me, one arm around my waist, and then lowers me again, inch by divine inch, over his erection. The stretch is just as breathtaking as that first time, but he takes it slow, giving me time to adjust, and as I settle down onto him at last, I let out that breath in a long sigh. "Okay?" he says, moving his arm up, so his hand cups my breast as he leans back and pulls me with him.

"Yes. You feel so good."

"Hmm… so do you."

He swivels his hips and I feel him move inside me… not hard, or fast, like yesterday in the shower, or on his desk, but gently, the tip of his arousal seeming to hit a spot that makes my body tremble already. I lean slightly to my right, so I can turn my head and look at him, desperate to ask what's happening… how he does this to me. But before I can utter a sound, he bends his head, covering my lips with his in a deep and passionate kiss. I feel him pinch my nipple, and at the same time, he moves his other hand down, his fingers rubbing against my clitoris.

I can't take that… it's too much, and I squeal into his mouth, breaking the kiss so I can throw my head back and scream, my body spiraling, out of control, in a heavenly swirl that takes a long, long time to slow, and eventually stop. When it does, I twist around again, looking back up at Hunter and he stares down at me, shaking his head. I'm about to ask what's wrong when he says, "You're incredible," and I smile.

I don't get the chance to tell him how incredible he is, because he places his hands on my waist and lifts me off of him. I'm disappointed and let out a slight moan, but he quickly slides out from under me and switches places, so I'm closest to the seat.

"You want me to sit?" I look up at him.

"No. I want you to turn around," he says, his voice a low growl.

"So I'm facing away from you?"

"Yes."

I do as he says. "Now what?"

"Kneel on the seat." I lean forward, putting my hands on the edge of the bathtub, and kneel. "Now bend forward."

I look over my shoulder, noting the heat in his eyes as I bend, clutching the side of the bath again. I'm looking directly at a bowl of shells, but I'm more distracted by the fact that my ass is above the surface of the water, and I hear Hunter groan as he lifts me and moves me to my right. Then he raises my leg. "Bend your knee just a little more," he says and I do, holding my breath, unsure what to expect, until he balances my knee on the edge of the bath.

"Oh… God…"

"What's wrong?" He sounds concerned, and I glance over my shoulder again. "Does that hurt?"

"No. I feel…"

"What?"

"Open to you."

The worry fades from his face and he smiles as he reaches down, his fingers parting my lips before he pushes one inside me and I gasp, rocking back against him, wanting more. He obliges, adding a second finger and I moan out my pleasure, just as he withdraws them, moving in closer and slamming his arousal straight into me. I scream with pleasure, water overflowing across the raised platform and down onto the floor as he pounds into me, harder and harder.

I want him so much, and I'm about to tell him that when he stills and lets out a strangled groan.

"Oh, fuck, Livia… you're gonna make me come." I feel him swell inside me and the jet of hot liquid pouring from him to me. I love how that feels and squirm back against him. After a few seconds, he falls forward, his chest against my back. "I'm so sorry," he murmurs.

I can't move, so I arch my back slightly. "Let me up, Hunter." He stands, giving me space to turn around and sit down on the seat. I look up at him, although he's staring out the window. "Why are you apologizing?"

He lowers his head, his brow furrowed. "Isn't it obvious?"

"No."

I hear him sigh as he sits on the edge of the bath, his shoulders slumped. "That wasn't supposed to happen."

"It wasn't?"

"No."

"Which part?" I ask.

He tilts his head at me. "The end part," he says. "I didn't mean to come so soon."

"That was soon, was it?"

"Yes."

"Well… I liked it."

He frowns. "You did?"

"Yeah. I like everything you do with me… to me."

He leans over, lifting me into his arms, and sits me on his lap. "With you, baby. Always with you."

I reach up, touching his cheek with my fingertips, the fine bristles spiking against my skin. "Never apologize for doing that."

"Even when it ends sooner than it's supposed to?"

"Even then." I smile. "I like the fact that I excite you."

He holds the back of my head, tipping me over slightly as he kisses me. "Never doubt that for one second, Livia."


"Shall we just have toast?" Hunter asks, as he puts the water into the coffee machine.

"I think it's probably wise. We need to start work, or we'll never get finished in time."

He nods his head. "There's not as much left to do as you might think, but I don't wanna be late leaving tonight… not when I've got Preston coming to see me at eight in the morning."

"No." I'm reminded of the fact that we'll go our separate ways when we get back to the city, and we won't get to spend tonight together, as Hunter reaches into the refrigerator, and at the same time, the door in the back wall opens, making me jump.

The stranger who enters stops dead, his mouth open, and looks from me to Hunter, and back again.

"Drew…" Hunter slams the fridge door, turning toward the other man as I realize this must be his brother. The similarities between them are now obvious. Okay, so Drew is maybe a couple of inches shorter than Hunter, but they've got the same coloring, although Drew is clean-shaven. Their eyes are definitely a similar shade of brown, though, and Drew's are still fixed on me. "What are you doing here?"

Drew turns to face his brother at last. "How many times do I have to remind you? I live here."

"I know that. But you're supposed to be in the Caribbean for another couple of weeks, aren't you? What did you do? Get down there, decide you didn't like it, and come straight back again?"

"Something like that," Drew says and looks back at me again, tilting his head.

"Oh, yeah… sorry." Hunter comes over, although he doesn't touch me. He just stands beside me and says, "This is Livia… my PA. We came down to work on an important proposal."

Drew nods his head, smiles, and steps forward, holding out his hand. "So you're Doreen's replacement. It's nice to meet you."

"N—Nice to meet you too." I struggle over my words. Doreen's replacement? I'm not sure how I feel about that, but what's worse is Hunter's introduction. His PA? I mean, I know that's what I am… but is that all I am?

It sure feels like it.

"Do you wanna stay and have some breakfast with us?" Hunter asks.

"No, thanks. But I'll have a coffee, if you're making some."

"Sure."

Hunter walks away from me and I watch him finish fixing the coffee and preparing our toast, while Drew comes further into the room and I sit down, feeling out of place.

"So, what was the real problem in the Caribbean?" Hunter says, pouring the coffee and bringing it over. He puts mine in front of me, but doesn't make eye contact, and just wanders back to the other side of the kitchen.

"A storm." Drew takes a sip from his cup, putting it down again on the countertop. "Although it wasn't just that. Three of the four models got sick as well, so the agency decided to cut their losses and cancel. I don't blame them. The hotel alone was costing a fortune."

Hunter butters some toast, bringing it over. "You're sure you won't have anything?"

"No. I ate on the flight."

"You mean you've only just got back?"

Drew sips his coffee again, and although Hunter sits beside me, he still doesn't acknowledge me. I try to take a bite of toast, but my mouth is dry and I can't chew, so I put it down again.

"I drove straight down here," Drew says. "I didn't dare go into the city."

"Why not?" Hunter asks.

"Because Ella sent me a message with her flight details. She got back on Friday evening. I knew if I went to my place so soon after her arrival, she'd probably accuse me of checking up on her. So, I thought I'd come home."

"She's back already, is she?" Hunter says with a smile.

"Yeah. No doubt we'll hear from her soon enough."

Hunter smiles, and although that sounds a little ungenerous, I don't know their sister, and they do.

Drew gulps down his coffee, and stands, making it clear he's leaving again. His visit has been brief, and I wonder if that's because he can sense the awkward atmosphere between Hunter and me. Let's face it, Hunter's essentially ignored me since his brother walked in the door.

"You're going?" Hunter says, clearly as surprised as I am.

"Yeah. I need to unpack and do some laundry." Neither of those are chores that couldn't wait, which confirms his desperation to leave.

"Oh… okay."

Drew looks over at me. "See you again sometime."

I nod my head and he glances at Hunter, raising his eyebrows just slightly before he leaves.

The moment the door closes, I get down from my chair, but Hunter grabs my arm, holding on to me. "Where are you going?"

"Anywhere but here."

He stands too, looking down at me. "What's wrong?"

Can he really be that insensitive? "What do you think? Does what we've done mean nothing to you? Do I mean nothing...?" My voice cracks and I stop talking.

Hunter sighs, shaking his head. "I'm sorry. I handled that really badly, didn't I?"

"Yes."

He pushes his fingers back through his hair. "I'm just... I'm just not used to being in a relationship, I guess."

"Seriously? That doesn't even make sense. We both know you had a reputation with women, and even if you're not that kind of man anymore – which I hope you're not – you can't expect me to believe you've never been in a relationship before."

"I didn't say never. All I said was I'm not used to it. I lived with someone for..."

His voice fades, his words echo through my head, mingling with memories of Friday evening... of the things he said then... the lies he told. I pull away from him and as he reaches out again, I push him back.

"Don't come near me."

He stares, shocked, but I don't hang around... I run.

I'm up the stairs in no time at all, turning left at the top and heading straight for my bedroom... not his. Although I haven't slept in here at all, I haven't moved any of my things into Hunter's room, other than my toothbrush. Instead, I've been coming over here to grab whatever I've needed, and my bag is still on the couch. I bring it back to the bed, picking up my laundry at the same time and dumping it inside. I drop my pink blouse and am just bending to pick it up from the floor when the door bursts open.

"There you are," Hunter says, a little breathless.

"Where else would I be?"

He glances at my bag, his eyes darkening. "Um… what are you doing?"

"What does it look like I'm doing? And do you mind? This is my room."

"I know, but it's my house." He steps forward. "Are you leaving me?"

"It looks that way."

I grab the blouse and head for the bed, although he cuts me off, glaring down into my eyes.

"I can't let you leave me when I don't understand why. If this is because of the way I behaved downstairs and the fact that I introduced you to my brother as my PA, then I've already said sorry… and I'll say it again, and again, for as long as you need me to."

"It's got nothing to do with that."

"Then I don't get it."

"I won't be lied to."

He frowns. "What am I supposed to have lied about?"

"You told me on Friday evening, before we… before we… came up here…" I can't say the words.

"Before we made love?" He does it for me.

"Yes. You told me you'd never been in love before. You said loving me was a first for you… but now you're telling me you've lived with someone?"

"Yeah, I did. But that doesn't mean I was in love with her."

I tilt my head. "Seriously? You lived with a woman, but you didn't love her?"

"Yes."

"Did you bring her here?"

"No. I told you, I've never brought anyone here before… or are you gonna accuse me of lying about that, too?"

I look up into his eyes, trying to see the truth behind them, but all I can find is desperation, and maybe fear.

"What did you do?" I ask, refusing to relent. "Did you spend your weekends apart?"

He shakes his head. "No. I stayed away, rather than bring her here."

"Why?"

"Because this is my home, and she didn't belong in it."

"But I do?"

"Yes." He grabs the blouse from my hand and drops it to the floor, then he puts his hands on my waist and sits me on the bed, kneeling in front of me. "Will you let me explain?"

"Why should I?" I feel entitled to ask.

"Because I love you, and because you said you loved me, and listening to each other is what people do when they're in love. After you've heard me out, if you still don't believe me, and you still wanna leave, I'll take you back to the city. But you're not walking out on me, Livia. Not like this."

He's breathing hard, and while I'm still angry and confused, I know he's right… at least about the listening part. I can't speak, though, so I just nod my head, and he takes my hands in his, sighing deeply before he speaks.

"Her name was Sadie," he says.

Did I want to know that? I'm not sure I did, although I guess it'll be easier to tell his story if she has a name.

"How did you meet?" I ask.

"In a bar. She worked there, and I went along one evening with a friend of mine… Austin." His eyes darken again as he says his friend's name. "It wasn't very busy, and she spent most of the evening talking to us. Austin was dating someone else, and had to leave early, so…" He stares up into my eyes, looking pained. "So, she came home with me."

"She spent the night with you?"

"Yes."

"But you didn't know her."

"I'm aware of that," he says with a sigh.

"I thought you said the reports of your past were exaggerated."

"They were... mostly."

"But not in her case?"

"No." I nod my head, although I'm not sure I like hearing that.

"And she moved in with you?"

"Yes. Six weeks later."

"Six weeks?"

"Yeah."

"And I'm supposed to believe you didn't love her?"

"I had my reasons for asking her to move in, and love had nothing to do with it. Besides, we didn't see very much of each other. She worked most evenings, and I was at the office all day."

"And you didn't mind that?"

"Not in the slightest. We got along okay when we were together, but we weren't together very much. Then, about a month later, my dad sent me away to Europe."

"So she moved out again?"

"No, she stayed. She'd given up her apartment, and had nowhere else to go. I wasn't sure how long I was gonna be away, but in the end I was gone for four months."

"Did you call her while you were gone?"

"Yes, but not all the time. It wasn't like that between us. I was looking forward to coming back and seeing her again, but that was because..." He stops talking and lowers his head.

"Because of what? Hunter?"

He looks up again. "Because I'd missed the sex."

"She... she was that good?"

"Not especially," he says, shaking his head. "But I'd been faithful to her while I was away... because I'm a faithful kind of guy, and I'd missed having sex." I sigh and he lets go of one of my hands, reaching out and cupping my cheek. "I'm sorry. This can't be easy to hear."

"It's not."

He stares at me for a moment or two and then lets his hand fall into my lap again. "I got home in the middle of the afternoon, and I knew Sadie didn't start her shift at the bar until around six, so I headed to my apartment and let myself in. She wasn't in the living room, or the kitchen, so I dumped my bag, assuming she'd be in the bedroom. The door was open, and that was when I saw her… with Austin."

I gasp, unable to help myself. "I thought you said he was dating someone else."

"Yeah. It seems Austin wasn't a faithful kind of guy."

"What did you do?"

"To start with, nothing. I was in shock, I think. I mean, I'm not that easily shocked, but…"

"Hunter… what are you saying? You keep telling me you weren't in love with her, but then you say things like that."

"I wasn't in love with her. I swear it. The reason I was in shock was because of what they were doing."

"Why? What on earth were they doing?"

He sighs and turns away for a moment. "I don't know how to put this."

"Why not?"

He looks back, tilting his head at me. "Because, my love… you're such an innocent."

"Not anymore."

A smile twitches at his lips. "Yeah, you are… believe me." He sucks in a breath. "When I said Sadie was with Austin… they weren't in bed together."

"Where were they then?"

"She was in a swing."

"I'm sorry?"

He smiles. "Not a child's swing… a sex swing."

"What is a sex swing?"

"How can I describe it…?" He frowns slightly. "It's a device, made up of straps and chains – and cuffs – that hangs from the ceiling. The woman can lie in it, either face up or face down, and the man can adjust the height to suit whatever he wants to do. She's fully supported by the straps, with her ankles and wrists restrained, and…"

"I get the picture… I think." I pull away from him, kneeling up onto the bed so I can shuffle backward. "Are you telling me you have one of these things in your apartment?"

He leaps up beside me. "No, of course not. They'd installed it."

"You're kidding me."

"No. I wasn't very happy about them making holes in my ceiling." He smiles slightly. "I mean, obviously I wasn't exactly thrilled that Sadie was strapped into the damn thing and that Austin was fu—" He stops talking. "Sorry. I didn't mean to say that."

"It's okay. I understand. Well… I don't, because I can't even imagine why anyone would want to do that, but there's no need to apologize." I sit down, crossing my legs, and he does the same, facing me. "What did you do, when you'd finished being shocked?"

"I think I coughed. I made a noise, anyway, and they realized I was there. In all honesty, I'm not sure who was more embarrassed; them or me. But because Sadie was strapped into the swing, she couldn't do anything, other than stare at me and blush. I suggested they get dressed and join me in the living room. It was fairly clear we were gonna need to talk, but I didn't want to do it while they were naked."

"That's understandable."

He smiles. "They came out a while later, hand-in-hand, and told me they were in love. They had been for ages, evidently... since before I'd gone away."

"So, she'd been cheating on you all that time?"

"Yeah."

"What about Austin's girlfriend?"

"I asked that question and he said he was gonna break up with her."

"You mean, he hadn't already?"

"No. Not that hearing any of that helped... with how it felt, I mean..."

His voice fades.

Oh, God... what's he saying now?

---

*Hunter*

I didn't blame Livia for running from me. How could I? I'd been an idiot.

Drew arriving like that really threw me... especially when we'd been having such a perfect time. Okay, so I'd screwed up in the bathtub. I was embarrassed that I'd climaxed so soon, but there was nothing I could've done about it. In that position, I was so deep inside her, and just the sight of my cock sliding in and out of her was too much. It was Livia's reaction that turned something disastrous into something magical. I mean... obviously, I had to explain what the problem was, because she didn't get it, but once she did, she was so understanding, I fell even more in love with her, if such a thing were possible.

The very last thing I expected was for my brother to walk through the kitchen door, unannounced, and I know I handled that really badly...

I never thought we'd end up here, though.

The fear I felt when I came in here and saw her bag on the bed... it was indescribable.

I knew I couldn't lose her.

I still can't.

"Hunter? I—I thought you said you didn't love her."

I look up at her again, hurt filling her eyes.

Why won't she believe me?

"I didn't."

"Then what do you mean, when you say it didn't help with how it felt?"

"I'd been faithful to her. I assumed she'd been faithful to me, so I felt cheated, humiliated. Like a lot of people in that situation, I felt inadequate for a while. But more than all of that, I felt angry."

"B—Because of what they'd done?"

"No. Because she'd proved my father right."

She frowns, confusion etched on her perfect face. "Your father? What does any of this have to do with him?"

I reach out, and although I want to hold her, I know I can't yet, so I take her hands again. "You were right about me..."

"When?"

"When you said I needed to step out from my father's shadow. I think I'd known it all along, but hearing you say it made me realize..."

"Realize what?"

"That I'd been doing things all my life, just to spite him. Sadie was one of them. Dad spent years criticizing my way of life, and for a long time, that made me live it even harder. I'm not proud of it, but I went through a phase where I never saw the same woman twice, simply because Dad had told me I needed to settle down. That's where the 'playboy' tag came from. The problem was, it was exhausting, and I didn't even enjoy it very much."

"But you kept doing it anyway?"

"Yes. I had to do the opposite of what he wanted. I had to rebel... at least until I met Sadie and realized there was another way to get back at him."

"Which was?"

"To date her. To date someone he'd really hate."

"So you went out with Sadie because you knew your dad wouldn't like her? Is that what you're saying?"

"That's exactly what I'm saying."

She frowns at me. "You used her?"

"Not really. I know it sounds that way, but it wasn't. I liked her, Livia, even if I didn't love her. She had a great sense of humor, she was easy to talk to, and like I said, we got along with each other... even if she was screwing my best friend behind my back. All the same, I knew my father would never approve of me dating someone who worked in a bar. I knew he'd never look beyond her job, or her background, or her address, and that's exactly what he did. Right from the moment he found out about her, he didn't disappoint. He'd never met her, but he immediately said she was bad news. That was when I invited her to move in with me."

"To spite him?"

"Naturally. After that, he told me she'd cheat, and then sent me to Europe hoping to prove himself right. The day before I left, he told me I might as well make the most of my time away, because Sadie wouldn't be faithful in my absence. I remember telling her about that conversation when I got home from the office that afternoon. I was due to fly out the next morning, and she reassured me she'd never cheat. She was lying, of course. She was already seeing Austin behind my back and proving my dad right in the process. When I fought with Dad about it, after I got back, I didn't mention that Sadie and Austin had already been cheating. Instead, I told him it was his fault for sending me away. I wanted him to realize what he'd done… even if he hadn't. I suppose I stupidly hoped he might regret his actions, and his words."

"And did he?"

"No. He just smirked and reminded me he'd predicted her infidelity in the first place, and wondered why I was so surprised by it."

"What did you do?"

"I told him I was done playing games, and I left."

"And after that?"

"Well… obviously, Sadie moved out of my apartment. I removed the sex swing and repaired the ceiling, and I went to work for Moss and Dixon. I didn't see anyone, though."

"Not at all?"

"No. I didn't date, didn't sleep around… didn't do anything. Not because I'd loved Sadie, or wanted her back, or regretted what had happened between us, but because I needed to reassess my life. All of it. I spent a lot of time wondering why I'd behaved the way I had… questioning my judgement and my decisions, and trying to figure things out. What happened between me and Sadie and my dad… it wasn't good. It made me doubt my relationships with everyone I knew. I questioned who I could trust. Not just lovers and friends, but everyone."

"That's not surprising, considering what your supposed best friend had done."

I shake my head. "It wasn't that. Obviously I was hurt and angry about Austin, but I—I'd always had problems with trust, ever since Mom left, and…" I stop talking and gaze into her eyes, then raise my hand and cup her cheek. She doesn't flinch. In fact, she leans in to my touch. "Do you know? I think you're the first person I've ever completely trusted."

I hear her gasp, her lips parting slightly, and her eyes glistening. Is she gonna cry? Part of me hopes so, if it means she'll let me hold her.

"Y—You...?"

"I trust you, Livia, with everything I have, and everything I am. It happened naturally, without me having to even think about it. Maybe that was because you understood me, straight off the bat, and because you've helped me to understand myself. I spent years trying to figure it all out, and getting nowhere, but you walked into my office and within days, you had it all worked out. You made me realize that looking back won't get me anywhere. I'm never gonna know why Mom left, and even though Dad's words are always gonna be there, they don't matter. Whatever his motives, he was just being cruel. As usual." I shift forward, getting closer to her. "Please believe me... I didn't lie to you, Livia. I couldn't. I love you too much to lie to you."

She shuffles a little closer to me. "Do you have any idea how much I value your love and the trust you're placing in me? It's not unfounded, Hunter. I couldn't lie to you, either."

I lean over and pull her onto my lap. She comes willingly, raising her face to mine, and I brush my lips against hers in a gentle kiss. "I wanna make love to you so much right now."

Her eyes sparkle, and she smiles. "I wish you could... but we've been up here for ages, haven't we?"

"Yeah, we have."

"And I guess we've still got a lot of work to finish."

"Unfortunately, we do."

She lets out a sigh, and I match it, kissing her again, before I lift her off of my lap and we clamber from the bed.

We hold hands all the way down to my office, and she takes her seat opposite me and opens the laptop, gazing at me across the desk. Something's wrong, though. I know it is. I can feel it deep inside me.

"Are you okay?" Livia asks, tilting her head.

"No."

She frowns. "What's the matter?"

"I can't work. Not like this."

"What do you mean?"

"I'm not gonna be able to concentrate. Something's playing on my mind."

"What's that?"

"We didn't get everything straight between us yet."

She looks a little fearful. "We didn't?"

"No." I get up again, going around my desk, and I take her hand, pulling her up and leading her to the couch by the window, where I sit with her beside me. "Y—You were packing."

"Yes. I'm sor—"

I hold up my hand, and she stops talking. "Don't apologize. That's not why I'm saying this. I—I just... you were packing. You were gonna leave me."

"I was angry, Hunter."

"You had every right to be, but you're missing the point."

"I am?"

I take her hands in mine. "Yeah. I can't lose you, baby." My voice cracks as I'm speaking, but I don't care.

She leans forward, capturing my face in her hands. "You're not going to. I'll never leave you. I promise. It would break me."

I grab her, our lips meeting in a frenzied kiss. "I can't..." I murmur into her.

"You can't what?" She pulls at my shirt, then fumbles with my belt.

"I can't lose you." I know I'm repeating myself, but I need her to understand what she means to me.

"You won't." I break our kiss and yank her top over her head, then claim her lips again, pulling down the cups of her bra and tweaking her nipples. "Please, Hunter… please…" I undo her jeans and she raises her ass off of the couch so I can pull them down, before I tear through her panties, ripping them at the seams. She squeals, then looks up at me. "I—I want to touch you. Please let me touch you."

"You don't have to ask, baby." She's breathless, but so am I, and I stand, unfastening my jeans and pushing them down, along with my trunks. She sits forward, wrapping her fingers around me, her eyes wide and locked on mine as she licks her lips. I think that's unconsciously done, but my dick twitches and she startles. "Don't panic. That happens when my cock gets excited."

"And it's excited?"

"Very."

"Because I'm touching you?"

"And because you licked your lips." She looks confused. "It's an anticipation thing."

"Oh. I see."

"Hey… there's no pressure. You don't have to do anything you don't want to."

"And if I do?"

"Then I'm not gonna stop you." She smiles and leans a little closer, opening her mouth and running her tongue around the tip of my cock. I undo my shirt buttons, sucking in a breath and gritting my teeth as she takes me into her mouth. "Oh… fuck, that's good. That's per—"

"Hunter? Are you in here?" A male voice rings out.

I pull back and Livia releases me, jumping up from the couch. "It's Drew."

I lean over and help her pull on her jeans. "What about my panties?" she whispers.

"Hunter? Where are you?" Drew's getting closer, but I ignore him.

"They're torn to shreds. Don't worry about them. Just do up your jeans." She nods and fastens them while I straighten her bra and then bend down, retrieving her top. "Here... put this on," I say, handing it over, before I focus on making myself look presentable. I've just about done up my jeans when Drew pokes his head around the door.

"Oh, shit..." He ducks back out again and calls, "Sorry."

I look down at Livia. Her top is askew and her hair disheveled. Frankly, she's never looked sexier, but now probably isn't the time to mention that. I finish fastening my belt, and even though my shirt is still undone, I call out, "It's okay. You can come in now."

Drew appears in the doorway again. I'd like to say he looks embarrassed, but he doesn't. He can barely control his grin. Livia leans up and whispers, "I'm gonna go upstairs." I nod my head and she darts across the room, ducking past Drew without another word.

I wait until the sound of her footsteps has faded into the distance and then turn back to my brother.

"In case you didn't guess, I screwed up my introduction before. Livia isn't just my PA."

"I guessed there might be something going on, just from the way she was looking at you, but I didn't realize you'd become a total cliché."

I'd expected him to call me that, but with things between Livia and me being the way they are, it rankles. "A cliché?"

"Yeah. You're just the same as Dad."

I step forward, seeing red. "Don't ever say that to me."

He doesn't flinch, despite my raised voice. "Why not? It's true. At least in this instance. Honestly... what's the difference between his relationship with Doreen, and what you're doing with Livia?"

"Let me think... I'm not married. I don't have children. Neither does Livia. Do you want me to go on?"

"No. But she's how old? Twenty?"

"She's twenty-one. And why is that relevant?" He opens his mouth to speak, to raise more objections, but I hold up my hand and he closes it again. "It's not fucking relevant at all, Drew."

"Okay. Calm down."

I fasten my shirt buttons. "Do you think I went into this lightly? You think I didn't consider Livia's age, and the fact that she works for me before I got into this? I even considered the similarities between my situation and Dad's, and I dismissed them, because I'm not him. Regardless of what you might think, I've never taken advantage of my position. It isn't like that. Livia loves me, and I love her."

Drew's mouth falls open. "Love?" he says, clearly shocked.

"Yes. Love. The kind of love where I can't live without her. Hell... I can barely breathe without her."

"I—I'm sorry. I didn't mean..." He looks so lost, I have to take pity on him, and I smile, which seems to help him relax, just a little

"It's okay. You weren't to know." I stare at him for a moment, both of us catching our breath. "Did you come over for anything in particular?"

"No... I was just wondering how late you're gonna be here tonight?"

"Not very."

"So you won't be here for dinner?"

I feel a little guilty. It sounds like he's looking for company. But I can't provide that. Not with the early start I've got tomorrow. "No. I'm planning on heading back to the city around six, assuming we can get all this work finished."

"You call that work, do you?" He grins, much more like his usual self now.

"We were… taking a break." I'm not about to tell him what's been going on this morning.

"Sure you were," he says.

I shake my head. "I'd better go find Livia, to make sure she's okay," I say, stepping forward, but he nods down at the couch behind me.

"I think you forgot something."

I look around and see her torn panties lying in the corner of the couch and snatch them up, screwing them into a ball and putting them in my pocket. Then I head for the door, but as I pass Drew, he grabs my arm and I turn to look at him. "I'm sorry I compared you to Dad."

"It's okay. I do it often enough myself."

"Do you think that's something you should stop?"

"Livia suggested I should try… so maybe I will."

He smiles. "I'm really pleased you've found someone special."

"Oh, she's special."

He lets me go, and I make for the stairs, taking them two at a time.

At the top, I wonder which way to go, but take a gamble and turn right, going to my room, and hoping for the best. Sure enough, Livia's inside, standing over by the window. She's straightened her clothes and her hair, and I sigh out my relief. This feels better than finding her in the guest room, even if she jumps out of her skin when I walk in.

"You okay?" I close the door behind me. She nods her head and comes over, putting her arms around my waist and clinging on. "I'm sorry about my brother."

"I guess he knows we're together now."

I lean back, holding on to her. "Is that a problem?"

"No." She pauses for a second. "But I've been thinking... I know we joked about locking your office door at work, and... and..."

"And making love on my desk?"

She nods her head. "The thing is, though, I don't want people to know we're seeing each other. I—I don't want them to think I'm sleeping with you because of who you are, or because you're rich, or because I'm looking to further my career."

"I don't particularly care what people think, but we can keep this a secret, if that's what you want. As long as we don't have any secrets from each other."

"Of course not."

"Okay. I'll tell Drew to keep it to himself." She leans in to me, resting her head against my chest and I stroke her hair. "Speaking of sleeping together... when we drive back to the city tonight, I was wondering how you'd feel about coming to my place?"

She pulls away, looking up at me. "I'd love to. But it's a little impractical. I don't have anything to wear for work tomorrow."

"Okay. Why don't we slide by your place first, so you can pick something up?"

She smiles, her eyes sparkling. "Do you know? I was thinking, only this morning, how much I was dreading trying to sleep without you when we get back to the city."

"Well... you won't have to, if you come stay with me."

She leans forward again, but then pulls back sharply. "Wait... your apartment... that's the place you shared with Sadie, where she..."

"No, it's not, babe. I moved."

"Because of what she did?"

"No. It had nothing to do with her. It didn't even have anything to do with the holes she made in my damn ceiling."

Livia chuckles and I pull her closer. "I only moved into my current apartment about a year ago, not long after Dad died, and the thing with Sadie happened a couple of years before that. The two events aren't even remotely connected... I promise." She nods her head. "Please... please don't feel threatened by her."

"Okay."

"And please say you'll come back to my place tonight? You're not the only one who's been dreading sleeping alone." I lean down and kiss her. "I've gotten kinda used to spending all my time with you."

"Me too."

"In that case, let's keep on doing it."

# Chapter Ten

*Livia*

When I asked Hunter if we could keep our relationship a secret, I never thought it would be so difficult.

We've managed it... but I honestly don't know how.

Keeping our hands to ourselves during the day is proving challenging. We've nearly been caught out several times... most notably on the day we heard the company had been awarded the contract by Ecstatic Sports. Hunter was understandably thrilled, and I was in his office when Preston called with the news. Once he'd put his phone down, Hunter jumped to his feet and lifted me into his arms, kissing me, like his life depended on it... only for Miles Hampton to walk into the room.

Fortunately, as he crossed the threshold, he was looking at a piece of paper he had in his hand, and Hunter and I were able to step apart before he glanced up. I don't think he noticed anything, and if he did, he didn't mention it, but handed the document to Hunter before leaving.

"We're gonna have to be more careful," I said, as Hunter pushed a stray hair behind my ear. I felt sure I was blushing, although he just smiled down at me.

"Okay... but for that to work, you'll have to stop being so sexy."

"I'm not sexy at all."

He grabbed me, his hands on my waist, and pulled me close to him, his arousal pressing into me. "Oh, yes, you are." His kiss was even harder, and as his hands wandered, I soon forgot where we were, my need for him overtaking my reason. "Still think you're not sexy?" he said as we pulled away from each other.

"I still think this is madness."

He shook his head. "No, it's not. It's love."

I had to smile then, although I went back to my desk... partly out of fear that we'd be caught, and partly because I needed to calm down before we took things any further.

It might be tiring, and a little nerve-wracking having to keep our secret, but it's also quite exciting. We have to snatch our moments together during the day, and while that might make them brief, it also makes them very intense.

Even my parents don't know about us yet. Their ignorance isn't my fault... if 'fault' is the right word. They've been busy over the last few weeks, and Mom's been so full of how much better things are with Dad, I haven't had the chance to tell her anything about Hunter.

When we spoke on Wednesday, I half expected her to ask if I'd be going there this weekend, but she didn't. She told me Uncle David and Aunt Elizabeth will be visiting, and I'll admit, I was surprised. It's the first time they've been to stay since Dad's stroke, and that feels like a big step.

Part of me feels guilty for not visiting them – even though I haven't been able to – but a part of me is just grateful today is Friday, because that means Hunter and I will be going down to Newport again. This will be our fourth weekend there, and I can't wait.

I'll admit, the first time we went back, I was a little nervous. Hunter had explained that, although Drew had gone on another assignment and wouldn't be there, Pat and Mick would. I was anxious about meeting the woman who'd raised Hunter since he was eleven… it was as close as I was ever going to come to meeting his parents.

I had no need to fear Pat's reception, though. She was perhaps a little older than I'd expected, but she was dressed exactly how I'd imagined a housekeeper would be, in a simple skirt and blouse. I was struck by how tiny she was, and in my heels I towered over her, although she greeted me warmly, holding out her hand as she stood at the door, her green eyes sparkling and a smile on her lips.

"You must be Livia."

Hunter had clearly told her about me.

"Yes, I am."

"It's good to meet you," she said, nodding her head before turning her attention to Hunter. "Do you want to take the bags up? I'll have dinner ready in twenty minutes."

"Thanks, Pat."

He took my hand, leading me into the house and straight up to his room. We'd been sleeping together all week, and made no pretense of me using the guest room. Once inside, he pulled me into his arms and looked down at me.

"Feeling better now that's out of the way?"

I hadn't mentioned my anxiety about meeting Pat, and I frowned up at him. "Why wouldn't I be?"

He smiled. "Because you've been nervous as hell all day." He leaned forward and kissed me. "But it's okay."

"I know it is. Pat's really nice."

He shook his head. "That's not what I meant. I was about to say, it's okay because I'm gonna feel the same when I get to meet your parents, so don't worry about it."

"You're gonna be nervous about meeting my mom and dad?"

"I'm not sure nervous covers it."

"Why?" That didn't make sense to me.

"What if they don't like me? What if I don't measure up to their expectations?"

I rested my hand on his chest. "You make me happy. That's all they'll ever ask of you."

"I make you happy?"

"Of course you do. How could you doubt that?"

"I don't... I guess." His eyes flickered with something I thought I recognized... something wild. "I was just wondering if there was anything I could do to make you even happier."

"You know I'd never object to anything you wanted to do with me, but Pat said we only had twenty minutes... about five minutes ago."

"I know." He held the back of my head, leaning in so his lips were pressed to my ear. "I've forgotten what lesson we're on now, but let me introduce you to the concept of the quickie..."

Before I could say a word, he pulled me over to his bed and spun me around, so my back was to his front. Then he quickly unbuttoned my jacket, throwing it onto the end of the mattress, and hoisted up my skirt, bunching it around my hips.

"Kneel on the edge of the bed, baby." I loved the way he gave me instructions, and I obeyed. "Now bend forward on all fours."

I did exactly as he said, and he ran his hands over my ass, through the thin material of my lace panties, before he tore through them, ripping them at the seams. I yelped, but felt a trembling heat build inside me as he used his legs to part mine. Then I heard his zipper and felt the tip of his arousal pressing against me.

"Look up," he said, and I did, letting out a gasp as I saw the two of us reflected in the mirror opposite... me kneeling and him standing right behind me. We both appeared to be fully clothed, but that didn't matter. I knew what was about to happen, and watching it made it even more exciting.

He grunted as he pushed inside me, his eyes never leaving mine, and I sighed out a moan of deep satisfaction.

"More…" I urged. "Give me more."

He slammed into me, harder and harder.

"Fuck… you're so damn tight." I wondered why he only ever swore in front of me when we were making love, but I wasn't about to ask. I was too busy trying not to lose my mind. There was something gloriously abandoned about just being taken, really hard and fast, watching him pound into me, forcing me further onto the bed with every stroke.

It didn't take long – probably only a few minutes – before I felt a familiar quivering right at my core.

"I'm… I'm…" was all I managed to say before I was overwhelmed by pleasure. It seemed to start somewhere deep inside me and radiate outwards, consuming me. I struggled not to make a sound, but seeing my face in the mirror and the wondrous ecstasy written all over it, I couldn't help myself, and I let out a wild scream. I saw the look of rapture on Hunter's face, felt him explode, filling me, as he groaned, murmuring his love, and whispering my name in stuttering breaths.

He pulled out of me and flopped down onto the mattress at the same time as I collapsed forward beside him.

"God… that was good," I whispered, breathing hard.

"It was." I turned my head as he pulled me closer, kissing me gently. "As much as I'd love to lie here and hold you for a while, and maybe do all that again… the whole point of a quickie is that you don't hang around."

"Oh… I see."

I went to get up, but he pulled me back down, rolling us over, so I was on my back and he was above me, nestled between my legs.

"Not so fast… I just need to say something."

"Oh? What's that?"

He sighed. "You make me happy, too, baby."

I brushed my fingertips down his cheek and he dipped his head to kiss me, although I pulled back before we got carried away. "We need to go downstairs." He rolled onto his back and I sat up and shimmied to the edge of the bed before standing. "Pat's cooked dinner. The least we can do is to be there to eat it."

He smiled up at me. "I think you might wanna straighten yourself out a little first."

I wandered to the mirror and let out a cry of surprise when I saw myself properly. "What happened to me? I looked okay just now."

He got up and came over, standing behind me, his hands on my waist. I smiled at his reflection, pushing my fingers back through my disheveled hair to straighten it a little. "You looked better than okay. You looked fantastic. But, your hair is the least of your problems, babe."

"Why?"

He chuckled. "Your skirt…"

I pushed it down and looked at myself in the mirror again. "It's so creased." He laughed out loud, and I turned to face him, gently slapping him on the chest. "Stop it."

"Why?"

"Because it's not funny."

"Yeah, it is."

I stepped back, gazing at him, and realized that he'd fastened his jeans again. "How can you look so unruffled, while I look such a wreck?"

"I don't know… but you're my wreck."

"I am?"

"Yeah. I'm the one who's responsible for making you look like this."

"In that case, I think you should help me smarten up, don't you?"

"Of course. As long as I'm allowed to mess you up again later."

I rolled my eyes at him, but he helped me nonetheless, choosing me a light summer dress from my bag and bringing it over.

I'd slipped out of my clothes and was standing, naked. "I'll need underwear," I said, looking at the dress he was holding.

"No, you won't."

"But…"

He moved closer, putting the dress on the bed, and pulled me into his arms. "You won't," he said, and I looked up into his eyes, seeing the fire burning within them, and turned, pulling the dress on over my head. He groaned as I straightened it and then shook his head.

"What's wrong?" I glanced down at myself, but couldn't see anything out of place.

"Nothing. It's just I didn't think that through."

"What?"

"You… not wearing any underwear."

"Do you want me to put some on, then?" I asked.

"No. But it's gonna drive me crazy knowing you're naked underneath your dress."

I leaned in to him, my arms around his neck, and we kissed, his hands reaching up under my skirt, settling on my bare ass, his skin against mine, and I moved closer, crushing my breasts to his chest.

He pulled back, breathless, and gazed into my eyes. "We either stop now, or I'm gonna rip that dress off of you, and fuck you… until your legs don't work."

He'd used the word 'fuck' before, but it had always been in the heat of the moment, and never in that context. I liked it. It sounded good, but so did driving him crazy all evening, and I grabbed his hand and dragged him from the room.

Pat was in the kitchen, and didn't give the impression she was waiting for us, although she turned around on hearing us enter the room, and smiled... first at Hunter, and then at me. It was only then that I remembered how noisy I'd been, and I blushed, although Pat didn't seem to notice, and Hunter led me over to the island unit, where we sat and ate the Teriyaki chicken and rice she'd made.

"When Hunter called to tell me he was bringing you with him for the weekend, he neglected to give me any instructions about what you like to eat, and what you don't... so I took pot luck," Pat said, giving him a rather pointed look.

I smiled at her. "I like most things, except tofu. My mom tried it in a stir-fry once, and it was horrible."

Hunter laughed. "You won't find much tofu in this house, so I don't think we need to worry."

"No, we don't." I looked up at Pat as she spoke, to find she was smiling over at us, with a kind of dreamy look on her face. I didn't know what that meant, but I was enjoying my chicken too much to ask.

I only met Mick briefly that weekend. He was working on something in his and Pat's apartment above the garage, but he came over to say hello. He struck me as shy, but avuncular; the kind of man who keeps himself to himself, with kindly eyes, and hair that was probably dark brown once upon a time, although it had turned gray.

The only down-side to Pat and Mick being at the house was that I missed those moments where Hunter and I did things together, like watching him make breakfast, or taking our dinner upstairs to bed with us. But it was a small price to pay, because we spent a lot more time on our own, doing the things we liked best.

After that, I thought I knew what to expect from our weekends in Newport... lazy mornings in bed, brunch in the kitchen, swimming in Hunter's amazing pool, lying together on a couch in the library, curled up and reading... and making love, all the time. But last weekend was different again. That was because my period started on the Friday afternoon. I didn't get the chance to tell Hunter before we left, and I spent the entire journey worrying about what to say. By the time we arrived, I was a nervous wreck, but the traffic had been heavier than the week before, and Pat had our meal ready upon our arrival. I had to sit through dinner, trying to eat, my nerves getting the better of me.

By the time we'd finished, I was a mess, and Hunter must have noticed because we didn't hang around in the kitchen. Instead, after we'd thanked Pat for a lovely meal – that I'd barely touched – he took my hand and led me upstairs, straight to his room.

"What's wrong?" he asked the moment the door closed behind him.

"I—I..." I couldn't think what to say.

He took me over to the bed, sitting me down, and crouched in front of me, holding my hands and gazing into my eyes. "Tell me, Livia..." He looked so scared, and I knew I had to find a way.

"It's just... my... my period."

He seemed relieved and let out a sigh. "It's late?"

He didn't appear fazed by that thought, and somehow that helped me to relax. "No. It's started."

"And why is that a problem?"

"I don't know... I mean, it might not be. I—I just wasn't sure if we could..."

He frowned for a second, like he was trying to work out my meaning, and then he smiled. "Oh... I see. You wanna know if we can still make love?"

I sighed. "Yes."

"That's up to you, baby. Do you want to?"

"I don't really know. It's not something I've ever had to think about before."

He nodded his head. "Do you wanna try?"

"I guess…"

He stood, pulling me up with him, and looked down into my eyes. "Before we go any further, are you in pain?"

"No. Does that make a difference?"

"Of course. If you'd said yes, we'd have waited a while… until tomorrow, or the next day, or whenever the pain stopped."

"Oh, I see."

"But, as it is… come with me."

He led me to his bathroom, and once we were both undressed, he took me into the shower, turning on the water, then raised one of my legs up, bending it over his arm.

"You're so fucking sexy… you know that, don't you?" I shook my head, and he smiled. "Well, you are. Now, if this hurts, tell me," he said, as he entered me. It didn't hurt at all, but he was gentle, considerate… and I luxuriated in him. When we came, it was even more intense than usual, and afterwards, he held me in his arms beneath the water.

"Does having my period mean we can only do this is the shower?" I asked, and he leaned back.

"No. We can carry on exactly as we were before."

"But… but won't the bed get messy? And won't we, for that matter?"

He chuckled. "We can use a towel… or we can limit ourselves to the shower, if you prefer." He kissed me. "Whatever makes you comfortable, babe."

I rested against him, my head on his chest. "You do, Hunter… you make me comfortable."

It might be Friday again, but it's still only lunchtime. Hunter's had a busy morning, meeting with the design team that are working on the new website for Ecstatic Sports, and although it ended about thirty minutes ago, I haven't disturbed him. I know he'll have a ton of work to catch up with. We may have won this new contract, but that doesn't mean there's been any let-up in the pressure. If anything, it's even greater than it was before… because now we have to deliver.

"Are you hungry?" His voice startles me and I turn in my chair to find he's leaning against his doorframe.

"Yes."

He reaches into his pocket for his wallet, coming over to my desk and putting it beside my keyboard. "I'd say we could go to lunch together, but that would probably give away our secret… and anyway, I've got about a thousand emails to go through."

"What have you been doing for the last half hour?"

"Thinking about you," he says. "Why don't you go down to the deli and get us something nice? Then we can eat together in my office."

I look down at his wallet. "You don't think that would give away our secret?"

"Not if we pretend we're working."

I smile. "What do you want to eat?"

He leans over, his hands on the arms of my chair. "You."

I shudder, thinking about that, and how good I know it'll feel. "I meant from the deli."

"I know… but I still want you. You taste better than anything I've ever eaten in my life."

He leans closer, his lips brushing against mine, the kiss becoming heated in moments. He pushes me back in my chair, and I part my legs as far as my skirt will allow, feeling Hunter's hand dust against my thigh. I hear a groan, and suddenly come to my senses, even though I'm fairly sure the sound came from me.

"What are we doing?" I break the kiss, and he stands, smiling down at me.

"Kissing?"

"I know… but I thought we were being careful."

"That was me being careful." He leans over again. "I miss you, Livia."

"We only made love this morning…"

"So? I need you again."

Oh, God… "I need you, too."

His eyes glint. "Tonight can't get here soon enough."

"It can't?"

He shakes his head. "No… the moment we get to the house, I'm gonna take you upstairs and fuck you so damn hard."

I suck in a sharp breath. "Oh…. please."

He stands upright, gazing down at me. "I'd better go deal with some emails, or something… although how I'm gonna think straight, I don't know." He walks away as he's talking, but when he gets to the door, he turns and winks at me, and I have to chuckle.

I wish we didn't have to wait until tonight. I wish he could take me back to his apartment right this minute. A smile twitches at my lips, because although I might be used to it now, I can still remember how surprised I was when he first took me back there. We'd gone to my place to collect some clothes, exactly as we'd planned, and Hunter had stood in my tiny apartment while I made excuses for my untidiness and found what I needed. Then he drove me across town to a huge apartment block. He carried our bags from the car, and that's when I got my first surprise, because when we got into the elevator, Hunter put a key into the control panel and then pressed the top button; the one marked with a 'P'.

"The penthouse?" I don't know why I said that in a whisper, but I did, and he smiled down at me, nodding his head. I felt even more embarrassed then, knowing where we'd just come from.

"Yes." He smiled at me.

"And does everyone in the building need a key to use the elevator?"

"No. But that's because I don't have a front door. Visitors have to come in through the main entrance and use the intercom."

I nodded my head, like this was completely normal, but as the elevator doors opened, my breath caught in my throat. Who needed front doors when they could step out into a lobby with marble floors and walls? There was a circular table in the center of the space, and opposite, a painting that appeared to be an original.

I stood still, trying to take it all in. "Are you okay?" Hunter asked, turning to face me.

I nodded my head. "Is that Newport harbor?" I said, looking at the picture, trying to distract myself from my surroundings.

"Yeah. There's a guy down there who paints local seascapes and landscapes. I commissioned him to paint that one, and a few others."

"To remind you of home?" I said, turning to look up at him.

He smiled. "Yeah. Exactly." He tilted his head to his right, and I strolled past him, into the biggest living space I'd ever seen in my life. Immediately before me were four enormous couches, in a pale gray leather, set around a low table. Beyond them was a modern kitchen, with dark gray units and a black countertop, which was completely clear of clutter. It was separated from the living area by a breakfast bar, which had four chairs neatly tucked beneath it. I could just about make out a formal dining space on the other side of the kitchen, although it was in darkness at the time, so all I could see was the outline of the high-backed chairs. The wall to my left was made entirely of glass, looking out over the city, and to my right was a staircase.

"Y—You have two floors?"

He grinned. "Yeah. The bedrooms are upstairs."

"How many bedrooms are there?"

"Three. Each one has its own bathroom, and there's a separate bathroom over there." He nodded to a door I hadn't even noticed, beneath the staircase. We stepped further into the room and he dumped the bags at the end of the couch. "Do you want to see the best part?"

"You mean there's something better than this?" I said, gazing around.

"Oh, yeah."

He took my hand and led me to another door, at the foot of the stairs, opening it inwards and flicking on the lights before standing back and letting me enter. My mouth dropped open, and I stared up at his smiling face, before gazing back into the room... at the shelves and shelves of books.

"You have another library?"

"Of course." He grabbed me then, pushing me back against the wall, and kissed me. Hard. "It's... so... good to... have you... here." He spoke between breathless kisses as he ripped my blouse and bra from my body, leaving them and his t-shirt in a trail, walking me backwards, further into the room, until we hit the couch, where he sat me down on its wide, flat arm. I was panting with need and reached out to undo his pants, but he got there first, releasing his erection into my hand. His eyes widened as I stroked him, while he leaned in and unfastened my jeans, waiting for me to raise my ass, so he could pull them down, along with my panties.

"Lie back," he growled, and I looked over my shoulder to see the arm of the couch was more than wide enough to accommodate me, letting myself fall back onto it. He pulled me forward a little, lowering his pants and trunks, and entered me, letting his head rock back. "That's so fucking good..." He looked down at me again. "You're so fucking good."

I smiled. "Can I see your bedroom?"

"Now?"

I nodded my head, smiling, and he took my hands, sitting me up, although he didn't break the connection between us, even when he lifted me into his arms. He kicked off his pants and shoes and I wrapped my legs around him as he walked us back out the door and straight up the stairs. His room was the last one we came to, and he opened the door, flicking on the lights and letting us in to the enormous space, which was dominated by his vast bed. I barely had time to notice the pale gray drapes, the wooden floor, or the crisp white bedding before he carried me over and lowered us to the mattress.

"You like it up here?" he said, moving inside me.

I ran my hands up his arms. "I like it anywhere with you."

He grinned. "I'll make you prove that... later."

He did, too.

Since then, I've only gone back to my apartment to collect clothes and check my mail. When we're not at his house in Newport, Hunter and I spend the rest of our time at his apartment, and he's made love to me in just about every room... on just about every surface. He even took me on the circular table in the lobby, one evening in that first week, when we got home from work, and he kissed me in the elevator. By the time the doors opened, he'd already started undressing me, and there was no way we were going to make it as far as the living room, let alone the bedroom.

It's been glorious, and just thinking about it makes me smile. It also sets my body on fire, and part of me wants to walk into Hunter's office and tell him to forget about lunch, and keeping our secret. I know that wouldn't be wise, though. In fact, it would be foolhardy. We can wait... at least until we get to Newport tonight. It's hot today, so maybe he'll feel like a shower... or better still, a bath, in that most perfect of bathtubs...

We could even have a dip in the pool...

"Tell Mr. Bennett I'd like to see him."

I startle, looking up at the man in front of me. I'd say he's in his early sixties, smartly dressed, in what appears to be an expensive suit, with salt and pepper hair and a deep tan.

"I'm sorry. You don't have an appointment, so..."

"I don't care about goddamn appointments. Theodore Bennett and I go way back. We're..."

"Did you say Theodore Bennett?" I interrupt him, frowning.

"Yes. This is still his office, isn't it?"

"No." Oh dear... this is awkward. "I'm sorry, but I'm afraid Theodore Bennett passed away."

The man's face pales. "But... but that's not possible," she says, pushing his fingers back through his hair and shaking his head. "I mean... I've waited all this time."

He's becoming agitated, and I get to my feet. "I'm sorry, but..."

"You're sorry?" He raises his voice, glaring at me. "You're fucking sorry?"

He's probably just under six feet tall and very intimidating, but I'm determined to stand my ground. "There's no need to speak to me like that."

"Oh? Really? Do you have any idea what I've..."

"What's going on here?" I jump at the sound of Hunter's voice. He's standing in the doorway to his room, just like he did a few minutes ago, only now he's frowning, his eyes darkened. I feel relieved he's here, but also a little ashamed that I couldn't handle this situation by myself.

"Hunter, I..."

The man turns to Hunter, his eyes narrowing. "So, you're Hunter Bennett?" he says. "You're all grown up. Who'd have thought...?" He saunters over, full of swagger. "I'm an old friend of your dad's. I'm in the city for a few days, and thought I'd drop by and see him."

"But Dad's been dead for over a year." Hunter looks confused, and I have to admit, I am, too. If this man was a friend of Theodore Bennett's, surely he'd have known about his death, wouldn't he?

"Hmm… your secretary just told me," the man says. "It's such a shame. I'd been hoping to show him what genuine success looks like."

Hunter's demeanor changes. He stands up straight, towering over the other man. "Who are you? What do you want here?"

The other man smiles. "I just told you what I want. I came to show my old friend Theodore what a proper businessman looks like. As for who I am…" He shrugs his shoulders. "I guess I can't blame you for not remembering. You were just a kid when I left town." The man pauses and Hunter frowns, waiting. "I'm Ken Bevan."

It's like all the air is suddenly sucked from the room. I don't know why, but that's how it feels and even though Mr. Bevan holds out his hand for Hunter to shake, he ignores the gesture, his face paling.

Mr. Bevan doesn't remove his hand, even after an abnormal length of time. He just stares at Hunter with a slight smile on his face. This is embarrassing, and I lower my eyes to my desk for a moment. Whoever this man is, he's obviously someone from Theodore Bennett's past… someone Hunter knows, too. There's something about him I don't like, and I wish he'd leave, although that doesn't look likely and I wonder if I should suggest they move into Hunter's office, just to break the interminable silence. I raise my head again, noticing that Hunter is now staring at me. I can't make out his expression, other than that he seems bewildered. Or is that upset? Or maybe angry? I can't work it out. All I know is something's wrong. Something's very wrong.

I step forward, wanting to help, and although Mr. Bevan opens his mouth to say something, Hunter ignores him, barging past and coming straight over to me.

"How could you?" he thunders and I step back again, fear coursing through me.

"Hunter? What are you saying? I don't…"

"Don't tell me you don't fucking understand." He shakes his head. "I knew your name was familiar."

"My name?"

"Yes. Your fucking name."

Okay. This is definitely anger. I can hear it in his voice… see it in his eyes. But behind that there's fear, and hurt… hurt, like I've never seen before. Tears fill my eyes and I reach out for him. He steps back, though.

"Don't touch me. Don't you dare touch me."

What? "Hunter, please… you're not making sense."

"*I'm* not making sense? That's rich, coming from you. Everything you've said to me has been a goddamn lie."

"That's not true. I've never lied to you."

He glares at me, breathing hard, and although I don't know what's going on, I've never been more scared in my life. I'm losing him, and I don't even know why.

## Hunter

I sit at my desk, wishing it could be evening already. I may have just told Livia I'd come in here and deal with my long list of emails, but I also told her I wanted to fuck her the moment we get to the house tonight... and that's too distracting.

She's always distracting, it seems. Even when she doesn't mean to be.

I can't help smiling when I think about last weekend and how nervous she was on the journey to Newport, how she barely said a word throughout dinner, and how scared I was by the time I took her upstairs... all because her period had started.

She was worried we wouldn't be able to make love, but we did, in the shower, and it was spectacular. It always is, and afterwards, once we'd dried off, we climbed into bed, and I held her in my arms. We were quiet for a while, but then she leaned up and looked at me, a troubled expression on her face.

"Can you explain something to me?"

"Sure." I'd explained quite a few things to her since our first time together, and I'd grown accustomed to her questions, and to answering them. I enjoyed it. To me, it brought us closer, and I gazed into her eyes.

"Why is it you only use certain words when we're...?" She let her voice fade, and although I knew what she was trying to say, I was intrigued.

"What words?"

"You know what words, Hunter."

I wracked my brain and then realized what she was talking about.

"Are we talking about when I use the word 'fuck', either in the context of saying I wanna fuck you, or when I'm telling you how fucking sexy you are?"

"Yes. Exactly that."

"Does it bother you?"

"No, not at all. I like it. But I've never heard you swear at anyone, no matter how provoked you are."

"I swear all the time, baby. It's just that I try not to do it in front of you... except when I'm inside you, or even thinking about being inside you. In situations like that, it seems I can't help myself. I have to say what I'm thinking... to voice my true feelings."

I think I've done that since the beginning... maybe not since we first met, but certainly since we got together. I've never held back on telling her anything, and that's why I'm going to ask her to move in with me. My plan is to do it tonight when we get to the house, and if she says yes – and I hope to God she does – maybe we'll come back early on Sunday and start moving her things over to my place.

I know people might say I'm rushing things, but she's practically living with me anyway, and I love her so much, I just want to make it official.

I take a breath and open my mail app, deleting the first few messages, before I finally come across one worth reading. It's from Keira, and I smile. I was going to chase her up, to see where her invoice was, but it seems she's sent it in at last.

It's no more or less expensive than I'd expected, and I click on the link to pay it, sending her a quick reply to thank her for all her help. I've just returned to going through my interminable list of messages when I hear a man outside, raising his voice.

"You're fucking sorry?"

"There's no need to speak to me like that." Livia sounds scared and I'm on my feet in an instant, rushing for the door.

The man standing by Livia's desk is a little under six feet tall, with graying hair and a tailored suit. He's glaring right at her.

"Oh? Really? Do you have any idea what I've…"

I don't know who this guy is, but I'm done with hearing his voice. "What's going on here?"

Livia startles, turning to face me, as does the stranger, who tilts his head slightly, like he's confused.

"Hunter, I…" Livia says and a slow smile appears on the man's face.

"So you're Hunter Bennet?" he says, interrupting her. He studies me, like he knows me, which I'm damn sure he doesn't. "You're all grown up. Who'd have thought…?" He moves closer, his gaze making me feel uncomfortable, the hairs on the back of my neck standing on end. Do I know him? There's something about his voice… "I'm an old friend of your dad's," he says, although I'm still none the wiser. He could be anybody. "I'm in the city for a few days, and thought I'd drop by and see him."

"But Dad's dead. He's been dead for over a year." Surely if he was a friend of Dad's he'd have heard by now.

"Hmm… your secretary just told me." I want to correct him, and tell him Livia isn't my secretary, but he doesn't give me the chance. "It's such a shame," he says, smirking. "I'd been hoping to show him what genuine success looks like."

He doesn't sound like a friend of my dad's anymore. He sounds more like an enemy, and I stand up, using my height against him. "Who are you? What do you want here?"

"I just told you what I want," the man says with a smile. "I came to show my old friend Theodore what a proper businessman looks like. As for who I am…" He tilts his head just slightly while shrugging his shoulders. "I guess I can't blame you for not remembering. You were just a kid when I left town."

What's he talking about? Why doesn't he just say his name? "I'm Ken Bevan."

My brain freezes, along with my blood, and the room spins. I can't think... I can't take it in. I'm not worried that this is Ken Bevan, or that he nearly ruined my father and our family... or that he's standing in front of me, holding out his hand like he expects me to shake it. What I'm worried about... the thought that's rushing through my mind... is that I've just remembered where I heard Livia's name before.

Ken Bevan's daughter was called that.

I recollect, he used to tell a story about his grandfather falling for an Italian girl during World War Two, and how he came home afterwards, but couldn't live without her, so he went back to Italy to find her. Her name was Livia, and Ken's wife liked it... or maybe she liked the romance of the story. I don't know, but either way, they named their daughter after her. I glance up to see she's staring at her desk. She's embarrassed... and rightly so. She's known of the connection all along. Hell, she probably got this job on purpose, and then seduced me, intending to get some kind of revenge.

And it worked, didn't it?

I lower my head for a moment, unable to focus. The pain in my chest is building, crushing the air from my lungs. I can't let it, though. I have to deal with this...

I take a breath, struggling to keep it together.

When I look up again, Ken Bevan opens his mouth, but I push him aside, walking straight up to Livia, my anger getting the better of me.

"How could you?" I yell, and she stumbles backwards. I can see the panic in her eyes, but I know why it's there now. She's not fooling me anymore.

"Hunter? What are you saying?" Her voice is so quiet and despite my best efforts, it still touches my heart. *Stop it. Remember who she is... what she's done.* "I don't..."

"Don't tell me you don't fucking understand." I sigh, shaking my head. "I knew your name was familiar."

"My name?"

"Yes. Your fucking name."

God, this hurts. How can anything hurt this much while I'm still standing? There are tears in her eyes and I have to hand it to her, she's putting on an excellent performance. She reaches out, but I step away from her. She's never coming near me again.

"Don't touch me. Don't you dare touch me."

"Hunter, please… you're not making sense."

Is she serious? "*I'm* not making sense? That's rich, coming from you. Everything you've said to me has been a goddamn lie."

"That's not true. I've never lied to you."

She looks terrified, but I know that's only because she's been caught.

"You're lying to me now… but I guess it's second nature to you."

I turn away before she can say another word, and although I hear her sob, I don't turn back. Instead, I look into the face of her father. He seems remarkably unfazed by the plight of his daughter, but that's Ken Bevan for you.

"Get out," I say in a more calm and monotone voice. I feel nothing for this man, so it's easier to be detached, although I'm tempted to tell him to take his daughter with him. The problem is, I need to speak to her again first.

Ken laughs, shaking his head. "It's a shame your dad died before I got to shake hands with him again. I'd have enjoyed seeing his face when he realized his plan had failed." I've got no idea what he's talking about, and I don't care. He turns, glancing at Livia, before he looks back at me again. "Still, you clearly didn't fall too far from the tree, did you?"

I want to call him back and tell him I'm nothing like my father, but he's already striding down the hall, and to be honest, he's the least of my problems.

I turn again, looking at Livia, who's clutching a Kleenex and dabbing it at her cheeks.

"Come into my office."

She glances up, frowning, and seemingly bewildered by what's gone on in the last few minutes, but I ignore her fakery and walk into my office. This conversation is necessary, but as it's going to be our last, we'll hold it in private. She follows me, and I close the door, walking around her and standing behind my desk. After a moment's pause, she takes her place opposite me, clearly still struggling with her emotions. I clench my fists, wrestling with my own feelings. I want to ask her why... how? What did I ever do to her? Did what we've had mean nothing? Not that it matters anymore. It's too late. The damage is already done.

"You're fired," I say simply.

Her mouth drops open, and she swallows hard, blinking at me as a tear falls onto her cheek. "I—I'm sorry, Hunter... I..."

"You're sorry? Is that all you've got to say? Sorry? You think that's going to cut it? You said you wouldn't lie to me, and I was dumb enough – blind enough – to believe you. Well... I'm not being dumb, or blind, anymore."

"Hunter... if I've..."

I hold up my hand, and she stops talking. "I want you to leave... immediately."

"Why are you being like this? What am I supposed to have done wrong?"

"*Supposed* to have done? Seriously?" I shake my head at her. "I'm not even sure you know the truth from a lie anymore."

"Why do you keep saying I'm a liar?"

"Because you are," I bellow, and she jumps.

"You said you couldn't raise your voice to me," she whispers, and I'm reminded of how it felt to want to protect her... not that she ever needed my protection.

"So? You don't think I'm entitled?"

"No. I don't understand, Hunter. I don't…"

"Stop it! Stop bullshitting me."

"You really want me to leave?"

"Congratulations. You've got the message at last."

She doesn't say another word, but walks away, out of my office, and I slump into my chair, my heart in pieces. I can't take this… it's too much…

I startle as she comes back in again, tears streaming down her face. Her purse is slung over her shoulder and she's carrying her phone and car keys, which she puts on my desk.

"Keep them," I mutter, but she shakes her head.

"N—No. They're yours."

I stare down at them, and then up at her again, the last few pieces of my heart crushing to dust.

"Just go, will you?" *It hurts to look at you.*

She clamps her hand over her mouth, stifling her sob, and runs from my office.

I watch her leave, knowing I'll never feel happiness or hope, ever again.

# Chapter Eleven

*Livia*

I don't wait for the elevator. I run all the way down to the parking garage, only then realizing I don't have a car here anymore. The car that was mine is parked in bay twelve, but I can't drive it…

"Oh, God…" I fall to my knees, bringing up my hands to cover my face, and I howl. The sound echoes around and around, but I can't seem to stop. It hurts so much, I can't move.

"Livia? Is that you?"

I jump at the familiar voice and look up, expecting to see Hunter. *He's come for me. He's really come for me. We're going to be okay.* Except, as I blink through my tears, I realize the man approaching me isn't Hunter at all. It's Drew.

I struggle to my feet and he takes my arm, holding it by the elbow, and looking down into my face. "Are you okay?"

"I'm fine."

"No, you're not. You're a long way from fine. What happened? Did someone hurt you?"

*Yes. Your brother.* "It's nothing, really." I pull my arm away, without making it too obvious, and step back toward the exit.

"Where are you going? You can't leave. Not like this."

I nod my head. "I have to."

He frowns. "What does that mean?"

"Ask Hunter."

I turn and start running again. This time, I make it out onto the street, although I realize straight away that I can't run all the way home.

I get to the bus stop, though, and only have to wait a few minutes for the next bus to arrive. While I'm waiting, I keep looking back toward the office, wondering if Drew will come after me... or if Hunter will. There's no sign of either of them, though, and before long, the bus comes and I get on, sitting down and staring out the window. I know I look a mess, but I don't care.

I'm not sure I care about anything anymore.

All I did was screw up over the guy who came to see Hunter's father, and he fired me. Why would he do that? It doesn't make sense. He didn't say as much, but it was clear he broke up with me, too. Words weren't necessary... not when he was looking at me like he hated me. Not when he told me to 'just go', like he did.

I struggle to fight back my tears, his words echoing around my head.

I thought he'd never hurt me. In fact, I knew it... like I knew I'd take my next breath. And yet, here I am... hurt and alone.

That just goes to show, I didn't know Hunter Bennett at all.

The bus stops outside my apartment, but it's only once I'm inside that it hits me...

There's nothing here for me... in every sense of the word. Most of my clothes, my toiletries, my heart, my life, they're all at Hunter's place.

I make it to the bed that's supposed to be a couch and sit down.

A sob leaves my lips, and I cover my mouth with my hand, stifling it. Once I start down the road of crying again, I know I won't be able to stop. Crying won't help. Instead, I get up and go over to the closet, checking what's still here. There are no work clothes… but that's okay. I don't have a job anymore. There are a couple of pairs of jeans, and a few tops, which I guess are going to have to suffice, because there's no way I'll go crawling back to Hunter… even for the things that are rightfully mine. I'll just have to make do, for now.

I turn around again, facing my tiny apartment, and it registers that I don't have to make do. I don't even have to stay here. It might be admitting defeat, but there's always another option.

I can go home.

The moment the thought crosses my mind, the decision is made, and I grab a bag from the bottom of my closet, throwing in my remaining clothes. The books that are still here – the ones I didn't take to Hunter's – and all the rest of my things will have to wait for now. For today, I just need to get out of here. I need to be somewhere I'm loved.


The bus pulls up in Falmouth at just after five in the afternoon, and I climb down, thanking the driver. He gives me an understanding smile, like he knows my life is over… although I'm not sure how. Maybe it's the shroud of sadness I'm wearing, or the tears that are still pooling in my eyes.

I've spent the journey counting. I didn't want to think, for fear I'd break down and publicly humiliate myself, so I counted… everything, from red cars, to trees, to street signs. It was a distraction, nothing more. The pain in my chest is just as intense as it was when I closed the door on my apartment, and I'm just as confused, too. I still don't understand what's happened… or why.

My parents' house isn't far, and I make it there in less than ten minutes, standing outside for a moment or two, and wondering how it came to this.

*Because you fell in love.*

Except love isn't supposed to end like this.

Love isn't supposed to end at all.

It's eternal.

The door opens, my mom appearing.

"Livia?"

The sight of her is too much, and the tears fall… not in a steady trickle, but in a torrent. Great sobs wrack through me and I fall to my knees.

"Oh, my God…" I hear my mom's footsteps at the same time as her voice, and then her arms come around me, lifting me to my feet, her eyes locking onto mine. "What's happened, Livia?"

She looks scared and I shake my head, trying to reassure her, although it doesn't seem to work. I nod toward the house and she guides me inside, where Dad's waiting, standing in the hall, his face a picture of concern, too.

"Livia?" He tries to reach out to me, and I drop my bag, running to him. I hear his stick fall to the floor, and then I feel him bring both arms around me. That will have been a tremendous effort for him, and I lean against him, feeling safe at last. He rocks me for a while, like I'm a child again, and I take a deep breath. This feels good. It feels better than good.

"Can you tell us what's wrong?" Mom asks from behind me and I turn, taking a breath, knowing how disappointed they're going to be.

"I've been fired."

I feel Dad stiffen and I look up at him. He's frowning, like he's more confused than disappointed. I can't blame him for that. I'm confused, too, and I was there when it happened.

"What on earth for?" Mom says.

"I—I don't really know. My boss said something about my name, but…"

"He fired you because of your name?"

"I'm not sure. It all happened after a man came to the office to see Hunter's father…"

"Who's H—Hunter?" Dad asks, stammering.

"He's my boss… or he was." He's also the man I love… the man I wanted to share my future with, the man I thought I knew so well. Except I didn't. Evidently.

"What did this man want?" Mom asks.

"He didn't say. I explained that Hunter's father is dead, but that just made the man furious."

"Why?"

I shrug my shoulders. "It didn't make sense. The man said he was an old friend of Hunter's dad, and yet he didn't even know he'd died. He started shouting at me, and I didn't handle things very well, because Hunter had to come out of his office. I guess that's why he fired me, but the things he said don't add up. It was all so weird. The man introduced himself. He was gloating about making a success of his life, or something, saying that he'd missed a chance to show Hunter's father what a proper businessman looked like. I can't remember—"

My mom suddenly pales, clamping her hand across her mouth.

"What's wrong, Mom?"

"Julianne?" Dad speaks at the same time, both of us staring at her.

She lowers her hand, her lips trembling. "I've just remembered…"

"What?" Dad asks.

"The name… Hunter."

"What about it?"

She turns to me. "What's your boss's last name?"

"Bennett."

She glances at Dad, who steps away from me, and I look up to see his face is just as white as Mom's.

"Oh, no…" Mom cries, shaking her head. "It can't be."

"Livia?" I turn to Dad as he says my name, confusion boiling up inside me.

"Yes?"

"Was Hunter's father called Theodore?"

"Yes, he was."

"And the man... the man who came to your office..."

"Ken Bevan, you mean?"

Mom howls and I turn to face her again. She's shaking. "No... please no." She looks up. "This can't be happening."

Dad moves away from me, hobbling over to Mom, and pulling her into his arms.

"It'll be okay," he says.

"No... she'll hate me."

"She won't."

"Who will hate you?" I ask, and Dad straightens, turning to look at me.

"Your m—mom thinks you're gonna hate her."

I frown, shaking my head and walk over, standing in front of Mom. "I could never hate you."

She looks into my eyes. "You say that now, but you don't know what I've done."

I can't think of anything she could do that would make me hate her, but she seems convinced and bites on her bottom lip, fear shining in her eyes.

"We're g—gonna have to tell her, Julianne," Dad says, sounding resigned.

I think I've gone beyond the point of confusion now. So much has happened that I don't understand, my brain has given up trying to process it.

"Shall we sit down?" Mom suggests, nodding to the living room, and although I think she's buying time, I nod my head. Dad will probably be better off in a chair... and looking at her, I think Mom will, too.

I grab Dad's stick, handing it to him, then lead the way, waiting for them to follow, and I take a seat on the couch, letting them get settled in their chairs, before I turn to look at Mom. She's playing with the hem of her blouse, rubbing it between her thumbs and fingers, and it's impossible not to notice her hands are still shaking.

Whatever this is, it's bad.

"This is all my fault," she says.

"What is?"

"Everything that's happened to you. I should have told you…"

"Told me what?"

"Who your real father is."

Okay… I want to wake up now. I've had enough of this nightmare. I clench my right fist, letting my nails dig into my hand until I feel it hurt, and I know I'm not dreaming.

"M—My real father?" I look at my dad, or at least at the man I've always called 'Dad'.

"I'm not your natural father," he says in a perfectly clear voice, not stammering at all.

"Then who is?"

"Ken Bevan."

"W—What?"

"Ken Bevan is your father," Mom says, like it needs to be said twice.

"But how? I mean… the man I met today was in his sixties."

She nods her head. "He was sixteen years older than me."

"Sixteen years?"

"Yeah. I met him when I was twenty-five." So he'd have been forty-one…

"How did you meet?" I ask.

"I'd just started working for a big law firm in Boston, and he came to us on behalf of his company to ask for advice."

"His company?"

She glances at my dad and then turns to me again, sucking in a breath. "Ken Bevan was the CFO at Theodore Bennett Associates."

"Oh, my God…"

She nods her head. "Ken came to see my boss, looking for someone to investigate a possible fraud inside TBA. I was quite junior at the time, but we met and he seemed to take a liking to me, and insisted that I should be hired to work on the case. I wasn't complaining. Professionally, it was quite an honor for someone of my age to be given so much responsibility. Personally, he wasted no time in charming me into thinking I was in love with him, and we started dating."

"Did you find anything wrong? Did you discover who was committing the fraud?"

"As far as I could tell, with the evidence to hand, no-one was. There were a few accounting anomalies, but Ken had answers for all of those, and there was certainly nothing concrete against anyone, so at the end of my time there, I wrote up my notes, filed my report and went back to my office."

"Did you carry on seeing him… socially?"

"Yes. Not as often as I had done, but we met up quite frequently… until I discovered I was pregnant."

She lowers her gaze, staring at the space between us. "With me?"

"Yes." She looks up again. "I called Ken and said I needed to see him, and when I told him I was expecting his child, he just stared at me, like he couldn't quite believe it."

"He thought you were lying?"

"No, it wasn't anything like that. It was as though he couldn't understand. He proposed, though, and we were married just a few weeks later." She shakes her head slowly from side to side. "That's when I saw him for the cruel man he really was."

"He hit you?" I sit forward.

"No. He was never violent. But he was mean, vindictive. His words…" She falls silent and Dad reaches over. She takes his hand and looks up at him.

"It's okay," he says.

"Is it?" She blinks and swallows hard, looking back at me again.

"Did you leave him?" I ask, still trying to make sense of everything.

She shakes her head. "I wanted to. Especially after you were born. That was when I discovered he was having an affair with someone at the office. It had been going on for some time, evidently… maybe even before we were married. I never got to the bottom of it all, and I never found out who she was, although by then, I didn't really care. I thought about leaving several times, but I had nowhere to go… and then, one morning, while we were having breakfast, the cops came."

"The cops?" This is getting more and more bizarre by the minute.

"Yes. They arrested him… for fraud."

"Fraud?"

"The same fraud I'd been hired to investigate."

"But you said there wasn't any."

She nods her head. "I know… because Ken had directed my inquiries to suit his own ends. That was part of his scheme… and one of the reasons he'd looked so shocked when I told him I was pregnant. He hadn't banked on that. His plans had been meticulous. He'd worked everything out, hiding his fraud and bringing me in to investigate, knowing how inexperienced I was, and that he'd be able to influence the report I created. He did a good job, too… so good that after Ken's arrest, Theodore Bennett wanted me charged as an accessory."

I clamp my hand over my mouth. What's she saying?

"What happened?"

"Fortunately, I'd kept my notes. I was able to show what Ken had done… how he'd manipulated me. The police exonerated me, and I helped them with their investigations."

"Which showed what?"

She takes a deep breath. "That Ken had been embezzling money from TBA for years. He'd defrauded them of millions of dollars, almost wiping out the company."

"So he was charged?"

"Yes. And once he saw the evidence against him, he confessed. There was no point in trying to deny it."

"You mean my natural father went to prison?"

"He was sentenced to fifteen years," she says, shaking her head. "That was the maximum allowed at the time. He'd admitted the crime, though. He'd pleaded guilty and paid back most of the money, so he should have been given a reduced sentence. I'm not trying to defend him, or what he did, but Theodore Bennett had friends in high places, and he wanted his pound of flesh."

"What does that mean?"

"It means that Theodore Bennett used his influence to ensure Ken paid the maximum price, and because he didn't get back every cent that had been taken from him, he insisted Ken's possessions were seized, including the house we were living in."

"You mean, he made us homeless?"

"Yes. It happened ever so quickly, too, with almost no warning. He didn't care about us. He just wanted revenge."

"What did you do?"

"You were only a baby, so I moved us out of state… here to Falmouth. There was a lot of publicity surrounding the case. Theodore Bennett made sure of that, and he painted himself as the victim, too. I didn't want to be a part of it, and I didn't want it tainting our lives. I found a job here, and rented a small apartment... and I divorced Ken as soon as I could." She sighs. "About a year later, I met Connor, and fell in love for real."

"So did I," he says, smiling at her, and then he turns to me. "Your mom told me her st—story, right from the beginning. It didn't change how I felt about her. I still knew I wanted to spend the rest of my l—life with her... so I asked her to marry me."

I turn to my mom. "You told Dad, but you didn't tell me?"

She blushes. "We talked about it..."

"And... and we decided against it," Dad says, finishing her sentence.

"Why?"

"Because we felt you didn't need to know."

I stare at him. "Really? Do you still feel that way now?"

"I'm sorry, Livia," Mom says. "This is my fault, not Connor's."

"He's 'Dad' to me, not Connor. He always will be."

"It's not your mom's fault. I—It was a joint decision and if we got it wrong, then we're sorry," Dad says, and I look over at him. His eyes are glistening, and I don't doubt that's because of what I just said.

I get to my feet and Mom looks up at me, panic filling her eyes. "Where are you going?"

"To my room. I need some time to think."

"You don't want to talk?"

I shake my head.

"L—Let her go," Dad says.

Mom stands, ignoring him. "Please, Livia... tell me you don't hate me," she says.

"I don't hate you."

It's true, I don't. But as I leave the room and grab my bag, I'm filled with so many conflicting emotions, I'm not sure how I feel.

I've gained a past I never even knew existed, and while it doesn't alter anything about my feelings for my dad, there's no escaping the fact that the man who came into the office earlier today has changed my life... forever.

———~~———

## Hunter

"What's going on?" Drew appears in my doorway, jolting me out of my nightmare, and then walks straight into my room, his face like thunder.

"How the hell would I know?" The only thing I'm sure of is that I'm never going to trust my judgement again... not after everything Livia's done. "What are you talking about?"

"Livia."

I sit up, staring at him. "What about her?"

"I've just seen her down in the parking garage, crying her eyes out."

"Don't worry about it. I'm sure it's all part of the act."

"What act?" He takes a seat opposite me, crossing his legs. "The woman I just saw wasn't acting."

"Don't be so easily fooled. She's good at it." She took me in.

"Good at what? You're not making any sense."

I lean back in my seat and focus on the pen that's lying on my desk, rather than looking at him. "I don't think I mentioned it at the time, but when I first heard Livia's name, I had a feeling I recognized it. Not her second name, you understand, just her first name."

"Well... I suppose it is fairly unusual."

I raise my head, looking at him now. "Exactly. I thought it was odd, but I knew I'd heard it somewhere before. I abandoned the idea, though, and interviewed her…"

"And fell for her?" he says, tilting his head at me.

"Yeah… and fell for her."

"And then you offered her a job?"

"I did. And I know that may not have been the wisest move in the world, but…"

"You couldn't help yourself?"

"Something like that." I pause, remembering that morning, and how she came into my office and blew me away, my chest tightening at the memory.

"Okay," Drew says, interrupting the thought. "So, you met her, and employed her. This is ancient history. What happened today?"

"A guy came in here. He wanted to see Dad. I didn't hear the beginning of the conversation, but the guy started yelling, so I went outside."

"To protect her?"

"Of course." Although I realize now, it was all part of the act; she didn't need protecting from her own father, did she?

"And?"

"And he introduced himself to me… as Ken Bevan."

Drew's mouth drops open. "The guy who defrauded Dad?"

"Yes."

He frowns. "What the hell was he doing here?"

"He came to gloat, I think. He said something about wanting to show Dad what a success he'd made of himself, or something. I wasn't really paying attention."

"Why not?"

"Because I'd just worked out where I'd heard Livia's name before." I take a deep breath, still wishing it wasn't true, even though I know it is. "She's Ken Bevan's daughter."

"What the fuck?"

"I know. I feel like such an idiot."

"What for?"

"Falling for her lies, of course."

He stares at me for a moment, like I'm from another planet. "What lies?"

"All the lies she told me." He's still staring, and I realize I'm going to have to explain. "It was obviously some kind of plan, cooked up between Livia and her father, which required her to get a job here. Hell... now I come to think about it, she thought she was gonna be working for Dad. She expected it to be him who was interviewing her."

"So? What does that prove?"

"Ken Bevan didn't know Dad was dead, and neither did his daughter. They probably thought they'd come up with the perfect plan, but they failed to do their homework."

"Yeah... or there was no plan in the first place."

"Don't be so naïve, Drew."

"I'm not. I might have only met your girlfriend a couple of times, but she didn't strike me as someone who was capable of something like this."

"She's not my girlfriend... not anymore." My voice cracks a little as a searing pain crushes my chest and I flinch against it.

"It hurt to say that, didn't it?" Drew says, letting out a sigh.

"Yeah, it did."

"So, you've broken up with her?"

"I've fired her. The breaking up part was implied." Mostly because I couldn't bring myself to say it. I still can't... not if it's going to hurt like that.

He nods his head. "Are you telling me you didn't even sit down and talk it through with her?"

"There was nothing to talk about."

"Right... so you just fired her, without even checking your facts first? Did you at least give her severance?" I shake my head, staring at the pen again. "Wow," he says. "That was mean. I don't blame her for crying now." I raise my eyes just slightly and they settle on Livia's phone and car keys. Drew clearly follows the line of my gaze, leaning forward and reaching out for them. "Are these hers?" he asks.

"They were part of her package. She gave them back before she left."

He stares at me for a long moment and then puts the phone and keys back. "What happened to you?" he says.

"What do you mean?"

"I apologized not long ago, for comparing you to Dad, but I'm starting to think I was right. You're behaving exactly like him. He was all about revenge, and an eye for an eye. But that's not who you are, Hunter. At least, I didn't think it was."

"It's not, but this isn't as simple as all that."

"Why the fuck not? You love her. You told me so yourself."

"I know. That's why it hurts so much that she's lied to me."

"She didn't look like she was lying just now. She looked like she'd just had her heart ripped out."

The pain in my chest intensifies, but I ignore it this time. "I'm sure she put on an outstanding performance for your benefit."

"It wasn't a performance."

"How do you know?"

"Because I found her on the floor of the parking garage. Well... that's not strictly true. I heard her first. It would have been impossible not to; she was sobbing so loud. I just followed the sound, and I found her, kneeling, curled up on herself... like she was broken. None of it was for anyone's benefit, Hunter. It was real."

It's my turn to stare. This can't be right. He must have made a mistake. Please... God...

I grab my phone and look up Miles Hampton's number, connecting a call to him.

"Hunter?" he says, answering promptly.

"I need to talk to you about Livia."

"What about her?"

I'm going to have to tell the truth… or some of it, anyway. "I —I've just fired her."

"You have? What the hell for?"

"I've discovered she's the daughter of someone who used to work here… years ago."

"You don't know that," Drew says, and I glare at him.

"And?" Miles says in my ear.

"The man's name was Ken Bevan…"

"Oh, yes? I've heard of him."

"Yeah, you would have done." Everyone knows what he did, even the people who weren't here at the time. "The point is, did you check her out before you interviewed her?"

"As much as I could in the time you gave me. But I focused on her previous employment. I didn't look into her parents. Why would I? Her surname is Hopkins, not Bevan."

"Hmm… she must have changed it." I guess that makes sense. I'd change my name if my dad was sent to prison.

"Do you need me to arrange her severance pay?" he asks. "I can liaise with her…"

"No." My voice is loud and my reply hasty. He can't fail to have noticed. "I'll deal with it, if you send me her bank details."

"I'm sure you've got better things to do."

"It's fine. Just send me what I've asked for."

I end the call, putting down my phone, and Drew tips his head to one side. "Are you always so rude to the people who work for you?"

"No. It's just Miles. He has that effect on me."

"Is that anything to do with Livia?"

"He had a reputation even before she started working here…"

"I'm sensing a 'but'."

I nod my head. "He used to hang around her, and she didn't like it."

"Neither did you."

"No. Not that it matters anymore."

"You keep telling yourself that, you might even believe it one day." He sighs. "Are you sure you're doing the right thing, Hunter? You guys were good together. Why would you treat her like this?"

"Because her father almost wiped out our entire family."

"So? That's not her fault."

I shake my head. "Maybe not. But why did she come here, if not to pull the same stunt?"

"Maybe it was a coincidence."

"I don't believe in coincidences. I certainly…" I'm cut off by the ringing of my phone and I glance down to see Ella's name on the screen. "It's our sister," I mutter, connecting the call, and putting it on to speaker.

"Hey," she says.

"Hey, Sis." Drew speaks before I can, and I put the phone down between us.

"What are you doing answering Hunter's calls?"

"He didn't," I reply.

"No," Drew says, when I fall silent, my mind still in turmoil. "I'm at Hunter's office, and you're on speaker."

"Oh. I see. Well, I'm sorry to interrupt your fascinating conversation, but I just wanted to let you know I've found myself somewhere to live."

"You have?" Drew sits forward, his smile giving away how pleased he is by her news. I guess this means he'll get his apartment back now.

"Yeah. I won't be moving in just yet, though, so I'm gonna head down to Newport."

"Okay. I was planning to go down there later this evening. Do you want me to give you a ride?" I sit back, watching Drew talk, recalling my plans for tonight, plans that won't be happening now… or ever.

"I was hoping you'd offer," Ella says.

"Why? Because you don't have a car?"

"Not yet. It's something else I need to sort out… sooner rather than later." She coughs slightly. "What time are you leaving?"

"Around six?" Drew says.

"Okay. I'll be ready."

"That'll be a first."

They both laugh, but I can't join in, and after a moment's silence, Ella says, "What's wrong?"

"What with?" Drew asks.

"Hunter. Is he even there, still?"

"Yeah, I'm here," I say.

"He's just not quite himself," Drew adds on my behalf.

"Who is he then?"

Drew tilts his head again, examining me, and raising his eyebrows slightly. "He's doing a mighty fine impression of our father, if you want me to be honest."

"What does that mean?"

"It means Hunter's being an asshole."

"Thanks," I murmur.

He gives me a fake smile. "Just telling it how it is."

"What's going on?" Ella says.

I'm not in the mood for repeating my story, and I shrug my shoulders, letting Drew know it's down to him.

He sits back in his seat, fixing his eyes on my phone. "You haven't met Hunter's new PA, have you?" he says.

"No. I've spoken to her, but never met her. Why?"

"Because she and Hunter… they…" He falls silent, presumably unsure what to say next, but Ella fills the gap for him.

"I knew it! I knew there was something going on between you."

"There wasn't," I say. "Not when I last talked to you."

"So this is a really recent thing, then?"

"It's been going on for a few weeks." I sit back, closing my eyes and shaking my head. Is that all it's been?

"Okay, so what happened?" Ella asks. "Clearly something did."

"Yeah," Drew says. "The thing was, Hunter was fairly sure he'd heard Livia's name before, but he couldn't think where, and this morning, Ken Bevan came into the office…"

"The man who embezzled all that money from Dad?"

Even Ella knows the story, and she was only tiny when it all happened.

"Yeah… and that was when Hunter remembered how he knew Livia's name."

"How?"

"Because it's the same as Ken Bevan's daughter."

"Right…" She's waiting.

"So, he fired her."

"Are you crazy, Hunter? You've fired someone for having the same name as the daughter of a man who stole some money from Dad?"

"No. I've fired her because she's Ken Bevan's daughter, and she came to work here deliberately… to cause some kind of trouble."

"How do you know that?"

"Because Livia isn't the most popular name in the English language. I mean… what are the chances of coming across two people who are called that?"

"I don't know," Ella says. "Zero, probably. But even if she is his daughter – which you don't know for sure, by the way – what on earth makes you think there was anything deliberate about her coming to work for you? I mean… Doreen left quite suddenly, but how was Livia to know that would happen?"

Drew nods his head, raising his eyebrows. "Good point, Sis." He glares at me. "Even you were taken by surprise when Doreen resigned, so how can you accuse Livia of planning this?"

"She was probably waiting for the right opportunity, and when Doreen left, she took it."

Drew frowns at me, but I ignore him, and Ella clears her throat. "That sounds pretty damn implausible to me, but even if we accept your theory, why has she waited so long to act? She's been there for quite a while now, and she hasn't done anything, has she?"

"Well… no."

"And what exactly was this revenge you're accusing her of?" Drew asks, jumping on Ella's bandwagon. "Has any money gone missing? Have you lost any clients? Had any adverse press?"

"No."

"And you said Ken Bevan didn't realize Dad was dead."

"No," I say. "Neither did Livia when I interviewed her."

"But you put her straight, surely?" he says.

"Of course."

"Then why didn't she tell him?"

"Maybe she forgot," I say, and he tilts his head, like he thinks I'm crazy.

"You think?" he says.

"It's possible."

"Maybe in your head, but if that's the case, why did they show their hand now?" he asks. "Surely it would have been more sensible to wait until they'd completed their task."

"You're assuming it was financial," I say.

"Are you trying to say it was personal?"

"It feels pretty fucking personal."

His eyes soften, and he sighs, shaking his head.

"Did they seem to recognize each other?" Ella asks.

"No… I don't think so. But they'd have had to pretend to be strangers, wouldn't they? Otherwise, they'd have given themselves away. And if you're right and I'm wrong, why did she never talk about her father? In the whole time she was here, she mentioned her parents, and talked about her mom, but never said a word about her dad."

"I imagine she had her reasons."

"Yeah… like her dad being Ken Bevan."

"You're paranoid," she says. "And you're being unreasonable."

I pick up my phone, holding on to it. "Okay then, why did she sleep with me?"

"Ooh… let's think. Because she liked you? Hell… maybe she even loved you. I don't know. Like I said, I never met her, but did she seem like someone who'd use sex to get what they want?"

She seemed like the polar opposite. Livia knew nothing about sex. It was one of the most endearing things about her. Her innocence was so beguiling.

"No, she didn't," Drew says.

"How would you know?" Ella asks.

"Because, unlike you, I have met her. It might only have been briefly, but in my opinion, she wasn't experienced enough to know how to use sex… for anything."

I stare at him, long and hard, hating that he worked that out, although I can't deny it's true.

"Drew's right. Livia wasn't like that at all."

# Chapter Twelve

*Livia*

I've had a terrible night's sleep. Actually, that's not true, because I haven't slept at all. I've spent the night in bed, thinking about everything that happened yesterday. Aside from the discovery that my father isn't my father, but is a man I've never met – at least not until he came into my office yesterday – there's the secrecy, the lies… and Hunter.

I lost count of the number of times I wished I could call him. I can't… obviously, because I don't have a phone anymore. But if I did, I'd call him, even now, in the cold light of dawn. I'd ask him why he did what he did, and said what he said, why he didn't bother to to talk to me before he threw me out of his office, and out of his life. I'd cry at him, too, and I think I'd also beg him to give us another chance, because I miss him so much.

Sleeping without him is impossible. Knowing I'll never be held by him, or kissed by him again, is unthinkable.

I get up, going into the bathroom to shower, and then I dress in jeans and a top. I leave my hair to dry by itself and wander into the kitchen. Mom's sitting at the table, a cup of coffee in front of her, and she looks up as I walk into the room.

"How are you?" she asks.

"Okay."

"You look like you haven't slept."

"That's because I haven't."

I fetch myself a cup from the cabinet and fill it with coffee, adding some milk.

"Don't go," Mom says as I walk back past her. "Please… stay and talk." I turn and stare down at her. She looks just as tired as I feel, and I wonder if she's spent a sleepless night, too.

"Where's Dad?" I ask, sitting at the end of the table.

"He's resting. I think yesterday's revelations took it out of him."

"Is he okay?"

She nods her head. "He'll be fine, as long as he takes it easy." I sip my coffee. "I'm sorry we didn't tell you, Livia."

"Why didn't you? I've tried to understand, but I can't."

"We thought it was for the best. Your father…"

"If you're talking about Ken Bevan, can you call him Ken? He's not my father. Dad is."

She smiles. "Okay. Ken didn't take the money for us. It wasn't to give us a better life, or anything as noble as that. He didn't care about us. In fact, he didn't care about anything other than himself. Don't get me wrong, he could be charming when he needed to be… but deep down, he was cruel, and mean, and heartless." She shifts in her chair. "When he was arrested, he was at home, having breakfast. They just barged in, went through his study, read him his rights, and marched him out of the house. I'd rarely been in his study. He used to keep it locked, but the police had made him open the door, and after they'd all gone, I went inside. They'd taken his computer, and a lot of files, but in the corner, there was a suitcase."

"A suitcase?"

She nods her head. "I opened it, and found it was full of his clothes… not all of them, but enough."

"You mean he was leaving?" I ask.

"Yes," she says, sighing. "And he wasn't taking us with him."

I drink down some more coffee, glancing out the window. Nothing she's said has surprised me. I only spent a few minutes with Ken Bevan, but he struck me as someone who was far more interested in himself than in anyone else.

"I'd forgotten Hunter's name until you said it last night," Mom says, and I look back at her.

"I noticed."

She smiles, although it doesn't touch her eyes. "I didn't even know the name of the company you were working for."

"No... I didn't mention it." I suppose if I had, none of this would have happened. But I was busy falling in love.

"Theodore Bennett had three children, didn't he?" she says.

"Yes. Hunter is the oldest. His brother is called Drew and his sister is..."

"Ella," Mom says, completing my sentence. "I loved that name."

"Did you know them?" I ask.

"I never met the children in person, but Ken talked about them from time to time. Obviously, I saw Theodore at the office when I was working there."

"What about his wife? Did you meet her?"

"No. She lived at their house in Rhode Island." She shakes her head, like she's remembering those days. "It's such a coincidence that you should end up working there."

"Hunter clearly didn't think so. He must have thought I got the job on purpose for some reason, presumably connected to Ken Bevan. Maybe he thought I wanted to steal more money from him, or something." It's the only thing that makes sense of why he fired me... why he spoke to me like he did.

"You love Hunter, don't you?"

Mom's question takes me by surprise and I say, "Yes," instinctively, because it's true. I do love him… even now.

"I thought so."

"How did you guess?"

"If you'd just been fired, you'd have stayed in the city. You'd have found a new job and moved on. You certainly wouldn't have let it get to you this much."

"I—I couldn't stay, Mom. I had nothing left."

"Because Hunter had hurt you?" Mom says, pushing her cup away.

"Yes, but also most of my things were at his place… and I can't go back there now."

"Oh… I see." I've never seen my mom look so embarrassed before, but there's a definite hint of a blush on her cheeks, and in any other circumstances, I'd probably smile.

"I miss him so much…" My voice cracks and she gets up, coming to sit right beside me, and takes my hand in hers. "I really do. But I'm so damn angry with him."

"That's understandable."

"Is it? Is it possible to love someone and be on the verge of hating them at the same time? I was lying awake last night, thinking that I wanna call him. I imagined tears and explanations. In reality, though, if he was standing right in front of me now, I think I'd yell at him for hurting me so much."

"In which case, I think it's a good thing you've come home. You've put some distance between the two of you."

"I didn't do that, Mom. He did. He broke up with me."

"Hmm… but how do you know he's not sitting in Boston, imagining tears and explanations, too?"

"You didn't see his face when he told me to go. You didn't hear his voice."

She squeezes my hand. "You need to make allowances, Livia."

"What for?"

"Hunter would have been old enough to know what was going on when Ken did what he did," she says. "This isn't a figment of his imagination, or a story that's been kept from him. It's not like it is for you. He lived it. He'll remember what happened."

"I still don't understand why that makes it my fault."

"It doesn't. But his family lost almost everything they had when Ken stole from them."

"And? They got it all back, didn't they? I've been to Hunter's home in Newport, Mom. Trust me, our house would fit inside it several times over. They're not poor, and they don't need our pity."

"I'm not suggesting they do. But we're not poor either. It may sound strange, but in a way, I'll always be grateful for what happened."

"Grateful?"

"Yes. If Ken hadn't stolen that money, I'd never have had to move here. I'd never have met Connor, and you'd never have had such a loving and caring father in your life. There's no way I can be anything but grateful for the life we've had. I know things have been harder since your dad had his stroke, but that's got nothing to do with the Bennett family, has it? And however you look at it, Ken stole from them. The money wasn't his to take. It belonged to Theodore Bennett, and he was the one who insisted we should lose everything, not his son. Be careful not to judge Hunter too harshly…"

"Like he's judged me, you mean?"

"Exactly. I'm not condoning what he's said or done, and I'm not saying you have to call him straight away… or even at all. I'm not saying you have to speak to him, if he calls you…"

"He's not gonna call."

"You don't know that. If he loves you as much as you love him, he'll call, and when he does, you need to think long and hard before you push him away. Love is fragile, Livia."

"Is it? I thought it was eternal."

She smiles. "Men have written poems and made speeches about how love is the strongest thing in the world… about how it endures, no matter what, and binds us all together. But what they fail to mention is that it takes little more than a breath of wind to shatter it forever."

---

## Hunter

For the first time in a very long time, I didn't drive down to Newport last night. I called Pat not long after Drew left my office and made up an excuse about having to work. I'm not sure she believed me. She knows I can work from there, if I have to. But she didn't argue.

Once that was done, I pretended to be busy, tried to kid myself I wasn't falling apart, and spent the rest of the afternoon replying to emails, and rejecting phone calls from just about everyone. I wasn't in the mood to talk. I'm still not, even though Drew has already called twice this morning. He left a message the second time around, to let me know he was just checking in, making sure I'm okay.

I'm not, and I can't see the value in calling him back to tell him.

It's my own fault. I know that. I knew it when I got back here last night and walked into my apartment, wondering why I felt so lost. The answer was obvious. It was because Livia wasn't here. It didn't help that the first thing I saw when the elevator doors opened was the table in the middle of the lobby. My mind instantly filled with images of the two of us falling out of the elevator…

I'd been kissing her and had already undone her blouse. As we tumbled out into the lobby, I pulled her jacket and blouse from her shoulders, and yanked down the cups of her bra, licking and sucking on her nipples, while Livia fumbled with my belt. We'd only been together for a few days; the whole thing was still a novelty, for both of us, but I'd been in meetings all day, and I'd missed her so much, I couldn't wait. I couldn't even wait two minutes to get her upstairs to my bedroom, so I lay her back on the table, pushing up her skirt, and unfastening my jeans at the same time. Then I rubbed my fingers over her, feeling her through her soaking panties, before I pushed them aside and thrust deep inside her…

The memory of her screaming my name, of coming hard inside her, was too much for me last night, and I staggered into the apartment, only to be faced with the couches, and yet more memories. I tried to block them out. But how could I?

We've made love in every room, on almost every surface.

There's no escape.

So in the end, I poured myself a very large glass of wine and sat at the breakfast bar, trying not to think about sitting Livia up there, and tasting her… and instead, I went online and, using the information Miles had emailed me, I sent her some money.

It wasn't what I wanted to do… not that I cared about the money. That wasn't the point. What I wanted to do, was to hold her in my arms, to beg her to tell me I'd been wrong about the whole thing… that I'd just made the biggest mistake of my life. It wouldn't have been an easy admission to make, especially as I'd been so sure of myself, but I'd have done it. Except for one minor problem…

If Livia was somehow able to tell me she'd had nothing to do with Ken Bevan, that the whole thing was a coincidence, and she'd never heard of the man before, I knew she'd never be able to forgive me for all the things I'd said and done to her.

It felt like a lose-lose situation. Either I had to hear that she'd planned it all – with, or without her father's knowledge – or I had to accept that I'd fucked-up, that there was no connection between her and Ken Bevan and that I'd lost her forever… with no-one to blame but myself.

I didn't want to face either of those prospects, so I drank my wine, poured myself another glass, and went up to the bedroom. My plan had been to shower and change, but I didn't get that far. I was halted by the sight of Livia's books, piled on her nightstand. I shook my head, telling myself it wasn't 'her' nightstand anymore, just like it wasn't her side of the bed I went to sit on… except it was. It always will be.

Putting down my wine, I picked up the books, studying the covers. The first was a romantic comedy, and I put it aside, taking up the second, which was a murder mystery. I was surprised by that, and thumbed through a few pages, my surprise diminishing when I noticed it was written in a light-hearted style. That was more like Livia…

The third book wasn't surprising at all. It shocked the hell out of me. It was a beginner's guide to social media advertising. I sat back a little, studying it, reading through the contents list. For a beginner's guide, it was fairly comprehensive, and I flipped through the first chapter, pausing when I noticed some penciled notes in the margin. The section was basically posing the question: do you need social media advertising? The answer they gave was obviously 'yes', otherwise there would have been little point in writing the rest of the book, but the authors had included some statistics that appeared to be fairly up-to-date, which supported their perspective. Alongside these stats, Livia had written, *'Check this with Hunter. Is it accurate?'*

She had checked it, too. I remembered her coming to see me last week, and asking me about online ad performance versus printed media, the cost implications, and the potential results. We'd talked for a while and I'd enjoyed our conversation. I'd enjoyed spending time with her. Period. I'd assumed it was connected to something I'd asked her to do for me... not because she was doing homework on her own time, without me even noticing.

Could it be?

Had she really just come to work for me?

I put the books back then, and lay down, resting my head on her pillow, inhaling her scent and letting the pain engulf me. I knew I'd never sleep lying there, but I couldn't bring myself to get up. It felt like I'd be leaving her behind... and I couldn't do that.

Darkness slowly fell, shrouding the room in shadows, and although I closed my eyes every so often, I didn't sleep. I kept recalling the look on Livia's face when I told her to leave. The confusion in her eyes, her tears, her words of innocence... they'd all felt like an act at the time. But had they been? Or was I wrong about that? I thought about Drew's description of Livia in the parking garage, broken and alone. Could it have been a coincidence? I couldn't tell... and as the night wore on, the more confused I became.

I knew I missed her, without a doubt.

I knew I loved her more than ever.

And I knew I was right about one thing... and so was Drew. There was no way Livia was capable of using sex to manipulate me. I didn't know how anyone could be as innocent as she was, but she was. And I loved her for it. I'll always love her for it... for her smile, for her purity, for her curiosity...

I don't know what time it was, but it was still dark when the city lights started to blur, and the realization of what I'd lost truly overwhelmed me.

As the first tear trickled down onto Livia's pillow, that was the moment I broke.

Broken or not, I've got up, showered and dressed. I've got a coffee, and I'm sitting on the couch.

I've got no idea what to do with my day, and I'm wondering whether I should drive down to Newport after all... except Drew and Ella will be there, and they'll expect me to talk. They'll no doubt tell me I've screwed up, too.

Maybe I have. I still can't be sure.

There's no doubting the fact that Livia is an unusual name, but I can't deny, she didn't seem to recognize Ken Bevan, and he certainly didn't acknowledge her. That could have been part of their act, though... so it's not conclusive. Did he really come to the office to catch up with Dad and gloat over his achievements? Or was there something more to it? Something connected with Livia? It didn't look that way... but again, I can't be sure. One thing I can't escape is the fact that she hasn't mentioned her father, ever since I've known her, although I'm still uncertain whether that's significant. Like Ella said, there could be all kinds of reasons for that, so it could be yet another coincidence, for all I know. The thing that's haunting me most, though, for all kinds of reasons, is Livia's reaction. Not to me, or even to her father – if he was her father – but later, in the parking garage. If what Drew says is right, does that make sense? It does if she's innocent, but if she's guilty, it makes no sense at all. There's no way she'd have broken down like that, if she'd just been caught in a lie, no matter how big the lie.

If she'd just been rejected by the man she loved and trusted, though...

"Oh, God..."

I get up, pacing the floor, struggling to breathe.

What should I do? I need to know the truth… and short of speaking to Livia herself, there's only one person I can think of who might be able to help.

I grab my phone from the table, looking up the number I need, and connect the call. It rings a few times and then I hear the familiar voice.

"Hunter?"

"Hi, Doreen."

"This is a surprise."

"Yeah… I, um…" I take a moment, recalling that life exists outside of my problems. "How's your grandchild?"

"She's just perfect," she says, and I can hear the smile in her voice. "She was born three days late, and she doesn't seem to understand the concept of sleeping at night, but babies don't, do they?"

"No." My answer isn't based on personal experience… just hearsay.

"I'm sure you didn't call to ask about little Phoebe, though," she says. "Has something happened?"

"In a manner of speaking."

"How can I help?" I sigh, unsure where to start. "Hunter? What's wrong?"

"Everything."

"Is it work, or something personal?" I've never spoken to her about my personal life before, but I'm going to have to now…

"Both… although it's more personal, I guess." It certainly feels that way.

"Is it to do with Livia?"

I sit down, stunned. "How did you know?"

"I saw the two of you together. It wasn't hard to work out."

I shake my head, struck by the irony that, for all our efforts, we couldn't even keep our relationship a secret from someone who's three thousand miles away.

"I fell for her," I say, surprising myself with my own candor.

"You're not going to tell me she doesn't feel the same, are you? Because…"

"No, it's not that. It's… well… it's that she's not who I thought she was."

"Meaning?"

"I think she's Ken Bevan's daughter."

The line falls silent for a moment. "Oh, of course… Livia." I almost feel relieved that someone else has seen the connection, except I'm not sure it helps very much. "I assumed her name was short for Olivia, so I never put the two things together."

"I knew it wasn't short for anything. She told me. But I thought her name was familiar right from the moment I first heard it. I just couldn't think what until Ken Bevan walked into the office yesterday lunchtime."

"He came to the office?" She's taken aback. I can hear it in her voice.

"Yeah. He seems to have made something of himself since he came out of prison and said he wanted to see Dad, to gloat, I guess… about a year too late."

"That sounds like something Ken would do." The bitterness in her voice is only thinly disguised. "How did Livia react?"

I suck in a breath, recalling the scene, and my role in it. I'm not feeling very proud of myself, and don't want to admit to what I've done. Except, if I don't, there's very little point in me having made this call.

"She didn't recognize him, if that's what you're asking… but I—I fired her."

"What on earth for?"

"Because it seemed like too much of a coincidence that the daughter of the man who almost ruined my family could come and work for us."

"Coincidences can happen, Hunter. And how do you know for sure that she is his daughter? You said she didn't recognize him."

"I don't know for sure, but Livia is an unusual name." Every time I say that, it sounds more and more like I'm clutching at straws, trying to justify my actions. I think Doreen senses that, too. I hear her sigh and can imagine her shaking her head or rolling her eyes at me, just like she used to.

"Okay. Let's assume for the sake of your sanity that they are related. I'd still find it hard to believe Livia came to work for TBA intending to cause trouble."

"Why?"

"Because she'd have been raised by her mom after Ken went to prison, and Julianne Bevan would never have condoned that kind of behavior."

"How can you know that?"

"Because she was as straight as a die. She worked for a law firm. That's how she met Ken in the first place. He hired her to come into the company as an independent investigator to look into the fraud he was perpetrating."

"You're kidding."

"No. But if you think about it, it was a clever move on his part. I don't know how old she was, but she was quite an innocent. Ken saw that too and wasted no time in persuading her into his bed." She coughs, and I wonder if she's blushing. I don't say anything, though. Right now, I'm struggling not to think about Livia's innocence, and what I've done with that. "I can remember seeing her around the office," Doreen says. "And she doted on him, which, of course, meant he found it even easier to manipulate her lines of inquiry. She'd have done anything he asked of her."

"I presume she found no evidence of fraud?"

"Absolutely none. Ken made sure of that. Julianne went on her way, and Ken started seeing one of the girls in the finance department. Some women found him charming, although he could also be the most obnoxious of men, and I remember he used to strut around the office at that time, like he owned the place."

"He thought he'd got away with it?"

"Yes. Until Julianne called him."

"You mean she'd found something after all?"

"Not in the way you mean. She'd discovered she was pregnant."

"With Livia?"

"Yes. I remember Ken was furious about it, but the next thing I knew, they were married. That surprised me, although your father said much later, after Ken was sent to prison, that he thought he'd only married Julianne because having a family would provide a better cover for him. It didn't work, of course, and personally, I wasn't so sure."

"You thought he loved her?"

"Good Lord, no. I always thought it had more to do with him still wanting to manipulate her."

"Over the fraud, you mean?"

"Yes, and in other ways, too. He treated her appallingly, you know?"

"He hit her?"

"Not that I'm aware of. But he always talked about her like he owned her... like she was dirt. And I know for a fact he continued his affair with that girl in the finance office. Not that I can ju—"

She stops talking, although I know exactly what she was going to say.

"It's okay, Doreen. I know about you and my father."

"Y—You do?"

"Yes. I haven't known for very long, but…"

"Oh, I see. The office gossips have been active in my absence, have they?"

"Something like that."

There's a brief pause. "I'm sorry, Hunter."

"You don't have to apologize."

"Except I do. Here I am criticizing Ken Bevan, but what your father did to your mother was no better… and I was complicit in that. I knew what we were doing was wrong."

"If you don't mind me asking, why did you do it?"

"At the beginning, it was quite simple. My husband had died, and I was lonely."

"And for Dad? What was his reason?"

"He assured me there was nothing left in his marriage. He said he and your mom lived completely separate lives."

"Was that true, though? From what I've heard, your affair with him started before Ella was born."

"Wow… the gossips really have been busy."

"Is that how it happened?"

She doesn't answer straight away, but I can hear her breathing. "Yes," she says eventually. "I can't recall what age you and Drew were when I started seeing your father, but it was before Ella was conceived."

"And you believed him when he said his marriage was over?"

"I did at the beginning, but to be honest, things were complicated."

"I can imagine they were. He was married."

"I know, but that wasn't the reason for our difficulties."

"What was then?"

"My daughter. I had to put her first, which meant your father could never stay the night, or be with us at weekends. He resented that, although he always maintained he couldn't leave your mother." That surprises me, but I don't get the chance to

304

comment. Doreen's still talking… "I never asked him to, Hunter. Not once. As far as I was concerned, he had responsibilities, just like I did. But I loved him, and I wanted us to make the most of the time we had together. I thought I'd convinced him to accept that." She pauses for a second, clearing her throat. "I think that's why I found it so hard when he came and told me your mom was pregnant. My reaction wasn't what it should have been."

"Why? What did you do?"

"I—I'm ashamed to say my first instinct was to question who the father was. That was unfair of me. I shouldn't have done it."

"Did Dad tell you it was him?"

"Yes. He was honest enough to do that, at least."

"What did you do, having it laid before you like that, knowing he'd lied to you about his relationship with Mom?"

"I handed in my resignation and told him I never wanted to see him again. He'd promised me the physical side of their relationship had ended when Drew was conceived, so I felt used by him, and devastated by what he'd done. I was ready to leave town and take my daughter with me, although I had no idea where we were going to go."

"What made you change your mind?" Something obviously did.

"Your father came to my apartment."

"He asked you to stay?"

"He begged me to stay. He told me Ella had been conceived during a moment of drunken madness."

"Did you believe him?"

"I didn't know what to believe, and I certainly didn't want to know the details. He said he couldn't live without me. He told me he loved me. I—It was the first time he'd ever said that to me."

"So you stayed?"

"Yes. I know that was probably weak of me, and foolish, too. But you do foolish things when you're in love, don't you?" It seems so. I've just fired the woman I love… and I'm beginning to wonder why. "We spent even more time together after that," Doreen continues. "And we were very happy… except…"

"Except what?"

"Except, later on, during those months after Ken Bevan was arrested. We weren't happy then, and there's no denying what happened during those few months changed everything."

"I can remember Dad being obsessive about the whole thing."

"The obsession itself had started way before Ken's arrest. Theodore had realized something still wasn't right with the company's finances, even after Julianne's investigation was completed, so he brought in people of his own, telling no one, except me. It took them a while, but eventually, they uncovered Ken's activities, and your father called in the police. From then on, he was like a man possessed. He'd been proved right. He was triumphant about it, and he wanted revenge. That was the only time – apart from when he told me about Ella's conception – that I doubted my love for him."

"You thought he should forgive Ken Bevan?"

"No. The man had stolen millions of dollars. He deserved to be punished. It was everything else that was so… brutal."

"Brutal? What on earth did he do?"

"He tried to have Julianne Bevan charged as an accessory. Livia would have been a baby at the time, but Theodore hounded that poor woman."

"What happened to her… to them?"

"Fortunately, Julianne was able to prove her innocence somehow, and she wound up helping the police. Your father wasn't happy about that, and kept trying to find ways of implicating her, even though she was completely innocent. He'd have gone a lot further, I think, if I hadn't threatened to leave him. I told him, if he didn't stop, he'd never see me again, and he calmed down a little. But he wasn't the same man after that. It was only a short while later that your mom left. He never explained her departure to me, but I've always assumed your father's behavior finally got too much for her."

"And yet, you stayed with him?"

"Yes, and then a few weeks after your mom left, your father asked me to move in with him."

"He did?" That's a surprise.

"I said 'no'… obviously."

"Because he wasn't offering marriage?"

"No. I didn't expect him to marry me. I didn't expect anything. Theodore wasn't the kind of man you expected things from." She's not wrong there. "Your mom's departure might have seemed like the golden opportunity for us. I think, if it hadn't been for the events surrounding Ken Bevan's arrest, it probably would have been. But I'd seen a different side to Theodore, and although I couldn't help loving him, I didn't want to expose my daughter to a man who could persecute another human being in the way he had." She pauses for a moment. "I know you never got along with your father. You hold him responsible for what happened… with your mother."

"Do you blame me?"

"No. Do you blame me?"

"No, I don't."

"Thank you." I hear her sigh, and wonder if she needed my forgiveness as much as I need answers.

"Did Ken Bevan know about your affair with my father?"

"Yes, I think so. He used to make snide remarks sometimes, when he knew your father couldn't hear."

"I see. That makes sense."

"What does that mean?"

"When he came into the office yesterday, there was a moment, just before he left when he looked at me, and then at Livia, and he said I hadn't fallen too far from the tree. He must have guessed... about me and Livia."

She sucks in a breath. "And you think that makes him right?" I hear her tut and imagine her rolling her eyes at me. Again. "I remember on the day I resigned from TBA, you questioned why I wouldn't stay, and I told you that, after your father died, I knew it was time for me to leave. You interpreted that as my loyalty to him, and in part, it was. I felt a duty to your father to see things through... because I loved him. Mostly, though, I needed to go because it was time for you to run the company your way, without the influences of the past clouding your judgment. It was time for you to step out from his shadow."

"Oh, my God."

"What?"

"Livia told me exactly the same thing."

"Then she was right. You are not your father, Hunter. I loved him, even when I knew I probably shouldn't, but you are a far better man than he could ever have been. You don't have a brutal bone in your body."

"I think Livia might disagree with you about that. I was vile to her yesterday."

"Then apologize."

"You think an apology will be enough?"

"It's a place to start."

"And if she won't forgive me?"

"Then apologize again... and again. She's good for you. Make it right, Hunter... whatever it takes."


*Whatever it takes...*

Doreen's words are still rolling around my head... and not just the ones about me and Livia. I might have known the bones of the story about her and my dad, but now there's some flesh to them, I have to admit, I'm surprised. I'd never thought my father was capable of love, but I think he must have loved Doreen, in his own way. Hearing that he'd refused to leave our mother was a surprise, and I can't make any sense of it. I would have thought he'd welcome the chance. As for the fact that he asked Doreen to move in with him, that was a revelation. Although I can't help wondering if her refusal may have fueled his resentment of us. He'd never have perceived that he, or his behavior, might have been the reason she said 'no', and it wouldn't surprise me if he'd believed his children had stood in the way of his happiness with Doreen. Still, I guess I'll never know now.

I've already decided to keep all of that to myself, though. Especially the parts surrounding Ella's conception. There's no way I want to risk her finding out she was the result of a moment of 'drunken madness', so the fewer people who know, the better.

As for what Doreen said about Livia... I know she's right. Livia was good for me. That has to be true, because if it wasn't, I wouldn't feel so lost without her.

I might not know who she is yet – not for sure – but that doesn't alter the fact that I love her, or that I need to apologize. I was brutal with her yesterday, and that's not who I am. It can't be... not if both Doreen and Drew say so.

Personally, I'm still having my doubts.

The thought of what I've done, of Livia crying in the parking garage, of the fact that I caused that... that I broke her, it all weighs too heavily on my mind, and I leap to my feet, pocketing my phone and grabbing my keys as I run to the elevator, stepping inside the moment the doors open.

I'm pretty sure Livia's going to slam the door in my face. I wouldn't blame her if she did, but I'll have to keep trying. There are questions that need answering. I need to know who she is, whether she's Ken Bevan's daughter, and why she came to work for me.

If I'm right, and there was some kind of conspiracy, we need to talk… Livia, and me, and maybe her dad, too. They need to tell me what was behind it all, and whatever it is, she and I need to find a compromise… a way through it.

If I'm wrong, I need to spend the rest of my life making it up to her… assuming she'll let me.

I park outside her apartment and head straight in, taking the stairs two at a time, until I get to her floor, and rush down the hall to her door. Once outside, I hesitate for just a moment or two, taking a couple of deep breaths, and then I knock.

There's no reply, so I knock again… and again.

The silence is deafening. She's not home.

I turn, leaning back against the door. I hadn't anticipated this, and I don't know what to do. Where can she be? Grocery shopping? It's possible. She wouldn't have had any food here, although she'd probably have gone out yesterday afternoon and done that… unless…

I let my head drop.

Of course…

She'll have gone home. It's what Livia would do. She'll be hurting, thanks to me, and going home would be a natural reaction for her.

What I don't know is exactly where 'home' is. Falmouth may be a small town, according to Livia, but I can't just drive up there and hope to find her. Fortunately, our personnel files are stored electronically, and I can access them remotely through my phone. I saunter down the stairs and back to my car, while logging in to the company's system, and wait while it brings up the files.

They're listed alphabetically, so I scroll down to 'H', which is another reminder that Livia's surname isn't Bevan. I refuse to read anything in to that, though, and click on her file, waiting while it opens.

I get into my car, switching on the engine, and find her next of kin, wanting to kick myself. I should have checked this out sooner… or better still, looked at it before I fired Livia.

I sit, staring at the screen for a moment. According to this, her next of kin is Mrs. J. Hopkins, and the address given is in Falmouth, Maine. That doesn't really help or tell me anything. Okay, so Doreen said that Ken Bevan's wife was called Julianne, and Livia's mom's initial is 'J', but that's hardly evidence of a conspiracy… and I'm learning the hard way not to jump to conclusions.

Instead, I tap the address into my Sat/Nav and let out a slight sigh when it tells me the journey time is going to be a little under two hours… although, that's assuming I'll be sticking to the speed limits…

An hour and thirty-five minutes later, I pull up in front of a gray-painted colonial, single-story house. There's a garage off to one side, and the driveway is empty, although I don't presume to park there, and leave my car on the street, walking up a narrow footpath to the front door. The lawn on either side is neatly mown, and the flower beds are brimming.

This time, I don't hesitate, or pause to take a breath. I just ring the doorbell. The drive up here has made me impatient to see Livia, although as I hear footsteps approaching, my heart pounds in my chest.

The door opens and I'm faced with a woman who shares Livia's coloring, her blonde hair tied up in a ponytail. She must be Livia's mom, and when she tilts her head and raises her eyebrows, I know for sure. Their mannerisms are the same, too.

"Mrs.… Hopkins?" I say, hesitating over her name.

"Yes?"

I nod my head. "Is Livia here?"

She looks over my shoulder, focusing on my car. "Are you Hunter Bennett?"

"Yes, I am."

She nods and then glances back into the house, pausing for a moment before she turns to me again, her brow furrowing.

"Livia's not at home, I'm afraid."

I can't call her a liar to her face, but we both know she's not telling the truth. I also know Livia must be just inside the house, out of my sight, but visible to her mom.

"What you mean is, she's not at home to me." She doesn't say anything, but her silence speaks volumes. "I'm not here to make trouble, Mrs. Hopkins. I just wanna talk to your daughter."

She glances into the house again and then looks up at me. "I'm sorry, but she doesn't want to talk to you."

I guess that tells me everything I need to know. Livia might not be slamming the door in my face, but she's getting her mom to do it for her.

I'm not about to give up, though.

"Okay," I say, raising my voice, so I know Livia will hear me. "In that case, will you tell her, if I got this wrong, then I'm sorry. Even if I didn't get it wrong... even if everything I think about her is true, I'm still sorry. I want to work things out between us, if we can. Can you ask her if she'll let me try?"

Mrs. Hopkins looks away yet again, and although her expression doesn't change, she stares into the house for a lot longer this time, before she turns back to me.

"She still doesn't want to…" Her voice fades, and I nod my head. It was what I expected.

"It's okay." She steps backwards, about to close the door, but I raise my hand and she pauses, tilting her head again. "Can you tell her I love her?"

She nods, but says nothing, and closes the door. I stand, staring at it for a full minute, before I turn and walk back to my car.

This might have been what I expected, but it still hurts, and I sit and stare out the window for a long time, gazing at Livia's home. Just knowing she's in there makes me feel closer to her, even if she doesn't want to know me.

I'm not sure what to do. I don't have any answers and I'm not ready to give up yet, although I can't see the point of knocking on the door again, or sitting here all night.

That doesn't mean I'm going home, though, and I pull out my phone, checking to see what hotels there are in the vicinity.

I find several in Portland, and call up the first one on the list.

"I need a suite for tonight," I say to the woman who answers the phone.

"Our Ambassador Suite is available. It's eighteen hundred and fifty…"

"I don't care about the price," I say, interrupting her as I tap the hotel's address into my Sat/Nav. "I can be with you in fifteen minutes."

"That's fine, sir. We'll look forward to seeing you."

The Ambassador Suite is perfectly acceptable. It has a living room, with a corner couch, dining table, and kitchen area. From there you can walk out through the glass doors, onto a balcony that overlooks the city. The bedroom, which is where I am now, has a king-sized bed, a dressing area, and…

"This is the bathroom." The bellboy who carried up my bag, opens the door in the left-hand wall, and switches on the light, although I don't go over and look. A bathroom is a bathroom, after all. And, in any case, I'm feeling pre-occupied.

Obviously, my mind is absorbed by Livia, and how I'm going to get her to talk to me, but on the way over here, I realized that, in my haste to stay and try to work things out with her, I'd forgotten that I didn't have a change of clothes. I was just wondering if the hotel had a laundry service when I suddenly remembered that I didn't need to worry. In the trunk of my car was the bag I'd packed yesterday morning to take to Newport. At least one minor crisis seemed to have been averted... until I opened the trunk, and saw Livia's bag, nestling beside my own. I don't know why I hadn't remembered it would be there, but I hadn't, and it hurt, removing my bag, and leaving hers behind. It might sound silly, but it felt like another disconnection between us, and I wasn't ready to face that. I'm still not, and I wish this bellboy would leave, so I can stop pretending I'm okay.

# Chapter Thirteen

*Livia*

Mom closes the door and turns to me, raising her eyebrows.

"You said I didn't have to speak to him." I blurt out my words before she can tell me I got that all wrong.

"I know… and you said he wouldn't call."

"He didn't."

"No. He drove all the way up here." She folds her arms across her chest. "He loves you, Livia. Even if he hadn't just admitted it, it was as clear as the nose on his face."

"Maybe he does. But I'm not ready to talk to him yet."

She lets her hands fall to her sides and comes over, standing in front of me. "That's okay. Just remember what I said."

"About love being fragile, you mean?"

"Yes."

"I'm feeling pretty fragile myself."

"Oh… come here." She pulls me into a hug, and I let her, only turning when I hear footsteps behind me, coming from the back of the house. Dad's still in his pajamas, even though it's lunchtime, and he's put on a bathrobe, although he hasn't done it up.

"Did I hear voices?" he says.

"Yes, but don't worry about it." Mom goes to him and pulls his bathrobe closed. "Shall we get you dressed?"

He gazes down at her and nods his head. "I fell asleep again."

"I know, but it's okay."

She leads him back toward their bedroom, and I lean against the wall behind me, letting out a long sigh. I never expected Hunter to come here. If I'm being honest, I never expected to hear from him again.

When I realized it was him at the door, though, I hid. That might sound childish, and maybe it was, but I knew if I went and spoke to him, I'd end up yelling… and probably crying. And I don't want to do either of those things. I want to do what he suggested. I want to talk… to work things out.

Except I'm not ready.

I know I should be heartened by him coming here, and by all the things he said, but if anything, it's just fueled my anger. Why did he have to hurt me so much, if he didn't mean it? Why did he have to push me away, if he was just going to pull me back again? It was confusing, and hearing him say he loves me hasn't helped. Part of me wanted to run out and throw myself into his arms… to kiss him and tell him I love him too. And part of me wanted to scream at him. His actions had hardly been those of a man in love… at least, they didn't seem that way to me.

Standing here won't achieve anything, though, and it's certainly won't help me work out how I feel. It's nearly lunchtime, and while Mom helps Dad to get dressed, I can make myself useful and fix us something to eat.

I push myself off of the wall and wander through to the kitchen, where I make some sandwiches and coffee, getting everything ready just in time for Mom and Dad to reappear.

"You sit at the table," she says, helping him into a chair. She sits beside him, looking exhausted, although he does too, and I carry the lunch over, setting it down in front of them.

"This looks l—lovely," Dad says, with a smile, although he struggles to pick up the sandwich, and Mom gets up and fetches a knife, cutting it into smaller pieces, which he finds a little easier. Mom has to hold his cup and help him drink, and I watch them, my heart aching. Dad was worse than this at the beginning, when he first came home from the hospital, but I was living here then. I could help more, and it's been years since I've seen him need this level of assistance. I left home because I thought he was better, but looking at him now, I wonder – yet again – how selfish I was.

Lunch takes a lot longer than usual because of Dad, but once he's had enough, I clear away so Mom can help him into the living room. She returns within minutes and sits back down at the table, her head in her hands.

"Are you okay, Mom?"

"I'm fine." She looks up again. I know she's lying, and so does she. She's not 'fine' at all.

"How's Dad?"

"Exhausted. Eating does that to him sometimes. He'll be a lot better when he's rested."

He only woke up an hour ago, but I don't comment.

"I know I've asked this before, but I'm gonna ask it again… would it help if I moved back here?"

She tilts her head, frowning at me. "Are you asking that because it would provide you with a good excuse for not working things out with Hunter?"

"No." At least, I don't think so. "I just keep thinking about how selfish I was to leave you. It's hard work, looking after Dad."

"Yes, it is. But as I told you the last time you asked me that question, he's not your responsibility. Neither am I. You have a life of your own, Livia, and you need to live it. Don't get me wrong, you're welcome to stay for as long as you need, but if you want to go back to Boston or find a place somewhere else, then you go right ahead and do it."

"Where would I go?" I sit opposite her, and she reaches out, taking my hand in hers.

"Are you saying it's over between you and Hunter?"

"I don't know. If he hadn't come calling today, I think the decision would have been a lot easier."

"It would?"

"Yeah. I think I'd probably have stayed here for a while, licked my wounds, found a job in Portland, and maybe moved there... so I'd be close by."

She narrows her eyes, but doesn't repeat her point about living my own life. She doesn't need to. The look on her face says it all.

"The thing is, he did come calling..." she says, leaving her sentence hanging.

"I know."

"And that complicates things?"

"I knew where I stood before."

"And where was that?"

"In the wilderness, broken... on my own."

She squeezes my hand. "You're never on your own."

I smile at her. "I know... but can't you see? Now it's so much harder."

She sucks in a breath, letting it out slowly. "Do you want to go back to Boston?"

"I enjoyed living there. I liked my apartment. But if I went back, would Hunter take it as a sign?"

"A sign of what?"

"That I wanted to re-kindle things between us."

"Don't you?"

"I don't know what I want, other than to talk to him... to understand what happened. But I can't do that. I'm still too angry with him to think straight."

"Anger rarely lasts very long. You're feeling bruised and hurt. Is there any reason you have to decide straight away? Like I said, you can stay here for as long as you want."

"I'll need to get a job, Mom."

"Hmm… but first you need to decide where that job is going to be."

"I know. And that's my point." I sit back, staring up at the ceiling. "I feel like I'm going round in circles."

"That's because you are. You need to take your foot off the gas and focus on just one thing."

"Hunter…" I murmur.

"Exactly. Until you've decided what to do about him, it's impossible to work out what to do about the rest of it."

She's right. I know she is. The problem is, I don't know what to do about him.

"There's one thing I ought to do, I guess."

"What's that?" She frowns at me.

"Get myself a phone. I hate feeling so disconnected."

I get to my feet, and she releases my hand, looking up at me. "Where are you going?"

"Into town… to get a new phone."

"Oh. You're going now?"

"Is that a problem?"

"No, of course not."

I sense it is, and sit down again.

"What's wrong, Mom?"

She sighs. "It's nothing…"

"Do you want me to stay and help this afternoon?"

Her eyes glisten, brimming with tears. "Would you?"

I take her hand in mine this time. "Of course. What do you need me to do?"

*

Mom wasn't very specific about the help she needed. I think she was too tired to remember what had to be done, but we worked it out between us and I spent the afternoon doing laundry, tidying the house a little, and changing the sheets on their bed, before I made us spaghetti bolognese for dinner. Mom suggested it, as Dad finds it easy to eat as long as it's cut up. He still struggled, though, and afterwards, she helped him to bed. She followed him, and although I sat up and watched a movie for a while, I was too tired to stay awake, and came to bed.

I surprised myself by sleeping. It was fitful, my dreams filled with images of Hunter. I woke up once, in a blind panic, fearful I'd never see him again, and it took me a while to close my eyes again. I did, though, and the next time I crack them open, it's morning.

I stretch my arms above my head, stilling when I hear noises coming from the kitchen. It must be later than I think, but there's no clock in here and without a phone, I can't even tell the time.

I need to rectify that, but for now I jump out of bed and head for the kitchen, where I find Mom and Dad sitting together at the table, both nursing cups of coffee. Dad looks so much better today, as does Mom for that matter, and they both smile up at me.

"We were starting to think we'd have to come wake you."

"Why? What time is it?"

"Nine-thirty."

"Really?"

Mom nods her head, smiling. "Why don't you go shower, and I'll fix us some bacon and eggs."

My stomach growls, just at the thought, and I dash down the hall, straight to the bathroom.

I take no time at all to shower, and I braid my hair rather than drying it, because it's quicker, and then put on the jeans I was wearing yesterday, and another top. I'm going to have to think about some new clothes, I suppose… but not right this minute.

Right this minute, the smell of bacon is driving me insane, and I go straight back to the kitchen, where Mom's just transferring the eggs to the plates.

"I thought I'd head into Portland this morning, if that's okay." I look at her as I'm speaking and she nods her head.

"That's fine."

"You don't mind me taking the car?"

"Of course not. We were planning a lazy morning, anyway."

"What are you going for?" Dad asks.

"A new phone… and I might see if I can pick up some clothes, too. Is there anything you need me to get while I'm out?"

"I can't think of anything," Mom says.

"But you will, five minutes after Livia's gone."

"Yeah, and because I don't have a phone, you won't be able to call and tell me."

Mom chuckles. "I can see the value of you getting a new one now."

We finish eating and, although I offer to help clear away, Mom won't hear of it and insists I go out and enjoy myself shopping. I don't have the heart to tell her I'm not capable of enjoying myself, but I thank her anyway and pick up my purse and Mom's keys before I call, "Goodbye," to them both and head out the door.

I'm halfway to the garage when I hear footsteps behind me, coming up the path, and I turn, gasping, when I see Hunter, striding toward me. He's wearing stonewashed jeans and a pale gray t-shirt. They're the kind of clothes he usually wears when we're in Newport, and for a moment, I'm mesmerized by him…

by the pain in his eyes, which I know matches my own. I'm still not ready for this, though, and I turn back toward the front door.

"Don't… please." He reaches out and grabs my arm, stopping me. "Please, Livia."

He sounds desperate, but what right does he have to take that tone with me, after everything he said and did?

"Let me go, Hunter."

He doesn't, but instead he turns me around, taking hold of my hand rather than my arm. "Don't ask that of me. I can't let you go."

"You didn't seem to have a problem with it on Friday, in your office."

He sucks in a sharp breath, like something hurt him deeply. "I know… and I'm sorry."

At that moment, the front door opens, and Hunter startles, stepping back and releasing my hand. I turn and see my father, who looks from me to Hunter before he steps outside, leaning heavily on his walking stick. Mom's behind him, and as he starts toward us, she puts a hand on his shoulder.

"Leave it, Connor. Come back inside. Livia can handle this."

Dad shakes his head, glaring at Hunter, his face darkening. "You're Hunter Bennett?" he says.

"Yes."

"I'm Connor Hopkins. Livia's father. Not her natural father, you understand, but her father, nonetheless. I—I gather you think my d—daughter might have gained employment in your company and started a relationship with you, in order to d—defraud you." Mom must have told Dad about our conversation, and he narrows his eyes, stepping forward slightly. "If you truly believe that, young man, you don't know L—Livia at all… and you're certainly not worthy of her. For your information, the man who cheated your father hasn't been a part of Livia's life since she was a baby."

"So Ken Bevan is her father? Her natural father, I mean?" Hunter turns his gaze on me, looking confused.

"Yes, he is. B—But what difference does that make?" Dad says, raising his voice slightly. "It doesn't excuse your b—behavior, if that's what you're thinking. Livia wasn't even aware of his existence until she came back here on Friday afternoon, crying her heart out, because you'd fired her, and she didn't understand why. H—Her mother and I had kept her identity a secret from her because we wanted to p—protect her… and if we were wrong in doing that, then we're sorry. For Livia. Not for you."

"Connor, darling… calm down." Mom tugs at his shoulder again. "Please stop this before you have another stroke."

Something flips in my head… a need to protect my dad, I guess, and I step in front him, facing Hunter, but putting myself between them.

"I want you to leave."

He lowers his eyes to mine. "Livia… please don't do this. I didn't come here to cause trouble for you or your family. All I want is to talk to you… to apologize. I jumped to conclusions. I —"

"Yes, you did… and now you've worked that out, you can go."

He shakes his head. "Don't you love me at all?"

"Of course I do," I yell. "But my love for you doesn't give you the right to judge me."

"I know. I realize how many mistakes I've made, but can you please try to understand what that man did to my family?"

"What did he do?" I say, unable to keep the sarcasm from my voice. "Did he steal a few of your precious millions?"

"No… well, yes, he did. But that's not the point. When your father defrauded…"

"He's not my father. I don't even know the man you're talking about." I step back slightly and point to my dad. "This is my father."

323

Hunter holds up his hands, surrendering to my outburst. "Okay. I'm sorry. I'll start that again. When Ken Bevan defrauded my dad, he took a lot more than money. He stole what little faith my father had in the world and changed him beyond recognition. I've told you enough already for you to know that Theodore Bennett would never have won any awards as a human being, let alone a husband, or parent, but from the day he discovered what Ken Bevan had done, he was never the same again. He became even harder, even more distant. It was only a few months after Ken's arrest that Mom left us. I don't know exactly why she went. You know that. But the two things have to be connected. She'd had years of being ignored, years of Dad being absent from the family home. I'm fairly sure she knew he'd been having an affair for most of their marriage... but for some reason, she couldn't take it anymore, and she walked away. Drew and Ella don't remember what it was like. I've already explained that neither of them remember Mom, or the fights, or her tears, or what Dad was capable of. But I do. I'm sorry, but what Ken Bevan did... it robbed us of our mom and broke us as a family. So, it wasn't just about the damn money, Livia... not for the three of us."

He stops talking, breathing hard, and I stare up at him, seeing the years of pain in his eyes.

"I'm sorry too, Hunter. I didn't know about any of this, and I didn't realize the timing of it."

He takes a half step forward. "I get that. At least, I do now. Please believe me, I'm sorry for everything I've said and done. I'm not my father... or I don't want to be." He closes the gap a little more, standing right in front of me. "I know I've hurt you, and I'll do anything to make it up to you. Just tell me what I have to do... what I have to say..."

I shake my head at him. "I'm not ready, Hunter."

"Not ready for what?"

"To forgive you. To trust you again. I need time."

He looks a little despondent, but takes a deep breath. "That's okay. Is there anything else you need?"

"I don't know."

He frowns. "Do you need me?"

"I just said. I don't know."

His shoulders drop. "Do you still want me to leave?"

Do I? "I think it would be for the best." Even as I'm saying the words, I doubt them. Sure, I'm angry, and I don't feel ready yet, but how are we ever gonna work this out, if we don't talk?

The problem is, I need to be calmer before we do.

He nods his head, although I can tell he's not happy. "Before I go, I've got something for you."

He doesn't wait for me to reply, but walks back to his car, opening the trunk and reaching inside. He pulls out my bag… the one I packed on Friday morning to take to Newport, and closing the trunk, he turns, coming back up the path again.

"I stayed in a hotel in Portland last night, and remembered I had my bag in the trunk. Yours was in there, too, and I realized you probably don't have many clothes with you."

"No. They're at your place."

He nods his head, putting the bag down by my feet. "Do you need anything else? I can bring it up for you… whatever it is."

"You'd drive all the way to Boston and back again?"

"Of course. Why? What do you need?"

"Nothing." *I just can't believe you'd do that for me. It's confusing. Too confusing to contemplate.* "I'm sure I've got enough things here. If not, I'll buy whatever I need. It shouldn't be very much, and I can just about afford it."

He frowns. "What does that mean?"

"I don't have a job, Hunter. You fired me, remember?"

"I know, but…"

"Please… I don't want to get into this now." I pick up the bag. "Thank you for bringing this."

"That's okay." I step away, moving toward my parents, but he calls me back and I turn to him. "Tell me we're not over, Livia… please?"

That feels like a very unfair question. "You can't ask me that now. You said you'd give me time."

He nods his head. "Okay… I'm sorry."

I walk toward him again, looking up into his eyes. He looks so sad, I want to hold him, but I can't. "I've never been in a situation like this before," I say, struggling to speak. "I—I've never been hurt."

"And you think I have? You can only be hurt by someone you love… and I've never loved anyone but you."

"I know. But I didn't hurt you. You hurt me, and now I don't know what to do, Hunter. I don't know how to feel."

"Then let me help you."

I shake my head. "Not this time. You've helped me with everything else, but I need to work this out by myself."

"Okay. If that's what it's gonna take, I'll give you some time." He reaches out, caressing my cheek with his fingertips. I almost moan out loud, but I hold it in. "And even if you didn't answer my question, I'm gonna tell you… we're not over, baby. I'm coming back for you."

He turns and walks away, climbing into his car and driving off.

I get inside the house before my tears really start to fall, but almost immediately, I feel my mom's arms come around me.

"It's okay," she whispers.

I look up into her eyes. "I did the right thing, didn't I?"

"If you're not ready to talk to him yet, then yes, you did the right thing."

"I just need to think, Mom. I need to be sure that when I go back to him, we're both doing it for the right reasons."

"At least you said 'when', not 'if'."

"Now I've seen him, I know I want him back. But we can't rush at it. I have to be sure of him. After everything he said before, I have to know he means what he's saying now."

"I'm sure he does." I turn at the sound of Dad's voice. He's standing by the door, having made his own way in, and Mom rushes to him, helping him take the last steps. "I know I was kinda harsh with him just now, but you're still my little girl, and I'm always gonna be harsh with anyone who doesn't put you first."

I wander over and put my arms around his waist, leaning against him.

"You have to remember, love's a two-way street," Mom says. I turn to see she's glancing at Dad, her eyes sparkling, before she looks back at me again. "You have to allow for the other person's insecurities… because I think that's what we're talking about here."

"It sounded that way to me," Dad says, and I nod my head.

"His mom left when he was eleven, and although he doesn't blame her, I think he felt abandoned." He always sounded that way whenever he spoke about it.

"His relationship with his father can't have been easy, either," Mom says.

I shake my head. "Hunter never got along with him, even before his mom left. Afterwards, they rarely saw each other, although I don't think that was a bad thing. From what Hunter's told me, I think Theodore Bennett was probably a very cruel man."

"I'm not gonna argue with that," Mom says. "I didn't know him very well, but he was ruthless in his pursuit of me, when he thought I was guilty of helping Ken, and when it came to taking back the property he considered was rightfully his…" She shudders and Dad moves over, letting her nestle against him.

"He told Hunter that his mom had left him and Drew and Ella behind because she didn't love them."

Mom and Dad both stare at me, wide-eyed, their mouths open. "H—He said that? To his face?" It's Dad who speaks first. I'm not sure Mom's capable.

"Yes."

"That's a d—diabolical thing for anyone to say."

Mom steps forward, coming closer to me again. "It sounds like he had a tough childhood."

"A tough adulthood, too. He was cheated on by his ex-girlfriend…" I let my voice fade, wondering if I should have said that, but Mom just nods her head.

"Ahh. That explains it."

"Explains what?"

"Why he finds it so hard to trust people. I'm guessing that, when he met you, he thought he'd found someone different. Discovering you're Ken Bevan's daughter probably made him feel as though his world had come crashing down around him."

"I know. I understand that. But even I didn't know who I was. So why did he blame me?"

"I guess he just assumed the worst."

"Hmm… and that's the part that hurts the most."

Dad moves forward too now, taking a little longer to join us. "Will you take some advice from me?" I nod my head. "Will you allow for the fact that people make mistakes?"

"This was a big mistake, Dad."

"It was. But that's all the more reason for giving yourself some time to work it out. One thing you can't do is to spend the rest of your lives throwing this back in his face. You have to be sure you've put it behind you, so you can move forward together."

"It's the only way," Mom says as I look at them, leaning against each other, their heads bent close, and I know they're right.

## *Hunter*

I take just over three hours to drive to Newport, which is roughly what I would have expected. I'm not in any hurry to drive away from Livia, so I stick to the speed limits all the way, and pull up outside the house just after lunch.

I thought about going straight back to the city, but couldn't face it without Livia. Now I'm here, though, I'm not sure this is going to be any easier. In fact, I think it might be harder... the memories are more difficult to take.

I climb from the car, closing the door, and pop the trunk.

"Hunter?" I turn, hearing my name, and see Pat coming down the steps from her and Mick's apartment, above the garage. She's frowning at me, looking confused. "What are you doing here?"

I wonder about using Drew's line and reminding her I live here, but in the end I just say, "It's a long story."

She starts toward me and I step away from the car, meeting her halfway as she looks up into my face. I know she can see right through me, and it's an uncomfortable feeling at the moment. I'm too ashamed of my actions, and too raw for close scrutiny.

"Do you want anything? I can..."

I shake my head. "No, thanks. I'm fine, Pat." That's about as far from the truth as anything I've ever said. "I'll fend for myself. You enjoy the rest of your weekend."

"You didn't bring Livia with you?" she says, glancing into my car.

"No."

She looks into my eyes, hers softening, and then she takes my hand, giving it a gentle squeeze. "Let me know if you need me."

Why did she have to say that? A lump rises in my throat, and I struggle to swallow it down. I can't speak, but I nod my head, and with a slight smile, she lets go of me and turns, making her way back up the stairs again.

I give myself a minute, breathing deeply, and then grab my bag from the trunk, closing it again, before I let myself into the house. It feels cool in here compared to outside, and I set my bag down at the foot of the stairs, soaking up the quiet stillness. I'm not willing to face my bedroom yet, so I make my way through to the kitchen to get a drink.

The glass doors are wide open, and I can hear voices outside.

"Why did you sleep with her?" That's Ella and I can hear the smile in her voice, even from here.

"Why do you think?" Drew's reply is typical of him, and although I'm not feeling very sociable, I can't ignore them, so I wander out and find them lounging by the pool. Drew's wearing black shorts and a very fine tan, but my attention is drawn to Ella... not because her bikini is only just decent, but because it's been so long since I've seen her. She's changed. Her dark hair is cut shorter, and I'd say she's been visiting a gym. She seems more toned than I remember. She notices me first and sits up, pulling off her sunglasses and smiling, her hazel eyes sparkling at me.

"Hunter? I didn't think you were coming down this weekend. Pat said..."

"I know. I changed my mind."

Drew sits up too, frowning. "Something's happened." He gets to his feet, coming straight over, and Ella follows. "This is about Livia, isn't it?" he says.

"Yes."

"Oh, God... what have you done now?" Ella rolls her eyes and I turn to her.

"I haven't done anything... at least, I haven't done anything wrong."

"That's what you think. Although I'd like to point out, you didn't think it was wrong to fire the woman you claim to be in love with."

"We all make mistakes."

"There are mistakes, and then there are mistakes. This is the latter."

"Let's go inside," Drew says. "I could do with a drink."

He leads the way, and I let Ella follow him, bringing up the rear. Inside, Drew goes straight to the refrigerator, grabbing some water, while Ella fetches three glasses, and I sit at the island unit. They join me, Drew pouring the water, and Ella passing it out, before they sit, either side of me. This feels ominous, and part of me wants to run and hide… although I don't know where I'd go. I feel surrounded by memories here, and while all of them are good, I can't face them at the moment.

Not when my future looks so bleak.

"What's happened?" Drew asks, taking a long sip of water before he turns to face me.

"I went to see Livia."

"At her apartment?"

I turn to him. "No. She wasn't there. She'd gone home."

"Home being?" Ella asks, and I turn the other way.

"Falmouth, in Maine."

"Okay." She nods her head. "So, you drove up to Maine…"

They're both waiting and I know there's no point in pretending nothing happened, when it so clearly did.

"I got there yesterday afternoon, and her mom answered the door. Livia was there, but she wouldn't see me. She wouldn't even come to the door."

"I don't blame her," Ella says.

"Neither do I." My reply seems to surprise her, but before she can say anything, Drew gets there first.

"What did you do next?" he asks.

"I found myself a hotel, and stayed there for the night, and then I drove back to Livia's place this morning."

"With what in mind?" Drew says.

"I had no idea. I couldn't see the point of knocking on the door again, so I just sat there for a while, thinking, and getting nowhere. Then, suddenly, the door opened, and Livia appeared."

"So you spoke to her?"

"Yes. Although she wasn't very keen on the idea. She was so hurt... so angry." I'm never going to forget the look in her eyes when she asked me to let her go. It's going to haunt me for the rest of my life.

"That's a surprise?" Ella's sarcasm isn't lost on me.

"No. Not at all. But then her dad came out."

"Her Dad?" Drew raises his voice slightly. "You mean Ken Bevan?"

"No." I shake my head.

"So, she's not his daughter, after all? You got it wrong?"

"No. I got it right. She is Ken Bevan's daughter... but he's not her dad."

"Whoa... hold on." Ella slaps her hand down on the countertop. "I'm confused."

"The man who came out of the house was Connor Hopkins. He raised Livia. He's her dad... in her eyes, and everyone else's. Ken Bevan was married to her mom and was there at her conception, but that's about as far as it goes."

"I see," she says slowly, like she's taking it all in. "So, was there a conspiracy between them?"

"No. Her dad explained to me, in no uncertain terms, that Livia had no idea about her background until Friday night, when she went home and told her parents what I'd done... and they had to tell her the truth."

"Meaning, it was all a coincidence… like we said." There's a hint of a gloat in Drew's voice, but I can't blame him for that.

"Yeah… just like you said. Her dad was getting kinda worked up, and her mom told him to calm down, in case he had another stroke."

"*Another* stroke?" Drew frowns. "Did you know about that?"

"Of course not. I told you the other day, Livia hadn't mentioned her father to me at all. I had no idea he was so sick, and I would have backed off then, anyway… except Livia came at me."

Ella puts her hand on my arm, and I turn to her. "She just wanted to protect her dad, Hunter."

"She was mad at me."

"She was entitled to be."

"I know. I get that."

"Is it over?" Drew asks, cutting to the chase.

"As far as I'm concerned, it'll never be over, but…"

"She doesn't feel the same?"

I shrug my shoulders. "I don't know. She said she's not ready to forgive me, or trust me, or to talk, and I've said I'll give her time…"

"Then that's what you have to do," Ella says. "I'm sorry, Hunter, but you're the one who screwed up. That means Livia gets to call the shots now."

It's strange, but I can't imagine Livia calling the shots. She's too shy.

"It looks like you're gonna have to be patient," Drew says, and I suck in a breath.

"I know."

"Why are you so down?" Ella says, and I turn to look at her. She's smiling up at me, and tips her head to one side. "At least she's giving you a chance."

"I get that, and I appreciate it. It's just… she's so hurt, and it's my fault."

"And you want to make it right again?"

"Yes."

Ella leans in. "Give her what she's asking for. It'll be fine."

If only I had her confidence. But I guess she didn't see Livia's face when she said I'd hurt her… or the look in her eyes.

I know I've said I'll go back, but I wish I had some faith in the outcome.

"Can we change the subject?" I say. I'm done talking.

"Sure," Ella says, sitting back again, and I turn to Drew.

"Who did you sleep with?"

He frowns. "Sorry?"

"When I got here, I heard the two of you talking. Ella asked why you'd slept with someone."

His face clears. "Oh, I see. It was a model."

"Really?" He's usually very hands-off with models, which I guess means she must have been special.

"Yeah… and now I know why I usually leave them alone."

"It didn't work out then?"

"That's one way of putting it."

"What happened?" I ask. "Did the client not like it?"

He shakes his head. "The client doesn't know about it, and in this instance, I doubt they'd care. They've got bigger problems to worry about."

"Like what?"

"Like re-arranging that shoot I had in the Caribbean."

"Is that likely to be a problem?"

"It is when all the models have taken on work elsewhere, and I don't have enough free time in my calendar for months."

"Which shoot was this?" Ella says, sipping her water.

"One I had when you were still in Paris," Drew explains. "It had to be called off because the weather was so bad."

"And because the models got sick, if I remember rightly," I say, finishing his story.

"One of them didn't." He lets out a sigh.

"I see. And can we assume the two of you found something else to keep you occupied?"

"Yeah. I didn't take it too seriously…"

"Do you ever?" Ella says under her breath, although it's loud enough for both of us to hear. Drew frowns, but I don't say a word. I can hardly judge, given my background.

"Maybe not, but when we got home, Lexi called and asked if I'd like to go visit her in New York, and with the shoot having been called off, I didn't have anything better to do, so…"

"Didn't you have another assignment lined up?" I ask. "I thought that was where you'd been for the last few weeks."

"I made that up."

"You mean you've been in New York all this time? With Lexi?"

"Yeah. I was due to be away for three weeks, and had allowed for editing as well, so I had plenty of time to kill. The problem was, when you took away the sun, sand, beaches and lack of clothes… it just wasn't the same. We both knew it almost straight away, and it was only a matter of time before one of us said something."

"I don't see the problem. Not if you both feel the same way."

"The problem is, I plucked up the courage to break it off with her last weekend… only rather than coming straight out with it, I told her I had to get back to Boston. That wasn't strictly true. I don't have anything lined up until next week, but I thought I'd make my escape and call her. It felt easier to end it over the phone."

"Coward," Ella mutters.

"I know. I'm not proud of myself, but my plan backfired anyway."

"How?" I ask.

"Because she said she was going there, too. I hadn't expected that… or the invitation she issued to a friend's birthday party. That was the last thing I needed when I knew I was about to break up with her. Only I couldn't think of a reason to get out of it."

"So you went?"

"Yeah. And when I was there, I met her sister… a—and I fell for her."

I can't hide my surprise and I lean back a little, staring at him. "You fell for her?"

"Don't sound so shocked. It might have been quick, but…"

"It's not the speed," Ella says, leaning forward so she can see him around me. "It's the fact that we're talking about you and love in the same sentence."

"Thanks." He lowers his head, and I turn and glare at Ella. She shrugs her shoulders, and I'm tempted to tell her to be a little more tactful. Okay, I may have been thinking exactly the same thing, but there was no need to say it out loud.

"I know how easy it is to fall," I say to him, and he looks up again, nodding his head.

"It just happened… in the blink of an eye. But now I don't know what to do. I spent the entire evening talking to Lexi's sister, not Lexi. Obviously, it was damn awkward when she realized who I was, but what could I say? I'd already fallen for her by then. I know she's the one for me, and I've broken things off with Lexi. It's the right thing to do, for all of us, but how can I possibly ask her sister out?"

"You can't," Ella says. "Even if Lexi doesn't care—which you can't know for sure, when it's her sister who's involved—I don't see how you can possibly hope to make it work. Her sister's gonna think you're the worst kind of player there is."

"That's what I thought." Drew shakes his head, letting out a long sigh before he turns to me. "I came to your office on Friday to ask your advice."

"Sorry. I wasn't having the best day."

"That's okay." He shakes his head. "But what I was gonna ask was, do you think it might help if I waited a while?"

I shrug my shoulders. "I think that depends on what you mean by 'a while'?"

"I don't know... as long as it takes, I guess."

I put my hand on his arm. "I know this is a new concept for you, but you could try making friends with her."

"Make friends?" he says, tilting his head. "With a woman?"

Ella laughs, and leans forward again, so she can see Drew. "It's not impossible, you know?"

"It is for me." He shakes his head. "I've never had a female friend in my life. I wouldn't know where to start."

"You could try calling her," Ella suggests.

"And then what? If I ask her for a coffee, or a drink, doesn't that make it a date?"

She rolls her eyes at him. "Only if you treat it like a date. You can just talk, drink coffee, and then go your separate ways."

He stares at her for a moment, like he's trying to fathom how that would work. "Surely, if we keep going for coffee, or drinks... or even dinner... that's just like dating, but without the sex."

"Oh, my God..." Ella's clearly getting exasperated and I hold up my hands, turning to Drew.

"Forget about sex and try calling her. See how she responds."

"To what?"

"You... you idiot."

He nods his head, although I wonder what right I have to give advice about dating, or women, given my current predicament.

In a way, I wish I'd been able to stay in Newport for a little longer, but responsibility beckoned, so I drove back to the city on Monday morning.

I surprised myself by spending the rest of Sunday afternoon and evening with Drew and Ella, and joining in the barbecue they'd planned, but in reality, I think I was just putting off that inevitable moment when I had to face the loneliness of my bedroom.

When I closed the door behind me, I was engulfed by memories, the sights and sounds of everything Livia and I had done in there swirling around my head. The room is swathed in our love, and there was no escaping it, even in my fitful sleep. I kept waking up, imagining she was beside me, the disappointment building every time I realized the bed was empty.

In the end, I was relieved to get up, and after my shower, I went downstairs to find Pat in the kitchen. There was no-one else around, and I sat while she made me some breakfast.

"I'm going back to the city," I said, and she turned to look at me, although she kept stirring the eggs.

"Today?"

"This morning. As soon as I've eaten."

She nodded her head and turned back again. "Will you be back next weekend?"

"I don't know. I'll call you."

She tipped the eggs onto a plate, adding some toast, and brought it over, putting it down in front of me.

"What's happened?" she asked.

I sighed. "I hurt Livia… badly. She's gone back to her parents' place in Maine."

"You've broken up?"

"I don't know. She said she needs some time to work out if she can forgive me, and if she can trust me again."

She frowned. "Y—You didn't cheat, did you?"

"No. It was nothing like that. But I screwed up, Pat. I really screwed up."

"Then you need to make it right again."

"I know. But first, I need her to let me."

She tipped her head slightly. "She might have asked you to wait, but don't let her make the running. Show her how much you want her back. Don't give her a reason to doubt that... not for a second."

"I don't want to crowd her."

"I'm not suggesting you do. But give her a few days... maybe a week, and then call her, just to see how she is. Don't pressure her for answers, but let her know you're thinking about her."

"Oh... I'm thinking about her."

Pat smiled then, and left me to eat my breakfast. Thirty minutes later, I was behind the wheel of my car, on my way back to the city. Ella and Drew still hadn't surfaced, but I asked Pat to let them know where I'd gone.

Since then, I've kept myself busy, and managed to get through the week.

It's been easier than I expected in some ways. Not having a PA has meant I've been rushed off my feet and haven't had time to think. I could have found a temp to cover, but the thought of anyone else sitting outside my office now is just wrong. So, I've worked late, which has helped, too. I haven't had to spend too much time at my apartment, and I've barely talked to anyone. Drew and Ella both called to check I was okay. It was good of them, and nice to know they care, but they wanted to talk about Livia... and I couldn't. I wanted to talk to her, and in the absence of that, I'd rather stay silent.

Some things have been harder than I'd thought. Seeing Livia's car in the parking garage every day is tough. It feels like a punishment... and a reminder of what I've lost.

It was only yesterday afternoon that I remembered I needed to call Pat, to let her know my plans for the weekend, and while a part of me hoped she might be busy, and I could leave a message, I wasn't surprised when she picked up on the third ring.

"How are you?" she said.

"I'm fine."

"Hmm... you sound it."

"Okay. I feel terrible, if you must know."

"And what are you doing about it?" It was typical of Pat not to let me wallow.

"Doing?"

"Yes. Are you sitting around feeling sorry for yourself, or are you...?"

"I've been working all week."

"And how does that help you get Livia back?"

"It doesn't, but like I said, I don't want to crowd her."

"Maybe not, but it's Friday. You've given her a week, or thereabouts... surely you can call her, can't you?"

Just the thought of hearing Livia's voice made my body shudder, and I wondered... how would she react? Would she tell me to back off? Or might she want to speak to me, too?

"I could..." I wasn't sure. Should I start with a text message instead? Would that be easier for her? I might have wanted to hear her voice, but... "Oh, shit."

"What's wrong?"

"I can't call her, or send a message."

"Why not?"

"Because she gave me back her phone. I don't have any way of contacting her."

"That's not strictly true. You could drive up there."

"And that wouldn't be crowding her?"

"Not if you handle it right, no. It won't help if you make assumptions about her."

"I'm never gonna do that again, Pat."

"That's not what I mean. What I'm trying to say is, you can't make her think you have any expectations. So, I wouldn't go tonight, if I were you."

"In case she thinks I'm expecting to stay?"

"Exactly."

"Do you really think this could work?"

She paused for a moment or two. "Put it this way… I don't think it can hurt."

I wondered if she might be right, and although we ended our call, with Pat wishing me luck, I was still undecided about what to do. It wasn't until this morning that I made up my mind… and that's why I'm driving up to Falmouth.

Because it can't hurt… can it?


I park outside Livia's house, noting the Chevrolet Camaro on the driveway. In a way, I'm surprised by her parents' choice of car. I'd expected them to have something a little more practical… but what do I know?

I'm feeling nervous now, but I've driven all the way up here, and I keep telling myself the worst that can happen is that Livia will tell me she's still not ready… so I'll be no worse off. In any event, unless I knock on the door, I'll never know.

I only have to wait a few moments before her mom answers, surprise registering in her eyes, although she hides it well, with a smile. This looks promising.

"Mr. Bennett."

"Call me Hunter, please." She nods her head. "Is Livia here?"

"She is." That's even more promising. She didn't even have to check this time. "Would you like to come in?"

I nod my head and step inside the house. "Thank you."

"I'm sorry about what happened the last time you were here... if we were a little harsh. My husband just wanted to protect Livia."

I turn to face her, noting that, with her hair worn loose like it is today, she looks even more like her daughter.

"I understand completely, and you have nothing to apologize for."

She smiles and steps into the house. "Please... come this way."

I'm actually being invited in? I can't believe it. My nerves vanish in an instant, replaced by excitement and anticipation... the longing to see Livia about to be fulfilled. Her mom leads me into their living room, stepping aside, and as she does, my eyes are instantly drawn to Livia, who's sitting on the couch... right beside Miles Hampton.

What. The. Fuck?

I glare at him as he turns, smiling up at me and raising the coffee cup he's holding. "Hello, Hunter. I didn't expect to see you here."

*Clearly.*

I look over at Livia, who's blushing, which doesn't surprise me in the slightest, and I wonder if her mom did this on purpose. Did she invite me in to show me what I've already lost? I ignore the pain in my chest and glance back at Miles again. I've never been a violent man, but I'd happily punch that smug grin off of his face.

"Is that your Camaro outside?"

"Yeah." He sits back now, looking right at home, and although I want to ask him why he's here, the reason seems fairly obvious to me. She's sitting beside him. I'm tempted to turn around and walk straight back out the door. Except I refuse to give him the satisfaction... or her, for that matter.

"Can I get you a coffee?" Livia's mom asks.

"Um… no, thanks." She frowns, presumably wondering why I've driven all the way here.

I'm wondering about that myself now.

Miles sits forward in his seat, putting his cup on the table in front of him. "Well… I guess I'd better be going." He looks at Livia's parents, her mom standing beside her father, who's sitting in a chair opposite Livia. "It's been so nice meeting you."

He stands, and Livia copies him, although it's her mom who steps forward.

"I'll show you out," she says, and he nods his head before turning back to Livia again.

"Thanks for today. It's been lovely. I'll see you again soon… hopefully."

*What the hell have they been doing?*

She doesn't reply, but just smiles, looking embarrassed, and as Mrs. Hopkins moves toward the door, he follows her, keeping his head down and refusing to make eye-contact with me.

I'm staring at Livia, and she's looking at the space between us, her hands clasped in front of her.

"I—I think I'll go lie down for a while," her father says, and he struggles to get up.

"Can I help?" I step forward, but he shakes his head.

"No, thanks. I'll get there."

I move away again and watch him stand, waiting while he gains his balance, and then takes his walking stick, gingerly putting his weight on one foot, and then the other, limping from the room.

Once he's gone, I turn back to Livia again. She's looking at me now, with her head tilted slightly to one side.

"Dad doesn't normally let people see him do that," she says.

"Do what?"

"Struggle. He hates the fact that he can't do things like he used to."

"Well, I guess he could sense the atmosphere and was just desperate to get out of here." I huff out a sigh. "I know how he feels."

She steps closer, glaring up at me. "What does that mean?"

"It means I drove up here so we could talk. I was gonna stay at the hotel again tonight, so we could try to work things out between us over the weekend. It's been hell without you, Livia. All I've been able to think about is seeing you again... and yet I get here and find you cozying up with Miles Hampton."

"Cozying up? Is that what you...?" She stops talking, her cheeks pinking. "How dare you?"

"Why was he thanking you for such a lovely time?"

"How the hell should I know? Maybe he enjoyed being here."

"When did he arrive?"

"Why? Are you wondering if he stayed the night?" Her eyes are on fire, her anger matching mine now.

"Well? Did he?"

"No. He got here about nine-thirty this morning, if you must know." So two hours before me...

"Did you invite him?"

"Of course not. But I didn't invite you, either... and as your opinion of me doesn't seem to have improved, I think it's gonna be better for both of us if you leave."

"That's just fine with me."

I turn and head for the door. Her mom's nowhere to be seen, but I guess she's decided to give us some space, just like her father did... not that it matters. We don't need space. We need a goddamn referee.

"I can't believe this," Livia says from behind me, as I open the door, and I turn to face her.

"What?"

"Do you know... I was gonna call you. I even went out and bought a new phone, and I looked up your number. I just needed to work out what I wanted to say. But if you're gonna accuse me of cheating, on top of everything else, there's really nothing left for us, is there?"

"I guess not."

I step outside, my feet carrying me to my car, even though my heart is telling them to stop... to turn back... to beg her forgiveness, yet again.

I hear the door slam behind me, and I know it's too late.

I've really blown it this time.

# Chapter Fourteen

*Livia*

It's been three hours since Hunter left and I'm still struggling to calm down.

I've come to my room because I can't face my parents' questions. They might have taken themselves off somewhere, but they'll have heard everything Hunter and I said to each other. We weren't exactly being quiet.

I turn over on my bed, staring out the window.

How could he think that of me? I've lost track of the number of times I've asked myself that question, but seriously... how could he?

Why would he think I'd want to 'cozy up' with Miles Hampton? He knows perfectly well that I don't like the man.

And to think... I was actually going to call Hunter this afternoon. I'd even told my mom. That's probably why she showed him straight into the living room; because she knew I intended to speak to him.

I startle at the sound of a gentle knocking on my door.

"Come in," I say and it opens. My mom appears, followed by my dad, the two of them standing on the threshold.

"Is everything okay?" Mom asks.

"No."

She comes a little further into the room and Dad steps up behind her. "We heard you and Hunter arguing."

I sit up, making room for Dad to perch beside me, while Mom goes over to the window seat, getting comfortable.

"I can't believe what he said to me."

"We gathered he didn't like Miles being here," Mom says, frowning slightly. Her confusion is easy to understand. None of this makes sense to me, either.

"No, he didn't. He accused me of cozying up with him."

"Cozying up?" Her lips twist upwards, although she quickly brings them back into line again.

"Yeah. He seemed to think Miles had spent the night here… or at the very least, that I'd invited him to visit. Well, I'm done being judged by him." My voice cracks as I'm speaking, and tears fill my eyes.

"Did you honestly believe Miles when he said he'd come to talk about the termination of your contract?"

"Of course not. There's nothing to talk about, and he didn't even mention the contract at all… not once he'd got his foot in the door."

"No. I noticed that."

Dad leans in to me. "D—Didn't that make you wonder?"

"About what?"

"Why he was really here?" I turn slightly, looking up at him. "Miles was so clearly interested in you. Hunter probably saw that, too, even if you didn't."

"And? That doesn't make me guilty of anything."

"No, but imagine how you'd feel if you saw Hunter with someone who you thought was interested in him. Even if it wasn't reciprocated, how do you think you'd feel?"

"Oh… God." I don't need to think, I already know.

"What?" Mom sits forward slightly.

"I've just remembered." I look over at her and she raises her eyebrows, waiting. "There was a woman…" I stop talking as I realize I can't tell them about the stalking. They'll be livid I've kept it to myself all this time, and I can't face going through it all again. Not now.

"What about her?" Mom says, prompting me.

"She had some business with Hunter, and the way he introduced her made me think she was an ex-girlfriend of his. He and I weren't seeing each other at the time, but I liked him… a lot, and I was…"

"Jealous?" Dad says.

"Yes, I was. I practically ignored him for nearly a week… until he explained the misunderstanding."

"That she wasn't his ex-girlfriend?"

"No. She was his brother's ex-girlfriend."

Mom smiles. "You see? It's easy to over-react… to misconstrue someone's actions."

"I didn't do anything wrong, though."

"And did Hunter, when he introduced his brother's ex?"

"Well… no." On the contrary. He was doing his best to help me at the time.

Dad puts his arm around me, pulling me in to a hug. "We're not saying H—Hunter was right to say the things he said, or that you're not entitled to be angry with him. B—But…" He looks over at Mom, struggling to talk.

"You told us he'd been cheated on," she says.

"Yes."

"I know what that feels like. Ken cheated on me, and although I didn't love him, I felt used and hurt… and totally inadequate." Dad sighs and she looks at him, smiling. "When I met your father, I made his life a misery for a while."

"N—Not a misery," he says.

"Okay… I made it very difficult."

"How?" I ask.

"I used to quiz him every time I saw him… wanting to know where he'd been and who he'd been with. If he was ten minutes late, I convinced myself he'd been with someone else. I never allowed myself to think rationally… that he'd been held up by a student, or a colleague, or even just traffic. No… it had to be that there was another woman involved. It went on for quite a long time until eventually your father persuaded me I didn't need to feel insecure anymore. He loved me, and he wasn't going to leave me. Not for anything, or anyone."

"You're saying that's how Hunter feels?"

"He might do… or at least a version of it. His father's attitude won't have helped."

I close my eyes, letting their words wash over me for a moment as I recall Hunter telling me about Sadie, and how he felt when he found her and Austin together. "I shouldn't have yelled at him, should I?"

"He made you angry," Dad says.

"Yeah, but venting that anger at him didn't help the situation. It just made it worse. I should have talked to him. I should have told him how it felt to be accused, and discussed it with him… calmly."

"Don't beat yourself up over it. This wasn't your fault."

"But it wasn't his either, was it? Not this time. Not really."

Mom smiles. "Why don't you call him?"

"And say what? Where would I even begin?"

"I don't know, but you have to start somewhere." She nods toward my phone, which is on the nightstand, just as it beeps and her smile widens.

"That won't be him," I say before she jumps to conclusions. "He doesn't know my number."

I grab the phone, flipping it over and look down at the screen. It's an email from my music streaming app, telling me that this month's payment has just gone through successfully, and I let out a sigh.

"What's the matter?" Dad asks.

"I'm gonna have to cancel this subscription before it goes out again. I can't afford things like music streaming right now."

I click on my web browser and wait for it to open, as my parents get up and start for the door. There hasn't been time to put my banking app on my phone yet, but I know from experience that, if I want to cancel a payment, I have to do it online. I input a pin number, and wait for my account details to come up, and then my blood turns to ice and I let out a slight cry, clamping my hand over my mouth. Mom's back with me in an instant, right by my side.

"What's wrong, Livia?"

"I—I don't understand."

"What don't you understand?"

"I—I haven't looked at my bank account since the day before Hunter fired me. I had some bills to pay, and I checked my balance first."

"And?" Dad comes over too, looking down at me.

"I had over five hundred dollars in my account."

"And you've got less than you thought?" Mom says. "Because don't forget, you paid for your bus ticket, and you've bought your phone."

I shake my head. "It's not less... it's more."

I hand her the phone and she stares down at it. "Oh, my God." She flops onto the bed beside me. "It must be a mistake. The bank... I mean..."

"What is it?" Dad says.

"The balance is two hundred and fifty thousand, four hundred and twenty-one dollars."

Dad sucks in a breath. "Did you say two hundred and fifty thousand...?"

"Yes." Mom looks back at the screen again. "There must be a payment into the account," she says, scrolling down.

"It's a bank error, Mom. I'll contact them on Monday and..."

"You don't need to," she says, sighing and handing me back the phone. "Look who sent the payment."

I glance down, my breath catching in my throat as I read the name 'H. Bennett' beside the amount.

"Hunter?" I say, looking back up at her again.

She nods her head. "And look at the date on it."

I do as she says, unable to hold back my tears when I read that the date of the payment was the day he fired me.

"H—He must think I'm so rude. I've had this money for over a week, and I haven't even thanked him." I haven't asked him why, either... and I probably need to, although I guess this makes sense of his confusion when I said I wasn't sure I had enough money to buy new clothes. He'd have known then that he'd put this money into my account... even though I didn't.

"I think maybe you need to put that right, don't you?" Mom says, just as the doorbell rings.

"I'll get it," she says, rushing from the room, and Dad puts his arm around me.

"He loves you, sweetheart. Maybe you just need to let him."

"I need to thank him, too."

He smiles. "Well, you weren't sure how to start your conversation with him, so maybe this is your answer."

"Hmm... maybe it is."

Mom appears in the doorway, carrying the most enormous bouquet I've ever seen.

"Sh—Should I be jealous?" Dad says, smiling.

"No. They're for Livia."

I put down my phone and take the flowers from her. There's a card buried in the foliage and I pull it out, reading the word 'Sorry'. That's all it says, but I know who they're from.

"Hunter?" Mom says, and I nod my head. "Shall I put them in a vase for you?"

"Yes, please."

She takes the flowers back, and Dad gets up. "We'll leave you in peace for a while."

I know they're going so I can talk to Hunter. It's what I want to do. It's what I need to do as well. But what if we end up fighting again? Maybe talking isn't the best idea. Maybe I should start off more simply… just with words, and not emotions.

I suck in a breath and pick up my phone. I've already stored his number in my contacts list, so I find it and type…

— *Thank you. Livia x*

It seems a good idea to keep it simple to start with, and I add the kiss as in instinct.

His response is immediate.

— *After what I did this morning, I didn't think I'd hear from you ever again, or that you'd be so gracious. I hope you like the flowers, though. xx*

— *I love the flowers. They're beautiful. But that's not the only thing I'm thanking you for. I just checked my bank account. I didn't realize what you'd done, and I'm sorry I didn't thank you sooner. x*

I send my reply, hoping it's enough, and he comes back straight away.

— *You don't have to thank me. Can I call you? I need to hear your voice. xx*

— *Okay xx*

It looks like words aren't enough. We need emotions, too, and I suck in a breath, holding my phone, although I only have to wait a matter of seconds before it rings.

"Hello?"

"Hi." He might have said he needed to hear my voice, but he wasn't alone. The sound of that single word makes every nerve in my body spark to life, and my skin tingles, my heart skipping a beat. I needed this, too. "A—Are you okay?"

"Yes, thank you."

I hear him sigh. This isn't going as well as I'd hoped. It feels awkward, and nothing like it used to be. "Do you remember when you said you liked me voicing my feelings?" he says.

"Yes." I was lying in his arms, in bed, in Newport... before it all went wrong.

"Would you mind if I told you how I'm feeling now?"

"No." I feel a little nervous, but I can't stop him. It would be selfish and unkind.

"I'm scared, Livia. Really fucking scared."

"What of?"

"That I've gone too far this time... that you won't be able to forgive me."

"Why did you assume the worst of me, Hunter? You know I'm not interested in Miles. You know I don't even like him, so why did you assume—"

"Because I overreacted. It seems I'm quite good at it."

"I guess you're not alone in that."

"How do you work that out?"

"My parents spoke to me. I was so angry after you left, and they wanted to help. They tried to explain how it might have looked to you, finding Miles here, even though there was nothing going on, and they reminded me of how I'd felt when Keira came into the office."

"They knew about that?"

"No, but I've told them now. Not in any great detail, obviously. I haven't told them what Lucian did, but they asked me to imagine how you'd have felt, and I realized I didn't need to imagine it at all. I—I treated you so badly over Keira, and you were so kind..."

"Hey… don't you dare blame yourself for this. It's my fault."

"We both made mistakes this time, Hunter. I should've talked to you, not yelled at you."

"You wouldn't have needed to, if I hadn't judged you so quickly… again."

He's not wrong there, I suppose, but there seems little point in going over the same ground now. We both know we got things wrong.

"Can we change the subject?"

"Sure."

"Why did you give me the money?" I ask. I need to know… to understand. "You paid it to me on the same day you fired me. I didn't expect anything, but even if I had, it would have been whatever the severance payment is, not a quarter of a million dollars."

"It wasn't about severance. It was about us. That's why the money's from me, not the company. Drew had told me he'd found you in the parking garage, crying. I didn't want to believe him at first. I was so convinced I was right, that you'd been lying to me… conniving with Ken Bevan in some way. But when Drew told me what he'd seen, and we'd talked it through some more, I started to wonder."

"But why pay me? And why so much?"

"Drew said I was behaving like my father…"

"You weren't, Hunter."

"Yeah, I was. I'd made it about me, not about us. I'd hurt you. Drew said I'd broken you. Even if I didn't understand what was going on, I had to do something. I needed to know you were gonna be okay… financially, if nothing else."

He's thinking so badly of himself, but I don't know what to say to make it better. If he were here, I'd hug him… but he's not. And I need him to be.

"Can you come over?"

## Hunter

I pinch myself on the arm. It hurts and I smile. This has to be real, even though I feel like I'm in a dream. Livia asked me to come over... and I'm already making my way to the elevator.

"Of course. But you'll have to give me a couple of hours. If I leave now, I can be with you before six."

"Why is it going to take you so long? You're only in Portland. It's not..."

"I'm not in Portland. I'm in Boston," I say, interrupting her.

"You went home?" She sounds surprised, and I smile. "I thought you were gonna stay at a hotel."

"I was. But then we had a fight. You told me there was nothing left for us... remember?"

"Yes. I'm so—"

"Don't you dare say 'sorry'. This is on me."

"I—I didn't realize you were gonna leave."

"Doesn't mean I can't come back."

"You mean, you'd really drive all the way back here again... for me?"

How can she still not get it? "I'll do whatever it takes, if it means I'm forgiven."

"I'm worried about you driving up here, Hunter. Maybe I should come to you. I can catch a bus, and..."

"I'm already on my way." The elevator door opens. "I'll be there as soon as I can."

"Okay."

"Livia?"

"Yes?"

"I love you."

I hang up before she can answer. It hasn't escaped my notice that she's avoided saying she forgives me, and I don't want to hear her struggling over saying she loves me. I'm not sure I could handle that.

It occupies my mind throughout the journey, though. Asking me to come see her, isn't the same as saying we're okay... or that I'm forgiven... or that she loves me, like I love her, and by the time I park outside her parents' house, I'm more full of nerves than I've ever been in my life. This feels like make or break... but what I'll do if it's break, I don't know.

I switch off the engine, sucking in a deep breath, which catches in my throat when I turn to see Livia standing on the doorstep, waiting for me. She's wearing jeans and a white t-shirt and is biting on her bottom lip, looking doubtful, and I climb from my car, walking straight to her. She stares up into my face, and for a moment, neither of us says a word. I'd like to think that's because we don't need to... but we do. At least, I do.

"You haven't said you forgive me yet."

"I know." She sucks in a deep breath.

"Is that because you can't? Do you need more time?"

She shakes her head, which ought to feel promising. Except it doesn't.

"It's because I need to tell you something." I wait, fear clawing at my spine. Are we over? Is this it? Did she get me up here to tell me to my face we're through? "Do you remember me telling you that leaving you would break me?" she says.

"Yes."

"Well, it did. Drew was right about that. It broke me, and..."

"You mean *I* broke you."

She shakes her head. "This isn't about blame, Hunter. I'm just trying to explain how fragile I am. I didn't know it before, but I do now... and I know I couldn't do this again."

"Neither could I. My heart is made of glass when it comes to you. But if you think you can forgive me, and you're willing to give us another chance, we'll never have to do this again... I promise."

She frowns. "Can it be the same, though?"

"Of course it can."

"But you know how it is when something gets broken and you fix it? Sometimes it's never quite the same again."

I bring one hand up, holding it behind her head. "It'll be the same. Who knows? It might even be better."

"Is that possible?"

"Anything's possible. Especially if I learn from my mistakes. Please... just let me try."

She tips her head again. "They weren't all your mistakes, and shouldn't we both be trying?"

"No. You just need to be yourself, exactly like you always were. I'm the one who needs to try harder... to prove you can trust me." I pull her close, my lips grazing her ear. "To prove how much I love you."

"You have nothing to prove," she whispers. "I know you love me... and I love you, too, Hunter. Just please... please don't break me again."

"I couldn't, baby. There's no way I can ever do that to either of us again. I need you too much."

She shudders in my arms, my cock hardening. "I need you, too."

I lean back, staring into her eyes, seeing the fire within them, and I know we're back... back where we belong. "God... I wanna fuck you, so damn hard."

She gasps, her eyes widening, and I bend my head, crushing my lips to hers. We've kissed so many times before, in so many ways, but it's never been like this. There's a hunger in both of us that won't be sated and we devour each other. Nothing exists, other than this moment... this wild, desperate moment, and she clings to me, her fingers twisting into my hair, her sighs meeting my groans. Time passes, the world moves on, but we're caught... together, until she pulls back, breathless, her lips a little swollen and her eyes alight.

"You want more?" I whisper, and she nods her head, a smile touching at her lips, a blush creeping up her cheeks. I have to smile back. At least one thing is exactly the same as it was before. She's still just as beguiling as ever. "We will... but I think we'd better go inside and see your parents, don't you?"

I feel her body sag in my arms, and I want to laugh; her disappointment is so obvious.

"You'll take me back with you tonight?"

I'm about to say 'yes', when I realize I need to be sure. "Where exactly would I be taking you?"

"To your apartment, of course. I'm only asking because you've driven backwards and forwards so many times today, I thought you might be too tired to make the journey again. But where else would I be talking about?"

"I don't know, but I'm guessing you still have your own apartment in Boston?"

"I do. But I'd rather come back to your place, if that's okay."

"Of course it's okay," I say, bending my head to kiss her, although I keep it brief. "I just needed to check, that's all. I'm not taking anything for granted, baby."

She smiles, nestling against me, and although I'll admit to being exhausted, I can't wait to get her home...

"Shall we go in?" she says, after a moment or two, and I nod my head, letting her go, but keeping a firm grip on her hand.

We make our way into the house, and I close the door, letting Livia lead us through to the living room, where her parents are sitting beside each other, in separate chairs. Her mom stands, although her dad remains seated, and I recall Livia saying this morning, how he hates for people to see him struggling.

"Mom... Dad... this is Hunter," Livia says. We've already met, but I don't blame her for making formal introductions. It feels appropriate, somehow.

"It's nice to meet you," her mom says with a smile. "Please, call me Julianne, and my husband is Connor."

I step forward, and as her father holds up his left hand, I switch, and shake with my left, too, before stepping back again, and putting my arm around Livia. She leans against me, like she wants to let her parents know she's okay with me touching her... not that they seem unhappy. They're both smiling.

"I want to apologize," I say and they look up at me. Livia does, too, confusion etched on her brow.

"What for?" she asks, and I lean in and kiss the tip of her nose.

"Nothing to do with you, for once." I turn back to her mom and dad, although I focus most on Julianne. "I want to apologize to you, on behalf of my family, for what my father did to you."

Julianne shakes her head. "It's ancient history now. Please don't worry about it."

I turn to Livia, smiling down at her. "I feel even worse now."

"What about?"

"About all the things I said to you... about blaming you for what happened. Your family are so gracious, and when I think about..."

She reaches up, placing her fingertips gently over my lips, silencing me. "You weren't to know, Hunter. You only knew the story your father gave you... just like I only knew what Mom and Dad told me."

She's right, but I think it might take me a while to forgive myself.

Julianne steps forward slightly. "I know you must be keen to get back to the city, and you've probably got a lot to do, but would you like to stay for something to eat?"

I assume she's talking to me, but then realize she's looking at Livia too. She's worked out already that Livia's coming home with me.

"We'd love to, Mom." Livia looks up at me, and then steps out of my embrace and moves closer to her mom. "Are you gonna be okay if I go back with Hunter?"

Her mom rests her hand on Livia's shoulder. "Of course we are, sweetheart."

"Why don't I take us out for dinner?" I suggest, and Livia and her mom both turn, looking at me.

"It... it's kinda tricky." Julianne glances down at Connor, and I wish I'd kept my mouth shut. Or at least thought about it first.

"We could order in, though, couldn't we?" Livia says, and her mom smiles.

"That would be lovely." She goes to Connor, crouching before him and taking his hand in hers. "Do you feel like pizza?" He nods his head, smiling, and she looks up at me again. "Is pizza okay?"

"Sure, but we can have anything you like."

She stands, coming closer and lowering her voice. "I know, but it's best not to give him too many choices... and pizza is easy for him to eat."

"Okay... pizza it is."

I pull out my phone, but once it's unlocked, I hand it straight to Livia to find a local delivery service, and make the selections for everyone. It seems simpler that way, and then she hands it back to me, so I can pay.

"While we're waiting," her mom says, sitting back down again, "why don't you go pack?"

Livia nods her head, taking my hand, and leads me toward the back of the house. I'll admit, I'm desperate to be alone with her, even if only briefly, but I pull her to an abrupt halt, noticing a room whose walls are lined with books.

"Is this your library?" I say as she looks up at me, smiling.

"Yes." She pushes the door open fully so we can go inside. "It's nowhere near as grand as either of yours, but…"

"I like it." I look around, noting the tidy desk in front of the window, and the couch that faces the bookshelves. "It's cozy." I study some of the books, which seem to be mostly about history, and then my eye settles on one with a familiar author. "Your dad wrote this?"

She smiles. "Yeah… he wrote quite a few of them. He was a lecturer in European History."

"Did this used to be his office?"

"Yeah. It's Mom's now…"

Her voice fades, and I pull her into my arms, all too aware of her sadness.

"Are you okay?"

She nods her head and pulls back, taking my hand again. "We should probably go pack."

I let her lead me from the room again, and down the hall to her bedroom, which makes me smile.

"What's wrong?" She's looking up at me and has obviously noticed my expression.

"Nothing… it's just that I sometimes forget how young you are."

She glances around the room, smiling herself. "Yeah… my dad decorated it when I was about fifteen and thought pink was the best color in the world."

It's not like a pink explosion in here, but there's no denying it's very girly.

I stay by the door, while Livia goes further into the room, grabbing her bag from the chair by the window, and putting it on the bed.

"Tell me about your dad," I say, watching her. "What happened?"

She's folding a t-shirt and looks up at me. "He was at work, reading through dissertations, when he realized he couldn't move his right arm."

"He was having a stroke?"

"Yeah, although he didn't know that at the time. Fortunately, a student came by, and was able to raise the alarm, otherwise things could have been…" Her voice fades, cracking slightly, and I walk over, turning her to face me and holding her close.

"How old were you?"

"Eighteen. I was about to graduate high school."

"But you weren't going to college, were you?" I remember her resume and am surprised when she nods her head.

"Yeah, I was. I had a place at Chicago."

"What were you gonna study?"

"History."

"Like your father?"

"Yes… exactly like my father. He'd studied there, too."

"Then why didn't you go?" I ask.

"When the time came, he was still in the hospital. I—I couldn't leave Mom by herself, trying to work, and visit him, and help with his rehab. I'd never have been able to live with myself, let alone study."

"So you stayed?"

"Yeah, and I got a job. I wanted to be here for them, but also to help financially, so Mom didn't have to worry."

"Do you still help financially?"

She nods her head. "Mom tells me not to, but I do it anyway."

I let her go, so she can get back to packing. "How long was he in the hospital?"

"Nearly seven months." She shakes her head. "At the beginning, he firmly believed he'd get back to normal, even though he'd lost the use of the right side of his body. Considering where he was, he's done amazingly well… but…"

"He gets frustrated?" I guess, and she sighs.

"Yeah, he does."

"That must be hard for your mom."

"It is. They used to be so close."

"They still are, Livia. Anyone can see that."

"I know, but their relationship has changed. Dad's focus has altered. Just getting through the day is a challenge. For Mom, it's different. She still remembers all the things they had before, and the life they'd planned for themselves. Only she doesn't even have ten seconds in the day to think about that, or herself. Her entire life revolves around Dad and whatever he needs. She puts a brave face on it, but sometimes, when she thinks no-one's watching, she looks so sad."

"She's mourning," I say and Livia spins around, staring up at me.

"Nobody died."

"I know, baby. She's not mourning for him. Her grief is for their relationship… and it's hard. What they had before has gone. Everything they were planning for has evaporated, and nothing can bring it back. And while it's nobody's fault, this isn't what they chose. She's reminded of that every day… probably every minute of every day, and that just makes it harder. It makes the grief eternal." A tear falls onto her cheek and I grab her, pulling her into my arms.

"I—I was only thinking the other day, after… after we broke up, that love's supposed to be eternal."

"It is, baby. It is." I bend my head and kiss her, just briefly. "Your parents are living proof of that." She sobs, her shoulders shaking. "Don't cry, Livia." I want to tell her I'll work something out to help them… but I need to think through how I'm going to do that, and I'm not about to make idle promises.

"I—I've been so stupid," she whispers into my chest and I lean back, looking down at her tear-stained cheeks.

"*You've* been stupid?"

She nods her head. "I should have realized better than anyone how easily life can be snatched away… that it's pointless to waste time arguing over things that don't matter."

I hug her tight. "We're not gonna waste any more time, baby… I promise."

There's nothing idle in that… nothing at all.


Livia's just zipped up her bag when the pizzas arrive, and we go through to the living room, eating there, rather than making Connor get up. Julianne helps him and it's easy to see how dependent he is on her, and how much love there is between them.

Time is moving on, though, and once we're all finished, I help Livia clear away the boxes, and collect up her bag, while she says goodbye to her parents.

Connor's got up in my absence, and he comes to the door to see us off, taking my hand in his when I thank them for their kindness.

"Y—You're welcome," he says. "And we'll see you both soon." He grips my hand firmly, staring into my eyes. He doesn't say so in as many words, but I think that's his way of telling me to take care of his daughter… although I don't need telling.

I hold Livia's hand all the way to my car, helping her into the passenger seat and putting her bag in the trunk before I wave goodbye to her mom and dad. They wave back, and then Julianne helps Connor inside the house, and I get into the car beside Livia.

"Are you okay?" I ask, starting the engine.

"I'll be fine."

"Sure?"

She nods her head, and I drive away, although I wait until we're on the freeway before I reach over and rest my hand on her leg. She startles slightly and twists in her seat, facing me. I know I said I wouldn't make promises, but I have to say something.

"It'll be okay, Livia."

"What will?"

"Everything."

She puts her hand over mine, and I smile. I still don't know how I'm going to make it okay for her parents, but I know I will.

They deserve it.


It's late when we get back, but as I help Livia from the car, all thoughts of tiredness are forgotten. All thoughts of everything are forgotten... except for getting up to my apartment as quickly as possible.

I stop to open the trunk, pulling out our bags, and Livia frowns, looking up at me.

"You brought a bag?"

"Of course I did. I told you this morning, I was gonna stay at the hotel. I just hadn't gotten around to taking it out of my car."

"Oh, I see."

She smiles and I close the trunk, taking her hand in mine, and leading her to the elevator.

Inside, I press the button for the penthouse, and then stand, looking down at her. She's gazing up at me, too, wide-eyed, her lips slightly parted, and I'm tempted to kiss her. I hold back, though. I may be impatient, but I need to get this right, and if I start something now, I won't be able to stop it.

The doors open and as we step out of the elevator, Livia glances at the table.

"You want to re-live old memories?" I whisper.

"Yes." She blinks, looking up at me.

"We will... but not right now."

I pull her into the apartment, dumping our bags, and then lead her up the stairs, opening the door to my room. She's breathless already, but so am I, and once I've closed the door, I spin her around, placing one arm around her waist, while I clasp her chin with the other hand, tipping her head back and kissing her. She comes alive, kissing me back... hard. Her hands wander up my arms, resting on my biceps, and she sighs in to me.

I pull back, looking down at her. "I'm so glad you're home." Without giving her time to reply, I reach down, pulling her top over her head, and then I unfasten her bra, releasing her breasts into my waiting hands. Her nipples are already hard and I lean in, biting one, which makes her squeal. I'm in a hurry, though, and I kneel, undoing her jeans and lowering them to the floor, along with her panties. She kicks off her clothes, along with her shoes and now she's naked, I feel I can slow down.

She's home at last.

I lift her and she wraps her legs around me, a smile etched on her lips. I know why, too. She loves being exposed like this... or 'open to me', as she put it. I love that, too, and I tip her onto the bed, kissing her again, before I work my way down her body, licking and biting on her nipples, and tracing a line of kisses across her flat stomach, until I reach my destination.

She parts her legs a little wider and I flick my tongue across her swollen clit. She bucks her hips, but I reach up, holding her down, licking her again, over and over. I lean back slightly and run my finger from her clit to her entrance, pushing inside her, before I gently bite on her, sucking her swollen nub into my mouth.

"That's so... so good," she mutters, as I flick my tongue over her again and again, her walls clamping down on my finger. She's close... I can feel it, and I add a second finger, which is all it takes to push her into a screaming orgasm. She writhes against me, even though I'm holding her down still, but I don't let up, no matter how wild she gets.

Eventually, she calms, her breathing returns to normal, and she stills. I kneel up, pulling my fingers from her soaking pussy, and raise my hand to my mouth, licking them clean. She stares at me, her tongue grazing over her lips, before I lean down and kiss her. She tastes herself – not for the first time – but there seems to be a hunger within her I've never seen before… and I want more.

I stand, quickly undressing, and then crawl up over her body, palming my cock and finding her entrance with ease. She raises her hips and I slide into her.

"Fuck… you're tight."

"You're huge." She sucks in a breath.

"It's been a while."

"I've missed you."

"Nowhere near as much as I've missed you, baby."

She reaches up, her hand cupping my cheek, and within seconds I'm hammering into her, although she matches me, move for move, breath for breath.

"M—More," she whispers. "Give me more."

I flip us over, so I'm on my back and she's straddling me. "You want more?" She nods her head. "Then take it… take whatever you need."

She raises herself up and slams down onto me, letting out a deep and satisfied groan, before repeating the process, over and over. I grab her ass, sitting up and she clings to me, her breasts crushed against my chest, as she grinds her hips, her sighs and moans building to a crescendo. I can't take much more.

"I'm gonna come… please, Livia."

As if at my command, she tips her head back, screaming my name, and I pull her down onto me, so I'm as deep inside her as I can be, when I fill her with everything I've got.

She's breathing hard against me, our bodies filmed with sweat, and I lie back down, bringing her with me, and then turn us onto our sides, so we're facing each other, still connected, still wrapped in each other.

"Can I ask you something?" I say, and she tips her head, looking up at me.

"Of course." Her voice is laced with fatigue, and I smile.

I pull her closer, holding her tight against me. "Will you move in with me?"

She leans up, a frown etched on her face as she rests her hand on my chest.

"You don't think we should slow things down? We've been through a lot over the last week or so. Don't you think we should take some time… get to know each other a little better…?"

"We already know each other pretty well, don't we?"

"You think?" she says, shaking her head. "After everything that's happened, I'm not sure I even know who I am anymore."

"Yeah, you do. You're Connor Hopkins's daughter. I've met him. He's a great man."

Tears well in her eyes, and she nestles in to me again. "So are you."

"I'm trying to be. It's not always easy, but I do a lot better when you're around. I need you here with me, Livia." She looks up at me and I cup her face with my hand, brushing my thumb along her bottom lip. "I'm not trying to rush you into anything, and if you really wanna slow things down, we can."

"How? How are we gonna take it slow if I'm living here?"

That sounds like she's saying 'yes' to my suggestion and I have to smile. "You can sleep in one of the guest rooms."

She frowns and lets out a sigh. "But I wanna sleep with you."

"I wanna sleep with you, too. I always did."

"So did I. I can still remember how much I dreaded having to spend the night without you."

"You don't have to… ever again. Tomorrow's Sunday, so we can start moving your things in, and…"

"Is this you not rushing me?" she says, although I can hear the tease in her voice.

"No, this is me not wasting any more time." She nods her head, smiling her acceptance. "It's the most precious thing we have, baby... apart from each other."

"And our love."

"And our love..."

# Epilogue

## *Livia*

I'd wondered if Hunter was joking when he said we were going to move my things the day after he brought me back to the city... but he wasn't.

We may not have moved everything on that Sunday, but we made a start, completing the task last weekend. I didn't have very much to move, and I'm sure we could have done it a lot faster if we hadn't continually been tempted to make use of my couch, that spent the entire time as a bed.

At one stage, I even suggested we should get someone in to help. We were lying, naked, curled up together in the twisted sheets.

"Why? I'm enjoying myself," Hunter replied.

"I think that much is obvious. But we're not getting very much done."

"Yes, we are. I'm learning a lot about you."

I rolled him onto his back then, lying on top of him. "Such as?"

"You're not great at keeping house."

I sat up, straddling him. "Well... thanks."

He chuckled, resting his hands on my thighs, probably in case I was thinking of getting up. I wasn't, but he didn't know that. "I wasn't trying to offend you."

"Oh? What were you trying to do?"

"Tell you what I've learned about you." He sat up, bringing me with him, and cradled me in his lap, looking down at me. "I know this is a couch, but I've never seen it as one… not even when we used to come by here before to collect your things, and even though most of your clothes are at my place, your closet is a disaster. Your books are all over the floor…"

"They're not all over the floor. They're stacked on the floor. There's a difference."

He nodded his head, then tipped me onto my back, nestling between my legs, and smiling down at me. "I'm not criticizing, Livia. I'm no good at keeping house, either."

"Really? Your place is immaculate."

"Yeah, because someone else does all that for me."

"I know they do in Newport, but…"

"They do here, too."

I frowned at him. "Seriously?"

"Yeah. Mrs. Edmonds comes in three times a week."

"How have I not noticed her?"

He bent his head, kissing me. "Because she comes in when we're at work."

"Does she do the laundry, too?"

"No. I do my own laundry… and yours too, most of the time."

I felt myself blush, realizing the truth of what he was saying. "You're right. I'm not great at all this… but I'll try harder."

"You don't have to. I love you, just as you are. Besides, I enjoy fooling around with your underwear… even when you're not wearing it."

I chuckled, and he kissed me, swallowing the sound, and although I asked if we ought to get up and get on with the job in hand, he told me there was no hurry… and we found a far better way to spend the next few hours.

Everything is done now, though, and I've officially given up my apartment and moved in with Hunter. The only thing I left behind was the bookcase. There was no point in building it, and he has enough space in his libraries for my books. So, I left it behind for whoever rents the place after me.

When we haven't been moving my things, and making love, we've been working. I thought we were busy before, but it's been even more crazy since I got back. There was quite a lot of work to catch up on after my enforced absence, but what made it worse was that Hunter had to fire Miles Hampton.

His decision had nothing to do with me, or with Hunter discovering Miles at my parents' place. It was entirely to do with one of the designers making a formal complaint about him.

She came to see Hunter on the Tuesday after I got back, and I could tell straight away that something was wrong. She was flustered and upset, and although she didn't have an appointment, I showed her into Hunter's office. He asked me to stay, which didn't surprise me, and when he turned back to the young woman, and asked why she'd come to see him, she burst into tears. I stepped forward, putting my arm around her, then Hunter and I waited until she'd calmed down so I could ask her name.

"Jenni Moore," she said, sniffling.

Hunter frowned, but then his face cleared. "You work in the design department, don't you?"

"Yes." She almost managed a smile, seemingly surprised that he knew who she was. "I've only been here for two weeks."

I knew Hunter didn't take responsibility for hiring the design staff directly, and left that to Miles, so I was just as surprised as Jenni that he'd remembered her.

"Can you tell us what's wrong?" I asked.

She turned to me, and then glanced at Hunter, and although I was tempted to ask if she'd rather speak to me alone, I couldn't see the point. It was him she'd come to see, after all.

"It's… it's about Miles Hampton," she said, and Hunter sat bolt upright.

"What's he done?" I could hear the anger lacing his voice, and although I wondered if that was connected to me, I sensed there was something more to it.

"H—He touched me."

Hunter stood, and I frowned at him, nodding back at his chair. Didn't he realize how intimidating he was? He quickly sat again, and I turned to Jenni. "Would you rather Hunter left us to talk alone?"

She shook her head, swallowing hard. "No… it's okay." She took a deep breath, looking down at her hands. "M—Miles came to see me earlier and told me I needed to go to his office."

"What for?" Hunter asked, keeping his voice quiet.

"He said there was a problem with my contract, but when I got there, he started talking about how much he liked me… and the next thing I knew, his hands were all over me, and he was trying to kiss me. I was telling him to stop, but…" Her voice faded and she gulped down more tears.

"Is that all he did?" Hunter asked, and I scowled at him. "I'm not belittling what's happened to you, Jenni," he said, speaking to her and not me. "It's just that I need to know if he did anything else to you? I need to know exactly what we're dealing with."

"Fortunately, his phone rang, and it distracted him enough for me to get out of there."

Hunter nodded his head and stood up again, although this time he didn't seem so threatening as he came around the desk, looking down at Jenni. "Do you want to go home? I can have someone take you?"

She nodded her head. "Would that be okay?"

"Of course. Do you have anyone who can be with you?"

"My mom."

"Good. If you need to take some time away from work, that's fine. I'll make sure you're paid in full. But rest assured, Mr. Hampton won't be here when you get back. You'll be safe to return here whenever you're ready."

She looked up at him, tears filling her eyes. "Thank you."

"What for?" He seemed confused by her response.

"For believing me. I wasn't sure you would. I thought you might side with him."

"I'd never side with anyone who'd do something like that," he said, smiling at her, and she nodded her head. "If you sit outside with Livia, I'll have someone take you home."

I escorted Jenni from the office and, sure enough, about ten minutes later, a smartly-dressed woman came and asked for her. Jenni went with her, and once they'd disappeared down the hall, I walked straight into Hunter's office.

"You arranged for a female driver?"

"I thought Jenni might prefer it," he said, looking up at me.

"And are you really gonna fire Miles?"

He nodded his head. "I've just finished speaking to one of the board members."

"Oh?"

"Yeah. I told him what happened and asked him to come here this afternoon. I'll need a witness, and in this instance, it can't be you." He tilted his head to one side, attempting a smile. "The guy coming in is called Patrick Malone and he'll be arriving around three. I've arranged with Miles to come by, too... at three-thirty."

"You didn't tell him why you want to see him?"

"No." He sighed. "I just wish I'd done something about him sooner."

"B—Because of me, you mean?"

We hadn't mentioned Miles since my return, but it felt like one of us needed to allude to the elephant in the room, and it might as well be me.

He got up, walking around his desk, and came to stand in front of me, cupping my face between both of his hands.

"No, baby. Not because of you. I hated seeing him at your parents' place, but I couldn't fire him for being there."

"Then I don't understand."

"There were rumors about him," he said.

"What rumors?"

"Nothing specific. That's always been the problem. I'd heard things about the way he spoke to female employees, and about the way he behaved around them sometimes, but no-one ever came to me with anything concrete. There was nothing I could act on, until now, but I wish I'd…"

I rested my hands on his chest. "This isn't your fault, Hunter."

He kissed me then… really hard, holding my body tight against his. I could feel his arousal pressing in to me, and although I was tempted to do something about it, I remembered where we were and pulled back.

"I thought we were being careful."

"Not anymore. I don't care who knows about us, Livia."

"But what if they…?"

"Let them think what they like. We know the truth. I'm yours… entirely yours, and I don't give a damn about anyone else's opinion."

I realized then that I didn't either.

Hunter fired Miles that afternoon in a heated meeting, after which Miles stormed out of the office without even a glance in my direction.

It was only later that evening, after we'd eaten, when I was lying in Hunter's arms on the couch in his apartment, that I remembered Miles's visit to my parents' house again, and I sat up, looking down at him.

"Miles used the same excuse with me, you know?"

"I'm sorry?" He looked confused, but I couldn't blame him. We hadn't talked about Miles or Jenni Moore since we'd left the office, so my statement must have seemed very bizarre to him.

"When Miles came to my parents' house, he told me it was because he needed to talk to me about my contract."

He sat up, still holding me. "That's what he said?"

"Yes. Although once he'd sat down with a cup of coffee, he never mentioned it again."

Hunter cupped his hand around my chin, his fingers caressing my cheek, and raised my face to his, our lips almost touching. "I know I didn't handle that very well, but I'm so glad I arrived when I did."

"You think he had something in mind? Other than discussing my contract?"

He looked into my eyes, like he was searching them. "Yeah, I do."

"But my parents were there."

"I'm not sure Miles would have let a detail like that get in his way."

I shuddered, and he held me closer, kissing me tenderly.

It was a relief to know Miles wouldn't be at the office anymore, but his departure has meant even more work for Hunter. He's had to interview candidates for Miles's job, and on top of that, we found out last week that we've picked up two more of Pemberton's former clients, too.

I guess that's why we're both relieved to be going down to Newport for the weekend, just for a rest… although I'll admit, I'm also nervous.

We haven't left Boston since we got back together, and Hunter's already told me that both Drew and Ella are going to be at the house. I've only met Drew in passing, and on each occasion it was quite embarrassing. As for Ella, I've got no idea what to expect.

"I've never been happier to see this place," Hunter says as he parks his car by the garage, switching off the engine and turning to face me.

"You miss it when we don't come here, don't you?"

"Yes, but it's been worth it to get you moved into the apartment." He tilts his head, studying me. "Are you okay?"

I nod my head, and he smiles, getting out. I can't admit my nerves to him. He'll think I'm being silly, and will probably say so. And while I know he'd be right, I'd rather just get this over with.

As he's helping me from the car, the front door opens and Pat appears, smiling broadly. She doesn't say anything straight away and waits until we approach, Hunter carrying our bags.

"It's good to see you," she says, looking at me, not him.

"It's good to see you, too."

She turns her attention to Hunter, the look on her face speaking volumes. There's love in her eyes, and an element of pride, too, as she smiles up at him.

"Drew and Ella are out by the pool," she says.

"Good for them." Hunter's reply makes her chuckle, and I have to smile myself. "We're gonna go freshen up."

Pat stands aside, letting us enter, and Hunter leads me up to his room, closing the door behind us.

"It won't hurt to keep them waiting," he says, turning to face me. "Unless you'd rather get the formal introductions out of the way first?"

"No, it's fine."

He reaches out, pulling me close. "Don't be nervous."

"Is it that obvious?"

"Yes. But Ella's gonna love you. I promise."

I'm not so sure about that, but I'm also intrigued by something else. "Did Pat know about us splitting up?"

He nods his head. "Yeah, she did."

"What did she say? Did she blame me?"

He frowns. "No. Why on earth would she blame you? I didn't tell her exactly what I'd done – unlike Drew, and Ella, and Doreen – but I told her I'd screwed up."

"Wait a second… did you say Doreen?"

"Yeah." He looks down for a moment before raising his eyes to mine again. "Don't be mad at me, but I called her. I needed to understand what had gone on between my father and yours."

"Between your father and Ken Bevan, you mean. He's not my father, Hunter." He nods. "What did she say?"

"All kinds of things. She explained what happened, and how Ken used your mom to manipulate the inquiry into his own fraud, and how my father had been ruthless in his pursuit of what he perceived as justice."

"Against my mom, you mean?"

"Yeah. She also told me about her affair with my father."

I put my arms around his waist, hugging him tight. "Was that hard to hear?"

"Not as hard as you might think. I already knew some of it, and it was good to hear the truth behind some of the rumors."

"Was that it?"

"No. She told me you were good for me… and I should do whatever it took to make it right between us again."

"She said that?"

"Yeah, she did."

"Is that why you came to see me?"

"The first time? Maybe… a little."

"And the second time?"

He shakes his head. "If anyone had any influence over that decision, it would have been Pat. She told me not to make you do the running. You'd asked for time, but Pat said I shouldn't let you forget I was here… waiting."

I bring my hands around, resting them on his chest. "I wasn't likely to forget that."

"Maybe not, but…" He sighs. "I'd hurt you, Livia. I…"

I place my fingers across his lips, his eyes widening slightly. "Enough, Hunter. I don't wanna keep talking about what happened. We both made mistakes." He opens his mouth, and although I let my hand drop, I narrow my eyes at him until he closes it again. "I screwed up, too… maybe not so spectacularly as you, but I forgot to make allowances… to be kind."

He shakes his head. "Oh, God… Livia."

"When I was staying with Mom and Dad, I was talking to them about trust, and love, and us, and my dad said we needed to be sure we could put our differences behind us… so we could move forward together. So, can we do that, Hunter? Can we just accept what happened, and leave it in the past? We both know we're not gonna do anything like that again, so we don't need to keep talking about it, or thinking about it anymore."

"After tonight, there's nothing I'd like more."

"Why after tonight?"

He smiles. "Because I think my brother will want to score a few points. It's in his nature, and he won't be able to resist telling me how close I came to losing you, through my own stupidity."

I lean against him, looking up into his eyes. "Then he'd be wrong."

"He would?"

"Yeah. You were never gonna lose me."

"It felt like I had."

I shake my head. "We love each other far too much to stay lost."

He smiles, his eyes shining, as he bends his head and kisses me.

## *Hunter*

I was wrong about one thing.

Drew is not in a point-scoring mood. In fact, he can barely crack a smile.

Livia and I came downstairs about twenty minutes ago, having taken a shower together. We might have needed to freshen up, but that wasn't the main reason for stripping out of our clothes and heading into the bathroom the moment I broke our kiss. I needed to hold her naked in my arms and look into her eyes when I joined us together.

We haven't spent the last few weeks agonizing over what happened, but we haven't been able to draw a line under it... until now. Hearing Livia say she wanted to put it behind us was perfect. It was everything I'd wanted to say myself, but didn't feel I had the right. Whatever she says, the mistakes were mine. The absolution had to be hers.

Maybe it helped that we're here in Newport. Not only is this where it all began, but we're away from the city... and over the last couple of weeks, we've been too busy to even think straight, let alone talk.

Firing Miles Hampton was a necessary chore, and although it wasn't pleasant, I was relieved to have some concrete evidence against him at last. He tried to argue his innocence, but then turned it around, saying Jenni Moore had been the one to approach him, and that he'd had to fight her off. I stuck to my guns, and he left my office, calling me all the names under the sun and threatening to sue me. I'm not worried... especially as I now know he tried the same trick with Livia.

His departure has left a hole I've been trying to fill, and I've got three potential candidates I'm seeing again next week. In between that, getting two new clients, and moving Livia's things into my apartment, we've been rushed off our feet. Okay, so we could have made that easier by hiring someone to move the contents of her apartment into mine, but like I said to Livia when she suggested it, I was enjoying getting to know her.

Aside from Livia moving in with me, and the fact that we're together all the time now, I'm also relieved we don't have to keep our relationship a secret anymore. We decided on that quite quickly… which is to say, I told Livia I was done being careful, and she agreed. The next morning, we walked into the office holding hands. There were a few raised eyebrows, but no-one said a word, and people seem to have gotten used to it now, which is a relief, because I'm not sure I've got the energy for sneaking around.

We're sitting outside on the terrace by the pool. I made the formal introductions when we got down here. Ella practically threw herself at Livia, which I think came as quite a shock, although she took it well. Drew was much quieter, but like I say, that sums up how he's been all evening. He didn't even want to commandeer the barbecue, like he usually does, and we left it to Pat to do the cooking. I'd have done it myself, but I knew how nervous Livia was, and didn't want to leave her alone with Ella, who hasn't stopped talking for more than a few seconds since we appeared in the doorway.

"When do you start work?" I ask, taking advantage of her pausing for breath.

"Not this Monday, but the one after, although I'm going back to the city early on Tuesday morning. Most of my furniture is being delivered in the afternoon… so I should probably be there."

"I think that would be wise, but how are you getting there? Do you have a car yet?"

"Of course I have. I've got a Mercedes convertible."

"Like mine?" Livia says, her eyes lighting up.

"I don't know. Is yours bright red?"

"No, it's gray." Livia sounds confused and I can't blame her.

"I think Livia was referring to the model, not the color," I say and Ella shakes her head.

"Don't ask me technical things like that. All I know is, it's bright red and gets me from A to B."

I laugh and glance at Drew, expecting him to make a remark of some kind… except he's staring into space, like we're not even here.

"What is it you're going to be doing? For your new job, I mean?" Livia asks, to fill the silence.

Ella lets out a sigh. "I'm not allowed to say. The people I'm working for are being ludicrously secretive about the whole thing. Anyone would think we were spying for a government agency, or something."

Pat brings over the steaks, putting them in the middle of the table, and giving Livia a smile, before she goes into the kitchen, returning with an enormous bowl of salad. She glances at the table, checking we've got everything we need.

"I'll quickly clear up, and then I'm gonna head over to the apartment, if that's okay?"

She looks at me, and I nod my head. "That's fine… thanks, Pat."

She smiles, glancing at Livia again, before she leaves. I know she's pleased to see her here again. Not as pleased as I am, obviously, but pleased.

We're helping ourselves to steak, when I turn to Drew. "Have you been keeping busy?"

He nods his head and sighs, and I'm tempted to ask what's wrong. I'm not sure he'd tell me in front of Livia and Ella, though, so maybe it'll have to wait. "I'm going to New York tomorrow morning," he says, surprising me.

"Is that for work?"

He takes some salad from the bowl, passing it to Ella, and then looks up at me. "No, it's not."

"Then why…?"

"D—Do you remember me telling you about Lexi?" he says, his shoulders dropping in something that looks like despair.

"The model you met in the Caribbean?"

"Yeah. She called this afternoon."

Ella dumps the salad bowl in the middle of the table again, and we all start eating. "I thought you broke up with her," she says.

"I did. She called to tell me she's… she's pregnant."

Ella drops her fork, and although I keep hold of mine, I put it down carefully and turn to face him properly. "She's pregnant?"

"Yeah." He takes a sip of beer and sits back, not interested in food.

Ella turns to Livia, giving her a slight smile. "Lexi is a model Drew dated for a while."

"Oh…" Livia looks across the table at Drew.

"'Dated' is probably overstating it," he says.

"And you didn't use a condom when you were with her, because…?" I ask. It feels like the obvious question to me.

"Because the first time we were together, I was drunk." He raises his voice. "I forgot."

"Okay." I hold up my hands.

"We didn't worry about it in the cold light of day because Lexi told me she was on birth control."

"Hold on." Ella leans forward. "If she was on birth control, how did she get pregnant?"

Drew pushes his fingers back through his hair, looking a picture of dejection. "If you recall, I told you that most of the models got sick on that assignment."

"Yes… but Lexi wasn't one of them."

"Except she was. What I didn't realize was that she'd been sick too, before I arrived. She passed the bug on to one of the other models and it spread from there."

I nod my head. "And because she was sick, her birth control didn't work?"

"Exactly," he says, turning back to me.

"But why are you only hearing about this now, all this time after the event?" I ask and he shakes his head, like he's still taking it all in.

"Lexi explained that she's been away on an assignment in California, and she didn't even realize she was late until she got home. She took a test, and…"

"It was positive."

He nods his head. "I never had to ask whether it was mine. She seemed to assume I'd have my doubts, and she assured me she hasn't slept with anyone since."

"You believe her?" I ask.

"Yeah, I do. We may not have been compatible, but she wouldn't lie to me… not about something like that. And anyway, she said she doesn't want anything from me; she just thought I had a right to know."

"She doesn't want anything from you?" I find that hard to believe.

"That's what she said. I've already told her that's not happening. That's why I'm having lunch with her tomorrow, so we can talk things through." He sighs again. "I feel like my life is over."

"Why?" Livia asks and we all look at her. She blushes and I take her hand in mine. "I'm sorry, but I don't understand. Even if you're not together, surely you can work something out, can't you?"

"That's not the problem," Drew says, struggling to hide his dismay, and I squeeze Livia's hand.

"Like Drew said, he and Lexi were never that serious about each other, but he broke up with her because he met her sister at a party... and fell for her."

"Oh, I see." She looks at Drew again. "Did you do anything about that? After you'd broken up with Lexi, I mean?"

"I called her. Lexi's sister, I mean."

"You did?" Ella's as surprised as I am, only I'm better at holding it in.

"Yeah. I know you said I should wait, but I couldn't. Not for very long. It was driving me crazy. I needed to see her."

"And did you?" I ask.

"Yeah. I took her for coffee, but I kept it friendly, like you suggested."

Ella turns to Livia again. "We told Drew he couldn't hope to ask Lexi's sister on a date so soon after dumping her, but he could try making friends instead."

Livia nods her head, and we all look back at Drew. "How did it go?" I ask.

"It was perfect," he says. "We talked for hours. I've seen her twice since, and we were gonna meet up again, except I had to go to Hawaii for a few days. My flight was delayed, so I only got back here late last night... and then today I got the call from Lexi. I was gonna..." He stops talking, shaking his head. "Oh, what's the point? There's nothing I can do about it now, is there?" He looks at me, desperation filling his voice. "We can't even be friends anymore, can we? Not when Lexi's having my baby."

He has a point. It was difficult before, but now...

A silence descends over us and we eat our steaks, although I don't think any of us are very enthusiastic about food anymore.

Drew makes his excuses, returning to the guest house as soon as he can, and Ella leaves too, giving us both a smile.

"It's lovely to meet you at last," she says to Livia.

"You, too."

She goes into the house, and I turn to Livia. "Sorry about all that."

"Will Drew be okay?"

"I'll talk to him in the morning, before he leaves."

"You'll have to get up early, won't you? It's a long drive to New York."

"It'll be fine."

"I don't mind if you wanna go talk to him now."

"I'm not sure he's in the mood for talking." I get to my feet, pulling her with me. "And anyway… I've got plans for this evening."

"You have?" She looks up at me, a smile tugging at her lips

"Yes, I have."

I pull her toward the doors, closing them behind us, and I lead her through the house and up the stairs, into my bedroom. Once inside, I sit her on the bed.

"Can you wait here for a minute?"

She tilts her head to one side, frowning slightly. "Um… okay."

"I won't be long. I promise."

She nods her head, and I grab my bag, heading for the bathroom, where I set out everything, while running a bath. It takes a little longer than I'd expected, but roughly ten minutes later, I return to Livia, who's exactly where I left her.

I pull her to her feet, kissing her briefly, before I unzip her dress, letting it fall to the floor. Her eyes are wide, sparkling, and she breathes heavily as I remove her bra and panties, and then quickly strip off myself.

"Is there a reason we're getting undressed in here?" she asks.

"Yeah. Clothes could be dangerous in the bathroom."

"Dangerous?"

"You'll see." I turn her around. "Close your eyes." She looks up at me. "Close your eyes," I repeat and she does so, letting me take both of her hands and walk her into the bathroom.

As we cross the threshold, I tell her to open her eyes again, and she lets out a gasp and smiles, staring up at me.

"I—It's beautiful."

I'd hoped she'd like it, and I gaze around at the candles. There are over fifty of them, scattered around on every surface, including the floor. There are rose petals in the bath, too, and she leans in to me, her naked body pressed hard against mine. I don't want us to get distracted, though, so I take her hand, helping her into the bath, and then climb in behind her, my arms and legs wrapped tight around her.

"This is perfect," she murmurs, twisting slightly and looking up at me. I know she expects me to kiss her, and I will... but not yet.

"I've been meaning to ask you something."

"Oh?" I wonder if she can guess what I'm about to say. Somehow I doubt it.

"It's about your parents."

Her brow furrows, and I know I've confused her. "My parents?"

"Yes."

"You ran us a romantic bath to talk about my parents?"

"Not exclusively, but yes. I want to help them."

She turns completely now, kneeling in front of me. "Is this out of guilt... because of what your father did?"

"Maybe... a little. But mostly it's because you love them. They're important to you, and that means they're important to me, too. What's happened to them is horrible, and if I can make their lives easier, then I want to at least try."

She sighs, sitting back on her ankles. "I feel bad about leaving them."

"I know you do."

"And I hate that we haven't been able to visit them. Everything's been so crazy since we got back." She waves her arm, splashing water over me. "And this is your home. You want to come here on the weekends."

I nod my head. "But you'd like to be able to see more of them?"

"Of course."

"How do you think they'd feel about moving house?"

"To Boston?" She frowns, looking uncertain.

"I was thinking of Newport."

"Oh, I see…" She thinks for a moment. "They'd love it here, but surely property is really expensive, isn't it? Although I guess I could help them out. I could use some of the money you gave me…"

"Or not. That money's yours, Livia. Everything I have is yours." Her eyes widen, but I realize I'm getting ahead of myself. "I—I was thinking of building them somewhere here, in the grounds. I—I hope you don't think I'm being premature, but I've had some plans drawn up already, for a three-bedroom house…"

"A house?"

"Yeah, but don't worry. I noticed how much your dad struggled, and realized that getting from room to room must be difficult for him, so I found an architect who specializes in designing accessible properties. It's all on one level, and open plan, with no steps for your dad to negotiate. Nothing's finalized, though. Your parents can make any changes they want." I twist my legs around, kneeling in front of her, and take her hands in mine. "Mick would take care of any maintenance issues, and Pat could keep your mom company, and help with your dad, if necessary."

"And I could see them every weekend?" she says, her eyes sparkling.

"Yes."

"But what about Mom's work?" Livia's happiness dims, and I pull her closer.

"She can give it up, if that's what she wants, or at least choose her hours."

"How? They wouldn't have any money. The royalties from Dad's books are minimal, and…"

"Hey… stop worrying. I'll take care of it. Starting now."

"Now?"

"Yeah. Your mom shouldn't have to worry about earning a living, while she's having to care for your dad, too. That's a full-time job in itself, so I'll set something up to make it easier for them… financially."

"You mean, like an allowance?"

"Something like that."

She blinks a few times, and even in the dim candlelight, I can see tears welling in her eyes. "Y—You'd do all that? For my parents?"

"I'd do it all… for you."

She smiles. "It sounds perfect, Hunter. And really generous. But I think we'll have a hard time persuading my mom to accept. If you suggested it to her, she'd see it as charity."

I nod my head. I'd seen this coming, and to be honest, it couldn't have gone better if I'd written a script.

"Do you think she'd see it as charity if I suggested it as your fiancé, rather than your boyfriend or your boss?"

"My fiancé?"

"Yes." I twist around, reaching behind me into the bowl of shells, and I pull one out. Nestled inside it, exactly where I left it earlier, is the diamond ring I bought a few days ago, and as I turn back, Livia sees what I'm holding and gasps.

"You've got a ring?" She looks up at me. "You planned this?"

"I did. Say you'll marry me? Please?" I take the ring from the shell, holding it out to her, and she offers me her left hand. "Is that a yes, babe?"

She nods her head, gazing into my eyes. "It's a yes, please."

I place the ring on her finger, and after a quick glance at it, she throws herself at me, water splashing everywhere as we kiss, and the lights across the harbor twinkle in the night sky.

*The End*

Thank you for reading *Mistaken Identity*. I hope you enjoyed it, and if you did, I hope you'll take the time to leave a short review.

Printed in Great Britain
by Amazon